The Awful Truth About Dead Men

by

Terry Sykes-Bradshaw

To Dad . . . who started it all by teaching me that nothing is so serious that you can't laugh about it. I wish you were here to read the book. I just wish you were here.

To Mom . . . who supported me through the creative journey, one comma at a time. And who never got credit for her jokes. Until now.

Acknowledgments

Writing a book is not the piece of cake I assumed it was when I started this one. For a variety of reasons, it took me over a decade to get the book in print. If left to my own slacker ways, *The Awful Truth* would still be languishing half-finished in my computer or desk drawer. Without a little, oh okay, a lot of support, love, encouragement, and the occasional threat, it never would have happened.

I owe huge thanks to so many people . . .

. . . the two Kathys . . . my daughter, Kathy, who inspired me by printing the original manuscript in book form and presenting it to me as a Christmas gift. And, my sister, Kathy, who conspired with me and held my hand every step of the way. She has been my backer, emotionally and financially, from the moment inspiration struck, and I could never have achieved this without her. As a friend, you are the best. As a sister, you are amazing.

. . . my mother, Elinor, because I can never say thank you too many times, for the red pen she used to slash all of the grammatical errors and wayward commas she could find. I couldn't have asked for a better Grammar Policewoman.

... my friends (and you know who you are) for allowing me to steal their identities and use them for my own selfish purposes.

... the members of The Second Tuesday Writers' Group for putting up with me reading endless chapters.

... the DeScribers, Keena, Tanya, and Agnes, for always being available.

... Chris and Helen who pitched in when life got crazy.

... Alyssa who never failed to laugh me up.

... my entire wacky family for giving me so much comic material.

And last, but certainly not least, I want to thank my husband, Bill, who didn't bug me to get a "real" job and never complained when I served him cold cereal for dinner.

Love and thanks to you all.

Prologue

Dead. Stone cold dead. As in not breathing. As in lying in a pool of blood. That's how I found Captain Fairweather that afternoon. Dead, dead, dead. Not that I've had any previous experience with dead men or anything, but after I prodded him with my foot and hissed his name several times, I knew. I was, if you'll pardon the expression, dead certain.

I confess that I didn't handle the situation very well. I backed into the corner of Captain Fairweather's cabin and froze with my hands clasped over my mouth. I tried to scream but it came out a meek croak. The cabin was dim and stuffy and I struggled to breathe. "In," I coached myself. "Out." Finally I broke the spell and bolted for the cabin door. I tugged frantically at the door handle with a shaking hand. When it finally turned I took off as if I was being chased by a knife-wielding madman. I lost my footing on the polished wood floor and slammed into the wall, but didn't dare stop.

I hit the deck running and burst into tears. As my four friends, Mary Linda, Ellie, Sandra and Julie gathered around me, I sobbed, "He's dead. He's dead." Ellie patted me on the back and I wiped my eyes with the back of my hand.

"What's the matter?" Sandra demanded. "Who's dead?"

"Let's get the Captain," Mary Linda said. "Maybe he can help."

"No," I wailed. "You don't get it. The Captain is the one who's dead. I saw him."

"You saw him?"

"Yes." I sobbed. "He was lying on the floor of his cabin."

"Are you sure he was dead? Maybe he was napping," Julie said.

"No-ooo," I cried. My voice cracked. "He was all blo-ody."

They stared at me blankly. And why not? I was totally unglued. I mean, women from Ohio don't usually stumble over dead men. Sandra met my eye. "So, what you're telling us is that you found Captain Fairweather lying on the floor of his cabin in a pool of blood?"

It *did* sound a bit farfetched. "I think so."

"Well, then," Ellie said, "I think we'd better go to his cabin and check it out."

I would have preferred to lower myself into a pit of writhing snakes than to go back to that cabin, but I knew I had no choice. I had to suck it up and prove to my friends that the captain of our chartered sailboat was indeed a corpse. The five of us crept down the hallway to the Captain's cabin in the stern of the ship. The door was latched and only the creaking of the masts from the deck above disturbed the deathly silence. We jumped when Julie kicked over a wastebasket sitting in the hall and it clattered to the floor, the lid rolling under our feet.

Ellie whispered, "The door's locked, isn't it? He's sleeping or something."

Sandra tugged on my arm. "Let's just go."

"No." I shuddered. "I left this door wide open. Somebody or something closed it."

I jiggled the handle and discovered that the door was unlocked. I eased it open and, with my friends glued to my backside, I inched into the cabin. And . . . it was empty. No body. No Captain Fairweather. No murder weapon. Nothing.

"Where is this body?" Sandra demanded. "See, he isn't dead. He isn't even here."

"What do I know?" I said. "I'm not familiar with corpse protocol. Maybe he wasn't dead after all. Maybe the dent in his head wasn't a fatal wound. Maybe it was a cruel prank. There's only one way to find out. Find Captain Fairweather and he can explain."

So we scattered to search the ship. But we couldn't find Captain Nigel Fairweather anywhere. Our mood was bleak as we clung together on the deck as the watery late afternoon sun began to set and the tropical breeze freshened. The huge sails looming above us luffed in the breeze and the ship rocked on the swells. Dissipating rain clouds from the storm earlier scudded across the sky. Here we were somewhere in the Atlantic Ocean and the captain of our ship was, at the very least, missing, and if I was correct, dead. No one uttered a word.

"I think we have a problem," I said finally.

Chapter One

No one ever blamed me, but I know none of it would have happened if I hadn't opened my big mouth. Not that I dragged anyone kicking and screaming onto that ill-fated cruise. But still . . .

Before I explain, let me introduce myself. I'm Kate Kelly. Sometime writer. But more often, not. I'm addicted to Jazzercise, tennis, popcorn, cheesecake and *All My Children*.

And our story began one miserable January day. Ellie, Julie, Mary Linda, Sandra and I were sipping coffee at the Win-Slow Perk after our Jazzercise class. Snow swirled across the parking lot and we shivered as icy blasts of wind shook the steamy plate glass windows. The weather in Winslow, Ohio, was god awful.

"I loved the workout today," Mary Linda St. Clair said. "She's a great instructor. I could almost see my thighs getting smaller."

"Yeah, as if you need to worry about your thighs," Julie Wright said. "I'd need to do twelve solid hours of crunches to make a dent in this." She pinched her stomach ruefully. "And even then I don't think it would make much difference."

"You guys are insane," Ellie Francis said. She shoved up the sleeves of her pale pink sweater and fingered the bracelet that matched her sparkly pink earrings. "You know we're only in it for the coffee afterwards."

"Ha," Sandra Klein interrupted. "I disagree. It's all about the clothes."

"It's always about the clothes for Ellie," I said. "And she looks so darn cute in those exercise outfits."

Sandra smoothed her already sleek bob and grinned at us. "If I didn't love her, I could almost hate her. I can't pull off her look when I'm all slimey."

"We know you hate to sweat," Mary Linda said. "But sweat becomes you."

Our longtime friendship had been forged in our Jazzercise class. From the beginning we had bonded with each other. We called it "our sweat connection." Of course, after many years that friendship extended way beyond Jazzercise. We had seen each other through good times and bad . . . births, deaths, weddings, weight gain and bad haircuts. We owed our sometimes precarious grip on sanity to our coffee and therapy sessions after class.

Today was no different than a thousand other days.

A blast of frigid air blasted us as the outside door opened and two snow-covered customers blew in. I moaned. "I've got to get out of this place. I need to see the sun. I need to wear my sandals. I need to . . ." Before I finished my sentence the five at us looked at each other with a single thought dawning simultaneously.

"We need a vacation," I concluded.

"A girls only getaway," Sandra said.

"No husbands. No children," Julie said.

All trying to speak at once, we suggested and dismissed vacation destinations. Someplace warm, we agreed. And unique. We rejected visits to Florida or Hilton Head . . . too ordinary; California . . . too far away; and the Caribbean . . . too expensive. Suddenly I sat up, sloshing coffee on my hand. "I've got it. The perfect vacation. A chartered sailboat!"

On a blustery Ohio day the lure of warm tropical breezes gently rocking our own private sailboat was enticing. It took some convincing. Sandra objected, preferring the luxury of a "real" cruise. Julie and Ellie agonized over child-care arrangements and Mary Linda was reluctant to leave both her business and her new husband, Don. But my powers of persuasion are formidable. Or maybe I'm just bossy. Before we finished our third cups of coffee I had persuaded them that we wanted, no, we needed, to go sailing. Now it was up to me to find a sailboat that was available and affordable. So we gathered up purses, tucked ourselves into our winter jackets and, with visions of palm trees dancing in our heads, we launched the great sailing adventure.

As I drove home with sleet hitting the windshield, I fantasized about tropical breezes and blue ocean waves and tanned deckhands serving margaritas and piña coladas. The more I thought about it, the more determined I was to make this trip happen. First things first, of course, which meant I had to let my husband, Scott, in on the plan. I didn't have to get his permission to go on a vacation, but it couldn't hurt to have him agree. Not to mention that

I would feel less guilty leaving him behind in the grey gloom of winter.

When Scott walked in the door that night, I was waiting with wine poured and my sales pitch prepared. "Hey," he exclaimed when he saw me. "What are you doing here?"

What he really meant was why wasn't I playing tennis or at Jazzercise or in my studio working on a magazine article or a column for our local newspaper? Not standing in our kitchen dressed in jeans with a glass of wine in my hand. He probably should have known that something was up, but adorable as he may be, and that is pretty adorable, Scott can be clueless. He tends to be so preoccupied with problems at his company that it would take some pretty outrageous behavior on my part to make him notice.

"Hi," I said, oozing sweet wifely devotion. "Have a good day?"

He stowed his coat and his bulging briefcase in the closet. "That deal with the people from Donaldson is look-ing pretty good and . . ."

He rambled on about his day while I handed him his wine and steered him into the family room. We settled on the couch and, after he ran out of office information to share, I broached the subject of a sailing cruise. "We thought it might be a good idea for the five of us to get away from all this nasty weather," I told him. "And you won't believe what a great idea we had. How about one of those crewed sailboat cruises? Doesn't that sound perfect? Just the five of us. No kids. No hassles."

And Scott, being Scott, said, "That sounds nice, dear."

If you're clever, you've got a man who not only thinks it's fantastic that his wife is cruising with her girlfriends, but also thinks he came up with the idea.

Chapter Two

It's amazing what five determined women can accomplish in a short time. Particularly when they are suffering from winter phobia and cabin fever. The lure of warmth, sun and sandals spurred us into motion. Decisions were made. Plans formulated. Shopping for necessities such as the perfect bathing suit and sandals was completed. A mere six weeks after our brainstorm, I was packing for a ten-day cruise in the warm waters off the Florida coast.

As I was trying to decide what I absolutely had to take, I was not in the best of moods. I had lined up twelve pairs of shoes and was regarding them indecisively when the phone rang. Delighted to have a diversion, I picked it up.

"Kate," Ellie cried, "I don't know if I can do this. Robbie has the sniffles and Ted is tied up in a meeting and I don't know if he'll be able to go to the band program that Michael has on Friday and Kevin's teacher called and they need a volunteer in his homeroom . . ."

I waited for her to run out of breath and then said, "Calm down, sweetie. It will all work out. Ted is the boys' father and he needs quality time with them. With you hovering all the time, he never gets to bond. It will be fine. They will be fine. And we need you."

Ellie, who rules her house with an iron hand in a ruffled oven mitt, has a terrible time untying the apron strings, let alone actually cutting them.

"Ted can take charge," I assured her. "They will live without you and the rest of us will end up wearing unsuitable color combinations if you don't come. How will you live with the guilt of knowing that four women might be found wearing earrings that didn't match their outfits? Can you deal with that?"

Ellie laughed. "I guess not."

I fielded several more frantic calls from the rest of the crew that afternoon and said appropriately calming things to each of them. I was attempting to cram one final pair of shoes into my bag when Scott poked his head around the corner. After 25 years of marriage, he knows that my packing mode is at best cranky and at worst hysterical. So he approached with caution. "Hey," he said with a tentative smile, "are you still at this? I thought you would have finished hours ago."

By that time I was fed up with packing and wanted to say goodbye properly. So when he put his arms around me and began to kiss the spot on the back of my neck that drives me crazy, I didn't resist. Much, much later I got up and zipped my bag. Ready or not, I was going on vacation.

Chapter Three

"**H**ey, gang, here we are at the gateway to paradise," Julie announced as she pulled up in front of the Cleveland airport terminal. "Please watch your step as you debark and be sure to take all of your personal belongings with you."

We were laughing as we fell out of Julie's SUV and haphazardly heaped our luggage on the sidewalk. We staggered inside to the check-in counter while Julie sped off to park. We acted like a gaggle of schoolgirls as we made our way to the counter and one by one presented ourselves to the helpful ticket agents. By the time Julie joined us and checked in herself, we were somewhat organized, although no less giddy. And we were still giggling as we navigated the security lines and headed for the gate.

"Hey," I announced as we waited to board our flight for Fort Lauderdale, "look what I have." I dug around in my bag and produced a handful of papers that I displayed in a fan.

"What's that?" Sandra asked. "Looks like lottery tickets."

"Nope," I assured her, "better than that. What I have here is the reward for having a husband who travels a couple of weeks out of every month. Ladies, I have coupons for those cute, little bottles of booze that you get on the plane."

"But," protested Ellie, "it's only eight o'clock in the morning. Who drinks at this hour?"

"We do," chorused the other three. "Bloody Marys would definitely hit the spot."

"An excellent way to begin this vacation," Julie said.

And it was not much later that we were comfortably settled on our 767 with Bloody Marys in hand, ready to set off on a once in a lifetime adventure.

Sandra nudged me awake as the Captain announced, "We are about to land in Fort Lauderdale. The temperature is a sunny 75 degrees. Please put your seats in the upright position and return your tray tables to their original position. Please remain seated until I turn off the seat belt sign. Once again, First Officer Cramer and I would like to thank you for flying Delta Airlines today."

Groggily I opened my eyes and leaned across Sandra to peer out the window. "Palm trees," I breathed. "I see palm trees."

"Not to mention sunshine," Ellie chimed in. "Beautiful, warm sunshine."

"Tropical breezes," added Mary Linda.

"Tropical drinks and tanned deckhands," Julie joked. And we laughed as we settled back for the landing.

8

The man waiting for us as we emerged from security was good looking . . . really good looking. He appeared to be of Hispanic descent with dark hair and eyes and a tanned, well-muscled physique. He held a sign reading "The Kelly Party", and paced as he awaited our arrival. We were in good spirits due, in large part, to the number of little bottles of airline booze that we had consumed.

Julie, who was doing a good deal of smirking that morning, elbowed me and stage-whispered, "Take a look at that guy. I think he's waiting for us. Talk to him already. You're the linguist."

Indeed, I had considered majoring in Spanish at one time and had a minimal, and I emphasize minimal, command of the language. "Buenas dias, Señor," I said smoothly with, I thought, just the right amount of flair. "Estamos la fiesta de Kelly." I figured he would get the drift. When he looked at me inquisitively, I added, "Me llama Señora Kelly y ellas son mi amigas."

At this point, our escort took pity on my feeble attempts at conversing in Spanish and said, "Hey, I'm Antonio Moreno. Call me Tony. I'm here to drive you to the *Mirage.*"

My friends burst into laughter upon hearing Tony's very American accent. "I take it this means you speak perfect English," I said.

"You could say that," he replied. "I went to Northwestern University."

Chagrined, I allowed Tony to pick up the bag I had dropped on the floor and followed him as he led the way to baggage claim.

A short time later the five of us, all our belongings, and Tony were crammed into a bright red Jeep Cherokee. The side of the Jeep was emblazoned with ornate gold letters advertising "Sunshine Tours." It was a gorgeous, warm, sunny day in South Florida and Tony entertained us with a running commentary on the scenic highlights interspersed with bursts of vitriolic Spanish aimed at other drivers.

We rode in dazed silence as Tony maneuvered his way around traffic with the deftness and speed of a race-car driver while chattering nonstop. He appeared to take no notice of the color of traffic lights or of other vehicles as he careened from one lane to another. Even Julie was unable to dredge up any smart comments as she and the rest of us clung to our seats expecting at any moment to end up in a pile of twisted metal and hysterical Spanish.

It was difficult to appreciate our surroundings under the circumstances, but I did catch an occasional glimpse of a palm tree or a red-tiled roof. It was warm in the Jeep, in spite of the air-conditioning, due in part to the nervous perspiration of five women who expected to perish in the not-too-distant future. I was considering my family's response to my demise when Tony pulled up at a very small marina and came to a screeching halt.

The five of us sat in a state of mute thankfulness for a few seconds before we frantically opened the doors and tumbled out. "Oh, my God, I'm alive," exclaimed Sandra.

"My entire life flashed before my eyes at least five times," Mary Linda said.

"I know what you mean," breathed Ellie, "I figured Ted was going to have to raise the boys himself and would bring them up on a steady diet of McDonald's."

I turned to Tony who appeared to find amusing the disheveled and even prayerful state of his passengers. "Muchas gracias, Señor," I said with as much sarcasm as I could muster. "We are so grateful to you that we are here alive and in one piece."

Tony just grinned and began tossing our luggage into an untidy heap on the sidewalk. "No problem, ladies. Always at your service."

Julie recovered enough to respond flippantly. She batted her eyes. "I'll certainly take that offer under advisement."

Our "brush with death" had rendered us momentarily oblivious, but as we regained our wits we began to notice our surroundings. We were standing in a small parking lot in front of a smallish white building. The sign on the front read, "South Florida Landings. We Launch Your Adventure." It housed an office, perhaps a couple of restrooms and a vending machine or two. Beyond the office building a series of three well-worn docks extended into the water. Each dock had smaller docks running at perpendicular angles to the longer one, making a set of boat slips on each side. The marina was small, with space for only a dozen boats, but well-maintained. Flowers surrounded the office building and flower boxes lined the docks. Only four boats (or should I call them yachts?) were currently docked there. In the end slip was the largest sailboat, our home for the next ten days, the *Mirage*. With the sun glinting off its twin masts and the water lapping against the lovely green sides, the *Mirage* was an awesome sight.

"What could we have been thinking?" Sandra whispered.

As we contemplated the trim sloop, I asked myself the same question. What on earth had we been thinking? Such a small boat and so much ocean. Not exactly a paradise for claustrophobics. At that moment, I would cheerfully have traded the *Mirage* for a Holiday Inn without a single backward glance. There couldn't be enough Dramamine or Valium in the world to make the next ten days tolerable.

About the time I had decided to turn and run, a tall figure emerged from the back of the *Mirage*. A well-built man in snug-fitting blue jeans sauntered down the dock toward us. His white t-shirt accented his well-developed pecs. As he approached, my friends were struck dumb by his good looks. Even Julie couldn't think of anything to say.

"Hello, ladies," he said in a voice which simply oozed arrogance. "I am Nigel Fairweather and I am the Captain of the *Mirage*. We'll be seeing a lot of each other in the next few days."

While my friends were mesmerized by the Captain's nice neat buns, he shot me a calculating look and I stared into the coldest blue eyes I had ever seen. I actually shivered in the hot Florida sun. Nigel Fairweather was gorgeous, but frankly, he gave me the creeps. Obviously, my feelings were not shared by the others. As each introduced herself to the Captain, she, there is no other word for it, began to fawn over the man.

"So, you're the captain," said Ellie.

"Oh, yeah, baby," Julie breathed into my ear.

"We're going to be such good friends," Sandra put in.

Mary Linda giggled and fluffed her hair.

"How did I get so lucky?" Captain Fairweather said. "My guests are not usually as beautiful as you all."

I took a step back and tried to distance myself from my drooling friends and the smarmy Captain. I never have such an immediate reaction to someone as I had to Nigel Fairweather. And while I wished I felt as comfortable in his presence as my friends, he made me uneasy and

I couldn't shake the feeling. Somehow I knew that Captain Nigel Fairweather was not a nice man.

"This is my crew," Fairweather said, pointing to an unassuming couple who had followed him onto the dock. "This is Miguel, my right hand man, and this is his wife, Martha, who does the cooking. Incidentally, Martha studied at the Cordon Bleu in New York City and will make you ten pounds heavier before you leave. If you don't get too seasick." He chuckled insincerely at his joke.

The good Captain explained that Miguel spoke little English, but that Martha was an American and could translate for us.

"The three of us," he said, "will do all the work. This is your vacation and I want you to just lie around in skimpy bikinis and drink rum drinks and enjoy yourselves. Leave the sailing to us."

That chuckle of his and the lecherous looks he gave my friends were like fingernails on a blackboard. I was debating the wisdom of simply smacking him, when he deliberately caught my eye. Since I am taller than the others, they missed his tight-lipped grimace. I felt like he was trying to tell me something. Or maybe to warn me.

Tony finished unloading the Jeep and turned to bid us farewell. "Well, amigas, that's about it. Captain Fairweather will take mighty good care of you. Enjoy your voyage and I'll be here next week to pick you up."

He smiled and tipped his cap. I had taken only a couple steps toward the Mirage before some weird intuition made me glance back over my shoulder at Tony and caught him chewing his bottom lip and staring after us. Then he shrugged, hopped into the Jeep, and sped away, narrowly missing a Porsche parked in the lot.

I grabbed Sandra's elbow. "Did you see the look on Tony's face?" But she was already following good Captain Fairweather as he herded us toward the *Mirage*. Miguel lugged our bags to the boat and Martha drifted off to check on the groceries that had been delivered earlier. I was left standing alone gazing after Tony and the speeding red Jeep.

"Now what?" I asked myself.

Chapter Four

It wasn't long before Julie, Sandra, Mary Linda and I were sprawled in lounge chairs on the deck taking advantage of the afternoon sun. The others chattered and soaked up rays and I pretended to read a paperback novel while I kept an eye on Captain Fairweather. Suddenly I saw a look of cool calculation and lurid appreciation cross his face. I pivoted in my chair and saw that Ellie had finally emerged from her cabin.

Julie choked on her drink and began to sputter as she, too, spotted a defiant Ellie standing there in two strips of gold that could charitably be called a swimsuit. I have gold chains that offer more coverage.

It took only a second for Julie to recover enough to let loose with a wolf whistle that could have been heard in Chicago. After a moment of dazed silence, the rest of us began to talk at once.

"Good Lord, Ellie," Sandra exclaimed. "Whoo-eee!"

Mary Linda added, "Well, at least you've coordinated your bikini with your earrings."

"Yes," Sandra teased, "but the earrings are bigger than the suit."

I commented, "Actually, you do look great. Naked but great."

Poor Ellie. She blushed and reached for a t-shirt that one of us had flung on a deck chair. Mary Linda reached out and snagged Ellie's wrist. "Hey, girlfriend, you bought it, you wear it. Don't cover up because of us." She tugged on the bottom of her conservative suit and frowned. "I wish I had the figure to pull that off."

"Yes," I said, "if you've got it, flaunt it."

Ellie's face was as red as if she had been sunbathing all day. "I just wanted to be different."

"You got that right," Julie said.

Martha, with Miguel in tow, materialized on deck just then. Miguel wore a look of glassy-eyed admiration. "Dios mio," he muttered to himself.

Martha pursed her lips disapprovingly and elbowed Miguel in the ribs. Still scowling she relented and offered Ellie the plate of snacks she had in her hand. "Try one of my crab puffs," she suggested. "I can jot down the recipe for you if you want."

Ellie grabbed an hors d'oeuvres as if it was a lifeline. She scooped a drink sporting an umbrella off a nearby table and sank into a lounge chair looking like she wished she could disappear. Captain Fairweather had not spoken since Ellie showed up on deck, but his chilly blue eyes remained fixed on Ellie's barely clothed body. When he noticed me watching him, he shrugged and yawned. Then he winked and slid his sunglasses over his eyes.

My stomach did a flip flop. I wished that he would go away and leave us alone. I didn't like one single bit the covert looks that Ellie was casting his way. If I didn't know her better, I would have said she was flirting with him.

The other women rapidly got over the shock of seeing our little Ellie in a bikini. Julie pulled her straw hat down over her curls and gave Ellie a sidelong glance. "Hope you brought a lot of sunblock."

Sandra settled back into her chair and picked up the magazine that she had been reading. "Oh, look," she said, "here's Madonna in a bikini just like Ellie's."

The four of them huddled with their heads together scanning the magazine. I picked up my margarita and took a sip.

It was a magnificent day. Warm sunshine, no humidity. Paradise. From my deck chair I could look up and see the twin masts of the *Mirage* silhouetted against the brilliant blue sky. A slight breeze rocked the sailboat and the sea splashed gently against the sides. The *Mirage* was a ninety-foot sailboat with three double cabins, a triple cabin, and a single cabin below deck. There was also a comfortable, if somewhat compact, salon area where we could take meals or relax with a book if the weather turned rainy. Martha and Miguel had one of the double cabins and the Captain lived in the single cabin. My friends and I were in two of the other cabins. It was a cozy arrangement which could lead to becoming new best friends with the crew by the end of the sail. I didn't like Captain Fairweather at all, but, I told myself, he's just a leering chauvinist type. And it *was* a pretty revealing bikini. Quit worrying and drink your margarita. You're on vacation after all.

It wasn't long before the gentle rocking combined with the effects of the margarita lulled me to sleep. I don't know how long I drifted, peacefully dreaming of tanned deckhands with snow shovels in their hands, before I woke up. The sun was slipping lower in the sky and the breeze had picked up a bit. I felt a chill and I opened my eyes and observed Captain Fairweather keeping vigil. I jolted upright. Julie poked a drink umbrella into my midsection. "Wake up. It's five o'clock somewhere. And that somewhere is here."

"Oh, look," Mary Linda said. "Martha has prepared another plate of goodies and here she comes to give us her recipes."

Mel was correct. Martha was headed our way bearing a platter of delicious smelling and looking treats as well as a pad of paper. "Ladies, I have some tasty avocado and bacon bites as well as grouper with a special sauce and mushroom caps stuffed with lobster. Let me jot down the recipes for you."

Martha had a penchant for sharing her culinary genius. You could almost believe that she would have been handing out recipes for seafood gumbo as she went down with the Titanic. Ellie scribbled down the details on a cocktail napkin, while Mary Linda and Julie stuffed their mouths with an assortment of delicacies.

Okay, I told myself for the last time, this is going to be fun. I was almost convinced.

While we gobbled appetizers and sipped tropical drinks, the sun sank lower into the sky. As we ate the sun sank into the ocean setting the waves ablaze with reds, pinks and oranges.

"Wow," Mary Linda sighed, "we don't see sunsets like that in Ohio."

Captain Fairweather approached us from behind. "That's our official welcome to South Florida. We do that for all our tourists."

Ellie, Sandra, Julie and Mary Linda tore their eyes away from the sunset and gushed at the Captain like schoolgirls. I could only shake my head. Frankly I couldn't see the attraction. I suppose I had to admit that Captain Fairweather was good-looking. But I decided that he believed he was so irresistible to women that he couldn't imagine that a woman would *not* be attracted to him. But I wasn't. Not my type. Not at all.

Captain Nigel Fairweather was tall, about six feet two, and built like an athlete. Nice pecs, muscular arms and legs, and (so shoot me, I noticed) a cute butt. I guessed he was in his late thirties. Days in the Florida sun had tanned him a nice golden color and he had sexy squint lines around his deep blue eyes. Squint lines which would be called crow's feet in a few years, I groused. All in all, I supposed, a rather nice package. That is, if you liked the overconfident, I-am-a-Greek-god, type. Obviously, my travel companions did. They lounged in seductive poses on the deck chairs and sucked up to him. They acted like they hadn't seen a sexy guy in ages. They all have husbands, for crying out loud. But as Julie whispered to me, "God, he's gorgeous. I could stuff him and put him on my mantle," I figured they were going to look but not touch. I hoped.

With the disappearance of the sun, the wind picked up and it got chilly on deck. Delicious aromas wafted up from below and no one wanted to pass up another round of Martha's culinary concoctions. So, we hastily gathered our things and retired to our respective cabins to change for our first dinner on the boat.

Anticipation ran high as Julie, Mary Linda and I shed our swimsuits and donned shorts and shirts. We had debated our attire. Should we dress up or go with casual? Who dresses up for dinner on a sailboat? That question was answered when we met in the salon. Ellie does. She had on what can only be called a "slut" dress. Bright red, cut so low that one prayed that she didn't fall completely out of it, it clung to her body in places that aren't often clung to. Skimpy straps were all that came between Ellie and total toplessness. She staggered on five-inch heeled red pumps and had, true to form, matched bright red hoop earrings to her dress. The success of her gold bikini had definitely gone to her pretty blonde head.

Her cabin mate, Sandra, shook her head sadly. "I tried, you guys. I truly did. I told her that she looked like a 'ho'. But she doesn't care."

"Who made you guys the fashion police?" Ellie demanded.

Julie added, "A 'ho'?"

"You do know what that means, right?" Mary Linda asked.

"Ha ha." Julie grinned. "I just thought perhaps we were being a bit harsh on poor Ellie. We all know that she was a slut in high school."

"Eleven prom dates." Sandra giggled. "Definitely a slut!"

By now Ellie was beginning to look sheepish. "Okay," she said. "I'll go change. You guys cannot take a joke."

A chorus of "no's" met this declaration and Ellie was once again enjoying the limelight. She might have retreated to her cabin to change into something more comfortable and concealing if Captain Fairweather hadn't appeared at that moment. The appreciative look in his eye was enough to stop Ellie in her tracks.

"Why, Miss Ellie," he drawled, "I thought were going to dress for dinner not undress."

Ellie looked uncomfortable, but decided to tough it out. "Indeed, Captain," she replied sweetly, "I thought I would try to liven up the evening."

"Oh, you have certainly accomplished that," he said with a smirk. "Please don't run off and change on my account."

Oh, gag me, I thought. Can he be any more obvious? But Ellie was eating up the attention and the moment for her to retreat had passed. Martha surfaced and beckoned us to take seats at the salon table that was now laden with delicious dishes. We sat down and began to sample yet another round of Martha's goodies. By the time we had completed a meal of gumbo, grilled yellowfin tuna, a seafood rice pilaf, hot buttery rolls, a vegetable stir fry and polished off almost an entire Key Lime pie, all we could do was groan and stagger out to the deck. Holding our stomachs, we collapsed into deck chairs.

"If we eat like this every day," Mary Linda said, "I'll have to replace my entire wardrobe when I get home. Either that or spend a month at a spa."

"I'm with you, Mel." Julie groaned. "I haven't eaten so much in one day since I was twelve and went to Girl Scout camp."

"Well, I'm not going to worry about it," Sandra said. "The woman is a genius."

The conversation was congenial, the five of us in vacation mode. The *Mirage* rocked lazily and the sky sparkled with stars. We were far, far away from Winslow, Ohio.

It had been a very long day and soon we were feeling sleepy and ready to try out our bunks. One by one we headed below. All but Ellie. She was engaged in an animated discussion with Captain Fairweather. If I had been more alert I might have wondered about the two of them, but as it was I was anxious to get to sleep. Tomorrow we would finally set sail. I couldn't wait.

Chapter Five

I awoke the next morning as the first shaft of sunlight slanted through the porthole. Surprisingly, I had slept soundly, lulled by the lethal combination of excess food, drink, and the gentle rocking of the ship. Combined with a fear of falling from the narrow confines of my top bunk, I had hardly moved all night. I am not usually one to awake with the early birds, preferring to join them for a late brunch, but this particular day I was ready for action at first light.

I hopped, not terribly nimbly, from my perch and lurched into the tiny head. I hadn't acquired my sea legs yet. I splashed water on my face, combed the tangles out of my short, choppy hairdo, and pulled on a pair of shorts and a Jazzercise sweatshirt. Grabbing a pair of kino sandals, I headed up to the deck to see what the day had in store. I passed through the galley where a pot of coffee sat on the counter beside a plate of tiny poppyseed muffins. I filled a mug with coffee and looked for a recipe card describing the ingredients of the muffins. Failing to find one, I took a sip of delicious coffee and went on deck.

It was still cool, but promised to be another warm day. The humidity was higher than the day before and I could feel my hair beginning to frizzle as I stood on the deck and breathed in the air. The seas were still calm and the sun was just beginning to rise. Those early birds were singing and I almost had to slap myself to believe that I was here. A mere twenty-four hours before I had been enduring a grey, overcast, snowy dawn, and now I was in paradise. I had just settled myself on the side of the boat, carefully balancing my coffee mug and dangling my feet over the edge, when I heard a throat-clearing behind me. I came close to tipping myself into the water as I jerked around to see Captain Fairweather, coffee mug in hand, standing behind me.

This morning he was dressed in a pair of ragged cut-offs and a tattered sweatshirt emblazoned with "The University of California". He was rumpled and unshaven but definitely hot. Okay, okay, I know I said he wasn't my type. But a woman can look, can't she?

"Sorry to have startled you," he apologized.

"Not at all," I replied with my usual wit. "Pull up a rail and join me."

The Captain swung his long legs over the side, and sat beside me swinging his legs and sipping coffee. He favored me with a speculative look. "You're up early this morning. I would have thought you all would sleep in."

"Me, too," I agreed. "But I guess I'm excited about setting sail."

"I have a few details to attend to this morning and then we'll get underway."

We sipped our coffee in companionable silence for a few moments before I admonished myself to make conversation. I wanted to know who were we trusting to safeguard our lives and our wardrobes. Okay, Nancy Drew, I exhorted myself. Investigate.

"So," I said, "have you been doing this captain thing for long?" Brilliant, I thought, what a clever sally.

"About seventeen years," he replied. "Ever since college."

"University of California?" I asked. Super sleuth can read a sweatshirt.

"Actually, sort of."

I waited for him to continue but he didn't say anything further. "Sort of?"

"Um hum."

Okay this wasn't getting me anywhere. Try another tact. "So, are you English? I mean a name like Nigel Fairweather sounds so British."

"Nope. My mother was a bit of an Anglophile. Loved everything British. Fish and chips. Trifle. Scones. The whole nine yards."

"Then where did you grow up?" The grand inquisition continued.

"Nebraska. Farm country. My dad was part Indian."

"Geez," I sympathized, "it must have been tough being a Nigel in Nebraska."

"I don't usually go by Nigel. My middle name is Edward so I've always been Ned."

"You can call me Ned," he continued. "My friends do."

I did not want to like this guy. But I couldn't seem to help it. I chattered about Winslow and my family and my job as a reporter and my friends' jobs and families as the sun rose in the blue, blue sky and Ned encouraged me. Some spy I would be, I thought. Some reporter. What has happened to my reporting skills. What is this guy doing to me? I sounded like a schoolgirl on my first date.

It wasn't too long before the rest of the party started stumbling on deck. Julie was the first to pop her head up the steps. Dressed in a flowing caftan-like garment in a bright floral print, her dark curls tied back with a matching scarf, she looked like a gypsy with a hangover. "Omigod," she moaned. "I am never. Ever. Ever. Never drinking again. I will throw up if I even see one of those stupid little umbrellas. And please, God, will you stop this stupid boat from rocking?"

She looked so comical and pathetic that both Ned (see, I was getting to know him already) and I burst into laughter.

"Poor baby," I said, "let me get you a nice soothing cup of tea. I bet Martha Stewart of the Seas will have just the thing to fix you up."

I slid off the side of the boat and headed below just as Sandra and Mary Linda were coming on deck. Both were wearing trim khaki shorts and white t-shirts with the Jazzercise logo cavorting across their busts. They looked scrubbed and healthy and ready to boogie. Unlike poor Julie.

"Have you tasted those muffins, Katie Pie?" Mary Linda asked. "They are to die for. I can't believe I want to eat again after last night. I'm starving all the time. Must be the sea air."

"We haven't even left the dock, Mel. Maybe it's the touch of almond paste in them," Sandra told Mary Linda with a wink. "We'll have to ask Martha for the recipe."

They tumbled up the steps like two exuberant puppies. Stretching and yawning, they took in the tropical scene.

"So where's Ellie?" Julie groaned.

"Still sleeping," Sandra said. "She didn't come to bed 'til late." Sandra gave the Captain a searching look. "How late did you guys stay out here?"

Ned hesitated. "I went down fairly early. She was still sitting in the deck chair when I left."

We looked at each other. That didn't sound like the Ellie we knew and loved. Something was going on with her, but I didn't want to think about it at the moment. I went to fetch tea for Julie.

Breakfast that morning was a veritable feast. By now we were all referring to her as Martha Stewart, and, indeed, Martha did live up to the billing. She set up a folding banquet table on deck and laid out so much food that the entire U.S. Navy couldn't have consumed it all. There were muffins, both almond and tiny, melting corn varieties. Sweet rolls. Omelets. Juices of several varieties. Fresh fruit. Bacon, sausage and tiny shrimp puffs. End-less pots of coffee. Toast. She even offered to make pan-cakes or French toast if we wanted to indulge. What was up with this woman? Death by breakfast? Even though we had vowed not to stuff ourselves again, we couldn't help ourselves. Only Julie, nursing her hangover, resisted. She huddled in her chair sipping hot tea, looking green. For the rest of us it was vacation, and vacation means eating and drinking. And buying new clothes in the next larger size. But who worries about that when presented with one of Martha's homemade cream crullers?

The Captain (Ned) disappeared after he ate a quick breakfast. Miguel put in an appearance and then he, too, vanished carrying as many muffins as he could fit in his large fist. The five of us took our coffee cups and lounged in the deck chairs enjoying the brilliant sun and cloudless blue sky.

"It doesn't get any better than this," Mel said, stretching lazily and reclining in her deck chair. "I'm so relaxed I can't keep my eyes open. Maybe I'll catch a quick nap."

"I imagine Don is missing you so much," Julie teased, "that he will smother you with gifts and flowers and stuff when you get back. Better rest up for that reunion."

"Ah, newlyweds," Sandra mused. "They do tend to miss each other, don't they? I'll bet Allen is so immersed in his latest merger that he hasn't even noticed that I'm gone."

"Oh," I said, "he'll notice when he can't figure out how to use that fancy new cappuccino machine of yours. He'll put out a SOS then."

"Absolutely," she agreed. "Meanwhile, he'll always have Starbucks."

"Speaking of which," Ellie said, "I think I'll give Ted a call and see if he made the PTO meeting last night and see if Michael got his science project finished."

Ellie was attired this morning in yet another of the seemingly endless array of slut outfits that she had brought along. She wore skintight white shorts and a tiny hot pink tank top with gold strappy sandals on her well-pedicured feet. But no matter how trashy she looked, she still sounded like the same Ellie whose apron strings bound her family to her as tightly as superglue.

"Speaking of Starbucks brought you to Ted and the kids?" I asked.

"Everything brings her to Ted and the kids," Mel pointed out.

"But," Julie said, "I think I'll give Robert a call as well. Before we set sail I should just touch base. Maybe Mr. Mom has the perfect hangover cure in his bag of tricks. Not that I could tell him I actually have a hangover. He'd definitely freak. I think."

The Great Sailing Adventure was about to begin, but before we could weigh anchor we all reached for our umbilical cell phones to call home. A little gloating about the weather here versus there, I thought, wouldn't be all that terrible an idea. And hearing Scott's voice wouldn't hurt either.

I have been married to Scott for not quite twenty-six years, most of my adult life, and I can't remember what it was like not to be married to him. We were teenagers when he rescued my sister and me from what we always tell people was sure to be a watery grave. My twin sister, Christine, and I had taken our small sailing craft out on a day when small craft warnings were issued and would have kept us ashore had we bothered to listen to the radio and hear them. Had we heeded those warnings, I would never have met Scott Kelly. Kind of the silver lining in the dark storm clouds.

The two oldest in the Stevens clan, Christine and I had left our two younger brothers, Billy and Brian, happily playing in the sand on the Lake Michigan shore while we set off in our bright yellow Sunfish. The four of us and our parents spent summers in a comfortable, but rundown, cottage in Northern Michigan near the town of Petosky. The cottage sat atop a hill overlooking Lake Michigan. A long set of wooden steps led from the hilltop to the beach. It was far enough that once we reached the bottom, we hated to clamber back up unless we had a very good reason. Say, the lure of the Good Humor man or a trip to town, but not simply to check weather reports.

My dad, Bill Senior, was the editor of the newspaper in our small Michigan hometown. Respected for his civic responsibility, he was also fun, funny and given to flights of adventure. He brought us up to believe that anything was possible. No feat too daunting. No height too high to climb. Our mother, Lori, was a bit of an adventuress herself. And while she didn't work outside the home, she was involved in all kinds of volunteer work. She was also admired for her successes on the tennis courts and golf course.

My parents liked to snatch us up and take off on the spur of the moment for outings of all kinds. We skied, hiked, camped, white-water rafted, and even, one scary time, contemplated jumping en famille from a plane before sanity was restored. No activity was deemed too difficult for the Stevens clan and we were taught to laugh at adversity and to persevere in the face of all obstacles. It was a fun, but exhausting, childhood. Many times I longed for an evening spent in front of the televison with a bowl of popcorn rather than pursuing some arduous athletic adventure. I was the self-described black sheep of our hyperactive family and I loved to read and to write. Still, I never wanted to be left behind, so I took part in whatever crazy stunt was dreamed up.

We were nineteen when we decided to take our twelve-foot sailboat out for an early summer sail. We hadn't been at the cottage long and the weather had been glum, grey and cold. When that June morning dawned and a glimmer of pale sunlight lit the morning sky, Chrissie and I decided to "Just do it!"

We had been sailing for years. Both of us were competent sailors and excellent swimmers. It wasn't the most enticing of days, but we rigged the sails, waded out into the lake and climbed aboard anyway. We were enjoying a leisurely sail, and had ventured out further than we intended, when the wind picked up. I was languidly holding the lines when they were ripped from my hand. I realized that the sky had turned black and scary as the boat heeled over and the sails hit the water. Chrissie and I were dumped unceremoniously overboard and under the crashing waves. Wet, surprised, and frightened, we struggled with the sails and the boat. Each time we attempted to right it, the wind would gust and over it would go again.

Two small specks on the distant shoreline, Billy and Brian were not going to offer much help. Rumbles of thunder sounded in the distance and an occasional streak of lightning lit up the sky. Big rain drops spattered on the water and we began to panic in a major way. At that moment of despair, we spotted a power boat bearing down on us. Rescue, thank God, was at hand. The sleek nineteen-foot outboard slid to a stop beside us and I looked up into the face of Scott Kelly. Even if I hadn't been about to drown, I would have viewed him as Sir Galahad in an outboard. His brown eyes were concerned and under his baseball cap I saw the cutest face. Not an auspicious moment to meet one's future husband. My wet hair was plastered to my head, the remains of zinc oxide decorated my nose and my bikini top was askew. I glanced down and realized that the man of my dreams was viewing more of me than I had ever allowed a man to see. One breast was exposed underwater while the other was only partially covered by the offending top.

Chrissie choked, not just because she had swallowed lake water, but with laughter at the look on my face. Scott tried to hide a grin and said helpfully, "You girls need a hand here?"

I tugged my top into place and tried to resurrect my dignity as well. "You guys are just in time. We are about to drown."

A wave smacked me in the head and I went under, swallowing water and making noises which sounded like, "Snork, snork." When I came up for air, Scott was in the lake beside me and tossed a line to his friend, Dave, in the boat. Dave hooked the line on the stern cleat and hoisted Chrissie into his boat. Scott and I rode on our Sunfish as Dave towed us to shore. With waves crashing over our heads and trying to capsize our little sailboat, we still managed not to drown and to exchange life histories in the process. By the time we beached the boat I was infatuated with Scott Kelly and, from the look in his eyes, he felt the same way.

From that day on we were almost inseparable and two years later, after we both graduated from the University of Michigan, we got married. In Scott I found an island of peace and calm after a tempestuous childhood. I moved from life with my impetuous family into a life with conservative, careful Scott. He was never afraid to attempt the same daredevil feats that were so important to my parents, but Scott never did anything without first making a "plan". And that made all the difference.

Scott was (and is) my security, my safe place, a hug whenever I need one. It was a relief to be able to take things at a more sedate pace, but eventually genetics . . . I guess that's what it is . . . will out. Of late, I was beginning to hunger for a bit of danger. Maybe this sailing vacation was an attempt to add a little excitement to my comfortable and uneventful existence.

Chapter Six

When Ellie reappeared after making her phone call to Ted, she had discarded her revealing outfit in favor of a black one-piece bathing suit with a pair of baggy shorts pulled over it. With her blonde hair tucked under a straw hat and big sunglasses perched on her pert nose, she was slathering sunblock on every exposed surface and greeted me with a cheerful, "Hi, Katie, how's Scott? Did he tell you about the storm last night? Ice all over the place. They cancelled the PTO meeting, so Ted stayed home with the boys and watched movies. Of course, he also didn't make them do their homework, but I guess it won't kill them."

She chattered on about Ted and the boys as if Ellie the Sexpot had never existed. Apparently she had reconnected with her inner-Mom.

"How are Robert and the girls doing?" I asked Julie.

She ran a hand through her hair and shrugged. "I'll be damned if I know. All of a sudden Robert is making like Mr. Mom. The same guy who couldn't find his way into the kitchen, let alone cook in it, is making pancakes for the girls. And humming. Alexa said Daddy was humming. Robert does *not* hum. I don't get it. The girls will probably need years of therapy after this, but I can't deal with it now. I'll think about it later."

"Good plan," Sandra said. "I'm not thinking about Allen this trip and I'm sure he's not thinking about me either." Her expression was dark. "I'm sure his mergers are keeping him plenty busy."

Mary Linda was quiet. Her dreamy expression spoke volumes about the success of her phone call to Don, any qualms she had about this vacation erased by talking to him.

"Ooh, Mel's got that newlywed look on her face again," cooed Julie.

We laughed and began to prepare for the launch of the *Mirage*. Martha showed up bearing a tray of Mimosas and Bloody Marys as well as an array of fresh fruits and juices. The quintessential bon voyage snack.

The sun was creeping higher in the sky, the time edging toward noon and the five of us were impatient to get going. I hadn't seen either the Captain or Miguel since breakfast and I was wondering what they were doing, when I was distracted by a long white limo pulling up to the marina dock. Out of the limo popped the driver attired in traditional limo driver garb. Black suit, hat and even gloves. He looked hot and out of place. He whipped open the rear door of the limo and from it emerged a woman who appeared to be a cross between Madonna and Carmen Miranda with just a touch of Charo thrown in. She wore a white one-piece jumpsuit and a wide-brimmed straw hat on the crown of which bobbed a bunch of fruit that included, a banana, a pineapple and the traditional cherries. Close to six-feet tall and with a drop-dead gorgeous figure, her huge sunglasses hid her face from our awestruck scrutiny.

The five of us had identical dumbstruck looks on our faces.

"Who on earth is that?" Julie asked, voicing everyone's thoughts.

Before we could figure that out, the other door opened and out came a small, nerdy man. Garbed in a white golf shirt buttoned to the neck and impeccably creased tan slacks, he was shorter than the mystery woman, slightly stooped and slender. He hurried around to the trunk of the limo and helped the driver remove luggage while the woman gazed around.

We watched this scenario unfold with our mouths open. The Captain chose this moment to make an appearance with Miguel close on his heels. "Ladies," he announced, "our final guests have arrived."

"Guests," I shrilled. "What other guests? We're supposed to be the only guests on this trip. Who are these people? What are they doing here?"

I heard myself shrieking and knew I was behaving like a shrew. Ned seemed to be enjoying himself way too much. He looked delighted at our shock. "Now, ladies," he said in an oily voice, "who ever told you that you were the only guests? You know we have that extra cabin and these nice folks are going to use it."

"What? Who are they? When did this get arranged? And why didn't you tell us sooner?"

"And spoil the surprise?"

Carmen/Madonna and her geeky companion picked their way down the dock while we watched in aghast silence. Towering on five-inch heels, the mystery woman cautiously avoided the cracks between the dock boards. Her protective escort had his hand on her elbow to guide her, while the driver staggered under the weight of their bags. Neither of the newcomers gave him a glance as they slid with regal aplomb up the gangplank and onto the *Mirage.*

"Good day, Captain," said the nerdy guy. "I am so sorry to have kept you waiting. Our plane was delayed. And then the traffic . . ." He trailed off apologetically.

"Not a problem at all," said the Captain. "We had a lot of things to take care of this morning and now that you are here we can get underway."

"Ladies," he said, turning to us. "I want you to meet our other guests, Mr. and Mrs. Livingston."

"I presume," he sniggered under his breath. He continued, "Mr. and Mrs. Livington, these are your fellow sailors."

Mr. Livingston smiled at us standing there like statues and said, "Allow me to introduce myself. I am Glenn Livingston and this is my wife, Svetlana."

Hearing her name, Svetlana whipped off her sunglasses and revealed a face which would, as someone once said, stop ships. In fact, it was quite literally stopping this one. She had high Slavic cheekbones and eyes the blue-green of the sea. She was stunning. She smiled at us with a childlike grin. "Da, I am Svetlana. I am wanting to be a friend. Yes?"

Ellie was nothing if not the perfect hostess and she reached out and took Svetlana's outstretched hand. "Welcome aboard."

Quickly Mel and Julie joined the Welcome Wagon crew. "You'll just love the *Mirage*," Mel told her. "And the food," Julie added.

Sandra and I exchanged quizzical looks and then wordlessly decided to go with the flow. We introduced ourselves to Glenn and Svetlana and tried to be as cordial as possible. It wasn't their fault they'd been dropped into our laps. Was it?

While Martha flitted about passing her goodie tray and Miguel was occupied doing something involving lines and cleats, I sidled up beside the Captain and muttered, "Um . . . er . . . Ned . . . I'd like a word with you please. Alone."

He glanced around at the deck party and realizing, I supposed, that no one would miss us, gestured to me to follow him below. He slouched into the galley and poured himself a cup of coffee, added a generous helping of milk and stirred it lazily. Leaning his long frame against the sink, he looked me up and down. "Well?"

I assumed that he knew exactly what I had on my mind, but if he was going to play dumb, I'd just play along with him. I would not give him the satisfaction of losing my composure again.

"The thing is," I began,"we thought we had the *Mirage* to ourselves. So what are we doing with Glenn and Svetlana onboard? Nice as they may be." I didn't intend to badmouth them just because they had been thrust upon us.

"I got a call last night," he explained. "You know how it is. Management knew that we had an extra cabin and it seems that the Livingstons were a last minute booking. They are extra cash in the coffers. What can I say?"

I considered my options. I really didn't think I had much leverage. I could, I supposed, make irate phone calls and demand that the newcomers walk the plank. But if I did, our departure would be delayed and the outcome would probably be the same. We were stuck with them. Truthfully, Glenn and Svetlana looked harmless enough, if you can call a six-foot Slavic beauty with killer looks harmless. Still, who would she seduce? Ned? Miguel? Glenn? And who cared if she did anyway?

"I know you aren't being honest with me," I said. "I could make waves."

He nodded and waited patiently. I hated the shrewd look he gave me, but we both knew I wouldn't insist that the Livingstons walk that plank, literally or figuratively.

"Okay." I gave in. "We'll make the best of the situation but if we get one bit less than what we paid for I'll have your head on a platter." Dramatic? Yes. And, as it turned out, we did get everything we paid for.

"I'll make sure everyone is okay with this," I added, "but I'm sure we can manage."

"Thanks," he said. And just for a moment I believed that he really was grateful. "Now I'd better get this ship underway. Yo ho ho and all that."

"Yo ho ho," I echoed.

Chapter Seven

Once the decision was made it didn't take Captain Fairweather long to get underway. The five of us and Glenn and Svetlana gathered on the deck to observe the proceedings. We all had cameras and dashed about taking pictures. Of each other and Martha and Miguel and even of Glenn and Svetlana who had changed into a tropical print bikini and wrapped a matching sarong around her flat abdomen. She was everywhere making new best friends. "I take your photo. Vat do you vant else for me to do?" She was like the new girl at school trying to convince everyone to like her. It was a tribute to her personality that we hadn't thrown her overboard when she appeared in her bikini.

Her skin was a mellow gold which attested to either a great tanning bed or days in the tropics. I was betting on the latter. And her figure was even more spectacular unclothed than it was in the white jumpsuit. Gorgeous as she was,

Svetlana had the demeanor of an eager puppy and not one of us could work up a good hatred. Glenn, too, had changed before we launched and was now wearing his golf shirt with a little crocodile decorating the breast pocket, black Bermuda shorts with deck shoes and black socks. He sipped a Coke and followed Svetlana with his eyes as she flittered about. His look was both paternal and, I thought, grateful.

Ned fired up the inboard engine in the stern of the boat and we chugged away from the little marina with the sails bunched at the foot of the masts and the breeze fluttering the loose lines. Ned steered the *Mirage* into deeper water where the breeze picked up a bit. When we got far enough out, Ned cut the engine and Miguel tugged on the lines to raise the sails. Far above our heads the sails caught the wind, billowed and filled and the *Mirage* began to move, heeling over slightly as she picked up speed. The full white sails looked like big clouds against the blue Florida sky.

"Yahoo," Julie cheered. "We're sailing!"

We toasted each us with Mimosas and bellowed as our glasses clacked together, "Here's to us. Here's to the *Mirage.*"

Svetlana beamed. "Here is to the perfect trip. And to new friends."

An hour later I was lying on my stomach on the bow. I had changed into my new, very expensive swimsuit and I wasn't sure of its success until I caught Ned's approving look. I slathered on SPF 45 sunblock and prayed that I wouldn't broil lobster red. I covered my "naturally blonde" hair with a baseball cap and was hypnotized by the crash of renegade waves against the hull. Ah, this is the life, I thought. Winslow, Ohio, seemed very far away.

My friends were perched in a row on the high side of the boat. They looked like tropical birds in an aviary. Wearing bright printed suits, big sunglasses and sunhats, they clung to the rail exhilarated as the *Mirage* skimmed over the waves. The sound of their laughter floated up to me as I lay motionless in the blazing sun.

Svetlana and Martha had quickly become fast friends and I observed them giggling like a pair of sorority girls in the galley. Martha was preparing yet another of her culinary specialties and Svetlana pitched in to help. She removed her sarong and dove up to her elbows into fresh pineapple. Svetlana was not your typical glamour girl. Gorgeous or not, she did everything she could to be one of us.

Glenn, on the other hand, seemed no different than he appeared. A rich, geeky guy married to a beautiful woman who may or may not have designs on his fortune. He responded softly and shyly when he was spoken to, but didn't initiate much conversation. Instead, he watched and listened with no detail escaping him.

At the moment, he was at the helm with Ned who was patiently explaining to him every move and piece of equipment. Glenn had an absorbed look on his face and asked an occasional question. Mostly, though, it seemed that he was happy to learn by following orders.

It was a jovial group that bright Florida midday as the *Mirage* bobbed on the aquamarine waves that splashed against the hull and bubbled behind us. In the wake of the boat a dolphin popped up now and then to frolic and then disappear under the waves. This was perfect. This was exactly what we had been hoping for when we left Ohio. I sighed and dozed off in the hot sun.

I must have slept for quite awhile because when I woke up the *Mirage* was sailing into a small cove. We were surrounded by white sand beaches fringed with tall palms that swayed gently in the breeze. A small bamboo hut was nestled in a cluster of palms. On second glance I realized that it was actually a beachfront bar. The beach itself appeared deserted although several boats bobbed at anchor on the gentle swells. One was a sailing vessel somewhat smaller than the *Mirage* and there were a few smallish power boats.

I sat up with a start and all but decapitated myself as the main mast swung hard from the starboard side to the port and the *Mirage* turned toward shore. "Where are we?" I called out to no one in particular. I scrambled back toward the stern, clutching the top of my suit with one hand and a side rail with the other. I dropped onto the deck and spotted Ned and Glenn doing something nautical with the ropes . . . er . . . lines.

"Hey," I called to them. "What are we doing here?"

"First port of call," Ned answered in a distracted tone, "Dolphin Cay (pronounced key, I learned later, but spelled 'Cay')."

"Oh." Brilliant repartee.

"Yep," Ned continued, "we'll be here overnight. Martha has quite a feast prepared and we'll enjoy a little shore time."

"Great. So where is everyone else?"

"Didn't want to disturb your nap," Glenn put in diffidently. "I think they went below to put on cover-ups or something."

"Yes," added Ned, "when we get anchored we'll take the dinghy into the beach."

At that moment the beach sounded great to me. I wasn't seasick but a hefty dose of precautionary seasick medication had left me feeling groggy. I could use a respite from the lulling seas. I hurried below to my cabin and grabbed a Jazzercise t-shirt and shorts and put them on over my suit. Stuffing a bottle of sunblock into my beach bag along with a mystery novel I had been meaning to read, I followed my friends back up to the deck.

"This is so beautiful," Mel cooed.

"Look at that sand and the palm trees," Ellie added.

"And is that a bar?" Julie asked. "With more little umbrella drinks? I can't wait."

Sandra tucked a lock of smooth dark hair behind one ear and settled her sunglasses more securely on her nose. She scanned the beach to determine if there was anything exciting going on.

"The beach scene could be very interesting," she said as she spotted a couple of guys in swimsuits head for the Tiki Bar.

We were all excited as we clustered around the dinghy. Ned, Glenn and Miguel had dropped the anchor and the *Mirage* floated about fifty yards offshore. Just a short row into the beach.

"Miguel will take you into the beach," Ned told us. "Martha is going to stay here and prepare the feast for later."

And her recipe cards, I snickered to myself.

"Glenn and Svetlana and I will take the second trip into shore and meet you there," he continued. "Head on up to the Tiki Bar for a drink or just lounge on the beach. Chairs and umbrellas are available for any of you girls who want them."

We scrambled into the dinghy, aptly named "No See 'Em", and, as Miguel rowed the little craft into the beach, I glanced around at the blue ocean, the white sand, the waving palm trees and the cute beach hut. I sighed. "This sure beats snow, sleet and slush. I wouldn't trade this for anything."

The five of us were drunk on sunshine, tropical breezes and the freedom of being away on an adventure.

The "No See 'Em" slid onto shore and we gathered our beach gear and tumbled onto the squishy sand. We helped Miguel turn the dinghy around and as he rowed back to the *Mirage*, we took stock of our surroundings. The beach looked very nice to me. Very nice indeed.

Julie and Sandra headed for the Tiki Bar to get drinks for us while Mel, Ellie and I headed for the umbrella guy. Soon we had arranged for three umbrellas and five beach chairs and settled in for an afternoon at the beach. The drinks were frozen, fruity and delicious. The sun was hot. And so were those guys in the swimsuits. We all agreed the day was perfect.

"That Tiki Bar is so tropical," Julie said as she passed around our margaritas. "It's just like in the movies."

Sandra slathered her slender figure with sunblock. "There are some very tropical men around as well."

"Where?" Ellie asked. One hand shading her eyes, she scanned the beach. "Men?"

"Whoa, girlfriend." Julie grinned. "Your inner slut is showing again."

As indeed it was. Literally. Ellie appeared to have brought an endless supply of revealing clothing. Today she was wearing a hot pink bikini that left little to the imagination. Her only concession to the sun was her big floppy beach hat and liberally applied SPF 50 sunblock.

In all the years I'd known her, Ellie had never been anything other than prim and proper. Some might say prissy.

She grew up with five brothers and had the art of feminine wiles down to a science. If there was a so-called good girl in our group, it was Ellie. That's why her choice of attire for this trip was so baffling. Certainly out of character. I was surprised to discover that she has a great body. Voluptuous where you are supposed to be. Not only that but the rest of her was fit and toned and, I dare say, sexy.

"So," I told her, "I'm noticing a new Ellie. What's going on with you anyway?"

Ellie turned red and not from the sun. "While the cat's at home, the mouse is gonna play." She narrowed her eyes. "I mean, I think I can try on a new persona if I want."

"Ah." Mel gestured at Ellie's bikini top. "So that's a persona. I wondered what it was called."

"Where do I get a persona?" I asked. "I've always thought I needed a persona."

"I think I need an extra large persona." Julie glanced at her own ample bust.

Ellie gave Julie a grateful look and, anxious to turn the attention away from herself, pointed at the "No See 'Em" returning to the beach. Miguel beached the dinghy and his three passengers, the Captain and Glenn and Svetlana, disembarked. It took all of our self-control not to gape in amazement at Svetlana. To be absolutely truthful, there was a fair amount of gaping going on.

Svetlana had chosen a yellow flowered thong bikini as her suit of the day. Her breasts were awesomely showcased in the skimpy top. At least a 36 D, her bosom resembled that of a figurehead on the prow of a Viking ship. Striking yet strangely immovable.

"Now that's a persona," Julie whispered to me.

"Boob job," I whispered back.

The thong bottom of her bikini covered only, shall we say, the bare essentials. Acres of golden skin were in plain view. And it was a stunning view which the males on the beach were enjoying immensely. Svetlana, unaware of the furor she was causing, loped, if a person can actually lope in four-inch platform beach flip flops, over to us. Her demeanor was not one of a beach goddess, but rather of a happy child delighted to see her friends.

"Hi, all," she called to us. "I am seeing you have the sun covers up. Da, I am needing a sun cover."

"She's got that right," Julie said from behind her hand.

"Glenn." Svetlana gestured at our umbrellas. "I am needing one of those." She pointed at our frozen margaritas. "And one of those!"

Glenn leapt, and I do mean that literally, to do her bidding. Before you could say "No See 'Em", Glenn had Svetlana set up under a big striped umbrella sipping a drink. He planted himself next to her and carefully removed his sandals and the black socks he was wearing. "Are you comfy, darling?" he asked. "Can I get you anything else?"

"No, dahlink," Svetlana replied. "I am doing with the drink and the cover so happy."

Ned chatted with Miguel, but missed none of the action. To me it seemed that he was keeping tabs on Svetlana. His gaze took in the dumbstruck looks on the sailors' faces and he frowned. Hmm, I thought, he doesn't like her on display. But maybe I was reading more into his look than I should have.

Miguel slipped back into the dinghy and rowed to the mooring where the *Mirage* rode the swells. Ned surveyed the beach and then dropped his lanky frame into the empty beach chair under my umbrella.

"Hi there, Katie," he greeted me. "What's happening?"

Well, gee, that's what I wanted to know. Now's your chance, I told myself. You're a reporter. Think like one. "Nada much. What's new with you?" For scintillating dialogue I just can't be beat.

"Um, so, Ned, do you have a family?" I persevered.

He gave me a shrewd look. "Yeah, I do. How about you?"

Brilliant reporter that I am, I decided to lure Ned into revealing facts about his life by entertaining him with stories of mine. Ned reached into the cooler and pulled out two cans of ice-cold beer. He popped the tops and handed me one and kept one for himself. Never much of a beer drinker, I accepted the can nonetheless. Kind of a good will gesture that I hoped would lead me to finding out more about our good Captain. I took a big swallow of beer and choked. "Well," I began, "I have a husband and two great kids." Half an hour later I was still babbling on about my family while Ned reclined lazily in the beach chair and nodded occasionally, asking a question here and there to keep me talking.

When I realized that I was doing all the talking and that Ned had contributed little about himself, I slowed down. I turned sideways on the lounge chair so that I could see his long frame. He had removed his shirt and was clad only in a pair of surfer swim trunks. He had, if not six-pack abs, at least a five and a half-pack. He was tanned from working in the sun and, I had to admit, quite gorgeous. A hunk. A stud muffin. You name it. I found myself warming up to him just a bit. Those blue eyes didn't seem quite as evil as I had first thought.

"So," I said as I paused in my life story, "enough about me. What about you?"

Ned looked at me as if he couldn't decide whether or not to confide any of his life details to me. Then concluding that I was harmless, he grinned and said, "Well, I'm divorced if that's what you're asking."

"Oh. So did your . . . um . . . ex object to your being away for such long periods?"

A shadow passed over his face and his eyes grew chilly. Then he shook his head. "I seriously doubt that she ever missed me all that much. She had her own life. I had mine."

Ah, I thought, score one for the reporter.

"What did she do?" I was surprised to find that I really wanted to know.

"Spent money," Ned said dryly.

"Meaning . . ."

"I made it. She spent it."

"Not a career woman then?"

"Oh, sure. She has a career as a gracious and well-mannered volunteer and celebrity hanger-on. A woman who does lunch and martinis. Lots of martinis." He sounded bitter yet resigned.

"Does a cruise ship captain make a lot of money?" I asked. Then hastened to add, "Not that it's any of my business and don't answer if you don't want."

"No," Ned said shortly. Then tired of my weak attempts to ferret out more information, he pulled his cap low over his eyes and fell asleep. Or pretended to. Didn't matter since he was through talking to me, busybody that I was.

Well, I mused, so our illustrious captain had been married to a woman who did little more than shop and lunch. Hmm. Interesting but not that unusual. No crime there. I was positive that there was a lot more to uncover. And I was just the woman to do it. I turned to my shipmates and tried to lure them into the warm ocean water.

Mary Linda and Ellie, their chairs side by side under one umbrella, had their heads together and were laughing at something in the fashion magazine spread out between them. They seemed to have no interest in anything going on around them.

Glenn was keeping watch over Svetlana as she napped on her beach chair. He kept darting inquiring glances at two sailors lurking nearby. Svetlana's magnificent breasts moved gently up and down as she slept, unaware that her cleavage was enough to make any red-blooded man sit up and take notice. Not to mention those long legs, beautiful face and golden hair. No wonder that Glenn was acting as a watchdog.

Sandra and Julie had wandered up to the Tiki Hut in search of drinks and action. I could see them chatting and, most likely, flirting with the bartender. They didn't seem to be making any move toward returning to our little umbrella enclave.

Left to my own devices, I got up and ambled toward the ocean. I wiggled my toes in the white, powdery sand and looked up at the cloudless sky. I sighed contentedly. The water was warmer than I had anticipated, so I waded in. Having grown up around water, it always has a soothing effect on me. So I allowed any concerns or suspicions I had been harboring about the Captain to just float away as I stood with waves splashing over my legs.

"Look! Dolphins!" exclaimed a voice from behind me.

Startled, I whipped around. Ned was standing a few feet away, his clean-shaven head shining in the sun.

"Will you quit doing that," I demanded.

"Jumpy, aren't we?" he commented.

"I wouldn't be if you didn't keep coming up from nowhere and scaring me half to death."

"Look." Ned pointed out to sea. Two dolphins were cavorting in the waves a short distance from shore. We watched together in what I can only call companionable silence for a few minutes. The impish dolphins were undeterred by the nearby boats and the few people watching from shore. One shiny grey fin would appear and then an entire dolphin would dart into the next wave. His buddy followed in his wake.

"They are so cute," I said. "My daughter, Casey, would just love this. She's crazy about dolphins."

"Mike, too," Ned answered.

"Mike?"

"My son."

Ah, ha! Another bit of information for my files. "You have a son?"

"Two. Mike and Trip. Twins."

I really was interested. I abandoned playing investigative reporter and thought like a woman trying to figure out what made this particular guy tick.

"How old are they? Casey is just twenty-one. She can't decide whether she wants to be an actor or a scientist."

Ned gave me that speculative look once again. He seemed to be assessing me and then with a rueful grin he told me, "The twins are seventeen. Can't decide what they want to do with their lives. That is besides surf, drink beer, chase girls and fish. Not necessarily in that order."

"I worry about them," he continued, "with me being so far away so much of the time and only their mother around to provide a good example." And he laughed scornfully.

Generally, I consider myself to be a pretty good judge of character and my first impression of the Captain had been resoundingly negative. Now, however, I was beginning to feel that maybe I had been hasty. I really believed he was sincere in his concern for his sons. After Ned turned to wade back to shore, I stood knee-deep in salty water for a few more minutes trying to figure out exactly what had just happened. For awhile Ned had seemed to be a doting father. Then he closed me out. Who was Captain Fairweather anyway?

As I stood in the water after Ned's abrupt departure, I watched with interest the activity on the *Mirage*. Martha and Miguel were busy loading an assortment of coolers and boxes into the dinghy. They repeatedly scurried below deck only to return with yet another item to be stashed in the boat. Finally Miguel hopped into the "No See 'Em" and began to row toward shore, leaving Martha onboard the *Mirage*. She was still surrounded by bags and boxes which I assumed were meant for the big feast that the Captain mentioned earlier.

Ned waded out to meet Miguel and pulled the dinghy onto the beach and both men started to unload the cargo. Glenn wandered over from where he had been chatting with the two bare-chested sailors and tried to help as well. He staggered under the weight of one of the boxes and nearly fell, but Ned steadied him, leaning close to say something. Both men laughed as Glenn recovered his balance and managed to get his burden ashore with no further mishaps. I could hear their voices and the laughter, but I couldn't hear what they were saying. They look like buddies, I thought.

Sandra was stretched out in her beach chair with her eyes closed. She sat up as I dropped into the vacant chair next to her. "Hey, girlfriend," I greeted her, "I think we're going to have some kind of a feast. There's enough stuff there to provision an entire army."

Sandra, as usual, looked cool and unruffled, not a single strand of her shiny bob was out of place, which made me feel messier and grubbier than I already did after a few hours of sand, sun and sunblock. She pushed her sunglasses up on her forehead and studied me. "I'll bet this will be an affair to remember."

"Can't be any more memorable than one of your soirees."

Sandra was famous in Winslow for her dinner parties and other gala events. Her husband Allen's law career had succeeded in no small part due to Sandra's social skills. Her attention to detail, the menu, the flowers, the carefully selected guests, made invitations to her parties among the most sought after in town. Once upon a time Sandra worked in Washington D.C. as an assistant to a congressman, and even after many years in Ohio she never quite lost her big city glitz and the lust for glamour. She yawned and we both watched curiously as Miguel struggled with both a second boatload of goodies and Martha as well. Once ashore, the pair began to set things up for the festivities.

The Captain sauntered over to our umbrellas and draped an arm around Ellie's shoulder. The look on her face spoke volumes. I thought she would either melt on the spot or jump Ned's bones or possibly both. The look on his face was indecipherable. "Lovely ladies," he said with his arm still around Ellie, "it's going to take awhile for us to get set up for the big feast. If anyone wants to go back to the *Mirage* to freshen up before dinner, Miguel will row you out."

He pointed in the direction of the Tiki Bar. "Or there are some outdoor showers behind the hut where you can just rinse off. Au natural." He looked at me and winked. What was it with him and his winking anyway?

Sticky with sunblock and salty from the ocean, I jumped at the chance to take a quick shower in the head in my cabin. I would welcome a change of clothes as well. Ellie, Mary Linda and Sandra decided to return to the *Mirage* too. Julie, though, said, "I'm way too comfortable in this chair to make the effort. One more of these drinks and I'll be asleep anyway." In fact, she did look as if she might nod off. "Kate, will you bring me my blue sweater and drawstring pants? I'll stay here and take a nap."

"Come on, Jules," Sandra urged, "a shower will feel like heaven." But Julie refused to budge. The rest of us collected our paraphernalia and clambered into the waiting dinghy. Miguel manned the oars and headed into the incoming surf. The *Mirage* looked welcoming as she rolled on the seas.

Chapter Eight

My shower on the *Mirage* was about the size of a broom closet and required major contortions to use it. I banged my elbow painfully and since the showerhead reached only to my chin, I developed a crick in my neck trying to shampoo my hair. In spite of that I felt like a new woman as I stepped into the cabin wrapped in a big, fluffy towel. Unexpectedly, I found I had no desire to get dressed and return to the beach for an evening of revelry. My bunk held a much greater appeal and I considered just climbing into it with a good mystery book and skipping the whole beach scene. At that moment, Mary Linda popped back into our cabin dressed in clean navy shorts and a snug fitting white t-shirt. With her blonde highlighted hair pulled into a ponytail, she looked like something out of a Gap ad. "You aren't ready yet." She pointed out the obvious with an accusing look. "Ellie and Sandra are dressed and we're waiting for you."

I glanced longingly at my tiny bunk. "I was thinking of staying here in my jammies with a book."

"Oh, no, you aren't," Mary Linda exclaimed.

I could have protested, but I was beginning to get my second wind and, truthfully, I was curious. Only a loser would miss this party. I slipped into a pair of denim capris and a pale pink tank top. I finger fluffed my hair, figuring I wouldn't even try to fight the humidity, slid my feet into sandals, and grabbed my denim jacket.

"All set," I said. "You can stop drumming your fingers now."

We hurried through the salon and galley and out to the deck where Miguel and our shipmates were waiting.

The beach scene was nothing short of amazing. Long tables were set up under the palm trees and flaming torches illuminated them. Closer to the shoreline several bonfires burned, tended by teenagers in white t-shirts and khaki shorts. The umbrellas had been replaced with short-legged sand chairs clustered around the fires. On the tables Martha had arranged an awesome array of food. Apparently she was expecting the *Queen Mary* to arrive sometime soon. It was a feast of mammoth proportions and no expense had been spared.

The Captain had issued invitations to the occupants of the other boats and there was a group milling about. The men wore tropical shirts and shorts, except for the two boaters we had seen earlier who were wearing muscle shirts and bike shorts. "Mood pants," Julie whispered sotto voce as she joined us. Glenn, as before, was engaged in earnest conversation with them, while Svetlana flitted about at Martha's elbow. Svetlana had done something complicated with her habitual sarong and looked like a mythical sea nymph. It was a magical setting and I was glad that I had decided to come.

Svetlana broke away from Martha and bounded over to greet us. "You are wanting the umbrella drink. Yes?"

"We are definitely wanting the umbrella drink. Lead us to them."

Svetlana led the way to a beach bar that had been set up near the food tables. The bartender from the Tiki Hut tossed drink shakers from hand to hand, pausing only to pour frothy tropical drinks into glasses adorned with slices of fruit. We put in our orders and then, drinks in hand, wandered over to the tables to peruse the buffet. It was a spread which offered something for everyone. There was a table of delicious appearing appetizers, a table displaying exotic fruits, an assortment of salads and rice dishes, and wonderful aromas of grilling meat and fish. The pièce de résistance, though, was the dessert table where an abundance of creamy and caloric concoctions beckoned the weak-willed and sugar-addicted among us. My pants felt tighter just looking at the goodies.

Ned came over to welcome us with a grin and a bow. "Greetings, oh fair ladies. Welcome to the feast!" He beckoned to a beach boy type bearing a tray laden with an assortment of appetizers. "Behold the puu-puu platter. Martha has outdone herself tonight. I personally recommend the crab puffs."

Mouth-watering smells emanated from the platter and we snatched the bite-sized hors d'oeurvres as if we hadn't seen food in a month. Two tow-headed little girls of about four and six ran around dodging beach boys bearing dishes of food. Their parents were from the small power boat anchored a short distance from the *Mirage*. A group of teenagers from another boat were preoccupied with each other. The girls giggled coyly while the boys flaunted their cool attitudes. It wasn't a large crowd, but everyone seemed to be having a fine time.

As the evening progressed the noise level increased and new best friends exchanged e-mail addresses as they swilled liquor in huge quantities. I was determined that I wasn't going to overindulge . . . in either food or drink. Some of my friends weren't operating within the same guidelines. Sandra was never without a drink in her hand, yet showed no obvious ill effects from all the alcohol she downed. Julie, on the other hand, seemed more restrained than usual, nursing a single drink and picking at the food. Ellie, as usual, fawned over the Captain who appeared to be relishing the attention. While Mary Linda was deep in discussion with the mother of the two little girls.

I noticed that wherever Glenn was so, too, were the two tanned sailors in their too-tight muscle shirts. At one point he introduced them to us, but I immediately forgot their names. Two strange boaters on a beach scarcely registered. Svetlana, Martha's right-hand girl, kept busy refilling plates and putting out more food.

It was a fun and festive evening and, to my surprise, and in spite of my earlier reluctance, I thoroughly enjoyed it. As the hour grew late, I found myself alone. Diet Coke in hand, I wandered drowsily over to claim one of the beach chairs in the shadows just beyond the light from a bonfire. I slipped off my sandals, scooched down in the chair and leaned my head back to look up at the starry sky and bright moon. Ah, bliss. I was absorbed in my own thoughts, wondering what Scott and the kids might be doing, when I realized that I wasn't alone. Two people huddled in the shadows nearby were so engrossed in their conversation that they didn't notice me. I remained motionless, not wanting to embarrass the couple by drawing attention to myself and, let's face it, I'm never one to miss an opportunity to eavesdrop. I slipped even deeper into my chair and tried to melt into the darkness.

My great detecting skills led me to believe that they had a more than casual relationship just from the way they gestured and leaned into each other. I sat bolt upright, however, and nearly capsized my chair, when I realized that I knew the pair lurking there. I recognized the vibrant red sarong before I recognized Svetlana herself, but it was when I heard the unforgettable deep voice of the Captain that I almost blew my cover. I gasped audibly and waited to be ferreted out. But the pair was oblivious to everything but each other and I remained undiscovered. What on earth could these two be discussing so intimately? I eased myself out of my chair and crept as close as I could without revealing myself.

". . . no possible way," Svetlana was saying.

Ned's response was an unintelligible mumble.

"You just can't . . ." Svetlana's voice carried over the sounds of waves breaking on the shore. "What about me?"

". . . can and will." I heard Ned say. "I'll handle it. Don't worry. It will all be fine."

"Just wait. Please. It will never work. I can't lose . . ."

Svetlana's voice drifted away and it was terribly silent all of a sudden. The only sounds were the crashing of the waves and the palm fronds soughing in the breeze. I strained to hear anything further, but it appeared that Ned and Svetlana had gone. I was stunned. Glenn and Svetlana had made no claims to know Ned. There had been no mention of any prior acquaintance. Yet the conversation, or part of one, that I overheard made it quite clear to me that Ned and Svetlana were not strangers.

Something else about the interlude was bothering me. I racked my brain but I couldn't quite put my finger on it. All of a sudden, I felt isolated and vulnerable. Shivering, I gathered myself together and stumbled toward the dwindling group still clustered by the large bonfire. Light and people seemed very comforting at that moment.

Mary Linda broke away when she saw me. "Where have you been?" she asked. Then looking more closely at my face she added, "You look like you've seen a ghost."

"I think I just might have."

I didn't want to go into the strange scene I had just witnessed right then, so I shook my head at Mel, warning her not to ask me any more questions. "Later," I whispered in her ear. Mel looked at me quizzically, and then shrugged and dragged me back toward the fire and our friends. Svetlana was there, her arm around Glenn's waist and her head on his shoulder . . . even though she had to stoop to get it there. My mind was in overdrive. I couldn't fathom the connection between her and Ned. And he was nowhere in sight.

Svetlana snuggled up to Glenn and asked, "Liebchen, would you be getting me a beer? I am thinking I am thirsty."

And then it hit me. If the woman on the beach actually was Svetlana, it dawned on me that she had spoken with no hint of an accent. Her speech had been as American as my own, but now it was pure ZaZa. I was perplexed. Suspicion may be my middle name, but I just knew that something weird was going on. I had no idea what, but I sure was going to try to find out. That's what we Nancy Drew types do. Solve mysteries. And here was one with my name on it.

The party began to break up soon after that. The other boaters drifted back toward their boats and Martha and Miguel began to pack things away. Glenn and Svetlana had wandered off and only the Captain, who had quietly reappeared, and the five of us were left standing around the dying embers of the fire.

"Oh," sighed Ellie, "this has been a perfect evening."

The rest of us nodded in agreement. "But I am so ready for my teeny, weeny little bunk," Sandra declared. "It's way past time for me to turn into a pumpkin."

"Well, Cinderella," Captain Ned said, "I'll row you ladies out while Miguel and Martha finish packing the picnic things."

We stumbled into the dinghy with a fair amount of alcohol-induced hilarity. Not that any of us were drunk, but we were enjoying a sort of happy afterglow. Or four of us were. I, on the other hand, was in a quandary. My brain was clacking along trying to distinguish between what I *thought* I'd seen and heard during the course of the evening and what really might have occurred. I was having second thoughts about the entire thing. Maybe I had just imagined it. Maybe it had been a couple from one of the other boats having a lovers' spat. How could I be absolutely certain that the couple was Svetlana and Captain Ned? And had known each other before the Livingstons set foot on the *Mirage* only this morning? Svetlana and Ned seemed like such an unlikely couple. As Ned rowed the dinghy through the inky black night, I pondered what I knew and concluded that I was undoubtedly making the proverbial tidal wave out of a ripple. I decided I was suffering from an overactive imagination. Again.

Of course, as soon as Mary Linda, Julie and I closed the door to our cabin, Mel accosted me, demanding to know what I had seen on the beach that had freaked me out. But, now that we were safely back on the *Mirage*, the entire episode faded further into unreality. I convinced myself and my friends that I hadn't seen anything incriminating at all. Even if it had been Svetlana and Ned on that secluded beach, what was it to me? I recounted the incident in as few words as possible. Then I summed it up. "But I don't know if it was they. I'm sure I'm making a big deal about something that's absolutely none of my business."

"Leave it to you to create a big mystery." Mel laughed.

Julie groaned dramatically. "The bigger mystery is why did I eat so much."

The topic of our conversation veered from the puzzling beach goings-on to a safer, and always enthralling topic . . . food.

Several hours later I awoke with a start from a sound sleep. Both my cabin mates were snoring softly. I sat up, or as close to sitting as I could manage in the cramped bunk, and listened. I felt a slight thump and the *Mirage* rocked at its mooring and then I heard a muffled splash. I peered through the small porthole next to my bunk and I could see a tiny piece of moonlit sky. I got on my knees and cupped my hands over my eyes. I saw a small path of bubbles on the surface of the sea leading away from the ship. I watched intently, my attention focused on the water. At last, not too far from the *Mirage*, I caught sight of a swimmer just breaking the surface. As I watched, the mystery person swam steadily away from the *Mirage* and toward another sailboat anchored nearby. I couldn't tell who it was but, curious, I wiggled out of my bunk and hurried up to the deck. In the clear night I saw a figure approach the other sailboat and hoist himself out of the water. It was a man. And I concluded that he must have been visiting one of my shipmates. Who could have been entertaining a late night visitor? One of my friends who I thought I knew so well? Or Svetlana? Or even sweet little Martha sharing her recipes and something else?

I contemplated the ocean for awhile and then turned to creep back to my cabin. I stealthily descended the few steps from the deck to the galley below and was moving through the salon when I stopped dead in my tracks. I was still in the dark recesses of the salon, but the pathway to the cabins was illuminated by small glowing floor lights. So I could see clearly a small figure standing with her hand on her cabin door, glancing back and forth as if to make sure the coast was clear. Ellie! In all her scantily clad glory . . . still wearing her sexy little sundress from the party. I gasped. What on earth was Ellie doing? Just getting "home" from her evening's activity? Given her wardrobe I didn't think she was just getting up for a drink of water. Frankly, I didn't know what to think. I tiptoed toward her, but before I reached her, Ellie opened her cabin door and slipped inside, leaving me aghast in the eerie darkness.

Chapter Nine

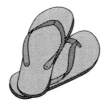

I tossed and turned most of the night. My bunk didn't seem big enough for both me and my nightmares. When I slept at all, I dreamed of the Captain and harems of women, of dancing dolphins with leering faces, of storm-tossed seas and drowning maidens. The first watery rays of daylight were just peeking through the porthole when I awoke feeling groggy and grouchy. Next to my head there was the telltale slap, slap of waves against the side of the boat and I recognized the soft flap of sails which meant we had set sail. I rolled out of my bunk, grabbed my hooded sweatshirt and stumbled in the murky half-dark to the head. I brushed my teeth and threw water on my face in an attempt to feel more alert. When that didn't help, I headed for the cabin door glancing back over my shoulder at my cabin mates who were still sleeping soundly. I turned the knob, tripped over the doorjamb, and lurched into the gangway.

I made my way to the galley and helped myself to coffee from the perpetually perking coffee maker. Coffee mug in hand, I climbed the stairway to the deck.

Ned was seated in the stern of the boat, absentmindedly steering the tiller, with a faraway look on his face. He was wearing a navy blue windbreaker with *Mirage* stenciled on it, faded jeans and a UC Berkeley baseball cap. He looked up and saw me as I cleared my throat. "Yo," he said with a brief smile.

"Yo, yourself." I handed him the coffee mug that he had left just out of reach.

"You're up early," he commented, accepting the mug. "Is this a new habit or are you always the early bird?"

"I hate to get up anytime before noon, but when I realized we were underway again I couldn't stay in bed. There's just something about early morning on the water."

Ned gestured at the sun which was just creeping up over the horizon casting a red and orange glow on the waves. "I love to sail before dawn. It's the best time of the day."

I nodded and we sipped our coffee and watched the sunrise, neither of us feeling the need to speak. Strange, I didn't feel the animosity for him that I usually felt. In fact, I found him to be downright mellow. I almost liked the guy.

"So, what's our itinerary for today?" I asked. "I know we're supposed to reach Key West tomorrow."

"That's the plan." Ned pulled on the starboard line and hauled the sail in a little to catch more of the increasingly fresh breeze.

I caught my balance as the boat heeled over and coffee slopped onto my shorts. I grabbed a fistful of napkins from my pocket and sopped up the spill. When I looked up

I caught Ned watching me with an odd look on his face. It seemed that he was going to confess some secret. Then he realized that I had seen him and he turned away. I shook my head in confusion and took a big gulp of coffee to give me time to regroup.

"I've never been to Key West," I said. "What are the best places to go? What's good for lunch and what bars are fun? And what about shopping?"

I listened absently as Ned filled me in on the wonders of Key West, but my mind was on trying to figure out his secrets. I was sure he had plenty of them. But then, who doesn't?

Balancing a mug of coffee and a slice of banana bread, Mary Linda was the first to pop unsteadily onto deck. She nearly lost her footing as the boat dropped into a trough and then climbed a wave. Clinging fiercely to her mug, Mary Linda dipped and rolled with the movement of the deck. "Whoa," she shouted above the noise of the sails flapping and the roar of the wind, "it's a bit breezy today."

The wind was now gusting ferociously, making the sails and lines snap and the *Mirage* fly over the seas. "Now this," Mel yelled, "is sailing!"

Ned gave her an approving look and a thumbs-up gesture before turning back to steering the *Mirage*. In her bright blue sweater and faded jeans, her face glowing and her eyes bright, it looked like Mary Linda didn't have a care in the world. As I caught a glimpse of her profile, I did a double take. "Wow, Mel," I said.

"Yeah, I know," she answered. "Boobs. Whoda thunk it, huh?"

"First Ellie gets a persona and now you have boobs. What am I doing wrong?"

Mel grinned. "Have you thought of a new bra?"

I punched her arm. "Or a boob job?"

She tossed her head sending her ponytail flying. "Honestly, Kate, I don't think I've ever felt like this. No one needs me. No one expects anything of me. Free at last. Thank God Almighty, Mel's free at last."

One by one the rest of our shipmates surfaced in various states of dress, and in some cases undress, and staggered on wobbly legs, trying to stay balanced on the heaving deck. Julie wandered up in the sweats she had slept in but none the worse for last night's revelry. Clutching a muffin as if it was a lifeline, she aimed herself toward one of the deck chairs and fell into it with a thump as the *Mirage* rolled in a sudden gust of wind.

"Whoa," she exclaimed, "it's rough. I didn't think about it being so rough."

"It is a boat, you know," Mel pointed out. "Boats have a tendency to rock and roll."

At that point Sandra and Ellie joined us. Both were dressed in shorts and sweatshirts and had taken the time to put on make-up.

"No weather too bad to not accessorize, huh?" I asked. "You two look like an ad for what the well-dressed boater should wear."

Sandra looked pointedly at me, raised an eyebrow and said, "And you look like the before picture."

I figured that Sandra was right and perhaps I should do a little fixing up myself. Before I had a chance to excuse myself, though, Glenn and Svetlana popped up from below. Glenn, as usual, was wearing a calm demeanor, Bermuda shorts and boat shoes. Svetalana glided toward us poised on three-inch heels. It was an astounding feat, if you'll pardon my pun. This woman was not the least bit clumsy as she made her way forward with Glenn in tow. She definitely had her sea legs, and I had to admit that they were pretty nice ones at that. Her greeting was cheerful as always, "Hello to my friends. And what a so nice day it is being."

It was a brilliant morning. The breeze had blown away the early clouds and the sky was a deep blue. The ocean was a matching aquamarine with the sun sparkling off it. A school of dolphins had come up in our wake and were playfully jumping out of the sea, their grey bodies glistening in the sun. Everyone else was focused on the ocean and the dolphins when I turned to find my camera and saw Svetlana catch Ned's eye and smile an intimate smile. He smiled back and his features softened. They held the gaze for only a few seconds before both turned away. I wondered if I had imagined it. But I knew I hadn't.

I hurried to our cabin, took one look in the mirror, and decided that some major repairs were needed. I showered, pulled on my favorite khaki capris and a bright red, hooded t-shirt and then attempted to apply make-up while maintaining a precarious balance on the rolling boat. I nearly took out one eye with my mascara wand before I decided that make-up and the rocky seas did not go hand in hand. I gave up my feeble efforts and settled for combing my damp hair and slicking on lip gloss. I felt infinitely more presentable afterwards. I grabbed my sunglasses and my baseball cap and headed back to the deck where yet another of Martha's feasts awaited me.

During my absence Ned had piloted the *Mirage* into a smallish cove and dropped anchor. In the shelter of the cove, we were protected from the sea breezes and the

Mirage sloshed from side to side on clear, glassy water. We were situated in the center of the 'U' shaped shoreline, surrounded on three sides by a glorious white sand beach edged by palm trees. The sun was rising higher and the temperature was a bit warmer.

With the *Mirage* at anchor, Martha set up folding tables on deck. Each table was covered with a cheerful floral printed cloth and matching tropical flowers were set out in gaily-colored vases. Scrambled eggs with brie and bacon, goat cheese and smoked salmon frittatas, banana-stuffed French toast, pancakes with a fruit compote and maple syrup, and fresh fruit and Eggs Benedict with portobello mushrooms were today's selections. Menus, of course, were displayed prominently.

My shipmates were greedily filling plates and raving about how delicious everything looked while Martha beamed in delight. Even Svetlana abandoned her role as self-appointed hostess and devoured a plate of eggs and French toast with gusto. "I am so much enjoying all of this so wonderful food," she said. "I am hungry like the beast."

Glenn hugged her. "Honey, I think you might be hungry like a bear. Not a beast."

"Oh, no," we interjected, "you, Svetlana, could never be a beast."

"Ah," Svetlana said, "I am always having the trouble with your English. I am not speaking it so pretty as you."

"You may not speak English as well as we do," Ellie soothed, "but you are so gorgeous that no one will ever notice."

For a split second a cloud crossed Svetlana's beautiful brow and she frowned. "Yes," she answered with a wry grin, "this is a problem of my life. No one is hearing what I am saying to them."

I glanced at Ned to see his reaction to Svetlana's comment, but he was busy with Miguel and seemed not to have heard her. Miguel headed below to carry out his orders and Ned turned to us. "Today we are scheduled to do a little snorkeling if anyone is interested. This cove is known for the tropical fish and clear water. It's the perfect spot for seeing the beauty that lies beneath the surface of the sea. As soon as you finish your breakfast, we can start getting ready to go in the water."

"I am wanting to do some of the skinny dipping," Svetlana volunteered.

Startled, the rest of us contemplated the glorious Svetlana and tried to imagine that body nude. It boggled the mind. Thinking, perhaps, about what was certain to be an awesome display, we exchanged amused looks and remained silent. It was an effort, but I think we were afraid to say anything because we knew we would burst out laughing.

"Um," Mel said. "Well, um."

"Well put, sweetie," Julie agreed. "Um, indeed."

We were all struggling to find an appropriate response when Glenn came to our rescue. With a grin that said he was enjoying our discomfiture, he put a hand on his wife's arm. "Honey, I think you mean skin diving, not skinny dipping. Skinny dipping is what you do *without* clothes."

Svetlana blushed and looked embarrassed. "Oh, no, I am doing it again." She put her hands over her face. "I am such not good at the talking in the English."

All of us hastened to assure her that we thought she spoke very well. Even Ned was amused. "I am liking the thought of her skinny dipping," he said in a low aside to Glenn, who just nodded.

That issue resolved, we spent the rest of the day snorkeling, sunbathing and snacking on Martha's culinary masterpieces. She flitted among us offering an excess of calories and fat grams that none of us were inclined to refuse. The day could not have been more perfect and the five of us congratulated ourselves once again on the success of our venture.

From time to time, I noticed the Captain and Glenn with their heads together consulting about lines or sails or something. It's a guy thing, I told myself. They looked really congenial sipping beers and laughing. Miguel was occupied with some other marine chores and took little notice of the rest of us while Svetlana resumed her role as Martha's helper and popped below deck frequently only to reappear with more snacks. All hands were content as the *Mirage* rocked at her mooring.

At one point during the long, lazy afternoon Ned suggested that we pull up anchor and set sail. That proposal was met with a decided lack of enthusiasm from the sun-baked and lethargic group. Even Ned didn't appear to be in favor of moving on. He put it to a vote and we unanimously decided to stay put until the next morning.

"I don't think I could hoist myself out of this deck chair if I wanted to," Julie drawled.

"Not unless it was to fetch another round of drinks?" Sandra asked hopefully.

"Nope, not even that would get me to budge my ample rear end," Julie said.

"I wish you would quit doing that," Ellie said firmly. "You are always putting yourself down."

"Look in the mirror, girlfriend," Mel added. "You are a gorgeous woman."

Julie blushed but was enjoying the spotlight. "Uh, huh," she said. "And actually, you guys, I have kind of a confession to make. I have an appointment to have liposuction when we get home."

"No way."

"Yep, way. I actually had it scheduled twice before and cancelled each time. Once the girls had the flu and once I just chickened out."

"Good," Sandra said. "You don't need to do something that drastic."

"Yes, I do," Julie wailed. "Look at me. I'm just a big old blob. I want to wear something fitted for a change. I am so sick of flowy things." Julie tugged at her loose caftan and pounded her fist on her stomach. "I hate how I look."

As the others discussed Julie's potential lipo surgery, I observed Captain Ned and Glenn. I knew I was trying to solve a mystery that possibly didn't exist. Ever since I was seven and read my first Nancy Drew book, I was hooked. I was determined to become the next Nancy Drew. My mother insists that I was an annoying child, always lurking in doorways and peering in closets seeking evidence of a crime. I prefer to think that I was vigilant. As I graduated from reading about Nancy Drew to Agatha Christie to more modern girl detectives like Stephanie Plum, however, I realized that my small Midwestern hometown was not a hotbed of criminal activity. The landscape was not peppered with corpses and innocent victims. So I amended my goals and decided that rather than being a private detective, I would write mystery novels.

I am always on the lookout for some bizarre occurrence. My friends scoff and tease, but I am convinced that one of these days I will happen upon a great mystery and through my brilliant deductive skills I will solve it. And here it was.

As the discussion flowed around me I studied the Captain and Glenn. With their heads together and deep in conversation, I was bothered by something. Some niggling detail kept eating away at me, but I couldn't figure out what it was. Two guys drinking beers and talking shouldn't be of any concern to me. At that point, Glenn said something to the Captain and he threw back his head in laughter. Glenn burst into laughter at the same time and it hit me. The two men had the same laugh . . . one that started as a deep rumble and then exploded into guffaws."

"Hah," I thought to myself. "Strange."

I didn't give it another thought that afternoon, though. I was too preoccupied with my friends. We were enjoying the exact kind of day that we had hoped for on that long ago morning when we formulated our Great Sailing Adventure plans. Who was I to spoil it all with stupid suspicions and made up mysteries?

Svetlana floated up from below with a tray of drinks and appetizers and offered them around. Then she made her way to the bow of the boat where Glenn and the Captain were engaged in comradely dialogue. Holding the tray, she carefully put one foot in front of the other in an effort to avoid spilling anything. She had nearly reached the two men when the boat rocked a little more energetically and she lost her balance. She struggled to keep her grip on the tray and almost fell, but the Captain caught her before either the drinks or Svetlana hit the deck. Still holding on to the Captain, she righted herself. I watched the byplay. Svetlana kept her hand on the Captain's arm and the look that passed between them was extraordinary. I know I sometimes live in a fantasy world, but to me that look sizzled with love and desire. Okay, so I probably read too many romance novels as well as too many mysteries, but I know what I saw. Quickly I glanced at Glenn to see if he sensed the connection too. What I saw amazed me. Glenn looked exactly the way a proud father does when he sees his children accomplishing something noteworthy. Glenn's look was simply not one your average husband would give a hustler moving in on his wife. No concern, no anger, no dismay. Nothing but that weird proud Papa look.

"Okay," I told myself, "now you really have lost it." I tried to refocus on the ongoing debate over Julie's liposuction and to ignore the three huddled cozily in the bow of the boat.

As the sun dipped lower and the late afternoon chill began to set in, Mel and I went below to change out of our swimsuits. I decided to share my observations with her and as we stretched out on our bunks, I broached the subject. "Mel," I began, "have you noticed anything unusual about the relationship between the Captain and Svetlana and Glenn?"

"Other than the fact that the Captain leers at Svetlana every chance he gets?"

"Well, there is that too. But I think it's more than that."

Mel pulled her hair off her neck and sat up in the narrow bunk. She looked at me and grinned. "Okay, Nancy Drew, what mystery are you trying to solve today?"

I tried to defend myself, but my reputation preceded me. Mel had every reason to be dubious. But I forged ahead, nonetheless. "Well, I'm not saying anything exactly, but haven't you noticed the hot looks that go both ways between the Captain and Svetlana?"

"No, can't say that I have."

"So, okay, then." I pursued my theory. "Have you seen any signs of passion between Glenn and Svetlana? Any looks? Any touches?"

Mel considered for a moment and then admitted that she hadn't.

"Me either," I said. "He acts like her father, for crying out loud, not her husband." A thought popped into my mind. "He seemed more interested in those sailor dudes in the mood pants than he ever has in Svetlana."

"Okay," Mel conceded, "I can see that. But that doesn't mean something is going on between the Captain and Svetlana. I've seen him give you and Ellie some pretty searing looks sometimes. Is there something going on with either of you and dear old Ned?"

"Well, not with me, that's for sure. But I wonder about Ellie."

Then we burst into hysterical giggles at the thought of our little Ellie hooking up with the Captain. She might be dressing the part of a slut, but underneath what little she wore she was still the prim and proper wife and mommy. Probably.

"I don't know why you don't just write the great mystery that you are always looking for," Mel said. "You'd save us all a lot of time and effort. Not to mention that you might achieve fame and fortune."

"I'll start working on it immediately," I said.

Mel and I returned to the deck, refreshed and dressed in sweatshirts and jeans, ready for another evening at sea. Mel convinced me that I was indulging in a fantasy, but I didn't know that I had created a tiny seed of doubt in her.

Chapter Ten

The next forty-eight hours were idyllic. The days were warm and sunny, the sky a deep azure, the winds light, and the ocean an enticing aquamarine. The nights were sultry and liquid with a sky full of stars and warm breezes. It was everything, and more, that we could have wished for.

The weather was so perfect we convinced Captain Ned to abandon his schedule. We were all excited to get to Key West, but at a leisurely pace. Captain Ned agreed. We sailed when we felt like it and we dropped anchor to swim or use the snorkeling equipment or the jet ski which was secured in the stern. All the while Martha plied us with exotic drinks and gourmet treats while Miguel, with his bronzed pecs on display, provided us with eye candy.

Ned, too, seemed congenial and relaxed, smiling more and leering less. Even Svetlana gave in to the languid mood and stretched out in a deck chair in a tiny red flowered bikini with a drink in one hand and a book in the other. Glenn alternated his attention between Svetlana and the Captain; bringing drinks and snacks to Svetlana and helping the Captain with basic boat duties. He seemed content to serve as butler/deck hand.

The second night at sea we all enjoyed yet another meal and then gathered under the starry canopy on deck chairs. Julie sighed and said, "I'm so stuffed that I may never look at food again."

The rest of us groaned our agreement. "I have to just stop feeding my face," Sandra added. "I will never be able to fit into any of my clothes at this rate."

Tugging on her waistband, Mel nodded. "I feel so fat. I seem to be expanding by the minute."

"We all feel that way,"Ellie said. "Let's just get over it."

"Yep," I said, "we'll be home soon enough and we can do double classes and eat nothing but lettuce leaves. Right now I intend to eat, drink and be merry and tomorrow I can diet."

Ellie said, "But I do intend to take home all of Martha's recipes and try them out on Ted and the boys." Another thought struck her and she exclaimed, "Why don't we see if Martha wants to publish a cookbook of all her recipes. We could call it 'From the Mouth of the Sea.'"

"No, no," Julie said. "From the Dolphins Mouth."

"How about Bait and Switch?" "Sea Shell Eat?" "No *Mirage*?" We called out titles.

"Speaking of books," Mel interrupted, "our Katie is trying again to write the great detective novel."

My friends groaned. "Not again," cried Ellie. "Who done it this time?"

"According to Kate," Mel explained, "Captain Ned and Svetlana are doing it."

"I never said that. I just think something weird is going on."

"And when didn't you?" asked Julie.

Sandra grinned at me. "Life is just one big mystery to you, Katie, and you want to be the one to solve it."

"Way too much Janet Evanovich and Sue Grafton, if you ask me," claimed Mel, naming two of my favorite authors.

"Wait, wait, wait," cried Ellie. "Back up the trolley. What do you mean the Captain and Svetlana are doing it? Doing what exactly?"

Julie laughed. "Ellie, sweetie, even you aren't that naive. Are you?"

"No, no," Ellie defended herself. "I just want to know what Kate thinks is going on. I haven't seen anything suspicious."

"You wouldn't," I said. "You're too sweet to see it."

Ellie frowned at the word "sweet". "I am *not* sweet. I am so sick of that word."

"Would you prefer slutty?" Julie inquired politely. "Cuz I've seen that little red number and it would certainly qualify."

For once Ellie didn't back down. "I prefer slutty to sweet, thank you very much. But my first choice would be sexy. It's about time I stopped being so damned sweet, isn't it?"

Mel patted her arm soothingly. "We love you just the way you are. And so does Ted."

Ellie glowered. "I'm not so sure about him."

Naturally we all leapt in to assure Ellie that, of course, Ted adored her and that she was alluring and sexy. Ellie didn't look convinced, but I think she was uncomfortable being the center of attention. "I still want to know what you've seen to make you think that the Captain has a thing for Svetlana," she said.

"Other than the fact that he can't take his eyes off her awesome cleavage?" asked Sandra. "The looks he gives her are positively smoldering."

I faced Sandra. "So, you've seen it too?"

"Why sure," she said, "but he looks at all women that way."

"Actually, I don't think he does," Julie said. "Have you ever seen him leer at Martha?"

We burst into laughter at the thought of tall, tan and mysterious Captain Ned snuggling up to the *Mirage*'s domestic goddess. After the laughter trailed off, I asked, "Am I the only one who thinks it's odd that Svetlana and Glenn behave more like brother and sister than husband and wife?"

Before anyone had a chance to answer, Glenn emerged from below with Svetlana clinging to his arm. "Did I hear my name being bandied about?"

"I am hearing my name as well," put in Svetlana.

The five of us exchanged chagrined looks, embarrassed at being caught gossiping about them. I stammered, "We were just . . . um . . . wondering where the two of you met?" Glib, as usual, I chided myself.

The pair sank into deck chairs and regarded us curiously. The conversation paused awkwardly as we tried to regain our equilibrium and then the chattering began again. Almost as if nothing had interfered. Well, I reflected, I'm not the only one who's suspicious. Sandra, too, had noticed the odd vibes.

No one wanted to call it a night, so we lingered on deck until the early morning hours. Captain Ned joined us and, to my disappointment, his behavior was unimpeachable. The perfect gentleman, he paid no more attention to Svetlana than to any of the rest of us and seemed to be in an unusually subdued mood. Other than an occasional exchange of enigmatic looks with Glenn, I found nothing in his actions to cause me any misgivings. All in all, it was a pleasant evening. A group of compatible people just hanging out under the stars.

Eventually Svetlana, who was falling asleep on Glenn's shoulder, excused herself and headed below with Glenn following in her wake. With the spell broken, the rest of the group shook off their lethargy and wandered below to their bunks. One by one they left until only Ned and I remained. We sat for awhile, neither of us bothering to speak. I looked at him and wondered what it was that had caused me to take an instant dislike. Only a couple of days had passed and I couldn't remember exactly what I had found so offensive. I believed he was your basic sexist male and while I didn't find that appealing, I was beginning to detect something quite different under that veneer. When he talked about his sons his demeanor was nothing like that of the man who greeted us with smirks and looks that implied he was imagining us parading around nude.

As we languished on the deck under the stars I felt that perhaps I had misjudged him. Had all of that leering been a masquerade? I could never quite shake the feeling that Captain Ned Fairweather had secrets and that he wanted to share them with me. I would have loved to have been taken into his confidence. Maybe he would confess his hidden passion for Svetlana. Or not.

Ned caught my eye and with an amused look said, "Do I have tomato sauce on my chin? Or perhaps a spot on my shirt? Or are you just overcome by my good looks? You haven't taken your eyes off me in the last fifteen minutes."

I blushed, which I hoped he couldn't see in the dark, and replied, "I haven't?" Brilliant rejoinder, I thought. "I'm just thinking about my kids and my husband. Sorry." Take that, you conceited jerk.

"Oh, so it isn't my devastating handsomeness that has you gawking at me?"

"Get over yourself, buster. You aren't *that* good looking!"

"Yeah, my wife didn't think so either." He shrugged.

Wife? My ears perked up. He had mentioned her before, but when I started to ask questions he had shut down. Maybe this time he would confess something to me. "Your wife? She must have been very discriminating."

"Well, she thought so anyway. I regret to say I wasn't the man of her dreams."

"So, who was?"

"Ironically, my father was."

"Hmm," I murmured encouragingly, hoping he would continue.

Ned reflected and then decided to confide in me. "We met in college. She was gorgeous and my hormones chased after her relentlessly. The thing is . . . while I thought I was pursuing her, it was actually the other way around. Alison came from a rather modest background. Her parents didn't have a lot and had to make a lot of sacrifices to send her to college. Particularly a college in California. My parents, on the other hand, were bloody rich. Mom came from a farm family, but Dad, well, dear old Dad is a captain of industry. Have you ever heard of Fairweather Electronics?"

I nodded.

"Well, that's Dad. CEO and founding father. And worth billions. Too bad he's a real son of a bitch, but that's another story. Anyway, Alison pursued me until I caught her, as the saying goes. She pretended to love everything I did. Boats and sailing and beer. We got married right after we graduated from college and I thought life couldn't get any better . . . stupid sod that I am. The ink was scarcely dry on the marriage license when she reverted to type. It appeared that my dear wife, with whom I was madly, passionately in love, or at least in lust, wanted nothing to do with me and my 'dinky little boats' as she called them. What she wanted was my money."

I made sympathetic noises and he continued. "I was devastated but I thought I could hang in there and she would see that I was as wonderful as she thought my dear father was. Thus, two sons. Unfortunately, my father divorced his third wife . . . my mom died a few years earlier . . . around the time that the twins were born. Alison saw her opportunity and put the moves on him. The rest is history. Alison and I got a divorce. She got most of my money and, as a bonus for putting up with me, she got my father as well."

At this point, Ned shook his head as if to wake himself from a trance. "I never tell anyone this stuff. Maybe it's the alcohol or maybe you're such an ace reporter that you can worm all the nasty details out of me. Whatever. I won't bore you anymore with the sordid details of my life."

"No," I protested. "I want to hear them. I mean, I'm always interested. I mean . . ." I trailed off in confusion. I didn't want him to think that I was hanging on every word, but I didn't want him to think I didn't care. His story explained some things about him. But I still had questions. His relationship to Svetlana, for instance.

"Well, that's enough about me." Ned gave a huge yawn. "I have bent your ear long enough. I think I'll head down to my cabin. Are you coming?"

"I wasn't bored at all," I said. "I think I'll just sit here a little longer and enjoy the quiet and the ocean."

"All righty then. G'nite."

"Good night."

I watched Captain Ned unwind himself from the low slung deck chair and stroll toward the steps leading down to the galley and the cabins. Clad in ragged jeans and a faded sweatshirt, his deck shoes tattered, he looked nothing like the wealthy man he professed to be. Or to have been. But then, truth is stranger than fiction. In my mind, anyway, they can be pretty much the same.

I was too tired to drag myself out of my chair and head below so I stayed put and basked in the tranquility. The water lapped gently against the hull of the *Mirage* while a loose halyard clanged rhythmically against the mast. I heard the far away cry of a mourning dove and was lulled into a deep slumber. As I fell asleep I heard the sound of laughter in the distance. Was it male laughter? Too tired to keep my eyes open, I drifted into sleep.

When I awoke I had no idea where I was or how long I had been sleeping. Disoriented and still half-asleep, I sat up, rubbing my eyes to clear the fog from my brain. Stiff and cold, I stretched cautiously. All I heard were the sounds of the night. No human noise intruded on the silence. I remembered the sound of male voices and laughter as I fell asleep, but I heard nothing now. Had I imagined it?

I shook my head wearily. My imagination never quits, I told myself. And even if I had overheard laughter, there were a million reasons for it.

I squinted at my watch and couldn't make out the time in the dark. Probably nearly three a.m. Way past time for me to be tucked into my bunk. I stood up and stumbled down the steps leading to the cabins. The little lights along the hallway lit my way as I tiptoed to my cabin. With my hand on the door, I glanced up and down the hallway and listened for any sounds which might have indicated that someone else was still up. I noticed a sliver of light coming from under the door to Ned's cabin. Curious. I fell into my cabin, clambered into my bunk and was asleep before I could manage one further coherent thought.

Chapter Eleven

It was late morning when I woke up in an empty cabin. Both Julie and Mary Linda were gone, leaving behind a rumpled bunk and a pile of discarded clothing. A glance at my watch told me that it was almost 10:30. I stretched as luxuriously as was possible in the cramped bunk and was surprised that I felt remarkably rested considering the lateness of the hours I had kept the night before.

The slap of water against the hull and the snap of the sails informed me that we had set sail once again. Not wanting to miss any action, I lurched from my bunk to the floor of the rolling yacht. Trying to get my sea legs, I staggered around the cabin and into the head. I decided that a shower would refresh me only to discover that no water was available. So I cleaned up the best I could and, feeling decidedly unattractive, pulled on my bathing suit with a sweatshirt and shorts over it. I stuffed my frizzling hairdo under my ball cap and tottered out of the cabin and into the salon.

I was surprised to find my four friends clustered cozily around the galley table. Martha bustled about as usual and chattered with Ellie and Sandra. To my utter amazement Ellie had on a bright orange t-shirt paired with hot pink shorts. Her ears were naked of any jewelry, matching or otherwise, and her hair could only have been styled with a mixer. The only fashion statement Ellie was making this morning was from the "don't list". But her eyes glowed as she jotted rapidly in her notebook and quizzed Martha relentlessly. Sandra looked on, throwing in a question of her own every now and then, while Julie and Mel lingered over cups of coffee.

I stood unnoticed for a few minutes. Ellie was absorbed in what Martha was saying, and the others watched in wonder as Ellie continued to grill Martha with prosecutorial aplomb.

"Hey," I finally said, announcing my presence.

They looked up and chorused, "Hey!"

"What's going on?" I asked. "Looks like a board meeting for the fashion impaired."

Ellie favored me with a cool glance before she laughed and admitted, "I didn't have time to accessorize this morning. Sorry." Her tone said she was anything but sorry. "I had this idea and I couldn't wait to see what Martha had to say."

I must have looked confused because Ellie hastened to explain. "See, Kate, I thought about what we said about a cookbook last night. I didn't sleep all night because I decided that we . . . I . . . could really do it."

"Go on," I encouraged her.

Emboldened by my interest, Ellie launched into an explanation of a cookbook that she could do in cahoots with Martha. Recipes from the sea. Photos. Tales and tails of the sea. She hurried on, her cheeks pink and her blue eyes alight with excitement and enthusiasm. I hadn't seen Ellie so impassioned since she discovered the secret ingredient in the Cheesecake Factory's chocolate chip cookie dough cheesecake.

"And that's where you come in." She paused to take a breath.

"Me?"

"Well, I don't write. But you do. And I know you could help write this and it would be so fantastic. We can sell a million, a gazillion, copies and become rich and famous and . . ." Ellie ran down, looking at me expectantly.

I'll have to admit that writing a cookbook hadn't even made the list of things I wanted to do. I love to eat, I do, but cook . . . not so much. My idea of a home-cooked meal is cold cereal, so what could I possibly contribute to the compilation of a cookbook? I said as much to Ellie.

"No, no, no!" she exclaimed. "Martha and I will do all the work. We'll get the recipes and all of that. You just need to write it down. Oh, and come up with a concept that will make this cookbook unique and marketable."

"Oh, is *that* all? It's just not that easy. If it was, wouldn't I have already published a best selling novel?" I told her in my best raining-on-your-parade voice.

Sandra decided at this moment to interject her opinion, as unwelcome as it might have been. "Katie, my love," she said in the grave tone of a doctor presenting a fatal diagnosis, "you can't say that you actually have tried. You've talked and talked and talked about writing 'your' book, but you have never given it much of an effort. It's always something. A vacation. A child in trouble. Tennis to be played. Jazzercise to be danced."

I was aghast. I stared at her speechless, because she had dared to voice what we all knew was the truth. I wanted to snap at her and tell her that I *was* working on that great award-winning book. I wanted to explain and excuse and deny. But I couldn't. She was telling the truth. As much as I had always planned to write a detective novel based on a crime that I personally had solved, I had only a few pages saved on a computer disk to show for it.

The others stayed silent, waiting to see what would come next. No one dared to venture a further opinion. Sandra was in this alone.

I fought back tears. "Okay, Sandra, you're right. I'm the world's biggest procrastinator. I have zero to show for all the promises I've made to myself. And to you guys."

Sandra looked as if she wanted to take back her accusing words. "You are one heck of a tennis player, though," she said, offering me a consolation prize.

She stood up and gave me a hug and Ellie silently handed me a mug of coffee and a slice of Martha's pineapple macadamia bread. Wisely she didn't pursue her cookbook idea, leaving me to digest it . . . a little cookbook humor . . . for myself.

Shaken from Sandra's unfortunately on-target assessment of my writing achievements, I decided to leave them and seek solace on deck. I was certain that as soon as I disappeared, I would be the topic of a conversation which I was better off not hearing.

I escaped from the stuffy salon into the fresh air still reeling from the truth. Captain Ned was at the helm guiding the *Mirage* as she sliced through the waves. The wind whipped my face and I slapped a hand onto my ball cap to prevent it from being blown away. It was a beautiful morning once again, but I scarcely noticed it I was so absorbed in my dismal thoughts.

The book? The one I always went on about? That was another story. A story I had yet to tell. Hardly more than an occasional thought, not even a legitimate pipedream, I worked on it sporadically when I had a burst of energy or when I couldn't figure what else to do. But I had never really dedicated myself to writing it. For me to say, I knew, that it was difficult to write and publish a book was akin to saying it would be tough to swim the English Channel. I was about as familiar with one as the other. I sighed and tried to push these unwelcome thoughts from my mind.

Captain Ned glanced over and then beckoned to me. "Kate," he called, "can you give me a hand?"

Why not, I thought, at least I can help someone else even if it isn't one of my best friends. "What do you need?"

"Can you take the wheel and steer the ship for a few minutes while I climb up the mast and secure that line that's flapping in the wind?"

I tipped my head back and squinted at the mast. Indeed, a line was loose and the wind was tangling it. "You want me to steer? I'm not so sure about that. Where's Miguel?"

"He's below and you told me you'd had some experience with sailboats, didn't you?"

I bobbed my head. "But the sailboats I sailed were like bathtub toys compared to this one."

The Captain patted me on the shoulder. "You'll be just fine. There's nothing to it. Just take the wheel and keep her going into the wind. Like this . . ." He positioned my hands on the wheel and stood behind me letting me get the feel of it. I was so engrossed in sailing the boat that I was hardly aware of Ned's arms around me guiding my hands. It did cross my mind that if anyone saw us, she would definitely get the wrong idea. Or maybe not. Now that I thought about it, I could feel his breath warm on the back of my neck and I could feel how strong and hard his body was against mine. Pay attention, Kate, I chastised myself. He is not coming on to you. He's teaching you to steer this stupid ship.

Impatient with myself, I jerked away and said irritably, "I've got it. Do what you need to do and get the heck back down here. I can't steer forever. Not unless you have a date in the Bermuda Triangle."

Ned chuckled and shinnied up the mast. I couldn't watch him because I was paralyzed. My hands were frozen on the wheel and I didn't dare look away from the glistening ocean. I was immobile for what seemed like hours before I dared to even breathe. Then it dawned on me that I was enjoying this. The wind whipped my hair and my sweatshirt billowed out around me. My sunglasses slipped on my nose and I risked capsizing the sailboat to push them back in place. I felt myself relax and then I began to relish the freedom of the moment. The sun, the sea, the wind, the boat.

I didn't even notice that Ned had completed his task and slid back down to the deck and was watching me. I jumped nearly a foot when he spoke from my elbow, "You're getting into this, aren't you?"

I grinned over my shoulder at him. "I had forgotten how great this is. I mean I always loved the water and I don't know why I haven't missed it long before this."

Standing on the deck of the *Mirage* with the wind in my face and a strange man with his hands on my arms, I suddenly realized that I missed the excitement, the thrills, of my childhood when no mountain was too high and no challenge too difficult. I was, it dawned on me, bored. Bored with the safe and secure and expected. I was in a rut and I wanted to break out of it. I wasn't sure how I was going to manage it, but I knew I had to try.

For the moment, I was enjoying being at the helm of the *Mirage*. Captain Ned stood at my elbow and offered brief suggestions and instructions, but otherwise I was on my own. It didn't take me long to gain confidence and soon I was in control, making small corrections as the wind gusted. The wind increased and I tugged the line in a bit so that we picked up speed. I felt as if we were flying over the water. I tossed my head and my cap blew off. I laughed in surprise and delight. This was fun!

Ned dropped into the captain's chair and watched me with the air of a teacher whose student has exceeded all expectations. He made a thumbs-up gesture and I responded with one of my own. We sailed for some time that way. With me in command and Ned standing idly by. Finally, I said, "I love this. How can anyone *not* love it? Your wife didn't like sailing at all?"

Ned shook his head. "Alison claimed that she got sea-sick, but I think it was more a matter of being sick of me."

"Turns out," he confided, "that she didn't mind boats at all. Just the little ones that I love. Alison is more the big cruise ship type. Give her a full service cruise liner with shops, restaurants, gambling, entertainment and other passengers to admire her and she doesn't mind sailing one iota."

"Kind of beneath her to sail on a ninety-foot yacht, huh?"

"You got it. My dad bought her an entire line of cruise ships and I haven't heard her complain about that." He slowly unclenched the fist he had made and stared at his hand.

"How about your mom and dad? If you were raised in Nebraska, it's kind of odd to develop a love of the sea, isn't it?"

"Not really. I got sick of all that corn. All those waving stalks. All that talk about corn borer beetles. Nebraska was way too corny for me."

I envisioned Ned riding a tractor through a cornfield. "I can see that. But no one else in your family longed to escape all that waving stalk stuff?"

I pictured his father, the captain of industry, striding through the fields in his business suit and I smiled to myself. Ned's next comment broke into my reverie and got my full attention.

"Only my little brother." He seemed lost in a daydream.

"Brother? You have a brother?" I asked, feigning an innocent interest.

Ned flinched. "What? No, I don't." He turned his back to stare moodily at the sea. Seconds later he stepped in front of me and took over the wheel. "I'll take it from here."

We were no longer having a friendly conversation. Ned had shut me out completely. I was sure that he had let the comment about his brother slip accidentally and I wasn't going to get any more information from him. Baffled, and more than a little curious, I turned to head below. I called over my shoulder, "Guess I'll go below for awhile. See what the others are up to."

He said nothing, his eyes fixed on the white-capped waves. I went to find my friends, puzzling over why it would be such a big secret to have a brother.

I found Ellie curled up on the bench seat beside the galley table with papers spread everywhere. Her blonde hair was disheveled and she ran her hands through it, chewing thoughtfully on the pencil she was holding. Her face scrunched up in concentration, she didn't notice me. I slid into the seat beside her and nudged her with my hip to get her to move over.

She looked up, startled, and exclaimed, "Katie you surprised me. I didn't hear you come in."

"Obviously. You are pretty much wrapped up in whatever you are doing."

She shoved the stack of scribbled notes aside and nodded. "The cookbook thing." She added almost apologetically, "I know you don't want to hear about it."

"Yes, I do," I assured her. "Sandra said some things about me that were sadly true."

Ellie crinkled her nose, screwing up her courage. "Well, Sandra kind of shoots from the hip. Speak now, repent at leisure."

"I can't disagree, but when she's right, she's right. I am a great big procrastinator."

Ellie started to protest, but I cut her off. "No, I am. Even though I have my reasons, that isn't good enough. So, tell me what you have in mind with this cookbook and how I can help."

She perked up and pulled out some of her notes. "Look at this one, Kate, and this one too." She displayed some recipes scrawled on scraps of notebook paper. "They are great. I mean you've been eating Martha's food and it's awesome. I started talking to her yesterday and she told me that she never just uses some recipe from a book. She adds her own little touches. Like that banana bread with the almond paste? Her idea."

I nodded sagely . . . I'm great with these food references. "Go on. It's past thyme." I nudged her. "Get it?"

"Ha ha. So, I'm thinking of a cookbook with all of Martha's recipes and maybe some others. But the thing is, it's been done to death. I can't quite come up with an angle."

"I hate to be the bearer of bad news," I had to tell her, "but you're right. It's probably been done. Off the top of my head, I don't have an angle either. But this is coming from someone who hasn't done much with her own ideas."

"That's okay," Ellie said. "If you're willing to discuss it that will be good enough for me. I doubt if I could pull off something like a real book anyway. It's a bit overwhelming to think about. I mean, Ted always says . . ."

"I don't care what Ted always says. He doesn't give you enough credit. He thinks all you can do is be cute but dumb. And you aren't dumb."

"I know, but . . ."

"No buts about it."

"I guess I do have the cute-but-dumb angle covered, don't I?"

"Ellie, honey, what was your major in college?" I asked. "Don't you have some business background?"

"Does being a legal secretary count?"

"Everything counts. So what was your major?"

Ellie's face lit up. "I see where you're going. Yes, I majored in business, but I also took a bunch of home ec courses because I loved it."

"Ah, hah. Business and home ec. Who better to do a cookbook?"

"Still, I don't have that angle," she groaned.

"Not yet, but we'll find something."

"You really think we can do it?"

"Yep, we don't have anything to lose. I'll help you as much as I can, but I also need to do my own thing. It's about time, wouldn't you say?"

"We'll be each other's support group. We won't let us fail."

"Hear, hear," I said, and we toasted each other with cups of cold coffee.

I left Ellie poring over her scribbles and headed to my cabin. Blaring music greeted me as I drew near. I yanked open the door and found my three friends dancing to music blasting from Julie's CD player. The song was one of my favorites from Jazzercise. They had formed a conga line, short as it was, and were trying to dance in the cramped space without crashing into the bunks. I burst into laughter at the sight.

"Hey, Katie," Mel whooped as she executed a bump and grind. "Jazzercise. You gotta love it."

Julie punched a button, another song began and I joined the conga line. When that ended, Julie started another and the four of us shook our booties until we were exhausted. Mel flung herself onto my bunk and, breathing heavily, Sandra and I collapsed on the floor. Julie turned the music down.

"Whew," Sandra said, "I needed that. I felt like a slug."

I high-fived Sandra and she looked relieved. "Then all is forgiven?" she asked.

"Well, duh," I said. "I wasn't mad. I *am* the world's biggest procrastinator and all you did was say it out loud."

"I didn't mean it," Sandra apologized. "I only . . ."

"Yeah, you did," I interrupted, "but that's okay. You were right. And besides, Ellie and I just had a long talk and we just might be able to do something with her cookbook idea."

Sandra peeked at her watch and exclaimed in surprise, "Guys, I didn't realize what time it is!"

We scrambled for our bags, books and other necessities for an afternoon of doing nothing more strenuous than lying in a deck chair. The *Mirage* was no longer moving at a rapid clip and I guessed that we were going to drop anchor and be served another feast a la Martha. I debated mentioning my odd conversation with Captain Ned, but I knew they would only think I was imagining things. Only I, it seemed, found Ned to be more than he appeared on the surface.

Coated with enough sunblock to protect a small village, I dropped into a deck chair with a sigh of pleasure and eyed the buffet that Martha, with Ellie's help, had prepared. It took all of my willpower to resist running over and filling my plate with one of everything. "Calories are not your friend, calories are not your friend," I recited under my breath. Svetlana, relieved of her duties as Martha's apprentice, materialized wearing a tiny silver bikini that melted down wouldn't supply enough silver for a thimble. And, as usual, she provided a vista which no male, except perhaps her husband Glenn, could fail to appreciate.

She glanced around at the assembled group, spotted an empty chair next to me, sank into it with a blissful moan and arranged her voluptuous form while the rest of us looked on mesmerized. Finally, she turned to me and exclaimed, "Whew. It is the day of total beauty. I am loving this day so much."

I murmured agreement and Svetlana gushed on, "The food it is looking delicious. I am not knowing if I can so much of it to eat. I am thinking I am getting the fat, how do you say it, butt?"

If there was anything Svetlana was not getting it was the "fat butt" and I told her so. "You," I said in my sternest mom voice, "are crazy. Your butt is not one bit fat."

I was not interested in discussing Svetlana's derriere, so I did what any self-respecting woman would do. I changed the subject. I blurted out the first thing that came to mind. "So, Svetlana, how long have you and Glenn been married and how did you meet?" Not exactly how I intended to broach the subject, but it did have a certain shock value.

Svetlana looked rattled for a moment before she regained her composure and turned guileless green eyes upon me. "I am not understanding," she said innocently, "the question you are making me? My English it is not so good sometimes."

"I didn't mean to be nosey. I just wondered how you and Glenn met."

Svetlana made several minute adjustments to the tiny silver bikini top, stalling for time. She gazed at me artlessly and fumbled with a strap. "I am thinking . . ." she began.

And then Glenn came to her rescue, a knight in a shining wetsuit. Dripping wet, he appeared from nowhere almost as if Svetlana had conjured him up. He planted a wet kiss on her silky cheek and slithered out of the wetsuit. With that accomplished, he made room for himself on the end of Svetlana's chair. "What are you two lovely ladies talking about?"

Svetlana gave Glenn what I interpreted as a grateful look. "I am so enjoying the beauty of the day. But you are making drips on my chair. Please to go away with yourself."

Glenn grinned cheerfully and gave her a damp squeeze. "Well, liebchen, would you like me to bring you some lunch?"

She waved her hand airily and laughed. "Oh, no, dear Glenn. Katie and I were just worrying about the fat butt. I am not wanting to get it. Nothing of that too delicious food for Svetlana."

As Glenn wandered off in search of a towel, he took a backward glance over his shoulder at the two of us. I was pondering my next inquiry when Julie and Sandra, bearing plates laden with food, plopped down on the end of my chair.

"You're not eating," Julie exclaimed. "You're not attempting a diet are you?"

"Now, my dear," added Sandra, "we'll have none of that. Remember our motto, eat, drink and be merry for soon we go back to Winslow, Ohio."

"I just don't want to be wearing clothes two sizes larger." I gestured at Svetlana. "Svetlana and I don't want to get the fat butt. Right, Svetlana?"

"Oh, for sure not," she agreed happily.

I reached over and took a piece of cheese from Sandra's plate. "There. I'm eating."

Ned's timely appearance interrupted our conversation. Clad only in ragged jeans and Topsider deck shoes, he was quite a sight. Working on deck had left him damp with perspiration and his well-muscled chest glistened in the sun. "Ladies," he said, "I believe we should discuss our itinerary for a moment." He paused to gaze at the mast and the sky before he turned back to us. "The weather is supposed to be decent for a couple more days. Then they predict a storm. If we pull up anchor and set out right now we can probably get to Key West the day after tomorrow."

"Or," he continued, "we could always use the engine."

"Oh, no," we protested in unison. "That's no fun."

"Okay, then," the Captain acquiesced, "here's what I propose . . . if we sail this afternoon and most of tomorrow, I'm thinking we can be down by Ramrod Key tomorrow night. Maybe further. Then we'll run in and have the next day in Key West. How does that sound?"

"Sounds great to us."

With those details decided we settled in for the rest of the afternoon. Ellie, finished with her hostessing, changed into a demure black one-piece suit and joined us. With a white sleeveless top tied at the waist over her suit and a wide-brimmed straw hat pulled over her hair, she was "our" Ellie once again.

Only Mel was missing so I volunteered to go down to our cabin to find her. It was cool and dim below and it took a moment for my eyes to adjust after the glare of the deck. As I stood blinking and enjoying the chill of the air-conditioned salon, I heard loud voices coming from one of the cabins. Curious, I crept down the hallway. The voices were louder now and sounded angry. Cautiously, I slid one bare foot in front of the other and held my breath for fear of making a noise and being discovered. I glided soundlessly past the door to my cabin and paused. The voices were coming from the Captain's cabin just beyond mine.

I looked up and down the hallway to see if anyone else was around and then moved stealthily to the door to his cabin. I unhooked one of my gold earrings, dropped it on the floor and then bent over. I hoped that if anyone happened along he or she would figure I was searching for my earring. Crouched on the floor by the door, I could now tell that there was only one voice. And to my great surprise, the voice was Glenn's.

"I'm positive that it was two million four and not a penny more," he was saying. "I've told you that."

There was a pause while Glenn apparently listened to someone else. I assumed that it must be a phone conversation. I eavesdropped shamelessly, all but putting my ear to the door.

"No, no, no!" Glenn shouted. "I will not do that!"

Then in a voice which was growing increasingly irritated. "No, Dad. I don't know. I haven't seen him . . . Yes, yes, yes . . . But, uh huh. No."

Brief silence. Then Glenn's angry voice again. "I absolutely do not know where he is, Dad. For all I know he's sailing around the world. I keep telling you that. Why? What good would he do you anyway?"

There was a pause.

"Okay, yeah. Right. Oh, sure," Glenn continued sarcastically. "The fair-haired boy who can do no wrong."

Another pause. My heart was beating so loudly I was certain that Glenn would hear it.

"Wait just a second. I've got it handled. I already talked to their people and it's all set. Two million four and that's a bargain."

Silence as Glenn listened.

"Oh, my God! Why can't you just trust me?"

The conversation was growing more heated by the second and I was riveted to the floor in fascination. I have no idea what I might have discovered if Mel hadn't chosen that moment to come out of our cabin. The boat lurched and Mel lost her grip on the door. It flew open forcefully and, with a loud bang, crashed into the wall. Mel stumbled out into the hallway and cried out in surprise, "Kate. What on earth are you doing out here?"

I stood up and whipped around at the same moment that a distraught Glenn jerked open his cabin door and glared at me. I had never seen Glenn in such a state. Rather than being cool, neat and put-together, he was disheveled and out of sorts. His normally well-groomed hair was mussed and his shirt rumpled and untucked. He was perspiring and his voice shook with anger. "What are you doing lurking out here, Kate?"

"I was just trying. . . . I mean I dropped my earring and I was looking and then Mel and then . . ." I stammered.

Glenn glowered at me, slammed the cabin door shut and stormed off down the hall.

"Wow," Mel breathed. "What was that all about?"

"I wish I knew," I said. "I really wish I knew."

I watched Glenn disappear into the salon and then whirled around, grabbed Mel's arm and yanked her into our cabin.

"Was that actually Glenn?" Mel asked. "I have never seen him so . . . well . . . undone."

"It was Glenn all right. But I don't know what's up with him. He was on the phone with someone, I think, and he was very upset."

"More to the point," Mel said, "what were you doing? Eavesdropping at that door is pretty bold even for you."

"I was coming to find you and I heard loud voices. It turned out to be just one voice. Glenn's. He seemed to be very angry with someone. I couldn't help it, I had to listen."

"Uh huh," Mel agreed solemnly, "you just had to. So, Miss Super Sleuth, what big mystery are you solving now?"

I shrugged. "I don't know. I can't help feeling that something fishy is going on. Svetlana's accent comes and goes. Glenn treats her like his kid sister. Ned, or whatever his name is, smirks at everything in flip flops and a skirt. And I swear that Captain Ned and Svetlana have some kind of a thing. And . . ." I stopped to catch my breath.

Mel reached over and hugged me. "You, girlfriend, are looking for trouble. I think your very overactive imagination is working overtime."

I frowned at Mel and then shook my head to clear it. "I guess you're probably right. Anyway, let's get out in the sun. What are you doing down here all by yourself?"

Mel indicated the best-seller lying on her bed. "Reading. And, I'll admit, I needed to get away from this togetherness thing for a few minutes. It reminds me of when I was growing up. No matter where I went there was always someone who wanted to know what I was doing." She looked at me meaningfully.

I laughed. "Okay, okay. I get it. Do you want me to leave you alone?"

Mel tugged on her bright blue swimsuit and a brightly flowered top and ignored my comment. She took a moment to smooth her hair and squint at her reflection in the mirror. "Is that another wrinkle?" she mused. "Yikes. I'm way too old to be . . ." Her voice trailed off.

I started to leave, but Mel stopped me. "Wait for me. I'll come with you. I've had enough of my own company. I was debating calling Don to tell him . . ."

"Tell him what? That you miss him like crazy and want to make mad passionate love to him as soon as you get home?"

"Not exactly. But I'm making myself nuts in here. Let's go find out what's happening in the real world. On deck."

Chapter Twelve

I could see that Julie was only half-listening to Ellie as she chattered on about her plans for a cookbook. And we had no sooner returned to the party on deck than Julie checked her watch, leapt up and, saying that she needed to use the head, disappeared below. When she didn't come back in half an hour, I decided to go below and see if she was all right. For days Julie had seemed distracted and preoccupied. We could all be laughing and talking and I would see that she had checked out. In her own world. I was worried.

Julie was lying on her bunk when I found her. "Hey, Julie," I said, "what are you doing in here? We're all making pigs of ourselves over some brie thingies and planning our expedition to Key West. I have been delegated to come down and bring you forth."

Julie rolled over and peered vaguely at me. "Umm. Give me a few minutes. I'll be right up."

I sat on the edge of the bunk and scrutinized Julie's face. "What's wrong?"

Julie shook her head and confessed, "I just called Robert."

"And?"

"And, I don't know. Something strange is going on with him and I can't figure out what it is."

Julie dragged her hands through her curly dark hair causing it to stand up around her face. Then she smiled a quavery smile and bounded out of the bunk. "Well, I can't do anything about it now. Lead me to those brie thingies. I'll think about Robert tomorrow."

"Wait a second," I said. "Tell me what's going on."

"Nothing. Everything is cool."

"Tell me or I'll blab to everyone else."

Julie had to smile. "You would, you little blabber mouth."

"So, give."

"Okay. It's Robert. I keep calling and I can't get him on the phone. One time I got Alexa and she said Daddy was baking a cake. Robert? I'd be less surprised if she said he was making a bomb in the basement. Well, I finally got him on his cell just now."

"And . . ."

"He told me he was making dinner. And he was so mean. I'm not that bad a cook am I?"

I assured her that she wasn't.

"And it wasn't just mac and cheese that he was making. No. He said he was making filet of sole with an almondine confit sauce on a bed of lilac leaves served with a berry rice mixture."

"He was making *what*?"

"Well, something like that. I don't know. He was just all weird and then we got cut off. I can't figure him out."

"I'm sorry, Jules. That doesn't sound like our serious scientist Robert. Maybe he's having a mid-life crisis."

"If he isn't now, he sure will be when I get hold of him." Julie glowered. She sniffed and rubbed her eyes. I handed her a tissue and she blew her nose. "There," she said, "I'm finished feeling sorry for myself. I need sustenance. And not any lilac concoction either. Give me Martha's most fattening goodie. And let's do it now."

She stomped out of the cabin with me trailing behind.

On deck all hands were in high spirits as Ned hauled in the lines and the sails filled, and we moved swiftly toward our rendevous with Key West. Mary Linda dug her Key West guidebook out of her bag and read excerpts to us. According to the book, Key West was the Capital of Tacky with something for everyone. That is, if you didn't mind jostling with crowds of camera-laden tourists and sweaty boaters or hand-holding gay couples. A tropical paradise with souvenir shops almost more plentiful than residents. Beer and margaritas by the gallon drum. A Mecca for those who are willing to do nothing or do everything; for those who want to fish, dive, kayak, sail, eat, drink, shop or even indulge in a little cultural exploration. Mary Linda looked up from her guidebook and lamented, "So much to do. So little time. I can't decide."

Sandra pushed her sunglasses up on her head and eyed Julie. "Hey, Jules, you've been to Key West haven't you?"

Julie nodded. "Yes, but it was a long time ago and things have probably changed a lot."

"When were you there?" Ellie asked.

"I think I was a freshman in college. I was there with my brother and his partner and my mom and dad."

I've known for years that Julie's brother, Daniel, is gay, but she seldom mentions him. I never thought she was ashamed of him, but more that there are some things that she just wanted kept private. But with this opening, I decided to find out more. "Were your folks uncomfortable being with Daniel and his partner?"

"Not hardly," Julie said. "The day Dan came out was one of the happiest days of their lives. If he had won the Nobel Peace Prize, I don't think they would have been more proud."

I have met Julie's parents, Eleanor and Harold Stein, professors at the small almost-Ivy League college in their New England hometown. I found them to be lovely people, but liberal to the point of exhaustion, as Julie explained it. It didn't surprise me to hear that Daniel's ultimate statement of nonconformity would please them, not upset them.

"Well," Sandra said, "that explains a lot about you, Miss Julie. You've spent your entire life trying to compete with Daniel's being gay. Probably you secretly wanted to be gay yourself."

"Not really, but I did have to compete with Dan for the cute guys. He's the pretty one in the family."

We laughed and continued to discuss the options for our day in Key West.

Svetlana wandered over and settled herself in our midst. "I am thinking," she announced, "that I am not doing the Key West at all. I am thinking Glenn and Svetlana might be on the boat staying. Sunshine and . . ." She winked suggestively. ". . . some time in the cabin we are doing."

I doubted that they would be doing anything more intimate than sharing the morning newspaper, but I had only my suspicious nature as proof. I managed to keep my mouth shut, although it was difficult. I really wanted to share my misgivings with the others, but I knew they would make fun of my feeble efforts at being a private eye. So I laughed with the others and kept my qualms to myself.

By the time Captain Ned hauled in the sails and dropped anchor it was nearly twilight. He said, "Everyone come up on deck. The sunset is going to be spectacular. I don't want any of you to miss it. I ordered it specially for you lovely ladies."

Ned seemed sincere in his desire to display for us the wonders of "his" ocean paradise. I yelled down the steps to the salon, "Hey, you guys. You've got to see this!"

It took mere moments for the five of us and Svetlana and Glenn to assemble on the deck of the *Mirage*. No one wanted to miss one of the trip's most unforgettable sights and, indeed, it was a gorgeous sunset. As the *Mirage* rocked gently at her mooring we gazed at the horizon where the huge glowing ball that was the sun dipped lower and lower. The sky was ablaze with orange and red light and grey streaks surrounded the blur of sun. It didn't take long for the orangy glow to sink beneath the horizon, leaving only a faint line of light against the darkening sky. Minutes later even that disappeared and it was dusk. I shivered in the sudden chill. My friends were still silent with their eyes fixed in fascination on the waning sunset. Something . . . call it a premonition . . . made me turn around and I intercepted a look of complicity between the Captain and Glenn, who stood with his arm draped possessively around Svetlana's tanned shoulder. It was only for a split second, and I first thought I had imagined it, but at that instant Glenn gave a thumbs-up signal and the Captain nodded. No one else noticed anything and the moment was over quickly. I shook my head. Had I really seen something pass between the two men or was I just imagining it, a product of too many umbrella drinks and too much sun? I didn't know and I really didn't want to think about it.

We gathered up our things and headed below to get sweatshirts or jackets. It was cooler than the previous night and the sky darker. I wanted to be in my cabin where there was light and warmth and laughter, but Ned put out a hand to detain me. "Wait a second, Kate," he said. "I need to talk to you." I abruptly pulled away from his restraining hand, but stopped and looked up at him. Ned was standing above me, silhouetted against the background of sky and sea, and his eyes glowed eerily. So, okay, maybe I am a drama queen, but that's how it seemed at the time.

"What do you want?" I asked, anxious to join the others.

"Well," he said, "we've made such good progress today. And the weather forecasts are for storms moving in sooner than they predicted before. So, I wondered if you ladies would object to us doing a little sailing after dinner tonight?"

"And you're asking me this because . . .?"

"I kind of got the impression that you were the group leader. And you are the only one who knows anything about boats."

I nodded. "Right. So we'd get to Key West tomorrow then?"

"Probably. The plan was to be there tomorrow night anyway, but this way we'd get you there a little sooner."

I shrugged. "Hey, you're the Captain. I'm not going to argue about how you sail the boat."

Ned's face registered appreciation for my easy acceptance. "What?" I asked huffily. "Did you think I'd object?"

Ned seemed to be considering saying something to me. I waited, looking past him at the sea and the few lonely stars which glittered in the night sky. At that untimely moment, Julie stuck her head out and called, "Hey, Kate, Martha's got another low cal feast spread out in the salon. Aren't you two gonna come down?"

The mood was broken and Ned said, "I'll be down in a few, Julie. Would you tell Martha to go ahead and serve. I want to rig the sails before I eat." He turned to me. "Go ahead, Kate. We can talk more later."

Unfortunately, we never did.

The salon was warm and bright, and Martha was setting out a variety of dishes which smelled delicious. My mouth began watering immediately. Although after all the food and drink I had consumed in the last few days, I couldn't have imagined that I would ever be hungry again. But I was. The others clearly shared my appetite as they were clustered around the buffet eagerly awaiting the signal to begin feasting. Even Glenn and Svetlana attacked dinner with unaccustomed gusto. Well, when in Rome . . . Not to be left behind, I grabbed a plate and began piling on delicacies. Plates of mixed veggies with intriguing sauces, platters of salmon encrusted with almonds and basil, big bowls of salad, a display of fruit which included huge juicy strawberries, grouper wrapped in phyllo, shrimp piled up and surrounded with cocktail sauce, rice pilaf with bits of sea bass mixed in. All of this to be followed by yet another sumptuous array of desserts, a veritable festival of calories, chocolate and creme. Truly a meal to die for.

Recipe cards for every dish were sprinkled across the table. Ellie busily collected all of them and stowed them in her purse. "Research," she whispered to me. "If she keeps this up the cookbook will write itself."

I just nodded. Ellie's cookbook was the last thing on my mind at that moment. All I wanted was to stuff myself with this wonderful food and worry about everything else later.

Ned came into the salon, hastily assembled a plate of food and then disappeared on deck with food in hand. I guessed his haste meant that he was anxious to set sail again. The rest of us might have lingered over our dinner, but Ned had obviously given Martha the word that speed was in order and she began clearing and stowing things as soon as everyone was sufficiently gorged. It didn't take long before the slap, slap, slap of water against the hull and the snap of sails announced that we were underway. Svetlana and Glenn vanished, so the five of us retired to our cabins, leaving Martha to her galley and Ned to his sailing.

It wasn't a rough night, so the *Mirage* sailed along smoothly. We relaxed in our cabins and planned our stay in Key West. We tried on and discarded a number of potential outfits in the search for the perfect one. And there was a lot of laughter and good-natured teasing. Sandra disappeared into the cabin she shared with Ellie and reappeared in one of Ellie's so-called "slut" outfits. She sashayed into our cabin in the red dress which was even tighter on her than on tiny Ellie. Staggering on four-inch heels, Sandra reeled and stumbled as we hit a trough. "I'm too sexy for this boat, this boat," she sang drunkenly. (How much had the girl had to drink?)

And Ellie was a good sport about it all. Blushing, she clapped and told Sandra, "I'll get you the earrings and the purse to match. Then you'll be set for a day, or night, of street walking in Key West."

"Ooh, I'll be so coordinated," gushed Sandra.

"Perfect for the sunset celebration at Mallory Square," added Mary Linda who had read about it in her ever-present guidebook.

"I love this dress," Sandra burbled happily. "I am so loving this dress," she continued in a perfect imitation of Svetlana.

"Sarcasm will get you everywhere," I said. "Svetlana is so loving everything. She's never met anything she didn't just 'to love'."

"You guys are just mean," Ellie chastised us, and then broke into uncontrollable giggles. "I am so not liking your doing that."

Finally, weary and anticipating a busy day in Key West, we decided to turn in. As I drifted off to sleep I was soothed by the movement of the *Mirage* skimming over the ocean. Voices and laughter just behind the wall next to my bunk caught my attention briefly. "Ellie and Sandra," I thought. More laughter. Masculine this time. Glenn, I wondered sleepily. Or Ned? Doesn't matter. And I slipped innocently into slumber.

Chapter Thirteen

I awoke early the next morning and realized that we were still under sail. Julie and Mary Linda were sound asleep, soft snoring sounds coming from their shared bunk. Anxious to find out just how close we were to Key West, I slid from my bunk feeling with my toes until I was sure I was on the floor. I pulled my grey hooded sweatshirt over my pajamas and lurched out of my cabin and up to the deck. There I discovered Ned at the wheel, still wearing the clothes he had on the night before. The sun wasn't even up and the breeze was brisk. Ned had the sails hauled in tight and the *Mirage* sped across the sea. Palm trees waved on the deserted shore. The world seemed to be empty of everyone except Ned and me. I wasn't sure if I wanted to break into his solitude or not, so I lingered on the top step and waited. For what, I'm not sure. Maybe for some signal that he saw me. Nothing. I smelled coffee and turned to go back down to the galley to grab a cup and practically jumped out of my skin. Mary Linda was just behind me, clutching her camera.

"God!" I screamed, startling both Mary Linda and Ned. "You nearly gave me a heart attack, Mel. I didn't hear you come up."

"Well, you nearly gave me one screaming like that," Mel shot back. "Where were you anyway? I said your name a couple of times and you acted like you were in a trance or something."

Ned waved from his perch. "You'll wake the dead if you yell like that." He checked his watch. "It's only six o'clock in the bloody morning."

"Sorry," I apologized. "So where are we anyway?"

"Sailing along nicely." He gestured into the distance. "Should make Key West by noon or so, I think."

Mary Linda, camera in hand, eagerly stepped onto the deck. She turned it on and began shooting rapidly. Training the camera on Ned, she called, "Smile, Captain!"

Ned grimaced and turned his back. "I hate having my picture taken," he said. But then he reconsidered and posed. He looked straight into the camera lens and grinned winningly. "But for you, my dear, I'll do it."

Mel took several shots of the Captain before turning her attention to the water, the waves and a dolphin who frolicked in our wake. While she was engrossed with her camera, I wandered over to the helm and plunked myself down on the bench that ran along the rail. With my arms propped on my bent knees, I watched Ned steer the *Mirage*. His movements were skilled and sure and I liked watching him. I would have liked to continue our conversation of the previous night, but he showed no signs of wanting to talk. So we sailed on, while Mel snapped away.

Ned informed us that we wouldn't drop anchor for Martha to serve breakfast. "This morning," he said, "you'll just have to make do with coffee, juice and muffins. You can get a big lunch in Key West or Martha can serve one onboard if you prefer. The wind is perfect and I hate to miss it."

"No problem," I answered. "I can't imagine that any one of us thinks she needs one of Martha's gargantuan breakfasts at this point. I'm still stuffed from last night."

He touched his cap in a half-salute. "Thanks," he said simply. Oddly, I was feeling that same strange connection to him that I had felt off and on throughout the cruise. I wanted to quiz him more about his background and his family, but couldn't find the words. I was proving to be neither the reporter I thought I was nor the detective I wanted to be. I would just conclude that Captain Nigel, "call me Ned", Fairweather was an obnoxious chauvinist, when he would let slip some secret which made me reconsider. When he spoke about his wife (make that ex-wife) and his sons, I sensed some elusive sadness in him which I was certain he would deny. I wanted to discuss all of this with my shipmates, but every time I brought up the subject they told me it was all a figment of my "overactive imagination." And, of course, other than my instincts, which had too often proved to be faulty in the past, I had nothing to go on. Nothing at all.

"Ned," I began hesitantly, "what are you thinking about . . ."

I was interrupted by Ellie and Sandra who materialized out of thin air bearing mugs of coffee and a basket of muffins. "Martha handed this to us," Ellie explained.

Sandra held out a mug of steaming coffee to Captain Ned and offered him the basket of muffins. He helped himself and then turned back to the task at hand, totally ignoring me and my questions.

Damn, I thought. In the grey early morning light surrounded by emptiness I might have been able to pry some information from the man. But surrounded by chattering friends, I knew he would be as impossible to pry open as one of the clam shells I found on the beach. My opportunity to be an ace detective had vaporized once again.

We didn't arrive in Key West early after all. Shortly after we demolished the basket of muffins, I noticed Glenn deep in conversation with Captain Ned. Glenn was explaining something while Ned, at the helm, appeared to be listening intently. With his eyes on the horizon, he nodded every once in a while in apparent agreement. Curious as always, I was trying to edge closer so that I could hear what they were saying when Miguel hurried to the helm and broke in, waving his hands frantically. Ned looked alarmed and turned the boat over to Miguel and hurried below. Obviously ill-at-ease, Miguel stood at the helm with his hands gripping the tiller until the Captain reappeared. After a hasty consultation, Ned dropped the sails and the three men retreated to attend to whatever crisis was brewing.

Soon Ned returned from his assessment of the "crisis" and beckoned me over. The look on his face freaked me out, so I hustled to his side to hear what I was sure would be dismal news. "Kate," Ned began, "I have some bad news."

"Yeah, I figured."

My face must have registered fear of impending doom, because Ned said hastily, "No, no, no. I'm sorry. It's not that bad."

I laughed nervously. "So, what then?" I expected to hear that the *Mirage* was sinking or that a massive tropical storm was bearing down or us or something even worse, so I was taken aback by Ned's words. "Well, we have to put in to a marina to check out a problem with the head."

"A toilet emergency?" I was dumbfounded. "You had me scared to death and it's a backed up toilet?"

Ned made a face. "I'm sorry," he apologized again. "I didn't mean to scare you. But, Kate, a backed up toilet is nothing to sniff at."

I burst into laughter. "It most certainly is!" The corners of Ned's mouth twitched and then he broke up too. The two of us totally lost control. We struggled to stop and then one of us would lose it again and the other would join in. I pinched my nose and waved my hand in front of my face saying, "Phew" and Ned cracked up. The two of us carried on like silly children until our mirth brought the rest of our shipmates scurrying to our sides.

"What on earth is so funny?"

"Well, we have this problem," he started and I couldn't stop giggling.

"Yes, Captain," I snorted, "explain to the nice people what you were telling me."

Finally, after a few aborted attempts, he was able to choke out an explanation. "It seems," he said, "that the water supply is being . . . err . . . contaminated and we have to check it out."

Miguel had discovered that the water system was compromised and the *Mirage* was in jeopardy of having no drinking water, no showers, and, worst of all, no usable toilet facilities. Ned explained that rather than continuing to Key West he would prefer to have the problem checked out at a little marina close by. "The owner is a friend of mine and I've had lots of work done there and it's cheaper and more reliable than in Key West."

Ned took one look at our disappointed faces and added, "It won't be too long and there's a restaurant on the dock that serves awesome rum runners and terrific food."

"But no shops," murmured Ellie, a woebegone expression on her face.

Ned put a consoling arm around her shoulder. "Not to worry. I won't keep you from the wonders of Key West for too long. It's just better to handle things as quickly as possible. No head, no shower, no shampoo."

We shrugged disconsolately and began to make alternate plans. "It's all about being on vacation anyway," Julie said. "What difference does it make where we are?"

Soon the *Mirage* was under way once again using the small diesel engine, and a short time later we docked at the Fresh Ketch Marina in Coconut Key. This marina was nothing like the one in Fort Lauderdale where we first met the *Mirage* and its crew. This seedy little place was forlorn and appeared unoccupied. As Miguel secured the *Mirage* to the dock, we looked around curiously. The dock itself was unpainted and in a state of disrepair with the pilings splintered and broken in many places. Numerous boards were missing which made walking a dangerous proposition. Several jaded pelicans eyed us warily from their perches on the dock and then, deciding that we were harmless, went back to dozing in the late morning sun. The sign announcing that we had arrived at the Fresh

Ketch Marina hung by one corner from the ramshackle little building at the end of the dock and banged rhythmically in the breeze.

"Lovely," I whispered, not wanting to disturb the unearthly silence. "Just marvelous."

At that moment Ned bounded up from below, his face and hands grimy and his white t-shirt stained. Sweating and looking annoyed, he bellowed, "Hank. Dammit. Where are you?"

From the shabby office popped a giant of a man whose unruly grey hair stood out around his face in a curly grey cloud. He was bare-chested and wore only a ratty pair of cut-off khaki shorts. On his feet he had a pair of disreputable sandals which perhaps dated back to the time of Moses. "Ned," the giant roared. "Good Lord, man, I haven't seen you in ages. What on earth are you doing here?"

At that he launched himself from the dock and landed on the deck of the *Mirage* in the midst of five very startled women. We withdrew instinctively from this unexpected visitor, while he looked us over with a pair of the merriest brown eyes I had ever seen. Grinning in delight, he winked broadly at Ned and said, "I see what you're doing, my man. Five lovely ladies at your feet. Didja come to share with me?"

The giant was so obviously good-natured that it was impossible not to grin back at him. He scooped Ned into a bear hug and when he released him Ned groaned in mock dismay. "Behave yourself, you big galoot," he said. "These lovely ladies are my guests." "My paying guests," he added with emphasis.

The five of us stood rooted to the deck in stunned surprise. Ned turned to us and made introductions. "Ladies, this is Big Hank Dayton, originally hailing from just out-side Topeka, Kansas, and the best boat hand in the Keys. No one knows boats like Big Hank."

Hank grinned and looked embarrassed. "Nah," he scoffed, "I just do my job. What brings you and the *Mirage* here, Ned?"

"Little problem with the water tank and the holding tank," Ned explained. "Wanted to get it taken care of before we head on down to Key West. Can't have my passengers thirsty and dirty, can we?"

The two exchanged an unfathomable look and Hank said, "Nope, can't have that. I'll have you fixed up in no time." They had started below when Svetlana, with Glenn in tow, materialized at the top of the steps. When he saw Svetlana, the shocked look on Hank's face was comical. He stared questioningly at Ned for a moment, and before he could say a word Svetlana rapidly assessed the situation and in her usual friendly puppy dog way cried out, "Where is it that the boat is being stopping, Captain Ned? And who is this your friend, so large?"

She smiled in delight and waited expectantly for an explanation. Behind her Glenn frowned and curved a restrictive hand around her upper arm. "Now, now, dear," he said, "let the nice man do whatever he needs to do. Let's not bother them." He tugged on Svetlana's arm and attempted to pull her back down the steps.

Svetlana flicked an irritated look over her shoulder at Glenn and then turned back to persist with her questions. "Who is the large man on the boat?"

Hank recovered his equilibrium and he gawked at Svetlana. "I'm just here to fix up this here boat, miss," he blurted, when he finally managed to speak. "Nothing to worry your very pretty little head about." Hank whistled softly and said to Ned, "You crazy son of a bitch."

Ned remained silent, the look on his face impossible to decipher.

Svetlana pulled free of Glenn and bounced over to us, bubbling questions. As we began to describe our circumstances to her, the three men vanished below, hopefully to solve our problem so we could move on to Key West before the day was over.

Suddenly alone on the deck, we looked at each other questioningly. "Well," Julie asked, "what do we do now?"

Everyone spoke at once. "Try the rum runners." "Let's explore." "Take a nap."

"Shut up, you guys," Mary Linda commanded. "One at a time. Personally, I think we should get off the boat and explore. No point in just hanging around here."

The rest of us agreed. "Sounds like a plan," I said. "What about you, Svetlana? Want to go ashore with us?"

Svetlana considered for a moment and then accepted the invitation. "First I must be checking with Glenn. I am needing to know if other plans he has for us. I am wanting just five minutes to ask him."

A few minutes later we were waiting on the deck anxious to go ashore and see what we might find besides a shabby, silent building. We had almost concluded that Svetlana wouldn't be joining us when she showed up. This was not, however, a Svetlana we had seen before. Dressed in cut-off jeans (which showcased her gorgeous legs admirably) and a white cropped t-shirt (I need not tell you what this showcased), Svetlana had pulled her hair into a ponytail and had a white baseball cap pulled low over her forehead. She peered out from behind huge dark glasses that nearly covered her entire face.

"There you are," Ellie hailed her. "We had about given up on you."

"What's with the outfit?" Sandra asked. "You look like someone in the witness protection plan."

Svetlana looked confused. "What means witness protection?"

"Never mind," Ellie said. "Ignore these jokers and let's get going."

The six of us clambered off the boat and onto the splintery dock. I observed that Svetlana was unusually subdued, but I assumed that she and Glenn had an argument earlier. His face had been stormy when he first saw Hank. None of your business, I told myself, and picked a path over the missing dock boards. "Careful," I cautioned my friends, "we don't need anyone spraining an ankle."

The rickety dock passed on either side of the decrepit office building, so we made our way around it to the back where we stood gazing at a wooden platform which sported two gas pumps and a weathered structure which proclaimed itself to be the Coconut Key Bar. In the doorway hung a bead curtain. To our left was an outdoor bar. A few grimy tables with soiled umbrellas were scattered near a huge wooden bar. We exchanged apprehensive looks and then, with a what-the-hell shrug, I led the way into the bar.

As we tried to get our bearings and decide if and where to sit, I noticed the bartender watching us curiously. Then concluding that we weren't going to bolt and run like a bunch of scared chickens, she hurried over. A large, blowsy woman with a mop of frizzled grey-blonde curls pulled into a messy top knot, she wore skimpy cut-off shorts and a halter top which clung to her enormous breasts and revealed a vast expanse of tanned midriff. The name tag pinned to her chest told us that her name was Flo.

"Welcome, Ladies," she greeted us with a huge smile. "What brings y'all to the Coconut Key?"

"We don't get strangers in these parts all that often," she added.

Since I had designated myself the spokeswoman, I told Flo that we were sailing on the *Mirage* and that we had put in to have Hank Somebody or Other make some repairs. "He and the Captain are trying to fix the problem and they said it could take a couple of hours, so we decided to explore," I said.

Flo seemed delighted at the news. "I'm so glad to see y'all. I don't get near enough company down here." She leaned closer to us and confessed, "Hank's my husband and I love him to bits, but I do get a might lonely sometimes."

She kept up a steady stream of chatter as she led us to a large picnic table in the rear of the outdoor area. As we sat down Flo passed out menus and grabbed napkins and silverware to spread on the table. We opened the menus and as Flo picked up her pad to take our orders, she spotted Svetlana who had hung back with her hat pulled low and her head down.

"Hey, doc," Flo exclaimed, recognition dawning on her cheerful face. "Haven't seen you down here in a long time. Still with Ned I see."

Svetlana seemed a bit flustered. "Oh, no," she said quickly. "I am not being here before."

Flo laughed. "Sure you were, honey. You were here with Ned."

Svetlana continued to shake her head. "You are being wrong. I did not to meet the Captain until my *husband* and I arrived to the *Mirage* in a few days ago. I am never being here before."

Taken aback by Svetlana's insistence, Flo reconsidered. "No, you're not her after all. I don't know what I was thinking." She shrugged and turned to the rest of us. "What can I bring y'all from the bar? I recommend the rum runners." She laughed. "But I make them and I might be prejudiced."

We all agreed to try the rum runners. Even Svetlana. And Flo hurried away to make them with an apologetic glance at Svetlana. The others were willing to accept Svetlana's denial, but they hadn't been on the beach that night when I heard Captain Ned and Svetlana arguing. And they hadn't heard Svetlana's clear, unaccented voice pleading with him. Now I was even more convinced that things weren't as they seemed. Still, I didn't have anything but circumstantial evidence to go on.

Flo served our rum runners with a proud flourish and we sat back to enjoy our drinks. The Coconut Key Bar was a typical Florida beach bar. The thatched roof offered protection of sorts from the sun, but wayward birds and other beach creatures roamed unrestrained. A lizard scuttled across my bare toes under the table and I jerked away in revulsion. Glancing overhead, I saw birds roosting and long palm fronds dangling precariously. The most interesting thing about the bar, though, was that the walls were decorated with dollar bills. Every square inch of wall space was covered with bills on which patrons had scrawled their names, the date of their visit, and messages of good will to Flo and Hank. I squinted in the dim light trying to read them. I wondered if I would recognize any of the names. Had any celebrities paid a visit to the out-of-the-way spot?

Flo kept any eye on us from her post behind the bar. I caught her gazing at Svetlana with a puzzled look, and I decided that I would have to find an opportunity to quiz Flo before we left. Meanwhile I sipped my delicious drink and scanned the menu to see what I might have for lunch. It offered your basic bar food. More grease than glamour, I presumed as I studied the choices.

Presently the lure of company was too much for Flo to resist and she dragged a chair over to our table and sat down. Leaning one elbow on the table, she interrogated us about our lives, our home, our trip. Obviously starved for female company, Flo was going to be our new best friend for the duration of our stay.

In turn, we learned her life story. Flo was happy to answer any questions about the tiniest detail of her life. "Hank and I came down here from Kansas about ten years ago," she began. "Just plain had enough of the snow and the corn and the small town gossip. We don't have no kids so it was just the two of us and we pulled up stakes and left in a big hurry. 'Course that was just about the time that Hank wrote that bad check and Sheriff McCauley told us to haul ass or he was bringing Hank in." She chuckled. "Anyways, we decided to head for warm weather and boats, cuz Hank always did love boats. Where but Florida? We hung out in lots of places. Fort Lauderdale. Key Largo. Even Key West before we heard about this bar and decided to give it a try."

My reporter's inquisitiveness kicked into high gear. "What did you use for money? I mean, you said you and

Hank left Kansas with nothing but the leather jackets on your backs and Hank's Harley."

"Yep, honey, you're right," Flo admitted. "That's another story. Let me bring y'all some lunch and then I'll tell you."

Before we could order, Flo suggested shyly, "How 'bout I just bring you some of my best stuff. I about never get the chance to do the cooking around here. But our cook, Randy, is off today and I'm a pretty good cook if I do say so myself."

"No problem," we concurred. "Sounds great. We are nothing if not flexible. Bring it on."

Flo collected our empty glasses and hurried away. She reappeared bearing fresh drinks and a platter of conch fritters and deep fried shrimp as well as some blue corn chips and a homemade salsa. "Munch on these while I prepare the food," she said.

Savory smells emanated from the platter and we all dug in. Svetlana removed her dark glasses, but kept her back to the bar. She picked up a conch fritter warily and sniffed it. "I am not knowing what this is," she confessed. "It is looking odd, but it is smelling yummy."

Our mouths full, we assured her that it was indeed tasting as yummy as it smelled, and Svetlana stuffed a fritter into her mouth. A look of pure bliss passed over her face and she leaned back in her chair and sighed. "Now that is tasting very yummy. I am not eating these kinds of things so often."

"Well, you definitely should," Mary Linda told her as she reached for a shrimp and dipped it in cocktail sauce.

"I am not eating so much the food," Svetlana confided. "I am not wanting the fat butt."

I groaned inwardly. More of the fat butt talk.

Svetlana went on, "I am the model and I am losing the jobs if I get the fat butt."

"Ah," Sandra said, "that makes sense."

"But," Ellie asked, "what about Glenn? Do you have to work? We kind of thought that Glenn had some serious money." Amazing what a few drinks and strange situations do to one's courage. Ellie would never have been so nosy under ordinary circumstances.

Svetlana, however, didn't seem fazed. Almost as if she was eager to pass on the information, she responded, "Yes, Glenn has the money. But Svetlana is working for herself to be proud."

"What is it exactly that you model?" Mary Linda wondered aloud.

Svetlana giggled self-consciously. "I am the model of the underwears. I am being in the Victoria's Secret once upon the time."

Abruptly, Julie choked on her drink and there was a flurry of activity as both Sandra and Mel pounded her on the back and handed her napkins and a glass of water. With tears running down her cheeks, whether from laughter or from nearly strangling, Julie covered her face with her hands. Her shoulders shaking, she said in a muffled voice, "Oh, God. Oh, Lord. Oh, boy."

The rest of us gawked at her and then burst into laughter. Poor Svetlana looked bewildered, unsure of what was so funny. Then she couldn't help herself and joined in.

We had barely recovered our composure when Flo descended upon us with trays of food and another round of drinks. All discussion was suspended as we filled our plates with the delicious array of Florida Keys cuisine. There were cups of conch chowder, platters of crispy grouper with fat homemade fries, bowls of salad topped with croutons and fresh shrimp, a plate of pulled pork and black beans and yellow rice and another of fresh mangoes and pineapple. Tasting everything, we praised Flo until she was blushing. I caught Ellie eyeing her and knew she wanted to get Flo aside and find out the recipes for all of these delicacies. I would have to be quick on the uptake to get Flo to myself before Ellie cornered her with her ever-present notebook in hand.

Finally stuffed, we sat back and smiled at each other. "Well, Captain Ned sure was right about one thing," Mel said. "The food here is amazing."

Flo looked up from clearing the dishes and offered us dessert and coffee. "Key Lime pie, y'all?" she asked. A chorus of yeses sent Flo rushing to the kitchen. She had no more than set huge slices of Key Lime pie and steaming mugs of coffee in front of us, when Captain Ned and Hank stomped into the bar. Sweaty and grease-covered, they converged on the bar and Hank stepped behind it to draw two draft beers. Both men downed the beer in two gulps and then Hank drew two more and both collapsed onto bar stools. Hot and dirty, they looked immensely pleased with themselves.

Ned beamed over at us. "Didn't I tell you that Flo puts out a good spread? Are you ladies enjoying yourselves?"

"You did and we are," I answered. "But what's up with the boat? Is it fixed?"

Ned shook his head. "Not yet. But we're gaining on it. Aren't we Hank?"

Hank grinned a smug grin. "You betcha we are." He addressed his wife. "Flo, Ned and me and them other two are needing a bite. Can you whip up some sandwiches for us to take back to the boat?"

"Sure thing, Hank." She planted a kiss on his grimy cheek and headed for the kitchen.

Hank slid off his stool saying, "Ned, stay put and entertain your lovely guests while I help Flo with the sandwiches. Grab another beer if you want one." And he strode toward the kitchen with Flo trailing in his wake.

"So on the boat is Glenn staying?" Svetlana asked plaintively, looking up at Ned. "I am hoping he is not too hard working."

"No," Ned told her, "Glenn is a big help. He's kind of dirty and didn't want to offend you by showing up without a shower. And, of course, he can't do that 'til we fix the water problem."

"What about Martha and Miguel?" I asked. "What are they doing?"

"They went over to the local market to check things out. And Miguel has been working on the boat. That's his job, after all." His tone said that I was asking stupid and unnecessary questions, but I was undeterred. This was my little mystery and I intended to solve it.

Ned was in his buttoned up mode and I couldn't pry a clue from him. I gave up and went back to the Key Lime pie, which, incidentally, was out of this world. The sly look on Ellie's face told me she agreed and wouldn't rest until she got Flo to divulge the recipe.

"How long 'til we can get underway again?" Sandra asked. "Do we have time to explore that market that you mentioned?"

"At least a couple of hours, I'd say. Plenty of time. It's not a very big market."

Flo returned and began refilling our coffee cups. Hank, carrying a bag of sandwiches, motioned to Ned to leave.

Flo watched Svetlana covertly while she circled the table, coffeepot in hand. When her gaze fell on Svetlana, she seemed perplexed. I was itching to get her alone.

Sandra and Mel decided that the market was enticing enough to persuade them to forgo the shade and relative comfort of the Coconut Key Bar. Julie was willing to go along just so she wouldn't be tempted to eat more food. Svetlana was eager to go and impatiently scooped up her sunglasses and her tote bag. Only Ellie was torn between her desire to shop and her desire to get Flo's recipes. Finally shopping won out and the four of them and Svetlana stood up.

"You know," I said, "I think I'll just stay here and have another cup of coffee with the rest of this divine pie." I smacked my lips. "You guys go on. I'll come and find you when I'm finished."

Ellie inspected me suspiciously, but went out with the others, hellbent on finding something to buy even in this Godforsaken spot.

Alone at last, Flo and I stared at each other in silence. She poured more coffee into my cup and then poured herself a cup and sat down. I toyed with my pie, trying to formulate a coherent question, but before my brain could work, my mouth took over. "You know Svetlana don't you?"

Caught off guard by my blunt approach, Flo got up from the table and went over to the bar to find sugar. Stalling, she stirred a spoonful into her coffee and took a sip. "Um," she said, "I guess I don't."

"Well," I persisted, "you sure thought you did when we first got here. You called her 'Doc'."

"Well, I was wrong." Flo refused to look at me.

"Come on," I urged her, "who did you think she was?"

Flo looked uncomfortable. "No one. Really. Me and my big mouth."

I had the feeling that she wanted to confide in me but something was stopping her. Hank? Ned? Svetlana, herself? I waited, sipping my coffee. There wasn't a sound in the bar. I decided to take a different tact. I leaned back and propped one foot on an empty chair. "Obviously you and Hank know Ned pretty well."

Flo fiddled with her coffee cup and then looked me straight in the eye. "We sure do. Ned comes by pretty often."

Well, well, well, I thought. "Tell me more," I prodded Flo. "Is he always alone or does he bring someone with him?" Too pushy, Kate, I warned myself.

Flo hemmed and hawed. "I don't know. Ned just shows up now and agin. And once he had this lady doctor with him."

Nonchalantly, I pushed on. "Doctor? How do you know?"

"He introduced her as Doctor . . . now what was the name . . . LaSalle? Laville? La . . . something."

"Hmm," I mused. "Well, our shipmate is Svetlana Livingston, the wife of Glenn and a model of . . . er . . . underwears." I giggled and Flo joined me. Both of us were relieved to break the tension growing between us. I had one final question. "Do you recall what Ned's lady friend was a doctor of? Medical doctor? Or what?"

"Don't know," Flo replied. "They just came in on the *Mirage*. Had a few beers with Hank and then left. This ain't the same woman. I made a mistake."

I wanted to continue my interrogation, but I could tell that Flo had revealed as much as she intended to. I stretched and yawned and pushed my plate away as I rose. "Geez, Flo, this has been awesome, but I need to move around a little bit. I think I'll wander over to the market and see if I can find the rest of the gang. Thanks for the wonderful meal and the company."

More relaxed with my questioning ended, Flo shoved her chair back and stood up too. Impulsively, she hugged me. "I've loved having y'all here. Come on back inside if the boat ain't fixed soon." She scanned the empty bar and then whispered, "Keep in touch, will ya? I'll write my e-mail down and you can let me know how the rest of the cruise and everything goes." She favored me with a meaningful look as she scrawled on a napkin. Then struggling with the heavy tray, Flo marched away leaving me staring at her sashaying backside. She knows something, I concluded. But what?

Peering outside I saw only the twin masts of the *Mirage*, sun glinting off the surface. The dock was deserted. Only the pelicans were in evidence and even they seemed uninterested in their surroundings. Satisfied that the *Mirage* was still under repair, I used the ladies room and then went to find my friends. I walked around the Coconut Key Bar and stood on the sun-drenched sidewalk. Across the dusty street was a rundown gas station and an equally dilapidated grocery store. Next to the grocery, about a half block away, was the market. It was set up on a corner lot with the grass worn away to leave only hard-packed dirt and a few scattered and unhealthy looking palm trees. There were about thirty different vendors, most of whom displayed fresh produce and seafood. Interspersed among these booths were others offering shells and shell jewelry, straw goods and an odd assortment of flea market type items. It was stifling on the unprotected sidewalk, so I hurried toward the market and the small amount of shade provided by the scraggly palms. It didn't take long for me to spot my friends. With Svetlana in their center they were as conspicuous as orchids in a weed patch. They were huddled in front of a booth whose display included a large selection of colorful shell bracelets, necklaces and purses. All of them were picking over the offerings as they tried to make decisions. Ellie clutched several white plastic grocery bags, apparently determined to single-handedly support the meager economy of Coconut Key.

They greeted me enthusiastically as I strolled up. "Hey, Kate, look at these great bracelets," Julie cried. "I'm gonna get a couple for the girls."

Sandra and Mary Linda were pawing through a display of rings, slipping them on and off their fingers, holding their hands up to admire their choices. "Come and see these rings," they said. "They are so cool."

I moved closer to Ellie and put my arm around her shoulder. "Hey, girlfriend," I whispered in her ear, "I left Flo all by herself. I think she might like to talk about recipes and cookbooks."

Ellie smiled her thanks and calling back over her shoulder, "I'm gonna use the ladies room at the bar," scurried toward the Coconut Key Bar.

I joined the rest in searching for the perfect souvenir. We spent the next hour perusing the offerings at various booths. Each of us bought a few inexpensive trinkets and haggled ineffectively with the vendors over price. We figured haggling was expected of us and as tourists we didn't want to disappoint the locals. It was a satisfied group of women (nothing satisfies like retail success) who headed back to the bar.

Ellie, scribbling in her notebook, was listening avidly to Flo who sat with one arm on the bar propping up her chin. Ellie, as fascinated with the colorful tattoo on Flo's arm as she was with her monologue, could not tear her eyes away from the fish (was it a marlin?) that decorated Flo's left bicep. As Flo flexed her arm, the fish appeared to jump. A mesmerizing sight, indeed.

When they heard us come in both women looked up startled. Ellie scrambled to put away her notes, but Flo beamed and whooped, "Lookee, here, you gals, lil Miss Ellie is gonna make me a star."

Ellie blushed bright red. "No, not really. I mean, I just thought her pie was . . . and I could . . ." Ellie trailed off in embarrassment.

Flo was having none of that. She clapped Ellie on the back and roared, "Don't be modest, gal. You are writin' a book." Flo was beside herself with pride and excitement.

The rest of us took in Ellie's shy discomfiture and Flo's gushing admiration and we chorused our approval. Even Svetlana had something to add. "I am thinking that so delicious pie needs on its own a chapter. I will be buying that book, Ellie. You will be making me have a friend so famous."

"Both of you will be famous," I said. "I can just see it now. The Today Show will bring Al Roker down here for an interview with both of you. Maybe Meredith and Matt will come along."

"Yes," added Sandra, "they'll be doing a cooking segment and they'll taste Flo's pie and just die!"

We passed the afternoon joking and planning, and it was late afternoon and the light outside was getting dimmer when the Captain and Hank finally showed up covered in grease and dirt. They charged into the bar full of boisterous self-congratulation over a job well done. Ned spotted us and hollered, "Why, there you are. Ladies, your chariot awaits!"

Flo hugged each of us tearfully as we said our goodbyes. I was the last to be hugged and she held me tight for an extra second. And I promised her that I would be in touch. It turned out that it would be much sooner than I could have anticipated.

Chapter Fourteen

It was nearly eight o'clock when the lights of Key West became visible on the horizon. As we got closer we could hear laughter and music across the water. Svetlana and Glenn and Martha came up on deck to watch the approach to port with us. The nearer we got, the more excited we grew. Captain Ned dropped the sails again and they puddled on the deck before Miguel hurried to gather them up. Ned started the diesel engine and we putt-putted past several moored sailboats to a vacant buoy and then secured a couple of lines to it. That task completed, he stood up and pointed to the shore. "Ladies," he announced, "there is Key West in all its seedy glory! All ashore that's going ashore, as they say."

Since it was now past dark and we hadn't had dinner, Martha was anxious to feed us more of her gourmet fare. Recipe cards in hand, she tried to tempt us. But we were beyond temptation. Or at least we weren't going to succumb to Martha's siren song. "No," we told her, "we'll pass for tonight."

As we gazed at the brightly lit shoreline full of temptations of other varieties, we didn't need to debate our plan of action. We, the Fabulous Five, were going to take Key West by storm. Quickly we changed into jeans and grabbed our jackets and begged Miguel to man the dinghy. "No problema, Miguel," Captain Ned interceded agreeably. "I'll take the No See 'Em in. I've got some things to do and people to see." He winked and I wasn't sure how to take that.

Neither Svetlana nor Glenn was keen on making the short voyage into Key West, preferring, they said, a quiet evening a deux. "I am so needing a nap," Svetlana said and nudged me. "After the day of so much eating and drinking." Please, I thought, I am not having another discussion about her butt, but Svetlana simply winked suggestively and wound herself around Glenn.

We said good night to the pair and scrambled into the dinghy. Captain Ned followed us and started up the tiny outboard motor he had affixed to the stern and steered the little craft past the collection of moored boats. When he docked the dinghy he said, "Here you are at the A and B Marina. Up there . . ." He pointed. ". . . is the Schooner Wharf Bar. Best rum runners around. And over there . . ." He pointed again. ". . . is the Lobster House. Good food if you're hungry."

Acting as a tour guide he continued, "Right down there you'll find the infamous Duval Street with its collection of t-shirt shops and bars and stores. Probably most will be

closing up now. I'll meet you all back here at . . . shall we
say . . . midnight?"

We agreed and Ned ambled off, leaving us on our own.

"First things first," Sandra said. "Let's go up to the
Schooner Wharf Bar. We don't need to drink, but we can
absorb some Key West atmosphere. I hear music."

We found three empty stools at the large wooden bar,
so Julie, Mel and Ellie sat while Sandra and I stood behind
them and checked out our surroundings. Even on a chilly
winter night the bar was full. A scruffy musician was strum-
ming a guitar and singing Jimmy Buffet songs while an
equally scruffy audience sang along. The bar was sheltered
by a palm frond structure and if you glanced up you could
catch glimpses of a starlit sky and patches of moonlight.
We ordered margaritas and scanned the menu. The bartender was a skinny woman of about thirty with dishwater
blonde hair in two braids and two keen brown eyes peering
from behind large horn-rimmed glasses. She reminded me
of a prosecuting attorney as she peppered us with rapid-
fire questions about where we were from and how we got
there.

Eventually we escaped from the bar and the bartender's
inquisition and wandered the streets to determine where
and what we were going to do the next day. We roamed in and
out of bars with names like Fat Tuesday and Hog's Breath
Saloon. At first we noted families sight-seeing the shops,
but as the hour grew later, we found mostly beer drinkers
still up and about. We perched on tall stools upstairs at the
Rum Barrel late in the evening, sharing a platter of conch
fritters and a single piña colada. With five straws stuck
in the drink it felt like a quintuple date. We giggled as we
jostled for a turn to sip. I had managed to maneuver my

straw into position and was preparing my assault when I glanced up and nearly toppled off the barstool. In the back of the bar were the two sailors we had met at the beach party. What were their names again? Gino and Skippy? I recognized them in their too tight muscle shirts and jeans that looked painted on. They were bidding good night to two other guys who looked like they frequented the same clothing boutiques, and preparing to pay their bill when one of them . . . Skippy? . . . looked my way and nudged his friend. Covertly, they studied the five of us and then, with their backs to us, leaned over and spoke to the two still seated. I watched them as they slapped a few bills on the table and nonchalantly strode toward the door. With my attention trained on them they couldn't do anything but stop to say hello. I had the feeling that they would have been happier to have just walked by.

"Hi again," one of them, was it Gino, greeted us. "So the *Mirage* is in town?"

Well, they obviously knew who we were, too. "Just got in tonight," I said. "How long have you been here?"

Skippy simpered. No other word for it. "This afternoon. We've been drinking since we got here."

"Um . . . staying long?" I asked, simply because I couldn't think of anything else to say.

"As long as it takes to meet every bar here."

"Well," Sandra observed, "it looks like you've had a good start."

The two snickered and leaning on each other for support staggered out of the bar. We exchanged looks and burst out laughing. Julie commented offhandedly, "Light in their loafers." I knew it was an observation, not a condemnation.

"And drunk as skunks," Ellie added.

"Or, at least that's what they want us to think," I concluded. "They seemed okay until they saw us. And then they started falling all over themselves."

"Hey, it's Key West," Mel said. "Weird things happen here all the time."

"They do?" Ellie asked.

"According to the books I've read," Mel said, "Key West is the Capital of Weird."

Tired after the long day and wanting to be rested for tomorrow's foray into the village, we started to stroll back to the dock, peering into the brightly lit bars on Duval and Front Street along the way. "Hey, you guys." Julie pulled us to a stop. "Look over there." She pointed across Duval at a bar. "My brother and his friends love that place. They say it's got the best food in Key West." We turned to see where Julie was pointing. Several gay couples were clustered on the sidewalk in front of Boys Will Be Boys. Music blasted from inside and one twosome hugged as they moved through the door.

A flash of recognition shot through me, and then I realized that the other four women were gaping in openmouthed shock as well. We stood glued to the sidewalk for a few seconds and then Julie, white-faced, dragged us away. "Let's get out of here. Now."

"Was that Glenn?" Ellie voiced what we were all thinking. "Was that *Svetlana's* Glenn?"

Julie hustled us down the street until we were several blocks away from Boys Will Be Boys.

"I say it was Glenn!" Sandra declared.

"Me, too," I agreed.

"No way," Mel argued. "It couldn't be."

"He's married to Svetlana!" Ellie was vehement. "It wasn't Glenn!"

Julie inquired thoughtfully, "I don't suppose any of you saw the other guy?"

We shook our heads. We had been too stunned to see Glenn going into a gay bar to notice his companion.

"Well," Julie said, "I can't be sure but I think it was one of the muscle boys from the other sailboat. The one we just saw at the Rum Barrel. Skippy."

"No." A chorus of denial. "Skippy? Are you sure?"

"No, not absolutely positive, but pretty damn sure. It's hard to mistake that spiky blonde hair and those jeans that look like they are part of him."

"Okay," Sandra said, "let's just say that it was Glenn and Skippy? What do we do?"

"Makes my suspicions about their relationship . . . I mean, Glenn and Svetlana's . . . look more real, doesn't it?" I asked. "I say we just keep our mouths shut. It really isn't any of our business, is it?"

The others agreed. It wasn't any of our business. Fascinating, perhaps, but none of our business. We straggled back to the dock where we bought beer and soda from the White Tarpon Bar, and sat on wooden benches by the water to wait for Ned's return. Each of us was lost in her own thoughts as we lingered there, listening to the water lapping and the sounds of Key West's nightlife wafting on the brisk night air. Ned hurried up, out of breath and distracted. Spying us, he wasted no time in shepherding us into the dinghy for the quick trip back to the *Mirage*.

Once onboard the long day and night as well as the overindulgence in food and drink caught up with us.

Reeling with sudden exhaustion, we bustled off to our cabins and collapsed into our bunks. I fell into an uneasy sleep where visions of Glenn and Skippy danced in my head.

The sounds of being in port with other boats awoke me early the next morning. I heard voices and motor noises from outside and, eager to explore Key West in daylight, I popped out of my bunk and into the newly repaired shower. I towel-dried my hair and was applying make-up when I heard Julie and Mary Linda. I poked my head into the cabin and called, "Good morning, you two little chickadees. Time to get up and see the world."

"Coffee," mumbled Julie sleepily. "I need coffee before I can see a damn thing."

"Coffee and then Key West," Mary Linda decreed. "Get up, Julie. Things to do. Places to shop."

I scrambled into khaki capris and a bright pink tank top, throwing a pink cotton jacket on over the top. I slid my feet into my sandals and headed for the salon where I could smell coffee and something cinnamon. "I'll bring you two coffee," I promised, "if you'll get your lazy selves up and at 'em. I want to see Key West and I'm not doing it alone."

"Get Ellie then," Jule grumbled. "She'll be ready."

Sure enough, when I entered the salon Ellie was already there efficiently copying the breakfast recipes in her notebook. Dressed in a bright-colored floral sundress and matching sandals, her blonde hair combed and shiny, she looked like an ad for Chico's, that trendy clothing store based in Florida. "I love your dress," I complimented her.

Ellie smiled with pleasure. "Thanks," she said, and handed me her notebook. "Look at what I've got so far. What do you think?"

I took the notebook and sat down with coffee and a muffin. As I flipped through Ellie's notes, I was astonished at what she had achieved. In her precise handwriting she had not only the recipes that Martha and Flo had dictated to her, but their life stories as well. Anecdote followed anecdote and as I skimmed through I was captivated. The stories were not only fascinating but also explained a lot about each woman and why she cooked the way she did.

"This is awesome, Ellie." I applauded her. "I am totally impressed. This goes way beyond a mere cookbook. I absolutely love it."

"Really? You do really?"

"Absolutely. Without a doubt!"

Suddenly bashful, Ellie explained, "I thought I could get recipes from different and unique women and tell their life stories and kind of work it all together. Would it work, Kate? You know publishing better than I."

"I haven't published anything myself except my columns in the paper. But I think you've got something there. It's really interesting and fun."

Ellie considered for a moment. "So, Kate, how'd you like to be in it? You're interesting and fun."

"Yeah," I concurred, "I'm totally fun, but I don't cook. My best recipe is the phone number for Primo Pizza. What that says about me is kind of frightening."

Ellie collected her notes and stuffed them into the cute straw bag that matched her dress. "I'm ready to hit the streets. I'm gonna research cookbooks and restaurants and see if I can't buy some souvenirs for Ted and the boys and . . ."

She was cut short by the arrival of Julie, Mel and Sandra who were all dressed, wearing make-up and ready to rock and roll. All by shortly after seven in the morning. A miracle.

We filled our mugs from the ever-perking coffeemaker and sat at the salon table planning our day. Impatient to get going, we didn't loiter over breakfast as we had most mornings. We were stacking our cups in the sink when Glenn bounded in. The last time I had seen him Glenn had been in a foul mood and cranky with Svetlana. This morning, however, it was a different Glenn. He greeted us with a chipper, "Good morning."

"Off to the big city?" he asked with so much sunny good nature that I half-expected him to burst into song.

"Yes, as soon as we can."

"Oh, indeed," Glenn said with a smug smile. "I think Svetlana and I will stay onboard this morning. It was so pleasant to have the ship to ourselves last night."

Had he really gotten lucky last night or did he just want us to think so? He was trying very hard to convince us. But his demeanor did convince me that he had no idea that we had seen him in Key West the night before. Of course, if it wasn't Glenn that we saw going into Boys Will Be Boys, then he wouldn't have any reason to suspect that we had seen him. I was assailed with doubts, but couldn't shake my suspicions.

Svetlana showed up at that moment, looking tired and stressed. Her beautiful green eyes were ringed with dark circles and her hair was uncombed and greasy. She wore a faded old bathrobe of an indeterminate color and reached for a mug with a shaking hand. But the voice was pure Svetlana. "It is a so beautiful morning, my friends. Are you for doing the Key West?" Her tone said she couldn't have been more delighted for us if we had been planning a visit with the Queen of England.

"Glenn says you are staying onboard with him," I said. "You can leave him here and come with us if you want." I was perhaps looking more for a reaction than for her company, but I wouldn't have minded if she had joined us. However, she cast an indecipherable look at Glenn and shook her head. "No, I am taking the rest this morning. I am the tired cookie."

Glenn gazed at us blandly. "Yes, perhaps we'll come over for the Sunset Celebration. I think Svetlana would get a kick out of that."

"Okay then, let's go, guys. Maybe we'll see you later. Have fun. Enjoy the day. Bye." And we filed out of the salon leaving Glenn and Svetlana to their own devices.

Miguel took us ashore in the dinghy, since Captain Ned was nowhere to be found. It was a still morning and the sea was a glassy, deep aquamarine as the No See 'Em skimmed along. The pink buildings and tall palms with the blue sky as a backdrop looked to our intoxicated eyes like a movie set. The moment our feet hit the dock, I announced, "It's not even 8:30, so I know just the place where I want to begin the day. Anyone else want to come along?"

"Where are you going?" they wanted to know. But I just smiled secretively and started walking. Like a group of ducklings following the Mama Duck, my four friends toddled behind me. I led them down Front Street and came to a halt in front of my destination. "There." I gestured to a small restaurant with a cedar shake roof. "The Two Friends Restaurant. The best breakfast in Key West."

"But we've had breakfast," Mary Linda protested. "I don't need anything else to eat. Food is the last thing I want."

"Okay," I conceded, "maybe we aren't exactly starving, but this is our only chance to have breakfast in Key West and I'm having it. And you, Ellie, can find new recipes and ideas for your cookbook."

"I'm in," Ellie surrendered. "You had me at recipes."

"Oh, all right." Sandra gave in as well. "Coffee for me and nothing else. I mean it. No more food."

"Me, too," sighed Mary Linda, her hand on her stomach. "Just a quick cup and then I want to do some serious sightseeing."

"I'll be there in a few minutes." Julie, with her cell phone in her hand, edged away. "I've gotta call Robert. He is totally making me crazy. I have to find out what's going on with him."

The four of us crossed the street and were seated at a table outdoors on the patio. We ordered coffee and croissants and made ourselves comfortable as we watched the early morning parade down Front Street. It was too early for the camera-laden cruise ship passengers or the parents dragging crabby children toward the next "fun" event. It was too soon for the honeymoon couples to be up and too late for the early morning joggers. Mostly it was locals getting started on the day. We watched the Conchs, as they are called, attired in floral shirts and locally-made kino sandals, as they greeted each other. A few boaters hurried by on errands. It was an engrossing pageant.

We were just finishing our first cups of coffee when Julie, her cheeks crimson with dismay, sat down. She grabbed the cup of coffee we had poured for her and took a gulp before she looked up with her eyes brimming with tears and said, "I don't know what's going on. I think he's having an affair. Or something."

"What happened?" we demanded, ready to tar and feather Robert as soon as we got our collective hands on him.

"Well." Julie took a breath and tried to calm down. "I called him at home and there was no answer. I didn't really expect there to be one. Same thing at work. Although that was kind of weird because it switched over right away to the lab switchboard and I just hung up. Anyway . . . then I called his cell and he actually answered."

"But he was all rushed and funny and didn't want to talk and there were all kinds of odd noises in the background. Music. And banging. And a woman's voice singing. . . ." She broke into wails of distress.

"Did you ask him what he was doing?" Mel asked. "What did he say?"

"He just said he was busy. And then I heard a buzzer. And then he got all frantic and said he had to go and something about something burning. And he hung up on me." Julie stared at her empty coffee cup with teary eyes. "He hung up on me. My Robert would never . . . ever . . . ever . . ."

Ellie got up and circled the table to give Julie a consoling hug. "It's probably nothing." She patted Julie on the shoulder. "Maybe he's just . . . baking?"

Julie's face would have been comical if it wasn't so sad. "Baking? Baking! Robert?" she exclaimed incredulously. "He wasn't even ho-ome!" And, sobbing, she put her face in her hands.

Now, and I think I speak for Mel, Ellie and Sandra, too, I was having a difficult time picturing Robert cheating on Julie. He just wasn't the type. His serious hazel eyes peered out at the world from behind wire-rimmed glasses and he had a perpetually preoccupied expression on his face. I had always assumed that he was solving some obscure mathematic equation in his head which prevented him from being actually present in the everyday world. I never doubted that he loved Julie and the girls. He might have viewed them as strange little creatures from a different realm, but he loved them in a bemused and often distracted way. I had seen Robert disappear into the mists of his own mind during a gathering of friends and family. He simply went away. I couldn't conjure up an image of Robert noticing another woman, let alone having an affair with one. It boggled the mind, but clearly Julie thought it was possible. And she knew him better than any of us. Or thought she did. Now none of us was sure of anything.

Four pairs of hands patted and hugged and rubbed and four pairs of eyes exchanged looks over Julie's bowed head which said "this could be serious." Soon, Julie sniffed and blew her nose on the tissue that Ellie handed her. "I'm sure you're right," she snuffled. "He's just . . . baking a cake. For his svelte new girlfriend. Not a fat blob like his wife."

Julie gave one last sniff, downed a croissant in two bites, brushed the crumbs off her hands and stood up resolutely. "Let's go see Key West." The rest of us followed suit and tried to sort out who was going where and with whom.

Ellie said that she was going to do some serious shopping and check out the restaurant scene as well. Mel offered to go with her, but Ellie resisted, saying that she wanted to do this on her own. I intended to go to the Kino Factory to check out the sandals and then perhaps to Hemingway's house. Mel and Sandra decided to tag along. Julie said that she was going to do the art galleries. We arranged to meet at one o'clock in front of Fast Buck Freddie's on Duval to go to lunch together. As we started to head in our various directions, I pulled Julie aside. "What about going to Boys Will be Boys for lunch?" I suggested.

Surprised, Julie stared at me. Then my true purpose dawned on her. "Why you sneaky little detective you. You want to see if you can find out if Glenn was there last night with that Skippy from the other sailboat, don't you?"

I just nodded. "Don't you think it's a good plan? You said it had great food so we wouldn't have anything to lose."

"You never quit, Katie," Julie said, happy to have something to take her mind off Robert's alleged two-timing. "Sure, it's a great plan. The Five Jazzer-tectives on the job. Actually, it will be fun."

Our first stop that morning in Key West had to be the Kino Sandal Factory. Kino sandals are a Key West tradition. Cheap, comfortable and made before your very eyes, they are one of the worst kept secrets in the Keys. I wanted to add a pair (or several) to my already extensive collection. We found the factory nestled in a brick courtyard just a few steps from the Hog's Breath Saloon. The place had all the ambiance of a shoe repair shop complete with eau de shoe polish. It didn't take long for each of us to select a couple of pairs. Then I tagged along after Mary Linda and Sandra as they meandered in and out of a succession of t-shirt shops and souvenir stores selling cheesy items for cheap and classier establishments selling expensive jewelry and designer clothes.

With the mystery of Glenn and Skippy and Svetlana much on my mind, I spent the morning scrutinizing my fellow tourists looking for clues of high crimes and misdemeanors. But I found no smoking gun. The only things smoking were some ribs at a joint on Duval and a motor-cyclist sneaking a cigarette behind Sloppy Joe's. Finally, I could have sworn my own feet were smoking too. I begged Mel and Sandra to take a break, but they spotted another jewelry store they had to check out, so I bid them a fond adieu and limped into Caroline's Outdoor Café for a restor-ative cup of coffee.

I settled myself at one of the outdoor tables and gave my order to the waiter. I breathed a sigh of relief and, with nearly an hour to kill, took out my cell phone to call my family. Finally, refreshed, I strolled blithely down the street toward our rendevous in front of Fast Buck Freddie's. I waited only a moment before Julie, puffing and sweaty from exertion, arrived at the same time as Mel and Sandra.

The four of us huddled on the sidewalk examining our morning's spoils. We had finished our impromptu show-and-tell and Ellie had still failed to show up. A half an hour after our appointed rendevous time, we were beginning to be concerned about her. We debated what to do. Mary Linda said, "Maybe she's lost. Maybe she's sick. Should we call the police?"

"That seems a bit extreme," Sandra said. "Should we just go on to lunch? She obviously got hung up somewhere."

Julie and I hesitated. "I hate to just leave her," Julie said, "but she knows where we're going. Doesn't she? Maybe we should try her cell."

Beginning to be alarmed . . . Ellie is never, ever late for anything . . . I was anxiously scanning the sidewalk in either direction when I saw her. "There she is!" I cried more loudly than I intended. I pointed. Indeed, I recognized Ellie's flowered sundress as she hurried toward us, but I couldn't see her face beneath the large, floppy and very orange sun hat she had on. She looked like she was hiding under a huge dayglo mushroom cap. Packages clutched in one hand and the other clapped to her head to prevent her outrageous hat from flying off, Ellie dashed up breathless and full of apologies.

"I'm so sorry," she panted. "I didn't realize the time."

We were delighted to see her and began to collect our things. A large couple clad in baggy, long shorts and over-sized t-shirts advertising that they ate at Sloppy Joe's bore down on us clutching gigantic dripping ice cream cones in their hands. Taking up most of the sidewalk, they were oblivious to everything except the messy chocolate. The five of us stepped into the street to get out of their way, but Ellie wasn't quick enough and suffered a body blow as the heavyset woman crashed into her. Ellie was nearly knocked off her feet and as she struggled to maintain her balance, she dropped her packages and her floppy hat flew off her head. Ellie screamed in surprise and grabbed for her hat. The rest of us pivoted to see why Ellie had screamed and stared at her in openmouthed astonishment. She glared back at us, daring us to make a comment about her newly shorn and now red hair. As we stood rooted to the sidewalk, Ellie's face crumpled and she burst into tears. Sobbing, she shoved the orange hat back on her head and sank onto the curb.

"Ellie," we exclaimed, "you've got a new 'do."

It was now Julie's turn to pat Ellie's shoulder, and we exchanged appalled looks over her head as she sat weeping on the curb. We took stock of her new haircut as we tried to comfort her. It was short, spiky, and a bold auburn with streaks of strawberry blonde. It looked like a strawberry sundae-colored parakeet had been upended on her head. It might have been funny if Ellie hadn't been so pathetic.

"I love it," Mel lied staunchly. "It's really cute."

"No, it's not," Ellie wailed. "It's awful!"

"I don't know why I did it," she blubbered, sniffing and rubbing her eyes. "What was I thinking?"

"No, no, no," we soothed. "It's so now."

Ellie was not comforted. "I hate it," she howled. "What am I going to do?"

At a loss for words, the four of us sat on the curb with Ellie, and took turns hugging her and holding her hand while she sobbed. Finally, worn out from her tears, she blew her nose and gave a shaky sigh. "Ted is going to just kill me."

"I actually think it looks cute," Sandra said. "Blonde is boring!"

"Gee, thanks," I said, mock offended. "You think I'm *boring*?"

Ellie pulled herself together and wiped her eyes, mascara snaking a black river down her cheeks. Shredding the crumpled tissue, she sat on the curb with her eyes downcast and her face half-hidden.

"And," Julie added helpfully, "hair grows. If you hate it, you can just grow it out."

At those words Ellie's eyes filled with tears once again. "That's not all," she lamented in a wavering little squeak. "That's not all."

"Well, what on earth else have you done?" Mary Linda demanded.

Ellie, with tears running down her cheeks, unknotted her pale yellow sweater and pulled it from around her shoulders. "Look," she muttered and gestured at her shoulder. On one shoulder blade a tiny rose sprouted!

"A tattoo!" We were horrified. "You got a tattoo?"

Ellie's sobs went up a notch in volume. She nodded, unable to speak.

"Is it real?" Sandra asked, incredulous. Ellie bobbed her head. "Well." Sandra stumbled trying to find the appropriate thing to say. "I've always wanted to get one myself but I never had the nerve."

"Really? Really, Sandra. You did?"

Whether or not Sandra had ever considered having a tattoo was beside the point. Any of us would have said whatever we could think of to offer any small amount of consolation to Ellie.

A passerby had been watching our little drama with interest and he drifted over to us. He was dressed in white linen pants, a bright blue linen tunic which reached his thighs, a pair of leather sandals and carried a navy leather "boy bag." He knelt carefully in the gutter, protecting the knee of his spanking white pants and caught Ellie's eye. "I've been watching you," he told her, "and I want you to know that I think you look simply *fabulous*. The whole package . . ." He looked her over from head to toe. "is perfect."

Ellie was so startled by his well-meant interference that she gazed back at him abjectly. "Really," she quavered, finding her tongue. "You do?" She was oddly willing to be consoled by a total stranger.

The stranger stood and putting one hand on his hip, waved a finger and said sternly, "My darling, you look stunning. Dry your tears and hold your head up high."

Ellie smiled a shaky smile. "Thank you."

He started to walk away and called back over his shoulder, "Where did you get the hair, darling. I mean it's totally fab." And he gyrated away. Superman in linen come to the rescue.

"Come on," Julie said as we stared after him, "let's go find some lunch. You could use a drink, Ellie." She offered Ellie her hand and pulled her up from the curb.

"We all could use a drink," we chimed in. And we set off toward Boys Will Be Boys, Mel with her arm around Ellie and Julie leading the way. Sandra and I brought up the rear, talking in low whispers so that Ellie wouldn't hear us. "Wow," I breathed. "I didn't see that coming."

"Me either," Sandra said. "Ellie sure has been one surprise after another this trip."

"What next?"

We were seated at a window table at Boys Will Be Boys by a flamboyant maitre d' dressed in a snug tank top with Boys Will Be Boys in rhinestones across his chest. He pulled out our chairs with a flourish, told us our server would be Wil ("that's Wil with one 'L'"), and flounced back to his post by the door.

The decor was a tasteful combination of tropical green, yellow and gold tones and the clientele was mostly gay. Our entrance attracted a great deal of attention. Julie, unfazed, studied the menu with casual indifference to the stir we were causing. Ellie was silent and brooding, but perked up considerably when our server approached our table. It was the kind stranger from the street and he was delighted when he saw us.

"Gracious ladies," he said. "I'm so glad to have you at my table. My name is Wil and I'm here to serve your every tiny need." He put a hand on Ellie's shoulder and said with concern, "Whatever you need, Cupcake, I'll bring it to you. You need special attention today."

In spite of herself, Ellie had to smile at him. "I'm feeling so much better now thanks to you. I think we need a minute and then we'll order drinks."

"Lots of drinks," she added.

Wil took our drink orders and disappeared, reappearing moments later bearing a large, frothy, pink drink decorated with a fruit kabob and a pink umbrella. He set it in front of Ellie with a grand gesture. "Something special for you, darling, on a special day. The day the new you emerged from her cocoon."

Wil fingered her short, gelled, red spikes of hair and guessed, "I'll just bet you were a blonde. A cute, prim little blonde." Ellie nodded. "Now you are a hot little redhead."

And when Wil noticed the rose tattoo on her shoulder, he practically exploded with rapture. "A tattoo, too! Simply stunning!"

With Wil attending to our every need, lunch was a splendid affair. The food was every bit as delicious as Julie had promised and, with Wil dancing attention on her, Ellie recuperated enough to tell us how she had become a redhead.

When she completed her tale, Ellie was relieved to find four pairs of sympathetic eyes trained on her. "I know it was stupid," she confessed, "but, I don't know, I've wanted to go red for ages and then the tattoo just kind of completed the look. I'm just so tired of doing what's expected of me all the time."

A woeful expression passed over her face and she looked ready to cry again. "Ted is going to kill me. And what will the boys think of their mother? And the PTO . . ."

"Personally, I think you were very brave," Sandra said. "I think you look fantastic. Besides, we live in Ohio. You can wear a sweater for the rest of your life."

Ellie laughed. "You'll have to admit that I'll get noticed. Quiet little Ellie is no more. Bold and daring. That's me in the future."

The melodrama almost made me forget my original purpose in coming to Boys Will Be Boys, but as we were finishing our lunch I decided that I had to ask the questions that I had come to ask. Wil was loitering near the bar with several other waiters, so I excused myself to go to the restroom. I edged into the bar and when I caught his eye beckoned Wil. Immediately he materialized at my side.

"Can I talk to you a second?" I asked.

"Sure. What can I do to help?"

"Well, I was just wondering if you were working here last night?"

"Last night? No. Why?"

I decided to take Wil into my confidence. "The thing is," I began hesitantly. "The thing is . . . we saw . . . or thought we saw . . . Or anyway . . . this friend of ours coming in here with someone. And I was hoping that . . ."

Understanding illuminated his face. "You want to know if anyone saw this friend with another guy. Right?"

"It's just that this guy, our friend . . . well, he's married. And we wondered . . ."

"If he was cheating on his wife," Wil finished. "Let me see if I can find someone who worked last night."

He spoke to the other waiters and then came back with a tall, dark-haired guy. "This is Jamie. He was here."

"What does your friend look like?" Jamie wanted to know.

I started to describe Glenn, but then had a better idea. "Just a second," I said and went back to the table. I returned with Mary Linda's camera in my hand. "Mary Linda has taken pictures of absolutely everything we've done on this trip, so I'm sure she has a picture or twenty of Glenn in here." I turned on the digital camera and scrolled through the hundreds of shots stored on it. "Wait, here he is!" I turned the camera so that Jamie and Wil could see the picture, a shot of Glenn and Svetlana on the *Mirage*.

Jamie squinted at the tiny image. "Can you blow it up?" I fiddled with the camera and then turned it around again. "Oh, yes," Jamie said. "He was here. That's Guido. Not that I think that's his real name or anything, but he always calls himself Guido when he's here."

"What? He's in here that often?"

Both Wil and Jamie nodded. "Yes, we've seen him lots of times. Not always with the same guy, but he's kind of a regular."

I scrolled through a few more shots and found what I was looking for. I showed both men a shot of Skippy and Gino on the beach during our first beach party. "Do you recognize these two guys?"

"Sure," they said. "Skippy and Gino. They have a sailboat. To hear them talk it's the *Queen Mary*."

I thanked both of them for their help and stood pondering for a few seconds. Glenn, call me Guido, Livingston, was a regular at a gay bar in Key West. And married to the scrumptious Svetlana. Wow, I thought, what a fascinating turn of events. I couldn't wait to fill the others in on all the juicy details.

After lunch we decided to go separate directions. I was anxious to see Hemingway's House before I left Key West, while the others had more shopping and sightseeing to do. A revitalized Ellie had a gleam in her eye that I knew meant she wanted to interview someone for her cookbook. With Wil as her more than willing servant and her notebook in hand, she headed to the kitchen to quiz Chef Rick about the Boys Will Be Boys cuisine. A worthy addition. We planned to meet for the Sunset Celebration at Mallory Square. Since sunset was at six-oh-three p.m. we agreed to meet at five-thirty.

At the last minute Sandra elected to forego shopping and accompany me instead. I was happy to have the company. We strolled along gossiping about Ellie's hair, Wil, and the Boys Will Be Boys bar. I filled her in on Wil and Jamie's revelation that Glenn . . . our Glenn . . . was a regular at that gay bar. We were so engrossed in our conversation that we strayed off the beaten track. I wasn't sure exactly where we were, but it was a pleasant street lined with clapboard houses and white picket fences overgrown with fuchsia and orange bougainvillea blossoms. The beautiful old homes were shaded by palm trees and banyans and presented an entirely different atmosphere than tacky, touristy Duval Street.

I was soaking it all in when, without warning, Sandra grabbed my arm and pulled me to an abrupt halt. "Stop, Kate," she whispered insistently. "Quick. Get down. Don't look now." And she dragged me down behind a cute, red Mini-Cooper parked there. Squatting awkwardly behind the car, I couldn't see a thing except the curb and the street. A pink, Think Pink, Key West taxi flashed by and I wondered distractedly where it might be going. Sandra held fast to my arm to keep me from rising. "Kate, it's Svetlana. Over there. And you'll never guess who she's with."

When I didn't answer, Sandra mumbled in a hoarse voice, "She's with the Captain. In front of that house over there." She gestured in the direction of the house across the street. I cautiously peeked around the bumper of the Mini-Cooper. At first I didn't see anyone. And then I caught a bright swirl of color. Svetlana. Tall, slender, the hem of her vibrantly colored dress fluttering in the breeze. Standing on the stoop of the old home, her back was to us and she was talking to someone in the house. At her side, a hand grasping her arm, was Captain Ned Fairweather in the flesh.

"Is it Svetlana?" Sandra mouthed. "I can't see her face."

"It sure looks like her. Wait 'til she turns around."

I can't explain our actions even now, but we hid behind that car while Ned and Svetlana presumably said their farewells to whomever was inside. It would have been simple to saunter casually by the house and express surprise at seeing the pair. But we didn't. Maybe it was because we were confronted so unexpectedly with the situation that we kept silent in our hiding place until the couple descended the steps, hopped into the Think Pink cab and vanished down the street. I wonder now what would have happened if we had shown ourselves.

As it was, Sandra and I slowly rose and dusted ourselves off, our eyes glued to the spot where we had last seen the couple. Could it really have been Svetlana and the Captain? If so, what were they doing together? And who lived in that house?

"Let's go over and knock on the door," Sandra suggested.

"And say exactly what?" I asked. "Do we just march up there and ask what Svetlana and Ned were doing?"

"I suppose not."

"Well, what then?"

"Something. Don't we have to do something?"

"Now you believe me," I pointed out. "I've been telling you that something odd is going on with them. And now . . ."

"So, I'm going to go over there then," Sandra insisted. "I'll think of something to say."

There was no stopping Sandra, so I followed her as she stomped up the steps of the genteel old home. She hesitated with her hand poised over the brass doorknocker. Then she raised it and knocked firmly. I held my breath and waited to find out what she might say to whomever answered. No one came. Sandra knocked again. After a few minutes, I let out my breath. "No one's answering."

"I'm giving it another minute."

Finally, though, we admitted defeat and retreated to the sidewalk where we stood staring up at the shuttered windows of the silent house. I glanced sideways at Sandra whose mouth was set in a straight, unyielding line. "Now what?"

She shrugged. "I guess we have to give up. But I would love to know who lives in the house and what the Captain and Svetlana were doing."

Our enthusiasm for Hemingway and his home had definitely waned, so we abandoned the idea of going there. Sandra argued that we should stand guard from a post across the street and see who might come out or go in. I was onboard with that plan, so we found an inconspicuous spot where we could observe the old house. The street was eerily silent with no passers-by and little traffic. It was a still and muggy afternoon and soon we tired of keeping watch. "Nothing is happening," Sandra said, disappointed. "Do you want to leave?"

I might have stayed awhile longer but it was hot. I had long ago stripped off my jacket and tied it around my waist. My tank top stuck to my back in sweaty patches. As we crouched in our hiding spot, I realized that this was a classic case of "be careful what you wish for." Here I was "investigating" a mystery and I was sticky, grumpy and thirsty. If this is what a private investigator did to earn her keep, I was certain that I didn't want any part of it. I was uncomfortable and discouraged and more than ready to abandon detective work for the day. "This detective stuff is really boring," I admitted.

Sandra said in an ill humor, "Well what did you expect?"

"This was *your* idea," I retorted in a huff.

"You wanted to see what happened as much as I did."

"Well, I'm ready to throw in the towel if you are."

Sandra, too, had enough. "Let's go find something cold to drink and get out of this sun."

I paused as Sandra and I started walking reluctantly away and turned to get one last glimpse of the stately old house. I know I have an overactive imagination. I've been told that often enough. But I would swear that I saw someone peering out of one of the windows on the upper floor. Then the curtain dropped back into place and the facade appeared undisturbed. I blinked and said nothing to Sandra. I was sure if I told her what I thought I saw that she would want to stick around and I was in no mood to do that.

We made our way back to Duval Street and luckily found an empty table at Sloppy Joe's. Throwing our packages on the table, we collapsed into chairs, the blast of chilly air from the air conditioner a welcome relief after a busy afternoon of spying. Sloppy Joe's appeals to tourists who sip overpriced drinks and bask in the ambiance of old

Hemingway memorabilia, but for Sandra and me it was simply a place to recuperate and review what we had seen and thought we'd seen.

Brushing my damp hair off my face, I asked Sandra to order me a Diet Coke and headed to the ladies room. When I got back to our table, Sandra had turned her chair sideways and was deep in conversation with two attractive guys at the next table. She looked up at my approach and made introductions. "Kate Kelly." She indicated me. "This is Bill. And Craig."

Both Bill and Craig were in their mid to late forties, I guessed, and wearing pressed khaki shorts and golf shirts. Neatly groomed and shaven, they presented an interesting contrast to some of the disheveled tourists and boaters lounging at the bar. Bill (was it?) had sunglasses perched in his dark hair and managed to look professional even in shorts. The other guy (Craig?) was equally impressive. His sandy hair was receding a bit, but his brown eyes were kind and his smile endearing.

"You're not going to believe this," Sandra said, "but these two nice gentlemen are Congressmen."

I murmured something appropriate along the lines of "huh, whaddya mean?" and she continued, "They are here vacationing with their wives who are spending their money at Fast Buck Freddie's. How about that?"

I wondered how Sandra had ferreted out this information, but I know better than to question her methods.

"And . . ." Sandra could hardly wait to share the pièce de résistance. "Bill is from Nebraska."

Ah, hah, I thought, now I know why she's so excited. Captain Nigel (call me Ned) Fairweather had told me that he was from Nebraska. Certainly, this Bill would have heard of Ned's father's company and maybe he knew about the family as well.

"Nice to meet both of you," I greeted them as I sat down. "I suppose Sandra has told you that the captain of our sailboat is from Nebraska."

"Actually, I hadn't gotten that far," Sandra said.

"Well," I told them, "our captain is Nigel Fairweather and his father owns . . ."

"Fairweather Electronics," Bill finished. "Big employer in our little state. Worth billions."

"Ned told me that he had no interest in the company and that's why he's working on a sailboat."

"Makes sense," Bill said. "Rumor has it that old man Fairweather is ill, though. I've heard Alzheimer's or cancer or something serious. I presume that this Ned would inherit the company."

"If he doesn't want it though . . ."

Bill looked thoughtful and tapped his fingernail against his very white, very straight teeth. "I have also heard that there's a brother involved in the company, but there has been a falling out of some sort. I'm not sure."

I pressed for more details, but Bill had told us everything he knew. I sat back and reviewed what information I had, while Sandra kept up the conversation with the two congressmen. Okay. So, I knew that Ned's father owned Fairweather Electronics and that he was ill or something and that Ned had a brother. Maybe. Ned had clammed up when I asked about the brother, but Bill said there was a falling out so maybe there are bad feelings and . . . On and on it went, my mind racing.

Soon it was time to meet the others, but Sandra begged off saying she preferred the air-conditioned air of Sloppy Joe's and intelligent political conversation to the circus of sunset at Mallory Square. We agreed that she would meet us at the dinghy dock at eight. I left her happily oblivious to all but the ongoing political debate with Bill and Craig, and headed off to see what the infamous Sunset Celebration was all about.

As I strolled toward Mallory Square, it was obvious that nearly everyone in Key West was headed in the same direction. Only a few diehards remained in the bars and stores while the rest streamed toward the celebration. Bearing cameras, the indefatigable tourists mingled with society ladies in tennis whites, deeply tanned weirdos, crusty old women and the beer-drinking college crowd. I wondered how I was going to find my friends in the crush. I needn't have worried since, as I neared the square, I heard Ellie's shrill voice over the din. "You . . . hoo, Kate. Over here." I found them easily, the fading sun's rays glinting off Ellie's red hair. The three of them were huddled at the edge of the large bricked area next to the water. As I got closer, I saw that Ellie had brought Wil with her.

I looked around curiously. More circus than celebration, the sunset was taking a backseat to the carnival atmosphere. Together we wandered around taking stock of the lady in chains and the flame-swallowing man. We were amused by a couple of white-faced mimes panhandling the crowd, while close by a man was putting his trained cats through their paces. Mary Linda, camera in hand, darted from one oddity to another, documenting it all. We kept one eye on the sun's downward progression as we took it all in.

There was a pushcart vendor selling huge chocolate chip cookies and we bought one and broke it into pieces to share. The huge cruise ship that had been docked all day in the square departed and we could see it cruising out to sea. This was supposed to give the tourists a better view of the sunset, but only a small amount of the horizon was visible. As the sun sank lower, the activity became more manic and music blared from nearby bars and restaurants.

I was at once appalled and delighted by the Sunset Celebration and I was writing a column about it in my mind when I looked up and saw, to my complete astonishment, Glenn and Svetlana making their way toward me. If I had harbored any doubts that I had seen Svetlana on the steps of that old home earlier in the day, they were now put to rest. Svetlana hurried toward me, waving frantically and calling my name. "Kate, oh, Kate. I am seeing you." And, I was not entirely surprised to see, she was wearing the same bright orange, flowered sundress that I had seen on our so-called mystery woman. I couldn't wait to tell Sandra.

"Hi," I greeted them as warmly as I could without gushing. "So you made it after all."

"Yes, I am just loving this sunset," Svetlana bubbled like a child. "It is being so . . . "She searched for the word she wanted. "How you say it . . . like the circus?"

"Totally," I agreed. "Have you two seen the Captain or Martha and Miguel?"

"No," Svetlana lied without batting an eye. "I have not been seeing the Captain since the morning."

Sure you haven't, I thought. Now what are you hiding? Glenn's blank expression told me nothing at all. As Julie, Mary Linda and Ellie, with Wil in tow, joined us, the conversation automatically shifted to Ellie's new 'do and her new friend. I caught Wil inspecting Glenn furtively, but he gave no outward sign of recognition. Glenn, in turn, shook Wil's hand and gave a very creditable portrayal of innocence.

As the sun sank into the ocean and the sky became a dark grey orange, we moved as a group toward the wharf. I walked by Wil's side. "So?"

"I've seen him at Boys Will Be Boys. I'm sure I have. But that doesn't mean that he's cheating on her." He elbowed me and jerked his head toward Svetlana. "Maybe he bats both ways."

We stopped in front of the A and B Lobster House. "Let's go in here," Julie said. "We have plenty of time to get dinner and still meet Ned at eight. Besides, if we're late, is he gonna leave us? I don't think so."

We trooped into the Lobster House for what we presumed would be our last dinner in Key West. It was a hilarious affair, mostly due to Ellie and Wil. Wil regaled us with tales of Key West life and history, while Ellie, her good humor completely restored, recounted the now valiant tale of the tattoo. Terror was the emotion that best described how she felt as she contemplated her choices. "So why didn't you just run?" Mel asked.

Ellie shook her head in recollection. "I think I was more afraid to leave than I was to stay. Something kept telling me, 'Do it. Do it!'"

"Did it hurt?" Svetlana wanted to know.

Ellie grimaced. "You bet it did. I thought I would cry. Actually, I think I *did* cry."

She craned her neck to see the little rose on her shoulder and finished, "I really cried when they held up a mirror for me to see and I realized what I had done. And then it was time to meet you all for lunch and I had to buy that

hat and I didn't have time to undo any of it. Even if I could have. And that's it. You know the rest."

She added for Svetlana and Glenn's benefit, "I met them all for lunch and was a sniveling wreck until he . . ." She beamed at Wil. ". . . came along and liberated me from my former self."

Wil blushed. "No, Cupcake, I just told you what everyone else already knew. You look hot!"

It was Ellie's turn to blush, but it was obvious that she was not embarrassed in the slightest. I had observed her as she checked out her reflection in the window and gave it an approving smile. The new Ellie had kissed the old Ellie good-bye and didn't miss her one tiny bit. She patted her new haircut and tugged one red spike into place. Preening like a peacock, Ellie reigned over the dinner party.

After we consumed the last morsel and were sitting over cups of after-dinner coffee, Wil took his leave. With hugs for each of us, even Svetlana, he said his goodbyes and insisted that we stay in touch. We exchanged e-mail addresses and phone numbers as well as assurances that we would call, write, come back to visit. With a final wave, Wil pranced out the door. I had the impression that Glenn was relieved to see him go, but I couldn't say why. Just a feeling.

Chapter Fifteen

We were tucked into the No See 'Em when Sandra came flying down the dock. "Have I got a few things to tell you. You will die," she said to me.

I started to ask her what she meant, but she put a finger to her lips and shushed me. "Later," she mouthed.

As I scrambled from the dinghy to the deck of the *Mirage,* I gave a final look at the lights of Key West and breathed in the damp night air blissfully. I was grateful to be back on the *Mirage* where it was peaceful and quiet. That is, until Martha came bustling up with her perpetual cheery smile and suggested an after-dinner drink or snack. Even though it was barely nine by the time the entire party was back on deck, we were tired after the long day ashore and declined Martha's offerings.

No sooner had Glenn and Svetlana disembarked from the dinghy than they disappeared toward their cabin calling good night. "I'll in the morning be seeing you," Svetlana trilled. Julie, Ellie and Mary Linda quickly followed suit, claiming exhaustion and the need to shower off the griminess of the day. Having secured the No See 'Em to the side of the *Mirage*, Captain Ned excused himself as well. That left only Sandra and me and Martha to revel in the solitude. A patch of moonlight shone across the water and the stars twinkled overhead. I sighed. This was what I came on this trip to experience.

I exchanged a contented look with Sandra. She was bursting to tell me about her evening, though, and stargazing was not on her agenda. Since I was anxious to learn anything new about the Captain, I went along when she accepted a bottle of wine and two glasses from Martha and motioned me to follow her to her cabin. "I have so much to tell you," she breathed, "but not here." We slipped down the steps, through the salon and into her cabin. Sandra closed the door behind her and stood with her back pressed against it and checked out the space she shared with Ellie. The cabin was empty and we could hear the shower. "Ellie's in the shower," she said. "We have at least an hour before she'll be finished."

"Maybe not. With that haircut, it won't take her anytime at all."

Speaking rapidly, Sandra replayed her afternoon and evening with Bill and Craig and their wives. I was interested in what she had gleaned about Fairweather Electronics, but that wasn't what was most on her mind. "I think I had one of those 'ah ha' moments," she admitted. "I was about to leave to meet you guys and it came to me."

"Like a bolt out of the blue," I said helpfully.

"Trite as that is. Yes. All of a sudden, I realized that I had been kidding myself for all these years. I was never okay with leaving Washington D.C. I never could just turn my back and walk away from that. Those guys, Bill and Craig, they have *my* life. The one I could have had and should have had. And I want it back."

I examined her face and waited for the derisive laugh that would tell me she was joking. But her dark eyes were serious. For the first time in a very long time Sandra was not putting herself and the life she lived down. No, she was going to change it.

Sandra explained that it had been a walk down Memory Lane talking with Bill and Craig. They told anecdotes about the Hill and even found a couple of acquaintances they had in common. A very small world. Bill was acquainted with Sandra's former boss who was now the Senator from the great state of Nebraska. Sandra loved catching up on the political world. The two wives joined the party soon after sunset and Sandra thoroughly enjoyed meeting both Liz and Tricia. It had been almost impossible to tear herself away to return to the *Mirage*. It came to her at that moment, as ominously as a thunderclap, that she missed this . . . the conversation, the sharing of views, the political intrigue. Suddenly Sandra understood how big a hole leaving Washington had left in life. And now she was going to go back. Maybe not to Washington itself, but definitely back to politics.

"And Allen?" I asked. "Are you leaving him to run for Congress and move back to D.C.?"

"Of course not, " she laughed. "That's almost the best part. When it came to me that I wanted to be part of the political scene, the first thing I thought of was calling Allen to tell him."

"And did you? Call him, that is?"

"I did." Sandra's eyes sparkled with excitement. "And we talked and it was so great. He actually listened to me. I know it was kind of sudden and all that, but he didn't call me crazy or try to talk me out of anything. He just said that we would work it out when I got back and he could see me in politics cuz I can talk him into anything."

"Uh huh." I was dubious. "And this means . . . ?"

"Allen suggested that I run for city council or the school board as a first step. And he's right. I loved being on the PTO. And I could replace that old fogey Alice McMurtry who's up for re-election this fall."

"Sounds to me like you've been giving this some thought."

"I have, but I didn't even really know I was," she admitted. And then uncertainly, "So, what do you think?"

I refilled our wine glasses and held mine up. "Here's to Senator Sandra Klein or Congresswoman Klein or someday President Sandra Klein. One day I'll say I knew her when." And we clinked our glasses together.

Coming out of the bathroom, a towel wrapped around her head and wearing Winnie the Pooh pajamas, Ellie asked, "What am I missing?"

"Long story, babes," I said. "Grab a glass and sit down."

Ellie had already fallen asleep on the cabin floor when Sandra and I, unable to keep our eyes open any longer, called it a night. All I wanted to do was grab some sleep, so I slipped out of their cabin and into my own. I tried not to make a sound as I opened the door and pulled it shut behind me. I could hear breathing coming from Julie and Mel's bunk and, in the darkness, I thought I made out two bodies. I considered just falling into my bunk, but I was certain that I would sleep better if I showered first, so I tiptoed into the head and turned on the shower. As I waited for the water to get hot, I examined my face in the mirror. I felt like I had aged about fifty years that day, but I didn't look any different than I had that morning. Same choppy blonde hair, same hazel eyes. Then I heard a thud behind the wall which backed up to the hallway followed by a shushing sound. I was naked and not about to investigate. Assuming I was imagining things again, I stepped into the shower.

Scrubbed and drowsy, I put on my pj's, rubbed on some coconut body lotion, brushed my teeth and crept back into the cabin. I allowed my eyes to adjust to the darkness before I glanced at the other bunk and was surprised to see only one still form. One of them, either Julie or Mel, was missing. I almost succumbed to the lure of my cozy bunk, but I needed to know who was not in her bunk. And why?

I slid my feet into the sandals I had just kicked off and wrapped myself in the scarf that Julie left on the chair. Stumbling over my own feet, I cursed under my breath and fumbled with the cabin door. Remonstrating with myself over this foolish venture, I yanked at the door. I peered into the hallway and, seeing nothing amiss, debated, once again, just going to bed. Ultimately, though, I inched into the hallway and shut our cabin door behind me. Squinting in the dim passageway, I felt my way. No one was in the salon. I put one foot in front of the other, feeling with my toes for hidden obstacles. At the stairway I hesitated and stared into the blackness searching for God knows what and then I bolted up to the deck.

The night had turned dark and the wind had picked up considerably. The sea was choppy and lines and halyards clanged against the masts as the *Mirage* bobbed vigorously. The temperature had dropped and I shivered under Julie's wrap and I had half-turned to go back to my warm bunk when I spotted her. Mary Linda was curled up on the bench next to the helm. Clad in pj's, she was enfolded in a blanket filched from her bunk. Bare toes stuck out and she was silent and motionless.

"Mary Linda," I whispered.

She poked her head up from under the blanket and looked at me forlornly. Tears trailed down her cheeks and she sniffed. Oh, not again, I thought uncharitably. But she needed me, so I hurried across the deck to sit by her side.

I was almost too exhausted to feel anything, but I said with as much sympathy as I could muster, "Hey, girlfriend, why are you out here all alone in the dark?"

Mary Linda was pathetic. She didn't say a word, just gazed at me with tears rolling down her cheeks. I patted her shoulder and waited for her to explain. Finally, she rubbed her eyes and said, "If I tell you something will you promise not to tell another single soul?"

"Of course not."

"The thing is," she said with a catch in her voice, "I think I could be . . . I'm afraid that I'm . . . pregnant."

I looked at her, stunned. "Pregnant?"

She nodded and blew her nose. "And I'm too old."

I kept up the patting. "No, you are *not* too old."

She shook her head. "I am. And what will Don say? He likes our life just the way it is. Maybe he'll just leave."

"Have you told him?"

"I was going to, but then I figured I would wait until I knew for sure. I bought one of those pregnancy test kits in Key West. But I've been too scared to use it."

"Would it help if I stayed with you while you did it?"

"Oh, would you? I don't think I can do it alone."

"You won't have to, sweetie. And Don will be thrilled. I promise."

To be honest, I couldn't promise that Don would be thrilled about an unexpected pregnancy. After all, he and Mel had only been married for two years . . . a second marriage for both. Mel's "starter marriage", as she referred to it, had been more of a teenage rebellion to grab her parents' attention than a love match. It only lasted long enough for her son, Paul, to be born. She and Don had been high school acquaintances, but when they met again at their twenty-fifth high school reunion, sparks flew. And after a whirlwind romance, they tied the knot in the elegant wedding ceremony that Mary Linda had always dreamed about. After two years the pair still acted like newlyweds, but I knew that Mel suffered pangs of insecurity and jealousy.

And there is something about the dark and the sea at night that can bring on the blues in the most chipper of people. I have suffered the deep sea blues more often than I care to remember. So I sat there with Mary Linda and watched the waves breaking and thought dire thoughts about life and the Captain and Svetlana and Glenn.

Eventually Mel sat up and declared that she was going to go back to bed and deal with her issues in the morning. Telling her that things would look better in the light of day (what did I know?) I followed her back to the cabin. We climbed into our bunks and I was asleep in an instant.

Chapter Sixteen

Howling winds and rain slashing against the *Mirage* awoke me the next morning after too few hours of sleep. The boat was bouncing crazily on the rolling seas, and I was hurled from my bunk as the *Mirage* took a steep plunge into a wave as I tried to climb down. I lurched into the head and pawed through my makeup bag to retrieve my stash of Bonine. I gulped one down without benefit of water. Then, as I mimicked a tightrope walker trying to maintain my balance on the rolling ship, I swallowed a second pill. No time to be conservative. The storm that Captain Ned had predicted days ago had arrived with a vengeance.

My brain numbed from lack of sleep and fearful of the onset of a serious case of seasickness, I made a beeline for some fresh air. The stuffy cabin wasn't going to help my stomach a single bit. I staggered around the cabin pulling on jeans and a sweater. I rummaged through my duffel bag and came up with the *Mirage* rain gear that had been fortuitously provided for us by the Sunshine Tour people. Sunshine, ha! Obviously they knew something about the weather that they hadn't shared with us. I stuffed my feet into sneakers and tottered up to the deck.

It was a dark and surly morning with ominous grey clouds scudding by and rain coming down in sheets. The *Mirage* climbed up one side of giant waves and then crashed into the trough below. To my surprise, it was not Captain Ned, but Glenn who was at the wheel. I was relieved that he seemed to know what he was doing. When Glenn saw me, he tossed me an orange life jacket. "Put that on!" I didn't waste a second in obeying him.

"Where's the Captain?" I called out, but the wind whipped the words from my mouth and blew them out to sea. It appeared that Glenn hadn't heard me. I tried again, this time with more gusto. "Where is THE CAPTAIN?," I yelled at the top of my lungs. Glenn said something in reply, but I couldn't hear him over the roar of the wind. Yikes, I thought.

I deliberated the merits of being cold, soaking wet and miserable over those of going below and being warm, sick and miserable and decided to brave the outside elements. Unable to sleep on the bucking boat, the others one at a time groggily poked their heads up the steps to check out the weather, and one at a time they vanished from sight to seek shelter in the salon. After I had been on deck for awhile I went below to get warm and find out how the others were doing. No one was feeling well and I was dispatched to bring my supply of Bonine for mutual consumption. Only Martha was unfazed by the rough seas and the bouncing ship. She was astute enough, though, to realize that her culinary skills would be unappreciated, so she passed out saltines and reassuring words instead. We were not a happy party. As Julie said so eloquently, "I didn't sign on for a bout of seasickness." And she fled the salon with one hand over her mouth.

I found that I fared much better outside with the wind and the rain in my face, in part because it took my mind off my rumbling stomach. Clinging for dear life to the side of the boat, seasickness was (I was sure) the least of my problems.

The morning passed in a blur and I hardly noticed the slackening of the wind and the calming of the seas. But gradually the storm dissipated leaving behind grey skies, a chilly drizzle and a gusty breeze that heeled the boat over nicely. I was now more hungry than sick and began to wonder what I could find to eat in the galley. I was thinking of coffee first and then maybe a slice of toast when a thought hit me with the force of a jackhammer blow. Glenn was still at the wheel of the *Mirage*, wearing his orange life jacket and Bermuda shorts, his attention riveted on the sea. Svetlana had been holed up all morning in their cabin. No one had seen her according to the hurried reports I got when I stuck my head down the steps to ask how things were going. More important, it dawned on me that I hadn't seen the Captain all morning either. I hadn't seen him since last night.

The group huddled around the table in the salon littered with empty tea cups and crumpled saltine wrappers was dispirited and disheveled. They looked only a little less green than before and looked up at me glumly. Ellie, her short red hair sticking up around her face like an Indian headdress, scribbled half-heartedly in her notebook, while Mary Linda tapped unhappily at her laptop. Sandra peered over Mel's shoulder at the screen and frowned in concentration. "Battery's almost dead," Mel informed her and Sandra grimaced. Julie was absent from this cheerful gathering, having retreated to her bunk with a cold wash-cloth and a bottle of aspirin. They looked so bereft that I couldn't help smiling.

"You guys are looking fantastic," I said.

No one deigned to reply.

It wasn't my fault that the storm had moved in. I wasn't the weather goddess after all. "Guys," I said, "storm's passed. It's not that bad out. Come and see for yourselves."

They looked at me sullenly and not one of them moved. I made another feeble attempt to cheer them up. "Hey, we're making great time. We should be in smoother water very soon." I was grasping at straws. At their continued stubbornly morose silence, I shrugged and started to go back to the fresher air on deck. Then, I remembered why I had come down and pivoted and stepped back to the table. "Has anyone seen Svetlana this morning?" They shook their heads as one. "What about the Captain? Anyone seen him?" More head shaking.

"Are you positive?" I persisted. "Cuz Glenn's doing the driving in case you weren't aware of it."

The three of them peered at me wide-eyed with alarm. "Glenn?" Sandra stammered. "H-he is?"

They were completely useless. But, one thing was certain, no one had seen Captain Ned and they were unaware that it was Glenn steering the course of the *Mirage*. The skies were clearing and a watery sunlight glinted off the rain-slicked deck. Still . . . this wasn't right. Something was wrong, I just knew it. Well, then I would just go to Captain Ned's cabin and find out why he wasn't piloting the boat through the storm himself. I wasn't one bit happy that the job had been relegated to Glenn, and I was going to tell him so. I marched with righteous indignation out of the salon and down the hallway until I reached the Captain's cabin. I stopped outside the door and took a breath. Then I raised my hand and rapped on the door. I waited impatiently. And I waited some more. I counted to ten and then banged on it again, harder this time. Nothing happened. I put my ear close to the door and listened for any sound. I heard nothing. So, I pounded on the door and shouted, "Ned? Hey, Captain, it's Kate. Can I come in?"

Still no answer. Now I was becoming more concerned than angry and tentatively I put my hand on the doorknob and turned it. The door wasn't locked so I very slowly opened it and peeked inside. And that's when I saw him.

Dead. Stone cold dead. As in not breathing. As in lying in a pool of blood. That's how I found Captain Fairweather that afternoon. Dead, dead, dead. Not that I've had any previous experience with dead men or anything, but after I prodded him with my foot and hissed his name several times, I knew. I was, if you'll pardon the expression, dead certain.

I confess that I didn't handle the situation very well. I backed into the corner of Captain Fairweather's cabin and froze with my hands clasped over my mouth. I tried to scream but it came out a meek croak. The cabin was dim and stuffy and I struggled to breathe. "In," I coached myself. "Out." Finally I broke the spell and bolted for the cabin door. I tugged frantically at the door handle with a shaking hand. When it finally turned I took off as if I was being chased by a knife-wielding madman. I lost my footing on the polished wood floor and slammed into the wall, but didn't dare stop.

I hit the deck running and burst into tears. As my four friends, Mary Linda, Ellie, Sandra and Julie gathered around me, I sobbed, "He's dead. He's dead." Ellie patted me on the back and I wiped my eyes with the back of my hand.

"What's the matter?" Sandra demanded. "Who's dead?"

"Let's get the Captain," Mary Linda said. "Maybe he can help."

"No," I wailed. "You don't get it. The Captain is the one who's dead. I saw him."

"You saw him?"

"Yes." I sobbed. "He was lying on the floor of his cabin."

"Are you sure he was dead? Maybe he was napping," Julie said.

"No-ooo," I cried. My voice cracked. "He was all blo-ody."

They stared at me blankly. And why not? I was totally unglued. I mean, women from Ohio don't usually stumble over dead men. Sandra met my eye. "So, what you're telling us is that you found Captain Fairweather lying on the floor of his cabin in a pool of blood?"

It did sound a bit farfetched. "I think so."

"Well, then," Ellie said, "I think we'd better go to his cabin and check it out."

I would have preferred to lower myself into a pit of writhing snakes than to go back to that cabin, but I knew I had no choice. I had to suck it up and prove to my friends that the captain of our chartered sailboat was indeed a corpse. The five of us crept down the hallway to the Captain's cabin in the stern of the ship. The door was latched and only the creaking of the masts from the deck above disturbed the deathly silence. We jumped when Julie kicked over a wastebasket sitting in the hall and it clattered to the floor, the lid rolling under our feet.

Ellie whispered, "The door's locked, isn't it? He's sleeping or something."

Sandra tugged on my arm. "Let's just go."

"No." I shuddered. "I left this door wide open. Somebody or something closed it."

I jiggled the handle and discovered that the door was unlocked. I eased it open and, with my friends glued to my backside, I inched into the cabin. And . . . it was empty. No body. No Captain Fairweather. No murder weapon. Nothing.

"Where is this body?" Sandra demanded. "See, he isn't dead. He isn't even here."

"What do I know?" I said. "I'm not familiar with corpse protocol. Maybe he wasn't dead after all. Maybe the dent in his head wasn't a fatal wound. Maybe it was a cruel prank. There's only one way to find out. Find Captain Fairweather and he can explain."

So we scattered to search the ship. But we couldn't find Captain Nigel Fairweather anywhere. Our mood was bleak as we clung together on the deck as the watery late afternoon sun began to set and the tropical breeze freshened. The huge sails looming above us luffed in the breeze and the ship rocked on the swells. Dissipating rain clouds from the storm earlier scudded across the sky. Here we were somewhere in the Atlantic Ocean and the captain of our ship was, at the very least, missing, and if I was correct, dead. No one uttered a word.

"I think we have a problem," I said finally.

Chapter Seventeen

"**O**kay, now." Mary Linda chewed on her bottom lip nervously. "Let's not panic. There must be some explanation."

"Personally, I think panic is in order." Julie twisted her wedding ring on her finger.

Ellie played with a single red, spiky lock of hair with a trembling hand. "Really, you guys, the Captain has to be around somewhere."

"Yeah, I'm sure he just stepped out to the store to buy milk," I said.

Sandra snapped her fingers in irritation. "We should find Glenn and Svetlana. You said, Kate, that Glenn was at the helm. Where is he now?"

It hadn't occurred to me to wonder about Glenn and Svetlana. We needed to find out why Glenn had been sailing the *Mirage*. And we'd have the answers and we could stop torturing ourselves with scary scenarios. I volunteered to retrieve them.

I bolted down the steps and raced through the salon frantic to have our fears put to rest. I froze in front of Glenn and Svetlana's cabin, consciously avoiding looking at the closed door to Captain Fairweather's cabin. I tried not to think about what I had seen, but I was haunted by the image of his still body lying on the floor. I pounded on the door. My voice shrill and tense, I called, "Glenn? Svetlana? It's Kate. We need to talk to you."

The words were barely out of my mouth when Glenn opened the door. I looked past him into the cabin and saw Svetlana perched on the edge of the bunk. I expected to see her ill and weary from her day in bed, but instead she seemed ready to burst with repressed energy. "Hel-loo, Kate," she cried as she bounded to my side. "I am being glad to see you." Glenn lounged silently against the doorframe, his eyes cold and unblinking.

Filled with trepidation, I babbled, "We have a big problem. We can't find the Captain. I saw him on the floor of his cabin awhile ago and he was dead. And now he's gone. And we don't know what to do." I sounded like an idiot so I clamped my jaw shut to stop myself.

Svetlana reached for Glenn and grasped his arm. Her face contorted with panic, she stared at him. For a few seconds they didn't move, their eyes locked and then Glenn said with unnatural calm, "What do you mean, the Captain is dead?"

"Yes, what are you meaning?" Svetlana echoed.

I recounted what I had seen and explained that we had conducted a futile search for the Captain. Still clutching Glenn's arm, Svetlana backed her way to the bunk and sank onto it. Glenn touched his finger to her cheek and then turned to me. "I think I'd better know more about all of this. Where are the others?"

I didn't answer that question, but asked him the one I had been mulling for an hour. "Glenn, when did you see him last? And why were you, of all people, sailing the boat this morning? In a storm? With no help? What do you have to say about that?" I was only slightly hysterical.

Unruffled, his brown eyes behind his thick glasses were unblinking. "Why don't we find the others and I'll tell you everything I know. No point in telling it more than once." He looked at Svetlana for confirmation and she just nodded.

Glenn offered Svetlana his hand, pulled her up and together they exited the cabin. I followed in their wake feeling even more frightened and confused. I couldn't shake the feeling that I had just been treated to a very practiced performance.

My shipmates had abandoned their post on the deck and reconvened in the salon. Martha bustled around pouring coffee. They looked up expectantly as Glenn, Svetlana and I entered the salon.

Ellie asked, "Have you seen Captain Ned, Glenn? Or you, Svetlana?"

Sandra drummed jittery fingers on the salon table and cast a sardonic look my way. I shrugged and waited to hear what Glenn had to say. He gathered his thoughts and mutely considered the uneasy group. He refused to take a seat and positioned himself near the steps, keeping himself stiff and upright. Finally, when I thought I might explode from frustration, he took a sip of coffee, wet his lips nervously, I thought, and began speaking.

"Where should I begin . . ."

"How about at the beginning," Julie snorted.

"Yes, the beginning." He exhaled. "When I woke up this morning, I heard the wind and the rain. It sounded ferocious. Svetlana wasn't feeling well and I thought I'd go to the galley and make her a nice cup of tea."

Svetlana gazed at him adoringly.

"But when I got to the galley, I decided to stick my head outside and check on the weather. The Captain was at the helm and it seemed like he was having a tough time even standing up out there. He was drenched and I figured he must be pretty exhausted."

He paused to collect his thoughts. "So, I got my rain coat and went up on deck to see if I could help. He told me to put on a life jacket. So I did. And I watched him for a little while. He was so wet and he didn't have on rain gear and he was shivering."

No one spoke. Even Martha halted pouring coffee to hear Glenn's next words. "And, then, he said . . ." Glenn hesitated. "He said that he was cold and wet and wanted to get dry clothes and maybe a cup of coffee and could I take the wheel for just a few minutes while he went below. And I said sure. I've been taking lessons from him, you know, and I thought I was up to the challenge."

We waited as Glenn fiddled with his glasses, wiping them on a handkerchief. He jumped when I demanded. "And then what? Come on, Glenn."

Glenn concluded in a rush. "And I took the wheel and I never saw him again."

For just a moment I saw in Glenn a little boy seeking approval that never came. I opened my mouth and then closed it. I couldn't believe what I was hearing. "You never even wondered where he was and why he didn't come back? And you just kept sailing without a single word to any of us. I was on deck with you most of the morning and *you never said a thing*." My voice rose, approaching hysteria and Glenn winced.

He jammed his hands in his pockets. "But I did, Kate. I did say something, but you didn't answer me and I figured you had gone below and checked and that he was ill or something. So I just kept sailing and waited for him to come back or for you to give me a message from him." He glared at me and one eye twitched.

I did recall that he had attempted to say something to me and I couldn't hear his voice over the storm. His story was believable if you looked at it like that. It's safe to say I wouldn't make much of a prosecuting attorney since I accepted Glenn's version of events without question.

Sandra pushed her hair behind her ears. "So what do you think happened to him then? If no one has seen him since early this morning . . . what time did you say?"

Glenn sounded defensive. "I didn't. But it was about five or five-thirty."

I checked my watch and exploded. "It's four now. That means no one has seen him in nearly *twelve* hours. Unless you count me seeing him lying on the floor of his cabin, stone cold dead!"

Svetlana shuddered. "So, Katie, where then is this body being? If he is dead, then where is the dead body?"

"I think I know," Mary Linda said.

We turned on her in astonishment. "You do? What do you know?"

Mary Linda drew a ragged breath. "Last night I was on the deck. You remember, Kate, I couldn't sleep . . ." Her eyes begged me not to tell her secret. I did the bobble-head thing at her and she went on. "And I thought I'd get some air and then I'd go back and be able to sleep. I curled up in the corner of the bench under the cover by the helm. All of a sudden, I heard this odd noise. Kind of a ker-thud or something and I peeked out. I know he didn't see me."

"Who didn't see you?" Julie glowered.

Mary Linda shrank into her seat. "It was a man. I couldn't tell who it was, but he had a big bag and I thought it must be Miguel and that he was throwing garbage over. I thought it was kind of gross. He . . . the man . . . kind of struggled with the bag. It seemed heavy. And then he got it up on the rail and he shoved it over. He stood there watching the water for a little while. And then he went away."

I launched a fierce cross-examination of my friend Mel. "Did you see his face?"

"No," she admitted.

"Someone threw something overboard in the middle of the night and you didn't try to see who it was?" I was amazed that she had so little curiosity.

"No," Mel said in a tiny voice. "I didn't."

"Well," I reasoned, my mind racing, "it couldn't have been the Captain's body then. Maybe it was a body. But it couldn't have been the Captain because Glenn says . . ." I glanced at him dubiously. ". . . that he talked to the Captain this morning. And I saw his body around two o'clock this afternoon."

"This is getting weirder and weirder." Sandra methodically shredded a napkin.

Suddenly, I recalled hearing that funny dull thud when I was getting ready to shower the night before. And the strange shushing sound. Mary Linda had been up on deck then. Which meant the timing was right. But if the Captain was still alive, then, who or what was in the bag Mel saw being thrown overboard? I described the sounds I heard to the others and we looked at each other with growing dismay.

"So what now?" Julie asked.

"I think we have to contact the authorities or something. Can we call 911?" Mel said. "We need to have some help on this."

The salon was deathly still with only the sound of the ticking of the clock above the galley sink. For a few long moments not one of us said a word. We hardly breathed. And then in the space of a few seconds, we all began to speak at once.

"I'm telling you that if we can handle PMS and hot flashes, then we can handle this," Sandra said.

Mel uncurled from her corner and sat up straight, while Ellie scribbled in her notebook. Julie shoved her chair back from the table and began to pace in the confined space. "First we have to check the boat again. Maybe we missed something the first time."

Ellie repeated as she scrawled. "Check boat."

"We need to look for some clue to what happened," I added.

Mel persisted with her idea. "And call 911."

"Call 911," Ellie echoed. And she scribbled some more.

Julie glared at Ellie and growled. "Stop that, Ellie."

"This is a murder investigation, for chrissakes," I said.

"Or a missing person," Mel insisted.

"Ladies, don't you think you are overreacting?" Glenn asked. "I seriously doubt . . ."

"Oh, God." I had an awful realization. "Glenn, who is sailing this boat? If you are here and the Captain is God knows where . . . dead or alive . . . are we just drifting aimlessly toward the Bermuda triangle?"

"Calm down, Kate," he said. "Of course not. I dropped the sails and put out the sea anchor before I went below to check on Svetlana. With no wind we won't go far."

"Not to point out the obvious or anything, but isn't it possible that we are dragging the sea anchor?" I did know a bit about sailboats, and it was a reasonable question.

Glenn's face reflected conflicting emotions. He didn't want to admit that I had a point, but he also didn't want to have the *Mirage* at the mercy of the seas. He gave me an enigmatic look and rushed up the steps. Svetlana followed him with her eyes. "I am after Glenn," she announced and dashed after him.

I wasn't about to let them out of my sight so I followed, hot on their heels. "Let's meet in our cabin and brainstorm. I'll keep an eye on those two and be down in a second."

"Good plan," Sandra said in a businesslike tone. And added, "I'll get the wine."

"Wine?" Ellie asked.

"Sure. We don't have time to make margaritas."

The first thing we needed to do was to call the police. The trick was to figure out how. In the brochure depicting the delights which awaited us on the *Mirage* (which I had devoured not long ago) one of amenities included was the ability to be in contact with land at all times. That meant a radio. I hadn't given it a lot of consideration during the cruise, but I was certain it would be somewhere obvious. When I reached the deck, Glenn and Svetlana were huddled under the cover which protected the helm. They were engaged in a heated dialogue and I crept toward them hoping to overhear something. I wasn't quick enough or quiet enough and they stopped talking before I got within earshot. Glenn pointed at the panel in front of him. "I was just telling Svetlana that we should radio for help." He gestured at the deep, grey blue sea surrounding us. "And the *Mirage* is just fine so far. I told you I put out the sea anchor. We are safe here."

Indeed, the boat was rocking placidly, but when I scanned the horizon, I could not see any sign of land. No palm trees, no sandy beaches. Nothing but cold, grey seas and gloomy clouds scudding across a dreary sky. Only brief patches of pallid sunlight broke through. It was lonely out there.

"Where is the radio?" Good question. "And where are we?"

"The radio is right there. And I don't know exactly where we are. The storm blew us off course." Glenn spoke with no inflection and inspired no confidence.

"Do you know how to use the radio?" I asked.

"Miguel must know how," Glenn answered in that same robotic tone.

I sprinted below to get him.

"No es posible, Señora." Miguel fiddled with the radio and threw up his hands. "Es rompido."

"Como?" I needed Martha to translate for me.

"The radio is broken. He can't make it work." Martha consulted with Miguel in rapid Spanish. "He says the storm must have damaged it."

Glenn seemed unperturbed by this news. I turned to Martha. "Ask him what he thinks we should do."

Martha spoke again in a rush of Spanish. "He says," she translated, "that we need to start the engine and go to shore."

"Shore?"

"Si, Señora." Martha twisted her skirt in her hand. "Miguel says that we need the engine. There isn't any wind."

Well, he was right about that. In the lull after the storm, there was no breeze. We would not be able to get anywhere under sail. The motor was our only option. But which direction would we go? With no radio to call for help, what good would it do to start the motor. We could go the wrong way and end up in the middle of the Atlantic. I hoped we could use the compass and at least set a course for the Keys.

Miguel waved his hands wildly and in a flood of Spanish exhorted Martha. My Spanish may be a little rusty, but I understood a word or two of his harangue. If I understood anything at all, and I was afraid I did, then Miguel wasn't any happier than I was. I pantomimed starting an engine and pointed at Miguel. He nodded and disappeared, leaving me gazing at the darkening sky and the bottomless sea. I wanted to sit down and cry.

Miguel returned and with much shaking of his head and frantic gesturing told Martha the awful truth. Before she could translate for him, Miguel looked me in the eye and said sadly, "The engine she is broke, Señora. No go. No go. Lo siento mucho." Believe me, I was sorry too.

"Can you fix it?" I asked Miguel. He shrugged, uncomprehending. Frustrated, I said to Martha, "Ask him."

Martha and Miguel conversed for a minute in rapid Spanish. Finally, Martha turned back to me and Glenn and Svetlana. "He says that he will try to fix the engine, but he thinks it was tampered with. There seems to be water in the fuel and it could have been put there deliberately."

Glenn interrupted her. "Who would want to do that?"

Martha repeated emphatically, "Miguel says that someone tampered with it. He can fix it if he has parts and some equipment. But we don't have that onboard. We need to find a port."

"Let me summarize," I said despondently. "We can't sail because there is no wind. We can't radio for help because it's broken. And we can't use the motor because someone messed with it. Basically, we're screwed." Succinct and to the point.

After a hasty discussion we agreed our best bet was the engine, and we hoped that Miguel could somehow get it to run. If not, the wind would have to pick up sooner or later. Meanwhile, we were at the mercy of the sea.

I trudged back to my cabin with the pit in my stomach growing rapidly to the size of, say, Rhode Island. All I wanted was to blink my eyes and nod my head "I Dream of Jeannie" style, and be back in my own bedroom in comfortingly boring Winslow, Ohio. I yanked open the cabin door and found the others sprawled on the bunks and floor. Discarded clothing littered the cramped area and two bottles of wine occupied the place of honor in the middle of the chaos. I regarded them warily and then I dropped to the floor and poured myself a healthy glass. I chugged half of it before I uttered a sound.

"So, here's the thing . . ." I brought them up to speed on the predicament we were in, withholding none of the horrible details. "Any ideas?"

Silence. Struck dumb, apparently, by the circumstances, they exchanged helpless glances. Did anyone grasp the trouble we were in or did they think it was some kind of Girl Scout scavenger hunt?

I cleared my throat. "Let me call to order this gathering of the Jazzercise Detectives. Until we can get some help from the authorities we need to see what we know and maybe figure out what happened to the Captain. Maybe if we talk about it we'll remember something we can use." Confidently, I waited for a response.

"This isn't a novel, Kate." Julie spoke with a hostile note in her voice. "And you aren't Stephanie Plum or even Nancy Drew. This is real life."

"I know that. But we have to go with what we've got. Come on, you guys, what do you know?"

Julie grimaced. "Besides that I want to go home?"

"Yeah, besides that."

Like a dam bursting we all began to speak at once. We may not have been private investigators, but we each had skills we could use. And one of the basic mom skills is sniffing out teenaged misbehavior. We'd have to use those abilities to ferret out the murderer. Not that we were willing to admit, at that point, that there had been an actual murder. Only I was convinced of that. But then I was the only one who had seen the "corpse."

Mary Linda suggested that we check our cell phones to see if anyone had service. So, even though we had already obsessively checked and re-checked, we dug out our phones. Nothing. No signal.

Julie tossed her phone down in disgust. "Where exactly would there be a cell tower out here?"

Mary Linda sighed. "So, we are on our own then. Unless . . ."

"What?" we demanded.

"You said the radio didn't work?"

I nodded.

"But I'll bet that the Captain had a radio in his cabin. He wouldn't want to have to do all his communicating from the one on deck? Would he?"

I jumped off the bunk. "I'm going to go and see."

Julie grabbed my arm. "Not alone. We stick together."

No one wanted to be left behind, so the five of us crept reluctantly toward Captain Fairweather's cabin. The hall-way was shadowy in the waning daylight and the floor lights were the only illumination.

"This is spooky." Ellie hung back unwilling or unable to move.

Impatiently, we pulled her along until we halted at the doorway. I inspected the door as if it could give me answers. Just a plain cherry wood door. Shiny brass fit-tings and door-knob. Nothing special. I gingerly twisted the knob expecting that it would be locked. But it turned easily and the door swung open. With my four friends crowding behind me, I entered. Nothing had changed since we last had been there. It was quiet . . . too quiet . . . and undisturbed. We peered around fearfully, half-expecting someone to leap out of the closet and shout, "Boo!"

The closet! I edged over and unlatched it. Inside, jeans, sweaters and rain gear were neatly hung on hangers on the left side. On the right was a set of drawers which went from floor to ceiling. Nothing seemed to be out of order. I looked over my shoulder at my friends who clung together behind me. Then I boldly pulled out the top drawer and gasped. Chaos. I watch enough television to recognize a drawer that has been ransacked when I see one. Nothing gets past us amateur detectives. Either that or Ned had been a much messier person than I thought possible. In rapid succession, I pulled open the other drawers. The same. All were a jumble of clothes and papers.

I whispered, "Someone was looking for something."

"Maybe he couldn't find the socks he wanted. Or his belt," Sandra said.

That didn't require a response, so I closed the closet door and let my eyes travel around the rest of the tiny, airless room. A desk was tucked into the space beneath a porthole and I marched over to it. The desktop was neat and orderly. Nothing seemed out of place. A computer keyboard occupied the position of honor. Carefully, I grasped the handle on the big drawer on the right and sliding it out discovered the radio we had been searching for. Triumphantly, I stepped aside to reveal my discovery. Mel elbowed me out of her way and lifted it from its hiding place. Then her face fell as she saw the jumble of wires exploding from inside the radio. With the wires in her hand, she exclaimed fearfully, "I don't think this is gonna work. Someone pulled all the wires out."

"Now do you believe me?" It was obvious to even the most skeptical that we were dealing with a very menacing something or someone. Whatever else we might know, this much was clear . . . we had gotten more than we bargained for when we signed on for this cruise. We held onto each other for support and comfort. The air in the cabin, heavy with fear, was stifling. The urge to bolt was almost overpowering.

Reason prevailed, though, and I said, "Well, we're here. Let's finish looking around. Then we can get the hell out of here."

It wasn't a big space and there wasn't much else to see. Hastily we peered under the bedding on the bunk and into the head. Nothing. Clueless, we abandoned our futile search and began tiptoeing toward the door. Without warning, Ellie tripped, over her own feet, I presume. She lost her balance and fell, landing with a thump on a small square of burgundy carpet in the center of the cabin. Startled, she began to leap to her feet and froze, her hand hovering in midair. She made tiny squeaks as she stared at her fingers with revulsion. "Argh."

We looked over her shoulder. "What?" "I don't see anything."

Ellie didn't move a muscle. "Look." She continued to stare at her hand. And then we saw what she was talking about. Ellie's fingers were stained with something red and sticky. And on the carpet was a damp stain. It looked like . . . could it have been . . . oh my God . . . it *was* blood. Appalled, we stared at each other.

It came back to me in a flash. The picture of the Captain lying motionless (and dead?) on the cabin floor was imprinted indelibly on my mind. And I knew . . . beyond a shadow of a doubt . . . that he had been lying on that very carpet that was stained with someone's . . . the Captain's? . . . blood.

"Ah, hah," I said feebly. "That proves it."

"No, it doesn't," Julie argued with not much conviction. "Maybe he cut himself."

"Or someone else cut him." Sandra retreated from the evidence. "We need to call the cops."

At that, we escaped from the Captain's cabin to the safety of our own.

While Ellie scrubbed her hands at the sink for the fifth time, the rest of us gulped the remainder of the wine. The *Mirage* scarcely moved so still and flat was the sea. No wind ruffled the sails that hung limply from the masts. We cracked open the porthole window to get a breath of fresh air and saw only the deepening dusk.

Our crime-solving skills may have been negligible, but we refused to get discouraged. Actually we got mad. This was our vacation, damn it, and we were supposed to be sunning ourselves and eating our way across the sea until we were fat and happy and ready to go back home. Whoever was messing with us should have known better. We weren't spineless ninnies after all.

It occurred to me that we hadn't seen Svetlana and Glenn in quite some time and I wondered how much they would share with us. If I was correct there was something odd going on with the two of them. Actually there were plenty of weird things going on.

"Let's think about Glenn and Svetlana," I proposed. "What do we really know about them?"

Ellie emerged from the bathroom still inspecting her hands with disgust. She frowned and volunteered, "I could ask Wil if he knows any more about Glenn. Or Skippy."

"Good idea. But we don't have any way to communicate with the outside world right now," I reminded her.

"Oh. When we do . . ."

"Wait a second." Mary Linda bounded off the bunk, her feet hitting the floor with a thud. Eagerly she dug in her duffle bag and straightened up waving her laptop. "This is wireless and runs on a battery. And I have a spare one with me."

We may mock Mel for her devotion to organization, but in this case we applauded her. Literally.

"Will that really work out here?" Sandra asked.

"What do we have to lose?"

"Don't get your hopes up."

Even if we could send an e-mail, would we send it to our families and tell them that we were trapped on the *Mirage* with a (perhaps) dead man and a murderer? Definitely not the kind of thing a loved one would relish receiving. "Having a wonderful time. Wish the cops were here. Because there's a murderer on the loose." Nope. Even my placid husband would freak out if he got that. And what could he do? He couldn't send the police because we couldn't tell anyone where we were. How about . . . "Lost at sea. Please send helicopters." Sure, that would work. Send one to the cops then. Since we didn't have an e-mail address, should we Google it. Farfetched and hardly feasible. Maybe the e-mail thing wouldn't work. We were back where we started. Nowhere.

"I have Wil's e-mail address," Ellie said. "Let's say we could get it to him, then he could inform the Key West police and they might have an idea where to look for us."

We all agreed that Ellie had a good idea . . . she would communicate with Wil as soon as it was possible. Meanwhile, we decided that we would be vigilant and digest every single detail we knew about the crew of the *Mirage* (Ned, Martha and Miguel) and the ravishing Svetlana and her enigmatic husband, Glenn.

We had been holed up in the cabin for hours so it was only sensible for someone to check up on the others onboard. I felt responsible for getting us involved in all of this, so I offered to seek them out. "I'll come with you," Sandra said. "You can't go out there alone. God knows what's going on."

"I'd be glad to have some company," I said.

So, Sandra and I left the others in the cabin and found Martha alone in the galley. She was fixing trays of food. Fearing that we might startle her, I cleared my throat to get her attention. If I had expected to see a frightened woman, I was mistaken. Martha looked up from her chores and smiled at us in delight. "You came to get some food," she cried, obviously thrilled that her services were required. "I was just making trays for Mr. Glenn and Miss Svetlana. I can make trays for you girls or I can serve dinner here in the salon." Either murder and missing captains were not an uncommon event for Martha or she was totally oblivious to the seriousness of the situation. No matter. Martha was so blatantly cheerful that I had to wonder if it was an act. Sandra and I exchanged bemused looks.

"I'm sorry, Martha," I apologized, "I don't think we're up to dinner tonight. The Captain having gone AWOL and all."

"Oh," she said, disappointed. "Oh, well, then."

"So, Glenn and Svetlana are in their cabin?" Sandra asked.

"Yes, I believe so. They asked for trays so I assumed . . ."

"Okay," I said. "Where's Miguel?"

"He's working on the engine."

"Any progress?"

She shrugged. "You'd have to ask him. He's been there since the wind died down."

She returned to her food preparations while Sandra and I ascended the steps to the deck. The night air was damp and cool and we shivered as much from the eeriness of the empty deck and motionless sails as from the chill. Not a breath of a breeze stirred the water, which appeared black and bottomless to our apprehensive eyes. Sandra clutched my arm with icy fingers and said in a barely audible voice, "No one's out here. Maybe we should go back inside."

I looked around me with trepidation and gave in. "Let's go."

We checked with Miguel in the stern to see if he had been able to repair the engine. Shirtless, with his chest and arms smeared with grease, he gave us a disconsolate shrug and shook his head. "No. Es limpido, Señoras. Muy mal." We didn't need a translator to figure out that Miguel wasn't having any luck.

"Buena suerte," I told him. "Good luck."

Glenn and Svetlana were eating dinner when we knocked on their cabin door. Neither seemed particularly surprised to see us. Svetlana was much more subdued than her usual ebullient self. She said nothing as Sandra and I stepped into the cabin and kept her head down with her eyes fixed on her plate. Frankly, I wanted to shake both of them. Either they were in a coma or they were totally unperturbed by our current predicament. They might not have been responsible for the disappearance of Captain Ned, but I suspected they knew something about it.

I figured I should be subtle about questioning them, but my nerves were shot and I wanted answers. I wanted an explanation and here they were consuming the meal like it was any old night. "Damn it, Glenn," I shouted, "aren't you two the least little bit concerned about what's going on? Here you are sitting here as calm as can be and the Captain is gone and I think he's dead."

Sandra tugged on my arm, but I forged ahead. "Talk to me, will you!"

Placidly Glenn put down his knife and fork and stared at us. "And what am I supposed to do, Kate? I'm a passenger on this boat just like you are."

"Well, first off, I think you should look the tiniest bit worried. Maybe sweat a little."

"Oh, believe me, I'm just as worried as you are."

"Well, you don't look it."

"I am," he insisted. "I have a board meeting that cannot be postponed and I have to be there. This is not at all convenient for me."

"Convenient?" I yelled. "Convenient? I'm sure that Captain Fairweather is sorry his death has inconvenienced you."

"Now, now," he tried to pacify me, "that's not what I meant. I'm sure the wind will pick up in the morning and we'll be able to get to shore."

"And you, the great boat person, know which way shore is."

"When the sun comes up, we'll be able to tell which way to go," he pointed out patronizingly.

At least he was correct about that, I realized. A bit mollified, I backed off. Sandra breathed a sigh of relief and wrenched me away. "Let's get out of here. We need to talk."

I gave one last look at Glenn and Svetlana who had gone back to their dinners as if they didn't have a care in the world. It was obvious that we weren't going to get any more information out of them. They were as closed up as downtown Winslow after eight p.m.

Chapter Eighteen

The five of us talked late into the night. Actually it was early morning before exhaustion overcame us and we fell into our bunks, the need for sleep winning out over the desire to keep watch. Bleary-eyed, I climbed into my bunk and pulled the covers to my chin. Sleep didn't come as quickly for me as for my cabin mates. I lay there for a long time, staring at the ceiling, my brain working overtime. I had missed something. I was certain of it and it niggled at my mind. Eventually I dozed off.

When I awoke the next morning, I was so confident that yesterday's horrific events were nothing more than a nightmare that I bolted for the deck. Barefoot and still in my pajamas, I ran to the stern and up the steps. Thank God. There he was. It *had* all been a nightmare. Captain

Ned was at the helm, his back to me, staring out at the still unruffled seas. "There you are," I called to him in relief. "You'll never believe what . . ."

And I stopped abruptly as he turned to face me. Of course, it wasn't the Captain. It was Glenn. I was dumbstruck by the resemblance to Ned. I'd noticed it before, I recalled, but never so clearly as in the early morning light. I had been positive that it was Ned. The same size, same height. And something familiar about the posture.

My heart sank to my toes as I realized my error. "You aren't the Captain," I told Glenn unnecessarily.

"Sorry to disappoint," Glenn answered.

"You haven't seen him then?"

"I hate to be the bearer of bad news, but I would be forced to conclude that he is gone. I can't speak to the dead part, but he is nowhere on the *Mirage*. Svetlana and I searched everywhere."

Crestfallen, I asked, "So, what do you suggest we do now?"

"I imagine the wind will pick up as the sun comes up. No matter how light the air is, I'll hoist the sails and try to make some headway."

"And you're in charge because . . ."

"Because I know the most about sailing and I'm the only port in this particular storm."

"I grew up on sailboats," I informed him with a touch of annoyance. "You can use my help."

He allowed that, yes, he would appreciate my help. There was a flash of the old, easygoing Glenn. And then Glenn in Charge took over. "I'll take care of things, little lady," he said. "Don't worry."

"I am worried, though."

"Why don't you go and get some breakfast," he suggested. "I'm sure Martha has cooked up a storm."

"That would be Martha all right. For her, the answer to any problem is the proper menu. I can't wait to see what she thinks is appropriate today," I said. "The Don't Worry We are Miles From Anywhere Menu."

With a flash of humor, Glenn responded, "The Lost in the Florida Triangle and it Might Be Our Last Meal Bill of Fare."

"Very funny." And I scurried below.

Sure enough, Martha fixed a banquet fit for royalty. She left no spoon unturned in her efforts to distract us. We emerged from our cabins hungry and grouchy to discover the table in the salon laid out with a smorgasbord of temptations. Eggs a la Hollandaise, blueberry pancakes, fluffy omelets made any way we desired, bacon, ham and petite sausages served in a glaze, a fresh fruit compote, buttery croissants, gooey pecan rolls, tiny muffins, freshly baked cornbread, cinnamon French toast with a warm maple syrup, freshly brewed coffee, fresh squeezed orange juice and hot chocolate served with dollops of real whipped cream. She must have been cooking and baking all night. That emergency generator must be really sizzling, I thought.

Wide-eyed with amazement at Martha's audacity, and at the same time overcome by the sheer size and variety of this repast, I imagined that Martha saw this as the only manner in which she could contribute. It was a celebration created with the intention of easing our minds, and, to Martha's credit, it worked like a charm.

All of *Mirage*'s passengers and Miguel, too, put aside our qualms and dug into the feast like survivors of a famine. We piled our plates and then returned for seconds. It was silent as, our mouths too full for conversation, we ate until we were uncomfortably stuffed. Occasionally someone would mutter, "Ooh, that's good" or "Taste one of these" or "Martha, you are a genius." But mostly we just chewed and swallowed and then chewed some more. Finally, when we couldn't force in a single bite more, we pushed our plates aside and confronted the facts.

In the morning's light things didn't look quite as grim as they had the stormy day and night before. The sun was attempting to break through the thin grey clouds and as a gentle breeze ruffled the sails, the tiniest ray of hope raised our spirits ever-so-slightly. As Martha cleared the dishes, we gathered on the deck to peer at the sky. As the sun rose higher, it seemed, our morale did too.

Miguel apologized for his inability to repair the motor. "Eees broke, Missus," he admitted, his eyes downcast. "No can feex. Lo siento mucho." He hovered near Glenn waiting for orders.

Eventually we were rewarded by a small increase in the wind's velocity. Glenn caught my eye, gave me a thumbs up gesture and began checking lines and halyards. He called me over and after he consulted with me, I turned to my friends and announced, "There's enough wind to give this a try. Glenn says we might not make much headway, but at least it's better than doing nothing."

"Let's do it!" they chorused. "Let's sail!"

Svetlana joined us on deck and we watched as Glenn hoisted the sails and the breeze puffed them out just a bit. I took the wheel while Glenn made some adjustments. I hope we know what we're doing, I prayed. And where we're going. With no other obvious options, we had to trust Glenn. Terrifying as that might be.

Glenn was as good as his word. He did know what he was doing and, it turned out, where to go. With Glenn navigating and the two of us alternating at the wheel, the *Mirage* sailed on slowly. The wind became stronger and the sky cleared as the sun climbed higher. The temperature edged up a few degrees and, after a day spent in the tiny, claustrophobic cabins, everyone wanted to be out in the open air. One by one we changed into our bathing suits and slathered on sunblock. No one uttered a word about the Captain and his absence. As the hours flew by we acted as if the Captain had never existed. Svetlana, too, was uncharacteristically quiet as she lounged in a deck chair. Our voices hushed, we chattered about trivia, afraid to break the tranquility with unsettling speculations. And, so it was that all hands were on deck when our rescuers appeared on the horizon.

At first we thought it was an honest-to-goodness mirage, a figment of our imaginations brought on by desperation, but as the boat motored toward us we realized that our saviors had, indeed, arrived. Our heroes were aboard a forty-foot powerboat rigged for fishing. While the captain piloted the boat from the tall fly bridge, the crew had its eyes trained on the fishing lines. They were so preoccupied, in fact, we feared they would cruise by totally oblivious to us.

As the sleek fishing craft drew nearer we waved and screamed, trying to arouse their attention. The captain waved cheerily back and returned to his business. I don't know whether they would have stopped or not, but Svetlana took matters into her own hands. She perched on the side of the *Mirage* and in her tiny yellow bikini was a sight no male could possibly ignore. Even if a fish was on the line. "Yoo, hoo," she called and waved her arms above her head, revealing a great deal of cleavage. "We are needing your help."

Five admiring male faces turned our way and as the captain steered his boat alongside, I could read the name stenciled in gold on the bow. *HONOR*. The Captain of the *Honor* cupped his hands over his mouth and hollered, "Hello, *Mirage*. Do you have a problem?"

As Glenn uncleated the lines, the sails puddled on the deck and we drifted next to the *Honor*. "May day. Yes, *Honor*, we do have a problem."

"What can we do to help?"

"We lost our radio and our engine in the storm last night. Can you give us a tow to port?"

"Roger. We'll toss you a line."

One of the fishermen threw Glenn a line and Glenn secured it to the bow of the *Mirage*. When everything was set, the *Honor* restarted her engines and began towing us.

"Where are we?" Glenn yelled over the engine noise. "We got blown off course last night and the GPS isn't working."

"Closest marina is the Fresh Ketch at Coconut Key. Are you familiar with it?"

"Yes," Glenn said curtly.

I waited in vain for Glenn to advise the other boat of the serious trouble we were in, but he didn't say a word. I sidled forward, careful to maintain my balance as the *Mirage* trailed behind the *Honor*. I stood next to Glenn with my eyes fixed on the stern of the rescue vessel and, without looking at him, asked, "Don't you think we ought to tell them about the . . . alleged . . . murder and the fact that Ned is missing?"

"No," he said defiantly, "it's none of their business. We'll inform the proper authorities when we get to the Fresh Ketch. No point in involving these Good Samaritans in our little drama."

I whipped around to face him. "Little drama? If this is a little drama, I'd like to know what you consider a big deal?"

"Now, Kate, just let me handle it."

As the *Honor* towed us to Coconut Key I couldn't help but reflect on how ironic it was. There is *Honor* after all, I thought, among thieves. Or perhaps I should say . . . murderers.

Chapter Nineteen

As we approached the Fresh Ketch Marina, I saw Flo standing on the dock waiting for us. Her frizzy, blonde curls were blowing in the breeze and one hand shaded her eyes. Apparently the Captain of the *Honor* had radioed ahead and Flo and Hank were expecting us. When we were a few yards from the dock, Hank hurried out of the office building and down the pier. One of the crew untied the line connecting us and tossed it to Hank who caught it and, in one practiced movement, wound it around one of the pilings.

The Captain of the *Honor* reversed his engines and maneuvered so that he was heading back out to sea. "Good luck, *Mirage*," he yelled. "You're in good hands with Hank."

"Thanks for the lift, Captain," Glenn called back. "We appreciate it."

I watched glumly as the *Honor* chugged away, already dismissing us in anticipation of catching some big fish. We, too, needed to catch a big fish, but not the same species. Ours was more a deadly shark.

Flo practically jumped up and down in excitement at seeing us again and said, "I didn't expect to see y'all so soon. Let's go up to the bar and I'll get y'all some snacks."

Before anyone could respond to her offer, Martha appeared from out of nowhere and with one hand on her hip said, "They won't be needing any of your snacks. I've got that taken care of."

"Now, now, Missy," Flo replied, "I didn't mean to imply that your snacks aren't perfectly dee-vine. I just thought they might like to get off that there boat."

Still in a huff, Martha mumbled something and disappeared below. Oh, fine, I thought. Now we are going to have the Snack Wars in addition to everything else. I debated going after Martha to offer reassurance, but decided I needed to be on hand for Glenn's explanation of our frightening circumstances.

Succinctly, Glenn laid out the facts for Hank. Both Hank and Flo listened, their expressions revealing nothing.

"Oh, my, you poor dears," Flo said when Glenn finished his tale.

Hank, on the other hand, self-importantly straightened his ragged t-shirt and rubbed a hand over his stubbly chin. "I am the police chief here in Coconut Key," he announced. "It's up to me to investigate any criminal activity in this here jurisdiction."

Glenn looked only mildly concerned at this pronouncement. "I've given you the facts, Hank. I guess it's up to you to make sense of all of it."

Then he added, "And, if it wouldn't be too much trouble, could you repair the *Mirage* and find us a way out of the Keys? I have an important meeting to attend and I can't be delayed."

Hank may have looked like a rube. And if he'd been wearing boots and a cowboy hat, I wouldn't have been surprised if he'd started to round up a posse. But he wasn't about to take any crap from Glenn. He stared him down until Glenn dropped his eyes. "I'll have you know that I am in charge here. And no one is going anywhere until I get some answers."

Flo herded us down the dock toward the bar. "Hank, sweetie, let's get these girls settled someplace more comfortable and then you can investigate to your heart's content."

She whispered an aside to me. "He just loves bein' a big shot. We ain't had no crime here in the whole while we been here. But Hank knows his stuff. He'll find out what happened to Captain Ned, Lord rest his soul."

Hank interviewed each of us separately in his office. When my turn came, I was amazed to see how tidy the inside of the ramshackle building was. A counter ran across the front of the building. On it sat an old-fashioned cash register and a variety of pens and pads. Behind the counter was a cork board on which a fishing calendar was prominently displayed as well as several notices and bills.

There were two offices. One just to the right was piled with an assortment of boxes and fishing equipment.

Obviously, it was being used for storage. The other office was the one Hank ushered me into. I was surprised to see an up-to-date computer on the orderly desk. It was on, and the screen saver flashed a series of boats floating on a placid sea. Hank gestured for me to take a seat and offered me a soft drink. I accepted a can of diet cola and when I was settled, Hank began his questioning.

"I guess I'd better get the formalities out of the way," he began. "Name, address and all of that."

I told him and waited for his next question. "Tell me what you know about the Captain."

I hesitated for a few moments to gather my thoughts. "I didn't know him all that well. Sometimes I thought he was a disgusting chauvinist. My first impression was that he was a very bad man. But in the last few days I've kind of gotten a different impression. I started to kind of like him."

Hank nodded sagely. "I believe you were the one who found him in his cabin."

"Yes, I did."

"Tell me about it. How did he look?"

"He looked dead," I fumed. "Dead as a door nail."

"Exactly how did he look," Hank persisted. "What made you *presume* (and he stressed the word) that he was dead?"

I described for him, in as much detail as I could recall, precisely what I had seen when I first opened that cabin door. Retelling it for what seemed like the millionth time really creeped me out. At Hank's urging, I put myself back into the cabin and I could see him, his body twisted bizarrely. I remembered the silence, the only sound the ticking of his wall clock. I could picture the dim light and the eerie quiet.

Hank nodded and took notes as I talked. When I finally ran down, he wrote a few more words and then put down his pen and calmly watched me. "Was there blood?"

I shuddered. "Yes, on his face."

"You said you kicked the, um, body?"

"Well, not kicked it," I objected. "I just nudged it with my toe."

"And he didn't move at all?"

"No, he kept lying there all dented and twisted. He wasn't napping."

Hank ran his hands through his wild, grey hair and tapped a finger on his chin. "I never said he was napping, but maybe he was simply unconscious."

I had to admit that I had no positive proof that he was dead. "But," I said, "if he was only resting, where is he now?"

"That, Missy, is the sixty-four dollar question, ain't it?"

Hank asked me a few more questions and then, concluding that I had nothing further to add, said kindly, "Why don't you head on over to the bar and see if Flo can't give you something a little stronger than that." He indicated the can of cola. "You could use it after what you all have been through."

"Hank," I couldn't leave without asking, "what do you think? Is he dead? There isn't any body."

"I'll find out what happened," he assured me. "Don't worry that pretty little head of yours."

Easy for him to say. Hank asked me to send in one of the others and I stood up, shook his hand and went to find Flo and the others. I stood on the dock gazing at the ocean for a few minutes before I went back to the bar. It was a pretty day. Blue sky. Sun bouncing off the water now that the storm had passed. I reflected on how our much-anticipated vacation had turned out. I wondered what Stephanie Plum or Nancy Drew would do. My idols were nowhere to be seen, so I would have to make do with my own detecting abilities. I had the uncomfortable feeling that Hank wasn't into solving the crime as much as he was trying to conclude the investigation.

It was a glum party that I found inside the Coconut Bar. Julie, Ellie, Sandra and Mary Linda sat around one of the picnic tables with untouched drinks in front of them. Svetlana and Glenn sat so close together they appeared attached. Flo fussed over the group, bringing food and reassurance in equal amounts. "Now, y'all," she was saying as I wandered in, "Hank will find out what's happened to the Captain. Don't give it another thought."

As if anyone could stop obsessing about the Captain.

"Hank wants to talk to everyone," I said. "Who wants to go next?"

Sandra jumped to her feet. "I'll go. Might as well get it over with."

She motioned me to follow her to the door. "Did you tell him about Svetlana and the Captain in Key West?" she asked. I nodded and she squeezed my hand with icy fingers and headed for Hank's office.

One by one they went to talk with Hank and one by one they returned, looking simultaneously relieved and frightened. When each of us had come and gone, Glenn rose and took Svetlana by the hand. "I'll go with you," he whispered. "He can talk to both of us at the same time."

Svetlana brushed his hand away and shook her head. "No, Glenn," she insisted. "I'll be talking for me. I'm being just fine."

She didn't look fine. She looked shell-shocked and there were dark circles under her beautiful eyes. But she rose gracefully and left without another word to Glenn. He took in the five of us eyeing him and silently stalked from the bar.

"Stranger and stranger," Julie murmured.

"You got that right," I said.

"Does anyone have any idea what's going on?" Ellie asked.

"Or when we might be able to go home?" Mary Linda persisted.

"According to Hank," I said, "none of us is going anywhere until he gets a lot more information. Don't look now but any of us could have done it."

"We're suspects?" Ellie squealed in dismay. "We can't be suspects. We're from Ohio."

We laughed. "That's right," Sandra said. "No one in Ohio commits a crime. Especially not a murder."

"Unless you cut into the line for the Millennium Force Roller Coaster at Cedar Point," Julie said. "That might be cause for murder."

"Okay," I said, "it's a given that none of us killed the Captain. And I'm also assuming that none of us threw him overboard or helped him escape on a jet ski. Right?"

They nodded in unison. I glanced over my shoulder to make sure that Flo was out of earshot. "I get the feeling that Hank doesn't really have his heart set on catching a killer."

"What do you mean?" Ellie asked.

"Here's the thing," I said, "I think that Hank knows more about this whole so-called mystery than he's letting on. Don't you think it's pretty convenient that he's the law enforcement agency and that the *Mirage* ended up here? We know he knows the Captain and I suspect he knows him better than he lets on."

The four of them digested my comments, but before anyone could respond, Flo flounced over and plopped down on one of the wood benches. Wiping her forehead with a paper towel, she announced, "Glenn is out there standing guard while Svetlana is with Hank. He looks like a pit bull. In a geeky kind of a way. What's up with those two?"

"We don't know exactly," I said. "What's your take on all of this?"

Flo wrinkled her nose and took a big gulp of Sandra's untouched drink. "Hmm. I just can't say."

Can't? Or won't, I wondered.

It wasn't long before Svetlana and Glenn returned, followed soon after by Hank. Hank solemnly regarded the five of us . . . exhausted and bedraggled in wrinkled clothes and needing showers . . . and reassured us once again that he would move quickly so we could leave Coconut Key. "I need to talk to the cook and the Spanish guy," he said. "And I'm gonna do a sweep of the crime scene. I need all you ladies to stay put and not mess with my investigation. Flo will keep you from gettin' thirsty or hungry."

His patronizing tone didn't do much for me or for the others, if I was reading the looks on their faces correctly. Still, we had no option but to agree to stay out of his way while he worked. Once Hank headed down the dock to the *Mirage*, however, we all started to talk at once.

"I don't know about you, but I'm not just sitting here," Mary Linda said. "I think we need to look into a few things on our own."

"I couldn't agree more," I said.

Sandra and Ellie nodded vigorously. "I'm in," Sandra said. "Me, too," Ellie added. Julie, too, was ready to take matters into our own incompetent, yet willing hands.

"But not here," I said, looking significantly at Flo behind the bar. And at Glenn and Svetlana who had isolated themselves at a table a distance away from us. "Let's go to the market. At least we can be alone."

We called to Flo that we were leaving and put some money on the table. "No, no," she protested. "I'm not takin' your money. Keep it. Just don't go too far. Hank may be needing to find you."

"We just need some air," I told her as we left.

The five of us wandered over to the market area. This late in the day there wasn't a lot of activity. A few of the vendors were just disassembling their booths, but most were gone for the day. I led the way to a patch of shade under a gnarled and twisted palm tree. I made sure no one could overhear us and then said, "Okay, who's got an idea?"

We discussed various alternatives and decided that we each could play a part. Mary Linda was anxious to get access to Hank's computer since her little wireless worked only sporadically. "I can find out a lot of information on Captain Fairweather," she said. "And, for that matter, I can probably find out some things about Mr. and Mrs. Glenn Livingston."

Sandra planned to call her former boss, the now-Senator from Nebraska, to find out what he knew about Fairweather Electronics and its founder, Captain Ned's father. Ellie thought Wil might have some information about Glenn that he could share with her. She wanted to send him an e-mail using Hank's computer. I was going to stay close to Hank and see if I could find out anything from him while Julie was going to hang out with Glenn and Svetlana.

It wasn't much of a plan, but under the circumstances it seemed like a way to go. It was far better than sitting around the bar sucking up rum runners and waiting for Hank's verdict. Besides we knew some things we hadn't shared with Hank. None of us, it seemed, had mentioned seeing Glenn and Skippy together in Key West or our suspicions about Glenn's so-called "secret life." Hank hadn't asked and we didn't volunteer. Now we were determined to uncover the true story before Hank closed the case and we had to fly home.

It was dusk when we concluded our impromptu meeting, and we were anxious to get started on our assignments. I realized that I was starving. With all the excitement I had barely eaten a thing all day. My stomach growled and I had a craving for some of Flo's conch fritters and maybe even (diet be damned) a big plate of home fries. I suggested that we get some greasy, comfort food and the rest perked up considerably at the thought. Hungrily, we turned as a group and made our way back to the bar.

But when we reached the door we ran smack into Martha standing guard in front. "Girls," she cooed, "I have a delicious meal prepared on the *Mirage*. I convinced Sheriff Hank to let me back in the galley and I have a menu fit for royalty."

"Gee, Martha," I explained, "we were just going to get some conch fritters and fries . . ."

She looked hurt. "I just thought you would enjoy a healthy meal." The emphasis on healthy.

I really didn't want to hurt Martha's feelings, but I wanted those darn fritters. Sighing, I said, "Oh, sure, Martha.

We didn't want to put you to any trouble so we were gonna get some food here."

Martha turned to Ellie. "And, of course, Miss Ellie, I have put all the recipes on cards for you." She'd found Ellie's weak spot.

"Come on, guys," Ellie said. "Let's go eat Martha's dinner. She's worked so hard and all."

I caved at that. And we started reluctantly toward the *Mirage*. I admit that I was feeling pretty uncomfortable about going back onboard. Now that the *Mirage* was the "death" ship, I pictured yellow crime scene tape and cops crawling all over. I shuddered at that image and trailed behind the others. I didn't want to be left behind, though, so I climbed onboard, took a deep breath and looked around.

It was a still night and the sea was glassy. Nothing seemed out of order. I saw no cops, no yellow tape, no blood, no body. Same old, same old. I followed the others to the salon where Martha had, indeed, set up a feast. We sat around the salon table while Martha bustled about putting out the food. It wasn't long before the delicious food and Martha's solicitous attention put as at ease and we chatted as we ate with more enthusiasm that I would have believed possible just a few hours before. By the time we had eaten our fill and were relaxing over coffee, the mood had lightened and we could almost (but not quite) believe that nothing unusual had happened.

"So," Julie asked, absent-mindedly stirring milk into her coffee, "where are we supposed to sleep tonight?"

"Good question," Sandra said. "I don't know about the rest of you, but I am not real excited about sleeping on the *Mirage*."

"You aren't?" Mary Linda exclaimed. "Our cabin is next to his."

"Well," I said, "I don't see any hotels in Coconut Key. Hank mentioned some beach cabins, but he said they were pretty rustic."

"Besides," Ellie said, "all of our stuff is on the boat. We'd have to pack it up and move it over to the cabins. I say we just stay here."

Naturally, we were a bit freaked out at spending another night onboard, but we agreed that it was the best plan. We wanted to keep an eye on Hank's investigation and the *Mirage* was the most logical place to do that. As much as we wanted to start our Jazzer-detecting, we were exhausted, so we pushed ourselves away from the table and retired to our cabins for the night.

Chapter Twenty

Early the next morning, Ellie and I showed up at Hank's office. His expression told us that he wasn't thrilled about being interrupted, but he opened the door and ushered us into his office. "What can I do for you pretty ladies this morning?"

Ellie flirted with him, outrageously batting her eyelashes and smiling up at him. "Why, Hank," she cooed, "I just want to send a few e-mails. I need to let my family know that we're okay."

Hank considered Ellie appreciatively. "Sure enough, Miss Ellie. Your family is probably plenty worried about a cute li'l thing like you."

She did some more eyelash batting. "Oh, Hank, I just can't bear being away from my three little boys. You do have e-mail, don't you?"

Hank couldn't think of any reason to deny Ellie's request, so he relinquished his seat at the computer and turned to me. "What's on your mind this morning?"

"Just keeping Ellie company," I answered. "And I also wanted to find out how your investigation is going. Have you found out anything?"

Hank shook his head. "You'll be the very first to know."

I kept my eye on Ellie who was typing rapidly. The plan was for me to keep Hank distracted so that he wouldn't see Ellie's e-mail. We weren't trying to hide anything exactly. Oh, okay, yes we were. And we probably could have used Mel's laptop, but she was already deep into her own research and we didn't want to interrupt her.

I kept up a running dialogue with Hank while Ellie finished her message and then stood up. "Thanks, Hank." She smiled at him. "I appreciate it." And we excused ourselves before Hank could ask any questions.

"So?" I said as soon as we were safely outside.

"I sent Wil an e-mail asking about Skippy and Glenn and asked if he knew anything else about either of them."

"Can't Hank access that e-mail?"

"Probably he could, but I deleted it and the address and then I deleted his trash bin just for the heck of it. He might not like it, but that's not my problem." Ellie beamed with pride at her cleverness.

"When Wil answers . . ."

"I told him to respond to Mel's address."

Breakfast at Flo's sounded good to both of us, so we found a table outside and sat down. Within seconds Flo hurried over and took our order for coffee, scrambled eggs and toast. No gourmet cuisine this morning. Just plain old food. I watched Flo as she poured coffee and brought silverware and something niggled at my mind. What was it that Flo had said that was bothering me? Trying to remember was frustrating so I gave up and dug into my eggs.

The bar was empty at this early hour, so we had Flo's complete attention. She saw to it that we lacked for nothing. She even brought over a basket of muffins. "I know these aren't as fancy as that Martha's," she said, "but I do make a mean muffin, if I do say so myself."

Ellie's eyes lit up. "Do you have the recipe for these, Flo?"

Flo grinned in delight. "You betcha I do. Let me grab a pen and write it down for you, honey."

Flo joined us and scribbled for a few moments. Then handing the sheet of paper to Ellie, she poured herself a cup of coffee and leaned back in her chair. "Do ya mind if I join you?"

"Of course not," I said.

"In all the years that me and Hank have been here," Flo said, "I've never met anyone like you girls."

We smiled and sipped our coffee. Flo put her elbows on the table and confided, "Most folks treat me and Hank like hired help. You know, just here to fix the boats and mix the drinks. But you all . . ." She looked like she might cry. "You all have been so dang nice. Miss Ellie there askin' me for my recipes. Why, nobody ever done that before."

"Thanks, Flo," I said, impulsively taking her hand. "We really like you and Hank."

"How long have you been here again?" Ellie asked.

"Why darlin', it's been nigh onto ten years," Flo answered.

And then I remembered what had been bothering me.

"Flo, what did you tell me about coming down to Florida?" I asked. "You said you and Hank left Kansas and came here and bought the marina. But you also said you were broke and Hank had written a bad check. So, how did you manage to scrape up the money to buy this place?"

Flo hesitated before she answered. Then deciding we could be trusted, she confessed, "It was tough all right. We were in pretty bad shape up there in Kansas and Hank shouldn't have wrote that check. So we come down here on the bike and when we saw the marina, well, it was just love at first sight. Hank always loved boats and I loved palm trees and the beach and the bar seemed perfect for me. So Hank sold the bike and got a bit of cash for it. But we still came up short. But this real good friend loaned us the rest of the money so we could buy the Fresh Ketch. We're payin' him back a bit at a time and he's been real patient about it. But we owe him big time."

I wanted to pursue this, but I could tell that Flo was uncomfortable. Before I could think of another question, Hank popped in and strolled over to the table. Putting his big hand on Flo's shoulder, he bent down and kissed her cheek. "Now, honey," he said, "I hope you aren't boring our friends with your chatter."

Flo leapt up and hastily gathered up our plates and started stacking them on a tray. "Do y'all want any more coffee or anything?"

"No, it was wonderful though," I said and put a twenty dollar bill on the table. She started to hand it back, but I wouldn't let her. "You have to let us pay, Flo. You can't keep giving away food and drinks."

"Just glad to have y'all here."

As soon as we were outside, I grabbed Ellie's arm. "We have to find the others. I just figured out what's been bothering me."

We found Mary Linda and Sandra in my cabin. Sandra had a cell phone pressed to her ear and Mel was focused on her laptop. Both looked up as Ellie and I burst in and collapsed on the floor. We waited impatiently for Sandra to conclude her call and when she did she said, "Wait til you hear what I found out. You're going to absolutely love it."

"And I have some things to tell you, too," Mary Linda added.

"Me, too," I said.

"Who goes first?" Ellie asked. "And where's Julie?"

"Julie's hanging with Glenn and Svetlana," Sandra said. "Should we wait for her?"

"No way," I replied. "I'm too curious."

Sandra began, "I just called my old boss and he told me about old man Fairweather. That would be Nigel Senior. He is pretty much a mean old tyrant. He's not very popular with his employees, but Fairweather Electronics makes tons of money so no one complains much. However, the Senator says that there have been rumors that he is more than mean. The rumor mill has it that the old man is a racist, bigot, chauvinist. And, get this, he hates gays."

She let us absorb this and then continued, "Bill was absolutely right about the old man being ill. The Fairweather camp has been pretty closed-mouthed, so no one is quite sure what it is. Could be either Alzheimer's or cancer. Or both. So he is about to be replaced as CEO. His son, Nigel, our esteemed captain, is in line to replace him. Unless, of course . . ." She paused. ". . . he isn't around."

The logical question popped into my mind. "So then who will replace him?"

Sandra smiled smugly. "That's the thing you will just love. It seems that there is a second son and he already works for Fairweather. He would be the logical successor except that he and the old guy don't get along. Some issues from the past or something. The Senator isn't positive but he thinks there might be some clause in his contract that could be a problem. He really doesn't know. He isn't friendly with any of the Fairweathers."

"That's great, Sandra." I complimented her. "So if Ned is missing or dead, then someone else gets the job. And I know for a fact that Ned had zero interest in the company. Or in his father. His dad actually stole Ned's wife from him. Have I mentioned that?"

We mulled over the information for a few seconds and then Mary Linda turned her laptop so we could see the screen. "Maybe this will shed some light on the situation," she said.

Mary Linda explained that she had gone online. Recalling that Captain Ned said he had gone to UC Berkeley, she started there. She didn't know what years he might have been there, but she made an educated guess and started hunting. Since Nigel Fairweather isn't a common name, it wasn't too tough to find him. She searched through his files and found the activities he had been involved in. Not too surprisingly, she discovered that he was a member of the sailing club.

"But look at this." Mel was bursting to show us the screen. "I found a picture of the sailing club. It's a little fuzzy, but I recognized Captain Ned. A younger Captain Ned. With hair. But still him. What I didn't expect was the guy in the back row almost out of the picture. Look at him and tell me what you think."

We peered over her shoulder, squinting at the fuzzy image. After only a moment we stared at each other in shock. "Oh, my God," I exclaimed. "Do the rest of you see what I see?"

Mary Linda answered for them. "I think it's Glenn. He sure looks like our Glenn. Not as geeky, but I still think it's Glenn."

Sandra and Ellie chorused agreement. "It's him. Definitely. It's Glenn!"

And I put what we were all thinking into words. "If Glenn and Ned were in the same sailing club in college, then why were they pretending that they didn't know each other?"

We debated letting Hank in on our discovery, but decided to keep quiet for the time being. "Oh, my gosh," I said. "I almost forgot what I was going to tell you guys. Flo and Hank got some money from a good friend to help them buy the Fresh Ketch. Flo says that they owe this good friend big time. And not just money. He came through for them when they most needed help, so they would do anything for him."

"I can check out the deed," Sandra said. "Either online or I'll make some calls. My cell phone bill is going to be killer when we're done."

"No sacrifice too great, huh?" Ellie asked. "Mel, I e-mailed Wil and gave him your address to respond. Have you checked e-mails today?"

"I'll do it right now."

But before she could check, we heard Hank's booming voice from the deck. "Ladies, where are you hiding? I need to talk to you."

We kept silent, but it was only a few minutes before we heard footsteps and then Hank banged on the cabin door. "Martha told me you were in here. Open up. I want to talk with you."

Reluctantly, I opened the door to reveal Hank who resembled a fire-breathing dragon. He motioned imperiously for us to follow him and then strode toward the deck. Like four little ducklings, we trailed in his wake as he climbed off the boat and marched toward the Coconut Key Bar. Inside, Glenn, Svetlana and Julie huddled around a table with a pot of coffee and three cups in front of them. They jumped as Hank shoved the flimsy door aside.

"What the . . ." Glenn exclaimed.

"Sit down, all of you," Hank ordered. "I just got some news from the Key West Police Department."

I thought Hank might burst a blood vessel he was so excited. Glenn looked ill and Svetlana had developed a consuming interest in her fingernails. Hank pulled a piece of paper from his back pocket and waved it. "The Key West police have found a body washed up on shore. They are asking all of the jurisdictions within a couple of hundred miles if they recognize it. They faxed me a photo."

Our eyes were glued to Hank as he thrust the fax in our faces. The Captain? It must be. What would he look like? Bloated and rotting, I presumed. Ick. I dreaded seeing the picture and so did everyone else.

"Well," Hank demanded, "anyone recognize this corpse of theirs?"

He handed me the photo and I almost fell off my chair. My face must have registered the shock and surprise that I felt. I didn't say anything and handed the photo to Sandra. When each of us had seen the photo, matching expressions of fear and loathing were on our faces. Yes, it was, indeed, a gruesome photo of a dead man. His features were hard to distinguish so bloated was his face, but I knew immediately that it wasn't Captain Nigel Fairweather. I, and each of the other passengers on the *Mirage*, recognized it . . . him . . . though. Skippy! Our beach party guest and Glenn's companion at Boys Will Be Boys. Who could have killed *him*? And why?

No one uttered a sound. Svetlana gave full concentration to her manicure while the rest of us gazed into space. Glenn clenched his fists and buried them in his pockets. Only Flo seemed unperturbed as she tidied the bar, rearranging the salt and pepper shakers and the napkin holders.

Finally Hank broke the silence. "Well . . ."

I rapidly considered what and how much to relate to Hank. I concluded that he couldn't be kept totally in the dark. Glenn shot me a threatening look, but I hurried on. "That's not the Captain, as you know perfectly well, Hank."

"I got that, but do you know who it is?"

"Yeah, we do," I admitted. "It's a boater that we met at a beach party that the *Mirage* hosted a few days ago." Actually, it seemed like a lifetime, but it had only been a few days.

Hank's eyebrows shot up in astonishment. "You *know* this guy?"

We nodded. Glenn held his breath, but none of us said anything. We were pretty sure that Glenn was unaware that we had seen him that night. Somehow we made an unspoken decision not to divulge his secret. As the silence stretched out, Glenn looked relieved.

Svetlana abandoned her inspection of her nails and added, "Yes, he was being at the party. His friend was being there as well."

With the ice broken we filled Hank in on the beach party. We informed him that Skippy and Gino had been sailing a small sailboat, and that they had joined us for the party. That much Hank could find out quite easily, and there didn't seem to be much point in trying to hide the fact that we had met Skippy.

Hank interrogated us for awhile, but finally concluded that we had nothing further to add. As he prepared to leave the bar I figured I would throw him something to chew on which might occupy him for at least a little while. "Oh, and Hank, we did see Skippy and Gino at a bar in Key West. They said hi and that was about it."

Skeptical, Hank gave me the once over. He was undoubtedly wondering what else we knew and weren't telling him. Then he shook his head in resignation and left. He threw us a parting shot. "The Key West cops will want to talk to you then. And . . ." He pointed at Glenn and Svetlana. ". . . you two. Don't even think about leaving."

I wondered why the others were covering for Glenn. We all had watched enough cop shows on television to know that lying to the cops is a very bad policy. However, I argued to myself, it's not that we lied exactly. Not really. We just didn't tell the entire truth.

Later that morning I ran into Hank onboard the *Mirage*. He and Miguel had just emerged from the engine room covered with grease. Obviously in a foul mood, Hank snarled at Miguel and glared at me. "Hi, Hank," I said as innocently as I could manage. "Wearing your other hat, are you?"

Perhaps a little ashamed of his surly behavior, Hank said in a more civil tone, "Yeah, and neither hat is particularly successful."

"Problems?"

"I'll say. First of all, this danged engine has been tinkered with. Not worth a heap of bolts the way it is right now."

This was news, but not entirely unexpected. "Do you think whoever killed the Captain also messed with the engine?"

"I never said the Captain was dead, now did I?"

"Not in so many words, you haven't."

Slightly appeased, he said, "Even if he is, I don't know who disabled the motor."

Miguel mumbled something to Hank in Spanish and then disappeared into the bowels of the *Mirage*. Hank started to follow him and then stopped. "Not to mention," he fumed, "that Key West is sending a couple of detectives to Coconut Key to interview you all about this Skippy fella. Just what I need, Frick and Frack from the Key West Department fooling around in my investigation. Just 'cause they're from the big city they think they can come here and take over."

Big city? Key West? Well, I guess it's all relative. And Hank vanished below.

Chapter Twenty-One
Julie

Julie had been hanging out with Glenn and Svetlana for hours and she was getting pretty tired of their company. They were nice enough people, she supposed, but all the pretense was wearing on her nerves. Glenn and Svetlana pretended they were a happily married couple with no knowledge of the Captain or what might have happened to him. On her side, Julie pretended to believe them. She felt as if she was living a one-act play.

Not to mention she had other things on her mind. Like Robert. She waited until she knew that the girls would be in school and then she excused herself and took her cell phone out to the dock. First she dialed home and, as she expected, got no answer. Rather than call Robert's private number at work, she decided to go through the main switchboard and get his secretary in the hope that she could give Julie more information about Robert's recent activities.

By the time Julie abruptly ended her conversation with Glenda, Robert's secretary, and snapped her phone shut, she had some answers but even more questions. Dazed she stumbled to the end of the dock and collapsed. Blindly she stared at the water trying to make sense of what she had just heard.

He'd been laid off? But why hadn't he told her? And where did he go every day when he was supposedly going off to work? What could he have been thinking? Did he think she wouldn't love him and support him if he didn't have a job? That was crazy. They had always been each other's biggest supporters. No, there had to be an explanation and she was going to drag it out of him. Right before she killed him.

Julie dangled her feet over the edge of the dock and brooded. If you got right down to it, she supposed, Robert hadn't lied. He just hadn't told her the whole truth and nothing but the truth so help him God. The trick was to get him to confess without telling him she already knew. Somehow that would make it better. Not great, mind you. Just better.

Julie hoisted herself to her feet and headed back to the bar to find Glenn and Svetlana and resume her detecting duties. Svetlana was sitting alone at a table her chin propped in one hand. Julie watched from the door for a few seconds before she went over to the table. Svetlana's shoulders were slumped and she slouched in her chair.

She toyed forlornly with one dangling earring and gazed into space with a vacant expression.

"Hey," Julie said and Svetlana jumped.

"Hey, back to you," she said glumly.

"Where's Glenn?"

"Oh, he is off doing the manly things. Checking on Hank and the boat."

Julie sank into the seat opposite Svetlana and groused, "Men. Can't live with them."

"I am thinking you are so right."

Needing a confidante and finding only Svetlana around, Julie continued, "Secrets. They keep secrets. Robert . . . my husband . . . has been keeping a big secret from me. And I just found out."

Sympathetically, Svetlana said, "I, too, am knowing about these secrets."

Julie's ears perked up. Svetlana had opened a door and Julie marched right through it. "Secrets?" she asked. "What secrets do you have?"

Svetlana was obviously having second thoughts and she played with the zipper on her hot pink sweat suit. "I am just knowing about this."

Julie figured if she shared her problems then maybe Svetlana would do the same, so she gave her the condensed version of Robert's perfidy. "And I just found out from his, I guess I'd have to say, from his former secretary a few minutes ago," she concluded.

Svetlana had remained riveted throughout Julie's recital, her sea green eyes concerned. When Julie finished Svetlana exclaimed, "You poor baby. I know exactly what you mean." Both women were flabbergasted at Svetlana's clear, unaccented voice. Svetlana stammered, trying to cover her mistake, "I am meaning . . ." She paused. "Oh, to hell with it. You got me."

Shocked, Julie said, "The accent is fake."

Svetlana laughed bitterly. "You got that right. I am the biggest, fattest fake in all of South Florida."

Julie was blown away by this admission and for a moment couldn't think how to respond. "Okay, Svetlana, you win in the keeping secrets category for today. I'll have to admit that you had me fooled. Anything else you want to tell me now that you've gone this far."

If she was remorseful at all she didn't show it. "Not especially. What do you want to know?"

What the hell, Julie figured. "Why have you been faking your accent? And, for that matter, what else have you been faking?"

Svetlana stuck out her hand. "I'd like to introduce myself. I'm Doctor Svetlana (Julie thought she detected the briefest hesitation here, but couldn't be sure) Livingston. Delighted to meet you."

Julie clasped her hand and shook it firmly. "Julie Wright. Pleased to make your acquaintance."

Svetlana shook her head. "Glenn sure won't like that I said anything to you, so will you keep it between the two of us?"

"I can't promise not to mention this to my friends. It's too big not to share."

"I suppose you're right." Svetlana shrugged resignedly.

"A doctor? Of what exactly?"

"Oh, I'm an MD. A plastic surgeon."

Julie, her mind working quickly, put two and two together. "So, Flo did recognize you."

"Uh huh."

"And you were here with the Captain? Ned?"

"Okay, now here's where I stop telling you my secrets," Svetlana said. "I can't get you involved in this any more than you are already."

"But . . ." Julie began.

"No," Svetlana broke in. "It's better that you don't know the whole story. I can tell you that our motives are pure, though. I may have faked a few things, but I had good reasons."

Julie considered this. "I don't know."

Svetlana looked her in the eye and pleaded, "Please, Julie. I can't explain more than I have. Please don't go to the authorities with this."

Julie made her decision. Somehow she trusted Svetlana. "Okay, Svetlana, I won't tell the cops. The last time I checked faking an accent wasn't a crime. It isn't any of their business. But, to be fair, I really do have to tell my nosy friends. They can be trusted, believe me."

"Okay, if you say so. And thanks. Maybe someday I can tell you the whole story. I hope so."

Julie stuck out her hand and Svetlana took it and they shook on the deal.

"Call me Lana," Svetlana said. "All my friends do."

Chapter
Twenty-Two

I found Sandra in her cabin slathering self-tanner on her legs. With her attention focused on the precise application, I had to clear my throat several times before she looked up.

"Hey," she greeted me.

"Hey, yourself. What do you think you're doing?"

"What does it look like I'm doing?" Sandra extended one leg and examined it. "I'm not going home without a tan. With the storm and now all this stuff with the Captain, I'm white as the damn snow in Ohio."

"God help us if we let a little thing like murder," I said with as much sarcasm as I could muster, "prevent us from getting a tan. What will people think?"

"They'll think that I look pale as a ghost," she said. "So I'm fixing that."

I looked down at my own pale legs and put out my hand. "Give me some of that. Why not?"

Just then Julie burst into the cabin nearly incoherent with excitement. She stopped in her tracks when she realized what we were doing. "Oh, great. Here I've been sleuthing like crazy and what are you two doing? Self-tanning."

We scrutinized our legs before asking her, "What's got you so excited?"

"Well, while you two were indulging in self-beautification rituals, I have been bonding with our dear friend Svetlana."

"Go on."

"And I have the most amazing things to tell you."

When Julie finished her story, Sandra and I chimed in unison, "I knew it."

I exclaimed, "From that moment on the beach when I heard her talking to Ned, I just knew something was going on."

Sandra added, "And when we saw Ned and Svetlana together in Key West coming out of that house holding hands . . . well, that was pretty clear proof."

"But we aren't going to the authorities with any of this," Julie said. "I promised Lana we wouldn't."

"Lana? Lana! When did she become Lana?"

Julie shrugged. "That's what her friends call her."

"And now you're her new best friend," I said. "Watch it, Julie, she could be big trouble."

"I promised," Julie said stubbornly. "We aren't telling."

Grudgingly, we conceded that we would keep this quiet. I was pretty certain Hank was well aware of the connection anyway.

The three of us were still discussing options as the acrid smell of self-tanner wafted in the air when Ellie and Mary Linda appeared. Sniffing the air knowingly, Ellie demanded, "Good idea. Give me some of that." Mel echoed, "Me, too." Our preoccupation with conjuring up a great tan came under the heading of diversion, I suppose, and it was working really well.

Ellie and Mary Linda concentrated on smoothing tanner on their legs for a few moments. Then Ellie said, "Oh, we found some pretty interesting things on the internet. First of all, I got an e-mail from Wil."

"You did? What did it say?" Sandra asked.

Mary Linda displayed the screen on her computer so that we could read it. I peered over Sandra's shoulder and we read the message in silence. Wil had written:

Darling Ellie . . .

I was so delighted to get your e-mail. Key West is simply too dull without you and your friends. Yes, I do have information about Skippy and Gino. Right before the big storm a couple of days ago they were in Boys Will Be Boys. I was working that night and saw them having a lover's spat. They were screeching so loudly that I expected a hair-pulling tussle to break out at any moment. Then Skippy stormed out in a big huff and I heard him say to Gino, "I don't care what you say. I'm doing it." Gino paid the bill and followed him. (They didn't even leave a tip which made me pretty pissy, but that's another story.) That was the last anyone saw either of them until yesterday when Skippy's body washed up on shore. The cops came around here and asked if we knew him and I had to

admit that I had waited on him, so they took me to iden-
tify the corpse. Yikes. Just too nasty.

I am afraid that I am a bit of a suspect in the murder,
but they haven't got any evidence to tie me to them, so I
hope it will all blow over soon. And Gino has disappeared
so he is probably more of a suspect than I am. I hope. I
don't know much more except I overhead Gino tell Skippy
he would be breaking the law.

Wil went on for a bit about Ellie's hair and made a few
beauty and wardrobe suggestions before he ended the e-
mail, "*Lots of love, Wil.*"

The five of us sat silently surveying our legs as they
took on a golden glow. Sandra opened a second tube and
handed it to me. "Do my back, would you?"

"That's just about enough with the self-tanner," I
exploded. "Let's focus for a moment on something other
than the golden aura of our bodies, shall we?"

Sandra winced. "Okay, so where are we in all of this?"

Mary Linda spoke up. "Before we go any further, there
are a few other things I found that you need to hear about."
She proceeded to upend a suitcase and arranged her computer on it. She reminded me of a professor about to lec-
ture. In fact, if she had begun with "Now, class," I wouldn't
have been surprised.

"Now," she began, "you have all seen the yearbook picture of Ned in the sailing club and the guy in the background that we think is Glenn."

We nodded.

"Okay, so I decided to do a bit more searching on the
Internet. As long as the battery held out, I thought I would

see what I could find out about Skippy." She paused, pleased with herself, and about to deliver the coup de grâce.

"Come on, Mel," I said. "The suspense is killing us here."

She grinned proudly. "So, I remembered that Skippy was wearing some kind of a muscle shirt with his . . . um . . . mood pants at the beach party. I don't know why I thought it was important but I did. I went through the shots I'd taken on my camera and found a good one of Skippy. He was wearing a shirt that said Dartmouth on it. I figured that was a good starting point. I went to the Dartmouth College website and did a search for guys named Skippy or Skip. You would be amazed at how many Skippys turned up. I couldn't believe it. Mostly from the East Coast. To make a long story short, I made a guess at the year and searched that way. Narrowed it down to about a dozen. Then I figured that 'our' Skippy might have been in the sailing club. Sure enough there is a sailing club at Dartmouth. I looked at photos for the last ten years and was about to give up when I found this one."

She turned the computer toward us and we leaned over it. The image on the screen was fuzzy and distorted. A group of young men and women in swimsuits and shorts was clustered around a sailboat on a beach somewhere. In the foreground one of the young men was looking over his shoulder at the camera and laughing. I squinted at the screen. The other three did the same. Then we looked at each other triumphantly. Skippy!

"Mel, you are a genius," I said. "But what good does this fuzzy photo do us? So now we know that Skippy was in a sailing club."

Mel looked like the cat that swallowed the canary. She fiddled with the computer before she displayed the screen again. "Because Skippy wasn't the only thing I saw in this picture. Look." She pointed. "See that guy off to the left almost out of the picture. The one in the baseball cap. Who does he look like?"

We peered at the screen trying to see what Mel was seeing. It took a few moments but suddenly it came to me. That guy looked like . . . could have been . . . was it possible? Was that . . . Glenn?

Julie stared at the photo in amazement. "Is that Glenn? I think it's Glenn."

We turned the computer this way and that and finally concluded that the distorted image certainly could be Glenn. But what was Glenn doing in a photo of the Dartmouth College Sailing Club? We had another shot of him at the Berkeley Sailing Club.

"Maybe you'd better explain what you think this means," I told Mel. I had a good idea, but I didn't want to be jumping to conclusions. Not alone anyway.

"When I first found the Dartmouth picture I didn't think it could actually be our Glenn. I mean we already had him at Berkeley in the first picture. I went back to the Berkeley website and double-checked my information. I did a search for Glenn Livingston and sure enough a Glenn Alexander Livingston attended the University of California at Berkeley from 1985 through 1987. I found an online yearbook file and did a search and found a senior picture of Glenn Livingston. It was definitely a younger version of our Glenn."

Mel paced around the cabin. "Then I figured that he could have gone to Dartmouth, too. Lots of people transfer from one college to another. So back I go to the Dartmouth website and search for a Glenn Alexander Livingston there. Nada. I tried just plain Glenn Livingston and found several but the years didn't coincide. I was getting frustrated when it came to me."

"What? What came to you?"

"The answer." Mel was beside herself with satisfaction. "I had this hunch and I played it."

Almost exploding, Mel played her trump card. "I did a search for a Glenn Fairweather. Bingo. I found him. Glenn Alexander Fairweather attended Dartmouth from 1983 through 1985. He was a member of the sailing club and the honor society. His major was economics."

We were stunned. I had seen the resemblance but not put two and two together. Mary Linda couldn't contain herself a single second longer. The silence was too much for her to bear. "The Captain and Glenn must be brothers," she announced. "How about that?"

"Oh, my gosh," Ellie said. "I can't believe it."

"It's true. It must be true."

"Well, what does that mean?"

"Brothers. No wonder they look alike."

"Then what are they up to?"

We debated the possibilities for some time without coming to any conclusions. We had plenty of ideas. I knew we were on the right track, but what should we do now?

"Let me summarize," I said. "We are fairly sure that Ned and Glenn are brothers. And that Glenn went to Dartmouth, but then ended up at Berkeley using an assumed name. Is that correct so far?"

The others murmured agreement. "So why would he transfer to his brother's college and use a phony identity? And how does Skippy enter into the equation? He went to Dartmouth too, so he obviously knew Glenn there. They were both in the sailing club."

"Then," I continued, "he meets up with Glenn again at that beach party and what?"

"They talk about old times and college days," Sandra said.

"And maybe Skippy says something like, 'Gee, Glenn, whatever happened to you. You just fell off the earth after our sophomore year,'" Julie suggested.

"Yeah, and Glenn said . . ." Ellie asked.

"Wait a second." I had an inspiration. "What if Skippy didn't have to ask? What if he knew what happened to Glenn? Think about it. Glenn transfers to another school and changes his name. He was hiding who he was. And maybe he was hiding for a reason."

"What if," Mel suggested, "Glenn did something at Dartmouth that got him booted out? If it was bad enough maybe he was trying to become someone else to get away from that."

"Whoa," I said, "I remember something I heard about Old Man Fairweather. Ned's dad and the CEO of Fairweather Electronics. Ned said it. His dad was the biggest homophobe in the entire world. He hated homosexuals. And we know . . ."

"That Glenn is gay," the others finished.

"Suppose that Glenn is in college having a gay old time, pardon the pun," I said. "And his dad finds out and what? And how does he find out? Glenn wouldn't have just announced it over dinner and drinks at the family mansion."

Mel flicked the switch on her computer. "Damn," she moaned. "The battery's dead. I have to change it. But when I do, I'm gonna go back to the Dartmouth newspapers' online archives and see if I can dig up anything involving

Glenn Fairweather during the years he was a student there."

Frustrated by this untimely roadblock, we fumed as we concocted possible scenarios from Glenn's student days. Finally, we realized that we were wasting time making guesses and decided to continue doing what we had been doing.

"Julie," I said, "Ellie and Mary Linda haven't heard about your chat with Svetlana. Maybe you ought to fill them in."

When Julie finished telling her story for the second time, total silence enveloped the cabin. The puzzle was coming together but several key pieces were still missing. We were anxious to find them and put them in place.

"How much of this do you suppose that Hank already knows?" I asked. "And the Key West cops have undoubtedly found out a lot about Skippy. Do you think they have made the connection with Glenn already?"

No one had the chance to answer before there was a knock on the cabin door. We stared at the door, willing away the unwanted intruder. "Who is it?" Sandra called. "We're in the middle of something in here."

"I need you ladies at the bar," Hank shouted through the closed door.

"Can it wait, Hank?" Sandra asked. "We're . . . um . . . indisposed."

"You need to get yourselves decent. Them Keystone Cops from Key West have arrived and they want to speak with all of you."

I marched over to the door and yanked it open. Startled, Hank peered into the cabin and sniffed the air suspiciously. "You gals aren't doin' drugs, are you?"

We erupted into laughter. Hank watched us with a perplexed look. Finally I stood up and took the tube of self-tanner from the floor and held it out to Hank. Still snickering, I said, "Yep, we're doing drugs. Want to join us?"

Hank flinched and gaped at the tube as if it contained an explosive. Then he grinned. "I guess you aren't doing drugs then?"

"Not unless you count getting a fake tan as doing drugs."

Hank shrugged. "Just get them pretty tanned legs of yours up to the bar to talk with them cops."

Chapter Twenty-Three

After years of watching cop shows on TV and reading detective novels, I recognized Frick and Frack, as Hank called them, right away. Good Cop and Bad Cop. Good Cop, who introduced himself as Kevin Something or Other, was tall, dark and a bonafide hunk. His eyes were a shade of deep brown and when he smiled he displayed even white teeth. He wore crisply pressed khakis with a black silk t-shirt and a beautiful cream blazer. Good Cop could have stepped directly from the pages of *GQ*. His partner, Bad Cop, on the other hand, was rumpled and haphazardly put together. His suit, at least ten years old, was a candidate for the Goodwill box. He was grumpy and out of sorts and told us his name was Steve.

Hank offered Good Cop and Bad Cop the use of his office to interview us, and we were each ushered in deferentially by Good Cop. Hank, however, wasn't leaving us alone with the interlopers, and he lurked by the door with an apprehensive and protective air about him.

Since I didn't really know much about Skippy and his erstwhile companion, Gino, I wasn't too concerned about the interview. With no hesitation I told them the story of meeting Skippy and Gino on the beach and how we ran into them later in Key West. Good Cop showed me the picture of Skippy's waterlogged body attired only in thong underwear and I identified him. Each of my friends had basically the same experience. While Hank kept vigil, we confessed that we had met the pair only briefly and couldn't offer much in terms of motive or suspects. None of us, it turned out, mentioned that we had seen Glenn and Skippy together in Key West. If they had asked I am still not sure what I would have done, but they didn't ask so I said nothing.

Bad Cop asked suspiciously, "So, Miss you *claim* (obviously implying that I was lying) that you never met the deceased before the beach party."

"Now, Steve," Good Cop said soothingly, "she already said she didn't."

But Bad Cop persisted. "So, it seems that the captain of your cruise ship has turned up missing?"

As soon as Bad Cop launched this line of questioning, Hank stepped in. "That's my investigation and I have talked to each of the ladies. I know what they know."

"Still with two dead bodies it seems unlikely that the murders aren't related," Bad Cop insisted.

Hank placed himself between me and the Key West cops. "That's enough. You can't be harassing this little lady. Not in my office. Not in my jurisdiction, you can't."

Good Cop apologized for his partner. "I'm sorry, Miss, if we have offended you. Obviously you aren't a suspect here."

I accepted his apology and after a few other questions about minor details, they dismissed me.

Good Cop and Bad Cop were closeted in Hank's office with Glenn and Svetlana when the five of us met in our cabin to compare notes.

"Who do you think killed Skippy?" Ellie asked as soon as we were alone.

"Gino?" Julie suggested. "A lover's quarrel with a bad end."

"Did you see the thong underwear?" Sandra asked. "Maybe they were fighting about Skippy's taste in lingerie."

We couldn't come up with a motive for someone to kill Skippy. We needed to know a lot more than we did.

Since Sandra and I saw Captain Ned and Svetlana in suspicious circumstances in Key West we decided we were going to get her aside and talk to her privately. We intercepted her as she was leaving Hank's office after her interview with Good Cop and Bad Cop. She was alone and preoccupied. I had to call her name twice before she noticed Sandra and me. When she did see us, her expression was resigned.

"Hi," I said. "What did you think of the Key West detectives?"

"I am thinking," she began and then stopped. She looked at us warily and then continued, "You know, don't you? Julie told you."

We nodded. "Julie told us that you're really a doctor. Is that what you mean?"

She shrugged. "That would be about it. It's complicated."

She looked over her shoulder at the closed door to Hank's office. I guessed that Glenn was still talking to Good Cop and Bad Cop. Svetlana appeared undecided about what and how much to say.

"The thing is . . ." Sandra forged ahead. "Kate and I saw you and Captain Ned in Key West."

Svetlana's eyes widened and she took an involuntary step backwards. "You did? Where?"

"We weren't spying on you, honestly," I said. "Sandra and I were walking down a side street heading for Hemingway's house when we saw you and Ned."

"Right," Sandra added. "We didn't expect to see anyone we knew and at first we weren't sure. The two of you were coming out of a house together."

Svetlana abruptly sat down on the edge of the dock and put her head in her hands. "I told him. I told him it wasn't safe. That someone would see us." She lifted her head, her green eyes pleading. "I know it's a lot to ask, but I'd really appreciate it if you didn't mention this to anyone. Or is it already too late? Have you told Hank or the cops from Key West?"

"No," we reassured her, "we didn't tell the cops, but we clued in Julie, Ellie and Mel."

"I wish I could explain all of this to you. I really do. But like I told Julie, it's better if you don't know anything. If I tell you and then you have to lie . . . well, it's just better not to know."

"Can you tell us anything at all that will help us to understand what we've gotten ourselves into?" I asked.

"Just what I already told Julie. I don't want to involve you guys in this. Please, please, please trust me," Svetlana begged. "Maybe someday I, we, can tell you the whole story, but not now. It wouldn't be safe for you. Or for us."

"Who's us?" I asked. "Is Ned alive? Or not?"

For a moment I thought Svetlana was going to confide in us, but as she began to speak the door to Hank's office opened and Glenn stepped out and spotted us. He strode in our direction. As Svetlana watched him approach, her face clouded over. "Trust me or not, I can't help that. But I can't say another word." She gave us one last imploring look and then stood up, turned on her heel and fled without a backward glance, leaving Sandra and me staring after her.

"That went well," I commented.

Sandra's reply was a grimace.

Sandra and I walked into a scene of jubilation a short time later. Ellie, Julie and Mel were beside themselves. Mel greeted us, "Guys. You just have to read this."

We peered intently at the screen of Mel's computer. A pin dropping would have reverberated throughout the tiny cabin as we quickly perused the page displayed. "*Sex Scandal Rocks School*" the headline blared. The article beneath was dated March of 1985.

The Dartmouth student body was shocked when President Joe Smith issued a press release disclosing a "sex" scandal involving at least a dozen undergraduate students. According to Smith, several upperclassmen had been "employing" some freshmen and sophomore men as so-called sex slaves. This homosexual bondage began as part of a hazing ritual and then, Smith said, "it just got out

*of hand." The names of the undergrads who were "slaves"
are not being released at this time.*

The article related the story in great (and perhaps
unnecessary) detail, but the gist of it was clear. Sandra and I looked at the others who were waiting for our
reaction. "Glenn?" I guessed. "Could Glenn have been
involved?"

"Think about it," Mel said. "That would explain a lot."

My mind was racing. "Try this," I suggested. "Let's say
Glenn hooks up with this slave ring. He's a naive under-
classman. I can picture poor, geeky Glenn just wanting to
fit in. And we are pretty sure he's gay anyway, so he gets
sucked into this thing. But Dad would have a hissy fit for
sure. I mean, he hates gays. Now not only is he forced to
see that his younger son is gay, but that son is messed up
in a major scandal at his college. What would Dad do?"

"Yank him out of school?"

"Right. Yank him out of school."

"And then what?" Ellie asked.

"Send him somewhere else, naturally," I said. "But now
Dad figures that he needs someone to watch out for poor
dumb, gay Glenn. Make sure he doesn't get into more trouble. Watch his backside, so to speak."

It dawned on all of them simultaneously. "Ned," I continued. "Ned is already at school at Berkeley. Dad sends
Glenn out there so Ned can keep an eye on him."

"And changes his name to protect him from being per-
secuted because of the scandal out East," Mel concluded.
"Makes sense."

"I doubt if he did it to protect Glenn," Julie said. "More
to the point, he did it to protect his own name."

"There would already have been a black mark on the name because Glenn was using his real name at Dartmouth," I said. "But at least he wouldn't drag it through the mud a second time. Not if he was Glenn Livingston."

"But that's not all," I went on. "Who was there at Dartmouth at the same time as Glenn?"

"Skippy!" they chorused.

"And so Skippy unexpectedly meets up with Glenn at that beach party. Maybe he doesn't recognize him at first. Different name and all. But then he gets it. He hangs out with Glenn for a while to make sure and then he thinks he can make a fast buck out of it."

"Blackmail?" Sandra asked.

"Makes sense, doesn't it? Skippy realizes that he's found the goose who laid the golden eggs. So, he decides to make Glenn pay. Gino, according to Wil, wasn't thrilled about the idea and tries to talk him out of it. But Skippy doesn't listen."

"So far, so good," Julie said. "But what next?"

"That's the problem," I admitted. "Someone killed Skippy. It could have been Glenn. Or Gino. Or even Svetlana, I suppose. Or someone else entirely. We have to find out who."

"We do?" Ellie's voice was shrill. "Why us? Why don't we just tell all of this to the Key West cops or Hank? We aren't private eyes."

Stubbornly, I said, "Personally, I think Hank's involved in this whole thing with the Captain, so I'm not sure I trust him enough to take this evidence to him. Not to mention, they can find it out for themselves as easily as we did. Might take them a day or two, but they'll get there. It isn't up to us to help."

"Why the hell not?" Sandra said. "Who made us in charge?"

"Do you or do you not want to get out of Coconut Key?" I asked. "We'll get out of here sooner if we do some detective work on our own instead of just relying on Hank and Good Cop and Bad Cop."

Very reluctantly they agreed to do it my way and not share what we knew. Not yet anyway.

Chapter
Twenty-Four

We were gobbling a platter of conch fritters and home fries, when Sandra hustled into the bar out of breath. "Guys," she wheezed, "we've got to talk."

I glanced at Flo who had stationed herself behind the bar in the perfect position to attend to our every need. "Right. Let's get out of here and go somewhere more private."

We trooped out of the bar and headed into the dusty village of Coconut Key. The street that ran in front of the marina was almost deserted. It was quiet and sleepy in the noonday sun. Sandra and I led the way toward the Seven-Eleven down the road, where we bought soft drinks and huddled around the grimy picnic table nestled under a lone palm tree.

"What did you find out?" I asked.

Sandra grinned, ready to burst. "It's definitely a matter of who you know."

"Give it up, girlfriend," Julie said. "What do you know?"

Sandra took a deep breath and began, "I called Bill from Nebraska and he told me that any deed had to be registered and that a record of it would be kept in Tallahassee. So, I called the Registrar of Deeds. After a bunch of transfers and being on hold I got a nice girl who was actually willing to talk to me. At first she didn't want to, but I convinced her that it was life and death."

We all have been on the receiving end of Sandra's persuasive powers so we could appreciate that the girl never had a chance.

"And she found the deed for the Fresh Ketch Marina and the Coconut Key Bar and Grill. Registered to Hank and Flo Dayton. But that's not all. There was another name on the deed."

Sandra paused for dramatic effect. "The name was . . . Nigel Fairweather."

Her announcement was met with stunned silence. I had half-expected the connection, but there it was in black and white.

"I knew it," I said. "I knew there was a connection."

"Which means," Ellie observed, "that Hank and Flo would do anything for Ned."

"Anything at all," Julie added. "Including helping him disappear."

"Wait, wait, wait," I said. "I saw him lying on the floor. Dead."

"But we never saw any body, did we?" asked Mel. "No definite proof that he's dead."

"Well, why would he want me to think he was dead?" I asked. A reasonable question. "Why not just disappear if that's what he wanted to do?"

"Good question," Sandra said. "But I have more information which might answer that. Bill said he had done a little snooping into the situation at Fairweather Electronics, and it seems that old man Fairweather is definitely very ill. He is hanging on by his fingernails. Which means, of course, that he'll be passing on the whole billion dollar corporation to someone."

"And," I put in, "Ned is the logical one. But he doesn't want it."

"Yes." Sandra nodded. "But there is the small matter of the brother. And there definitely is a brother. Named Glenn. And he is working for Fairweather in some capacity. Bill knows a guy who used to work there, and he told him there is a lot of friction between Glenn and the old man."

"Would that be enough to keep Glenn from inheriting the company?" Julie asked.

"I'm not sure," Sandra told her, "but there apparently is a clause in the old man's will that says that Glenn can't inherit unless Ned pre-deceases him, and that Glenn has to be married for five full years and living a respectable married life."

"Where on earth would Bill's guy have learned this stuff?" I asked.

"Apparently Bill's guy was pretty high up in the corporation and knows a bunch of inside information which he passed on to Bill. According to Bill, if neither brother can inherit, the company will be passed on to the wife."

"Oh, my God," I breathed. "That's Ned's ex and he hates her. He would never, ever allow her to inherit. Not if he could help it."

"Then why wouldn't he just step up and take the company and then put it in his brother's hands after the old man dies?" Ellie asked. "Seems logical to me."

"Let's see what we've got so far," I said. "Old Man Fairweather is the sole owner of a billion dollar corporation. He has two sons. One is Ned, who has no interest in the business. The other is Glenn and he works for the company. But, and this is the deal breaker, Glenn is gay and the old man hates that. So in order to straighten him out, so to speak, he holds the carrot of the company over his head and tells him he can only have it if he's straight. So Glenn marries Svetlana and lives a straight life and when the old guy dies, he grabs the company."

"But what I don't get," Julie said, "is why he can't just inherit and then come out of the closet."

"Because," Sandra said, "there are ten board members who have control over the situation. They are empowered to enforce the provisions of the clause."

"Something's missing," I said. "There is some part of this puzzle that we don't have yet. But we're gaining on it."

As we ambled back to the dock I glanced into the store windows. At Fred's Bait Shop, I observed a display of fishing gear piled haphazardly behind the dusty glass. There were fishing rods and reels and an odd assortment of other fishing related stuff of very little interest to me. I had walked by the shop when I suddenly stopped in my tracks . . . so abruptly that Julie nearly knocked me over.

"Whoa," she chided me, "you need to signal before you stop." She waited for an explanation.

I couldn't respond. I was lost in thought. Something in the Bait Shop window had triggered a memory. I stared into space willing the memory to surface and it came to me. Stuck in the corner of the window was a dusty scuba tank. As I gazed at it I was transported back to the night of the beach party. Was it only a few days ago? I remembered hearing a splash and seeing a trail of silvery bubbles across the quiet surface of the ocean and realizing that someone was swimming. I remembered seeing that figure pull himself up on the sailboat anchored a short distance from the *Mirage*. And I recalled thinking that someone onboard the *Mirage* had a late night assignation with the mystery man. At the time, I thought it was Svetlana or even Ellie, but as our adventure continued I forgot about it.

Now I could visualize the scene in intricate detail and it dawned on me that the sailboat anchored nearby had been Skippy and Gino's. Could it have been Skippy leaving the *Mirage*? Could the assignation have been with Glenn, rather than with one of the women? And how did that information fit into the puzzle?

"Oh, my God, you guys," I finally breathed. "I just remembered something."

They stared at me and waited for me to go on. "I saw a man swimming away from the *Mirage* on the night of the beach party. At the time I thought maybe Svetlana or even Ellie might have been doing a little late night partying."

"Me?" Ellie was indignant. "Kate, I'm hurt."

"Okay, okay," I soothed. "So shoot me for thinking you might have been having some fun. I saw you creeping back into your cabin way after the rest of us had gone to bed."

"That was our first night at sea and I missed Ted and the boys so much, I took my cell phone up on deck and called home. I didn't want you guys to know I was such a baby."

"But," I said, "I saw someone. A man. Swimming away. Who was it?"

Ellie wrinkled her nose in concentration and ran a hand through her hair, absently fingering the red spikes. Suddenly her eyes widened and she said, "Oh, my gosh. I do remember something. I hadn't given it any thought before, but as I was about to hang up with Ted, I saw Glenn. He was standing in the shadows looking out at the waves. I didn't see anyone in the water, but that could have been what he was looking at. I mean, it could have been Skippy."

"Are you sure it was Glenn?" Julie asked.

"Yes, it was Glenn. I'm sure."

"Why do you suppose Skippy was with Glenn that night?" Julie wondered aloud. "Do you think it was a date or was Skippy threatening him?"

"My guess is that it was just a date. I don't think Skippy would have come up with his blackmail scheme quite so quickly," I said. "Maybe he was just trying to find out if Glenn was who he thought he was."

"Does it really matter?" Mel said. "What difference does it make what they were doing? I think it's enough that they were together."

"Where was Svetlana during this so-called date?" Ellie seemed skeptical.

"If Glenn married Svetlana so he could appear to be living a straight life, she wouldn't care what he did with Skippy," I suggested.

Sandra, her dark eyes gleaming with excitement, gave me a high five. "Kate and I saw Ned and Svetlana together in Key West and she admitted they were together."

"And," I added, my mind working at lightning speed, "I *did* overhear the two of them having some kind of argument the night of the beach party. She was saying that he couldn't do something and Ned was telling her to back off, his mind was made up."

The five of us weighed this information for a moment and then I said, "Svetlana and Ned are together but she's married . . . in name only . . . to his gay brother Glenn. That way Glenn can stay in the closet, inherit Fairweather when the time comes, and Ned is off the hook, so to speak."

"Not," Sandra put in, "if Ned is alive, though, so . . ." Her voice trailed off as the five of us reached the same conclusion. "Ned has to be dead so the three of them cooked up this plot to make it appear that he is dead. Kate saw a 'body' in the cabin. Then Ned is gone. Presumption is that he's dead."

"Enter Hank," I continued the conjecture. "He owes Ned big time so he agrees to go along with the whole thing. He's in charge of any investigation into the so-called death or disappearance, so after an appropriate amount of time, he proclaims that Ned is dead and we all ride off into the sunset. Glenn takes over the company and lives happily ever after."

Ellie broke in. "That is *not* a fairy tale ending, you know. What about Ned and Svetlana? Don't they get to live happily ever after? And where does Ned go?"

"Yeah," Julie said. "Svetlana told me there was a good explanation for all of this, but I don't think we've figured it out yet. There's more to this story, I think."

"Don't forget about Skippy," Mel reminded us. "He really is dead."

The sun beat down on us as we clustered on the sidewalk. We were creating a bit of a disturbance so we moved our meeting under the awning in front of the Coconut Key Grocery.

"This isn't the place to be discussing this," Sandra said. "We need to find some privacy."

"Let's go back to the *Mirage* and boot up my computer," suggested Mary Linda. "There is something out of order and I want to find out what it is."

The *Mirage* didn't appeal to any of us. Visions of dead bodies lurked in every corner. But we hoped to escape prying eyes in the safety of our own cabins. Taking a collective deep breath, we headed back to the Fresh Ketch and the privacy of the *Mirage*.

When we reached the docks we found Hank and Flo waving good-bye to the Key West cops. Hank looked over his shoulder as he heard our sandals slapping on the dock. I caught the relieved look on his face before he turned away. Even Flo had nothing to say to us, and we mutely watched the boat become a tiny speck on the horizon.

Hank broke the silence at last. "Well, I say good riddance to them two," he said with some of his old geniality.

"Yeah," agreed Flo, her hand in Hank's. "Them two was nothin' but a big pain in the you know what. I called them the two dwarfs, Pretty and Pissy." She grinned at us, enjoying her own humor.

We laughed nervously and followed the receding yacht with speculative eyes. I didn't know whether to be relieved

or frightened. I knew Hank was involved in Ned's disappearance and possible death, but I just couldn't be afraid
of the gruff giant. I couldn't help thinking he had gotten
himself into a situation he wasn't very happy about.

Hank shook his head as if to clear it and announced.
"Now, you ladies and I have some things to talk about. I
know you know a lot more about this here dead guy than
you are letting on. We're going to have a nice long chat."

He tried to look stern and commanding, but I saw only
confusion and despair.

Sandra patted his arm and said, "Hank, we'll be glad to
tell you everything we know, but right now we are going
back to our cabins and change clothes and maybe take a
nice nap or something. It's been a long morning."

She was right. We wanted nothing more than to escape
to our cabins and we marched away, sandals rhythmically
slapping.

Chapter Twenty-Five

"**I**'m calling to order the meeting of the Jazzer-detectives," I declared as the group of showered and refreshed women draped themselves over the bunks in my cabin. Showers and clean shorts and t-shirts, however, couldn't disguise the stress taking its toll on us.

Sandra began the discussion. "I've been thinking that it isn't that easy to just be declared dead. I mean, I don't know Florida law, but you can't just decide that you are going to disappear and be proclaimed dead. There are little matters of money and insurance and all of that stuff. I think it's like seven years or something before that happens. Unless you have a body."

"Which, of course, we don't," I said.

"Hank is the law in these here parts, sugar," Julie drawled. "Can't he just do what he wants?"

"Not unless he has a body," insisted Sandra. "For insurance purposes, anyway."

"So, what if Ned doesn't care about the insurance?" Ellie asked. "What does he need insurance for anyway? If he's dead, he doesn't care, and if he's alive, well . . ."

"Um, guys. I found something interesting." Mary Linda looked up from her laptop screen.

We clustered around her peering over her shoulder at the indistinct image. "What do you see? It looks like a bunch of clouds," Julie said.

Mary Linda fiddled with the computer. "Now do you see?"

I squinted at the screen and managed to focus on the image. It appeared to be a yearbook picture from many years ago. With a little help from my reading glasses, I made out the inscription under the fuzzy picture. "Svetlana Malinowski. Pre med, biology, sailing club, track team, homecoming court." I scrutinized the grainy photo and then looked at my friends. "You look and tell me what you see."

One by one they stared at the screen and then wordlessly at each other. "By George, I think she's got it," Sandra said finally. "Proof positive that Svetlana was at Berkeley when Ned and Glenn were there. The years match up."

"Not only that," I said, "but they were all in the sailing club."

"Not to mention, the homecoming court," Julie groused. "Some people have it all. Looks, brains, and two rich guys."

"Do you think they all knew Ned's wife too?" I asked. "I know they, I mean Ned and his ex-wife, met in college."

"Who knows, maybe they all hung out together," Mary Linda said. "But what does it all mean?"

"It means," I concluded, "that something fishy is going on. I'm beginning to think that we aren't going to be able to find any evidence that proves anything one way or another. Maybe that was the idea all along. Captain Ned is swimming with the fishies and Glenn and Svetlana live a long and happy and very rich life. Or not. Svetlana and Glenn are either murderers or scheming to snatch the company from Ned's ex or something."

I threw my glasses on the dresser and stood up. "I'm going to Ned's cabin to see if I can find anything. Maybe the police overlooked something. I'm thinking that Hank isn't all that interested in evidence and he wouldn't let the Key West guys anywhere near the crime scene."

My announcement was met with a chorus of protests, but I insisted that I was going. I opened the cabin door and looked up and down the hallway. "All clear," I said and slipped out the door.

I had gone only two steps when my cabin door slammed against the wall and I jumped at least two feet in the air. "Sorry," a voice behind me said, "I didn't want you to be alone." Mary Linda hovered just outside the cabin.

Gratefully, I grabbed her hand and pulled her down the shadowy hallway to Captain Ned's cabin. The yellow crime scene tape still crisscrossed the doorway, but no one was guarding it. The two of us contemplated the cabin door. Then I turned and said in a quavery voice, "I'm going in."

Mary Linda shook her head. "No way, girl, you can't." She pointed at the yellow tape. "It's against the law or something."

"When did a little tape stop us?" With shaking fingers I pried some of the sticky tape loose. The noise echoed in the empty hall and we paused to see if anyone pounced on us. When no one did, we pulled a larger section of tape loose and then tried the door. It was unlocked. I hesitated for a moment, then took a deep breath and tiptoed into the cabin. It took a second for our eyes to adjust to the darkness. From what we could see nothing much had changed since our last visit.

The rug was missing, I noticed, and gestured at the empty space on the floor. Mary Linda frowned. "Evidence," I breathed. "Blood stains."

Her face registered horror at the thought. "Now what?" she asked.

I shrugged. "Let's look in the drawers and under the bed and in the closet. See what we can find."

Mary Linda tugged open the closet doors and smiled in approval at the orderly display of clothing. "Nothing changed here." Rapidly we examined the contents of the desk and the drawers in the tiny dresser. Someone had obviously been in the drawers. Where they had been in disarray before, now they were tidy. Piles of papers were stacked neatly. Socks, underwear, t-shirts, clothes, all folded.

"The cops have taken anything important," I whispered. "We're wasting our time."

I had an inspiration. I pulled out one of the desk drawers and turned it over, dumping papers unceremoniously on the floor. "Oops," I murmured. Nothing. More carefully I examined the other drawers and found what I was looking for on the final one. There was the remnant of scotch tape on the bottom of that drawer. "Look." I pointed.

Mary Linda was anxious to escape. "Right. Big clue. Let's go."

"No," I protested. "Something was taped here. This is a clue."

"Of what?"

"I don't know exactly. Something."

"Okay, so let's get out of here."

"Just a second." I sank onto the desk chair and ran my hands through my hair. Thinking furiously, I tried to figure out what Stephanie Plum might do. My eyes fell on a wastebasket stuck under the desk. It was wedged tightly into the back corner and barely visible. It could easily have been overlooked by a less than motivated policeman. Curious, I tugged at it until I managed to get it unstuck. It contained a candy bar wrapper, an empty beer can, a discarded toothpaste tube. Disappointed, I sifted through it and was about to give up when I pulled out a bank envelope. Naturally there was nothing in it. First Federal Bank of Berkeley was printed in blue letters on the front. I fingered it for a second and then turned it over. Scrawled on the back was "NH8FP6". Recognition dawned on me then. A confirmation number. For what? An airplane? A boat? A space ship? Anything was possible.

By now Mary Linda was frantically tugging on my arm, so I stuffed the wastebasket under the desk and pocketed the bank envelope. "Okay, let's go." I backed toward the door, Mary Linda clinging to me, and my eyes fell on the bunk across the cabin. At the head of the bunk was a small headboard and on it was a double picture frame. Two faces radiating health and teenaged good looks smiled out at the gloomy room. They could only be Ned's twin sons, Mike and Trip. I recalled the conversations Ned and I had about our families. I pictured the pride on his face when he talked about the boys, and, at that instant, I knew that Ned could not, would not, have willingly done anything to jeopardize their futures. He must be dead, I thought. He wouldn't just abandon those two boys to his ex-wife.

The little cabin was suffocating and fear hung heavily in the air. We gave the place one last glance and then backed into the corridor. "That was fun," Mary Linda commented. "I thought for sure we'd get caught."

"Me, too. But I have this . . ." And I showed her the bank envelope. ". . . and a pretty good feeling that Ned is really dead." The thought of Ned actually being dead made me sad.

We made our way back to our cabin where we found the other three exactly as we had left them. "So," Sandra demanded as we entered, "what did you find?"

Ellie gazed at us with concerned eyes. "How did it look in there? Was there any blood?" She wiped her hands on her shorts and shuddered.

"Nothing much to see," I said. I handed the bank envelope to Mary Linda. "I think that's a confirmation number written on there. I'd guess that Ned wrote it. Maybe for an airplane flight to somewhere. If he's not dead, he has to be somewhere. Can you do anything with it?"

Mary Linda fingered the envelope. "I can try." And she bent over her computer.

Sitting on the floor with my back against the bunk, I tried to reconstruct the events of the past few days, but I couldn't get past the vision of the Captain lying on the floor of his cabin with a dent in his head. I didn't want to believe it, but I was becoming convinced that Captain Ned was six feet under . . . water, that is. When the unnatural, hushed atmosphere became oppressing, I struggled to my feet and said, "I'm hungry. I'm going to go find something to eat."

"And drink," Sandra said, sitting up and pulling on a sweater.

Even Julie abandoned whatever dark and gloomy thoughts that had obsessed her for hours and hopped down from the top bunk. I glanced at the clock surprised to see that it was nearly six-thirty. Outside our tiny port-hole window dusk had descended.

"All's quiet," I murmured, but the words were no more out of my mouth than the silence was interrupted by the sound of a large motor boat and the laughter and conver-sation of ebullient males.

"What on earth . . ." Ellie cried. Before anyone could answer we heard a male voice calling, "Hello, Fresh Ketch. Hull-ooh, Dockmaster. Is anyone there?"

The five of us bolted for the deck. Approaching the dock from the sea was the *Honor*, the fishing boat that towed us to the marina. The captain and his crew of three waved and called to us. Company! And male company at that. All of a sudden things were looking up.

"Hello, there," the captain shouted when the *Honor* was a few yards away. "Where is the dockmaster? We thought we'd put in for the night if he has room."

"I imagine that Hank's up at the bar." I gestured toward the Coconut Key Bar.

Miguel materialized from nowhere. One of the fisher-men tossed a line to him and there was a flurry of activity as the *Honor* was secured to dock pilings. When the job was finished, the four men clambered from their boat onto the dock. They found cold beers in the cooler attached to the stern and joked as they drank and took stock of the surroundings.

We were delighted with this turn of events. The crew of the *Honor* provided us with a welcome diversion from murder and mayhem. The captain was a tall, fair-haired man who I guessed to be in his mid to late fifties. The other men were a bit younger. Perhaps in their late thirties or early forties. Tired and sweat-stained, they still were in high spirits.

I heard a shout and saw Hank hurrying toward us. His expression was constrained but welcoming. "Hello, Captain," he called. "What can we do for you?"

The captain stuck out his hand and Hank shook it firmly. "Well," the captain said, "we had a great day fishing. Didn't want to call it a day since we got a forty-pound wahoo on the line. By the time we landed him, we were ready for beer and some of Flo's famous conch fritters. Didn't want to take the time to run back to our slip in Key West. Looks like maybe you could put us up for the night?" He jerked his head in the direction of the numerous vacant boat slips.

"Yeah," Hank said. "Business ain't too good these days." He failed to explain that most people were avoiding the Fresh Ketch because of the so-called "death ship", the *Mirage*, tied up a few feet away.

"I'm Rob." The Captain introduced himself. "And this is Ken, Roy and Danny." Perhaps he used last names, but I was too preoccupied to hear them. I was busy trying to figure out how this unexpected visit could help us uncover more about Ned's disappearance and Svetlana and Glenn's involvement in it.

Hank, on the other hand, played the genial host to perfection. He pointed at the dilapidated office building.

"There's a little shower in the office that you can use and I can help with the catch if you want. We could clean some of it and Flo could cook it up for dinner."

Captain Rob and his cohorts accepted Hank's offer and they scattered either to shower or to attend to the fish. The five of us watched the activity with interest.

"Isn't this a fine kettle of fish?" Sandra said.

I grinned at her. "Who knows, maybe the *Honor* crew can help us solve our mystery."

"Let's give the mystery thing a break," she answered. "I'm in the mood for some fish and some fun."

I totally agreed. This was, after all, our vacation and it certainly hadn't gone the way we thought it would. Putting aside our investigation for one evening seemed like an inspired idea.

The men lugged the cooler holding the fish up to the bar and recruited Flo and Randy, the regular cook, to help with the preparation. There was much conversation and good-natured teasing among the four fishermen. The noise they made soon attracted Martha's attention and she popped her head out of the galley. To her credit she realized that the party was going to be at the bar and not on the *Mirage*, and she scrambled off the *Mirage* and approached Flo.

"I'd be happy to help with dinner," she offered diffidently. "I have loads of food onboard and I'd be more than happy to bring it up to the bar."

Spontaneously, Flo hugged Martha. "I'd sure love that, honey. I'm never one to say no to a cook like you."

A truce was declared in the food wars as the combatants put down their weapons of mass digestion in favor of a cooperative effort. The party in the Coconut Key Bar that night was lively. Food and drink was plentiful and the company compatible. The four fishermen were in good spirits after a day of successful fishing and the five of us were happy to have something to take our minds off the last few days. Flo and Martha, having achieved detente, worked in concert, laughing and sharing recipes. Ellie watched them with the gleam in her eye that meant she was thinking of her cookbook.

Even Svetlana and Glenn emerged from their self-imposed isolation in their cabin. Svetlana, her hair piled artfully on her head, wore a red and yellow print strapless sundress and three-inch platform sandals. Obviously she had made an effort to dress for a party. Glenn, on the other hand, hadn't shaved in days and wore a wrinkled pair of shorts and a stained golf shirt. His demeanor was glum and he looked far different than the neat, if not terribly fashionable, man who had first boarded the *Mirage*. The last few days had taken their toll on him.

Instantly, though, he remembered his good manners and strode over to Rob with his hand outstretched. "I'm Glenn Livingston. Glad to meet you. So you had a good day fishing, eh?" He gave every indication of being fascinated with Rob's rambling account of getting the fifty-pound (it kept getting larger and more impressive) wahoo aboard the *Honor*, hanging on Rob's every word and interjecting an occasional expression of surprise or awe. All in all, a good performance, I thought.

The jukebox pumped out music and Svetlana, as usual the center of attention, danced with one after another of the men. Laughing and flirting, her accent more pronounced than ever, Svetlana had the men fluttering around her like crabs to a crab trap. The five of us ate and drank and danced with the enthusiasm, if not the expertise, displayed by Svetlana.

"Ooh, I am having the fun," Svetlana exclaimed to one of the fishermen (Was it Danny?)

And laying on thick the accent, I thought meanly. At that moment she caught my eye over the top of Danny's head, shrugged wryly and grimaced. I winked at her thinking "whatever it takes to get you where you need to go."

Glenn wandered outside and slumped in a chair at one of the umbrella tables. Nursing a bottle of beer, he appeared oblivious to the scene of merriment. Pink-cheeked and laughing, Svetlana danced outside and over to his table. She gave him a quick hug, whispered something in his ear and then flounced off, her skirt twirling to show off her shapely legs.

Even Miguel abandoned his duties and spent the evening in the bar. Martha kept a watchful eye on him when she wasn't attending to the others, bringing him a plate of conch fritters and home fries and a frosty bottle of beer. Strangely, he paid hardly any attention to her, preferring to focus on the dance floor. At one point, Glenn wandered inside to refresh his drink and Miguel straightened and started to get up. Then he shook his head and sat back down. "Dios, mio," I heard him say to no one in particular. "Muy estupido."

It didn't take a Spanish major to understand what Miguel said, but what it meant I had no idea, and I certainly wasn't about to devote a lot of time and effort to figuring out Miguel of all people. Hindsight being 20/20 and all of that, I guess I should have.

It was nearly midnight before the party began to wind down. Two of the *Honor's* crew had said good night. The third was deep in conversation with Hank and from the gestures and laughter I could tell that the fish tale was being replayed in great and, more than likely, much exaggerated detail. A country song blared from the jukebox and the *Honor*'s captain and Svetlana danced a rollicking Texas two-step. Svetlana's face was flushed and her skirt swirled high on her thighs as she danced.

Late in the evening Flo vacated her post behind the bar, and she and Martha sprawled at one of the tables. A bottle of beer sat in front of Flo and Martha nursed a cup of tea. Heads together, they pored over Flo's cookbooks, one or the other scribbling feverishly on a piece of paper from time to time. Ellie, notebook in hand, wandered over and casually plopped into one of the remaining chairs. The pair were obviously delighted to include her. Periodically Flo's booming laugh would resonate over the music.

When I saw Mary Linda gathering her things and heading out, I caught her arm as she attempted to slip by me and said, "Hey, what's up? Leaving so soon?" She turned and one look at her face told me that she was not well.

"Are you okay?" I asked. Her face was greenish and her eyes ringed with dark circles. Perspiration beaded her forehead. Morning, or more precisely, evening sickness?

"I really don't feel well," she managed to choke out. "Not much doubt . . ."

Julie came up behind me at that moment and interrupted us. "What are you two . . ." she said and stopped. She glanced at Mary Linda's face and put her arm around her shoulder.

"Mel," she said, "I'm taking you back to the *Mirage*. You can't go by yourself. You look like hell."

"Well, thanks," Mary Linda protested with a touch of her usual spirit. "I'll be fine. You don't need to leave the party."

"No problem," Julie said. "I've had about enough fun for one night. I might give Robert a call. If I can't find him at home during the day, he certainly would have to be there at night. Or not."

At that point, Mary Linda pressed a hand over her mouth and raced from the bar with Julie hot on her tail. I started to follow but I was too slow and they escaped without me. I wanted to talk to Hank before I called it a night anyway. Maybe he would confide in me with a few beers under his belt and the festive atmosphere to relax him.

He was still engrossed in conversation, so I meandered over to the bar and sat slouched on a barstool, my head propped on my hand, to wait for him to finish. A glass of diet cola in front of me, I drew lazy circles on the bar with the condensation. My eyes were dry and gritty and I could barely keep them open.

Svetlana continued to dance with abandon, taking on any partner who was available, while Glenn hadn't moved from his spot at the umbrella table all night. You would have thought they were mere acquaintances rather than husband and wife for all the contact they had with one another. Miguel, on the other hand, had found his way to Glenn's table and was poised there looking as if he might bolt at the slightest provocation. He perched awkwardly on the edge of his seat, leaning toward Glenn with an avid look on his face. Either he spoke more English than he let on or Glenn spoke Spanish. Either way the two men seemed to my weary eyes to be having a tentative sort of conversation. I don't know exactly what it was about their postures, but I figured they weren't entirely comfortable. Maybe the language thing, I decided.

I must have drifted off for a moment because my head slipped off my hand and I was jerked back to a semi-alert state. Svetlana had vanished and Sandra was backed into a corner listening to Captain Rob expound on something. She broke free and slid onto the barstool next to me. "Hey, Cinderella," she laughed, "looks like your prince has come. Better grab him before you turn into a pumpkin."

I followed her look and saw Hank striding toward the bar. His frizzled grey hair and beard stood up more than usual and his tropical shirt had sweat stains under the arms. Worn kino sandals slapped the wood floor as he marched up and put a large, hairy arm around my shoulder. "Hey there, little miss," he drawled, "you havin' a good time?"

I couldn't help but grin at this giant apparition. "It's been great, Hank. Best time we've had in a while."

He looked pleased. "I wanted to talk to y'all tonight before all this . . ." His gesture took in the entire bar. ". . . began."

I nodded and Sandra leaned around me to get Hank's attention. "We need to ask you some questions ourselves," she said.

"We want to find out how the investigation is going and when we might be able to head home," I added. "This hasn't exactly been the vacation of our dreams."

"I'm sure sorry 'bout that," Hank said. "But you found yourselves kind of on the wrong ship at the wrong time, now didn't ya?"

"I can't argue with you there, Hank," I said. "But what's next?"

"Listen, ladies," Hank said, "I think we should table this discussion until morning. I have some news that might interest you, but now just ain't the time to be spillin' it. What do you say we meet here tomorrow morning and Flo can fix some pancakes and we can talk it all out. Might be some interesting developments by then."

Try as we might, Sandra and I couldn't wangle any information out of Hank. He refused to budge so we were forced to accept his terms. For the time being, anyway.

Chapter Twenty-Six

The party was breaking up by the time Julie returned with Svetlana. I did a double take when I saw the unlikely twosome looking like they shared some big secret. Julie broke away and hurried over to Sandra and me at the bar. I was eager to hear what she had to say. When we assigned Julie to double agent duty, we hadn't thought she would be so successful.

"Hey," she greeted us breathlessly. "Wait until I tell you . . ."

Sandra shushed her as Hank and Flo strolled over to bid us good night. "Shh," Sandra whispered in Julie's ear. "Wait until we get back on the *Mirage*. Then we won't be overheard."

Impulsively, I reached up to give Hank a hug and a peck on his grizzled cheek. Looking embarrassed, he swept me into a bear hug and said, "Don't worry. We'll get this whole thing straightened out and I'll have you on your way back to Ohio in no time flat."

Flo gave each of us a quick hug and a kiss on the cheek. "Come for breakfast early in the morning. Me and Martha are gonna make a feast." She grinned across the room at her new cohort.

"Sounds great," we said and drifted out of the bar. The *Mirage*, bobbing on the tide, appeared deceptively innocent in the waning moonlight. We scrambled back aboard and lost no time getting to our cabins. With Mary Linda already curled up in her bunk, the rest of us slipped into Ellie and Sandra's cabin where Julie brought us up to date on Robert's activities and her conversation with Svetlana.

"So," Julie said, "I called Robert's cell. Of course, he didn't answer, but I got voicemail and you'll never believe this . . ." Julie paused to let her announcement sink in. "It was for Robert's Kitchen."

Innocently, Ellie asked, "Robert doesn't have a kitchen, does he?"

"Well, he does now. And I think that he has a restaurant. It all fits. It's too damn strange, but it fits."

We discussed Robert for a few minutes before I asked Julie about Svetlana. "What's up with her? You two came out of the restroom like BFFs with some huge secret."

"BFF, humpf," Julie said. "You *told* me to find out about her and Glenn. Haven't I done that?"

"Don't get your knickers in a knot," Sandra said. "But the two of you sure looked chummy."

"Come on, Jules," I said, "let us in on the big secret."

Julie gave us an aggrieved look. She sighed. "Oh, okay. Svetlana basically told me that she and Glenn are in this up to their eyeballs. She said she couldn't tell me any more now, but that someday she would tell us everything."

"Oh, right," Sandra said. "I'm so sure."

"No, really," Julie protested. "I believe her. You didn't see how she looked when she told me that she really cared about Ned. She loves him. I know it."

Too tired to make much sense of any of it, we agreed to wait until morning to discuss it further. By then, of course, other developments took over and we didn't get back to Julie's story for some time.

I think I might have slept until noon. All I wanted was to pull the covers over my head and let the world stumble on without me. If Julie hadn't waved a mug of coffee under my nose, I might have done just that. I rolled over and rubbed my eyes as I tried to focus on the little travel alarm next to my bunk. Without my contacts in, though, it was just a blur. I squinted myopically at Julie and reached for the mug. "Ah," I breathed, as I tried to sit up without slopping coffee all over the bunk. "What time is it anyway?"

"Nearly nine," Julie replied. "And life is happening."

Mary Linda, looking rested and much better than the night before, was propped up in her bunk with her computer on her lap. She was absorbed in the screen and paid us no attention.

"Hank wants to see us all," Julie said. "He's already been here twice and Martha and Flo are cooking up a storm, according to him. He's like a man dancing on hot coals he seems so worked up. I've never seen him like that. Not that I actually know him all that well."

"You're babbling, girl," I told her. "I'm up already. Where are Sandra and Ellie?"

Julie grinned. "Well, duh, do you think little Miss Ellie would miss a single moment of Cordon Bleu meets Fried Chicken? She was up with the birdies and over to the bar before daylight."

"And Sandra?"

"Last I saw her she was on deck with her cell phone."

"Okay, I'll be with you in a sec." I scrambled from my bunk and, deciding to forego the luxury of a shower for the moment, I washed my face and put a copious amount of hair goo in my sleep-flattened hair. I applied a minimum of make-up, heavy on the mascara and lip gloss, and donned my favorite denim capris and a hot pink tank top. I topped it with my jean jacket to ward off the morning's chilly breeze and I was set to go in record time.

Mel, too, abandoned her computer and dressed in capris, hoodie and sandals. With her hair combed and wearing dark glasses, she looked no worse for wear. We gave each other a quick once over and meeting with each other's approval we followed Julie from the cabin onto the sunlit deck. It was another beautiful day. I took a deep breath and then squared my shoulders as I prepared to disembark from the sailboat. When I turned I was only a little surprised to see that the *Honor* was no longer docked next to the *Mirage*. Just a touch miffed because they hadn't even said goodbye, I scanned the horizon for the boat. It was nowhere to be seen.

"Well, looks like our neighbors left early," I commented. "Not even a goodbye note."

"Nope," Julie said. "They were gone when I got up. I have no idea when they left."

Sandra joined us and said, "And we meant so much to each other too."

"After all we've been through together." Mel sighed dramatically.

I shivered then and realized that our gallant rescuers had vanished into thin air and left us without *Honor* and among suspected murderers. I hurried toward the warmth and delicious aromas emanating from the bar's kitchen with my friends in my wake.

Hank was at the door and, acting once again as the gracious host, ushered us inside and offered us coffee, tea or orange juice. Hopefully he asked, "Would anyone prefer a mimosa? Martha brought us some really fine champagne."

Overhearing him, Martha hastened to interject, "Not that fine a champagne. But perfect for mimosas with Flo's fresh squeezed orange juice."

Sounded good to me and I accepted gratefully. Mel refused, saying, "Make mine straight orange juice, please, Martha. That's from Flo's own orange tree, I assume." Mel caught my eye and winked. The others didn't notice anything amiss and ordered mimosas all around.

Sandra stood next to me and we sipped our mimosas in silence as Flo and Martha scurried around arranging platters of food on a long, banquet-style table. Finally, Sandra whispered, "I made a few calls this morning and found out a few more bits of information about our dear friends the Livingstons."

"After we talk to Hank, you can fill me in."

"Are we going to tell him everything we know?"

"Let's just see what he has to tell us first. Then play it by ear."

Flo and Martha may have ostensibly put aside their differences, but they were still vying with each other for our favor, each pressing on us her own dish. "Have some of my French toast," Flo would urge us. "Or try some of these seafood omelets," Martha would respond. "Can I get you some home fries?" Flo asked. "Or perhaps some tiny macadamia muffins would be better?" Martha would interject.

It was gastronomy versus gluttony; cuisine versus home cookin'; cordon bleu versus comfort food. It was the culinary wars and we had been chosen, without our knowledge or consent, as the judges and jury. It wasn't a bad job and, what the heck, someone had to do it. But when we couldn't stuff in another bite, we begged for mercy and Martha and Flo began to clear the table.

Julie pushed her chair back and clutching her stomach groaned, "I can't believe I ate all that. Now I really need that liposuction."

Ellie moaned in sympathy. "Even purely as research for my cookbook, that was way over the top. I'll join you for the liposuction."

Sandra added dryly, "Do you suppose we could get a group rate?"

"Kind of a group suck and tuck?" I suggested.

Still complaining about how satiated we were, we settled back with fresh mugs of coffee to wait for Hank. He had raced off in the middle of the breakfast feast to take a call on his cell phone. We didn't have long to cool our heels before he showed up, cell phone plastered to his ear and a sheaf of papers tucked under his arm. He dumped his papers unceremoniously on the table, helped himself to a fresh mug of coffee and plopped down on a chair. He took several sips of coffee and regarded us over the rim of the mug. All was silent, the only sounds coming from the kitchen where Flo's booming laugh could be heard above the rattling of dishes and the splash of water.

We sat around the table like six players in a high stakes poker game. We eyed each other warily. I mumbled under my breath to Sandra, who happened to be next to me, "Know when to hold 'em, know when to fold 'em."

"Know when to walk away. Know when to run," she finished.

I was determined not to show my cards until Hank revealed his. The tension grew as Hank shuffled papers and sipped his coffee without speaking. We squirmed and exchanged worried looks as the silence dragged on. Finally Hank stacked his pile of papers and cleared his throat. "I have some interesting developments in this case," he began, and we all sat up a little straighter and listened.

"I know you are all anxious to have this cleared up so that you can get on with things," he said. "So, if you can bear with me a little longer, I can do just that."

Sternly, he continued, "I don't think you ladies have been 100% truthful with me. I think you are hiding some things I need to know." He frowned and then sighed heavily. "Am I right?"

No one uttered a word. Hank sighed again and said, "I got a call from them Key West cops this morning. It seems they found out something interesting when they took that rug from Captain Fairweather's cabin."

The roar of a boat motor was the only sound.

"And," I asked.

"And," he continued gravely, "they analyzed the blood stains on the rug. Not too surprisingly, the Captain's blood was there. Lots of it."

The five of us shivered and Ellie looked sick.

"But that's not all," Hank went on. "Someone else's blood was on the rug too. Care to guess whose it was?"

"Nope," I said, "we don't want to play guessing games. Tell us."

"Seems it was traced to one Reginald Anderson MacComber the Third. But I believe you all knew him as Skippy."

Our reaction was shock and horror in equal parts. "Skippy?" exclaimed Julie. "Oh, my God," whispered Mel. Ellie's eyes were huge, and Sandra and I just stared at each other as Hank's words sank in.

Hank scrutinized us and then, apparently satisfied that we really were as shocked as we looked, he went on. "So, why do we have the blood of that dead gay guy on the rug in the Captain's cabin?"

I shrugged and shook my head. Then, having been wordlessly appointed as spokeswoman, I said, "How did Skippy's blood get on that rug? He was found floating in the ocean."

"Pretty obvious, isn't it?" Sandra said. "The Captain either killed him or they both were killed by the same person."

I interrupted her. "Okay, now I guess we'd better tell Hank all of what we know." I looked at the others and they nodded.

"About time," Hank said.

"Here's the thing, Hank," I said, "when we were in Key West we saw Skippy and Gino at a bar together. Later on we kind of thought we might have seen Skippy with someone else. Maybe on a date or something."

All ears, Hank leaned forward and said, "Go on."

"Um . . . um," I stammered trying to decide how much to reveal. "Well, we thought it might have been someone we knew. Maybe."

Growing impatient with my stalling, Hank growled, "Spill it, Miss Kate. This here is police business you are messed up with."

"Oh, okay," I said in a rush, "we saw Skippy going into a bar called Boys Will Be Boys and we were pretty sure it was with Glenn."

A groan escaped Hank before he could stop it. "Damn it," he bellowed. "I told that little . . ." He bit his lip and then more calmly asked, "You sure about that?"

Figuring there was no reason to keep anything from him at this point, I went on, "Well, we weren't sure. We thought it was Glenn. So, the next day we went to lunch at Boys Will Be Boys and . . ."

"You what?" Hank shouted. "Don't you ladies ever think about little things like safety?"

"Whoa," I said. "There hadn't been a crime back then. No reason for us not to do a little amateur detecting."

"Not to mention," Julie added, "that my brother recommended the place and it has great food."

"And nice waiters," Ellie said. "Without Wil, I wouldn't . . ."

Mel put a restraining hand on Ellie's shoulder and she stopped.

"So, anyway," I said, "we asked some of the staff and they said that Glenn was a regular at the place and that he used the name Guido when he came in. We had some digital pictures on Mel's camera and they gave us a positive I.D. of Glenn."

Hank shook his head in despair. "Stupid, stupid, stupid," he muttered.

"What?" I asked.

Before Hank had the chance to explain, we were interrupted by Good Cop and Bad Cop, the Key (Stone) West cops, bursting into the bar with undisguised enjoyment at Hank's obvious discomfiture. Hank was plainly annoyed, but not terribly surprised, to see the two. "Look what washed up on our shore," he groused. "Debris."

"Great to see you, too, Hank," Good Cop said mildly.

"This time we brought a search warrant," Bad Cop said, taking control of the situation. "And the CSI guys, too."

"CSI, Key West?" Sandra asked. "Now that's a new twist on an old story."

Bad Cop glared at her and Sandra wisely took the hint and shut up.

"You got the lab report on the blood?" Good Cop asked Hank.

"Yes, I did and I was just tellin' the ladies about it."

I waited for Hank to tell them about Skippy and Glenn, but he said nothing further. He hesitated a moment and then offered to fetch Glenn and Svetlana from the *Mirage*. "We was just about to round them up anyway," he said. "I s'pose you'll be wanting to interview them again."

Good Cop nodded and Hank, relieved to escape, strode from the bar toward the *Mirage*, leaving us alone in the bar with Good Cop and Bad Cop. Good Cop looked every bit as good as he had the last time we saw him and Bad Cop was every bit as disheveled and out of sorts. Whether it was because it would have been rude to ignore them or because Good Cop was a hottie, I can't say, but Sandra hurried behind the bar, poured two mugs of coffee and offered them to the cops. Good Cop accepted the mug graciously with a warm, even flirtatious, smile at Sandra. Bad Cop snatched his mug with ill-disguised rancor and gulped it moodily while Good Cop chatted with Sandra.

Flo and Martha peeked out from the kitchen, perhaps debating whether to escalate the Food Wars to include competing for the approval of the Key West cops. Fortunately, or perhaps unfortunately, this semi-social atmosphere was shattered by Hank. He flew into the bar, his frizzled hair standing wildly on end, practically foaming at the mouth in fury. I had never seen him so undone.

"They're gone. Lock, stock and teeny bikinis. They vamoosed. Hit the road. Blew out of town!" Fury made him nearly incoherent.

"Who?" Good Cop demanded.

"The Livingstons. Glenn Livingston and that gorgeous wife of his. Their cabin is empty. They are plain and simple gone!"

Dumbfounded, we looked at each other.

Good Cop and Bad Cop turned and sprinted for the *Mirage* with Hank racing after them. Not wanting to miss the action, we dashed after them into the brilliant sunshine. The pelicans sunning themselves gave us the evil eye as we scurried past. Breathless, we arrived at Glenn and Svetlana's cabin where the Key West cops and Hank were already yanking open drawers and peering under the bunks. Hank held up a gloved hand as we approached. "Don't touch a thing in here. We're gonna dust for prints." He reveled in using traditional cop lingo.

Both Good Cop and Bad Cop wore plastic gloves and their two associates were setting up a fingerprint kit. We watched the cops at work for a few minutes before Hank shooed us away explaining, "You're just getting in the way. Why don't I come and talk with you a little later." He pointed his finger at us and said severely, "Stay around here. I don't want you vanishing on me neither."

We reassured him and retired to my cabin to discuss the latest in a seemingly unending series of unbelievable events. "Can you believe this?" Ellie asked. "This is getting to be like a TV show."

"Yeah," Sandra said, "a bad one."

"Let's concentrate," I said. "We have two more pieces of information. First, Skippy's blood on that rug, and, second, Glenn and Svetlana running."

"Why do you think they took off? And how?" Julie asked.

"The how is fairly easy," I said. "I think they rode off into the sunrise on the *Honor*. Svetlana was pretty busy last night flirting with the guys. I'm betting she convinced them to take Glenn and her with them when they left."

The others nodded. That theory seemed to work. "But why?" I wanted to know. "Julie, you talked to Svetlana last night. Any clue why they would leave so suddenly?"

Julie furrowed her brow and ran her hands through her black curls. "Not really. She promised to let me know what this was all about. Some day. But I didn't get the feeling they were about to go missing."

"Maybe," suggested Mel, "it was more what they had to lose by staying. Could they have known that the cops from Key West were going to show up? And could they have known about the bloodstains?"

"Mel," I exclaimed. "You've got it!"

"What?" the others demanded.

"The bloodstains. They knew Skippy's blood was on the rug. They couldn't have known exactly when the authorities were going to find out, but they sure did know that eventually it would happen. So, the *Honor* presented an opportunity to escape. And they took it."

"That means . . ." Sandra surmised, "that Glenn and Svetlana knew about Skippy's murder. They could have done it. Either one of them could have done it."

"So that Skippy couldn't pursue his little blackmail scheme?" asked Mel.

"Yep, I'd bet on it," I said.

"Think back, Mel, to the night we heard the noises. Something or somebody being thrown overboard? It's possible it was Skippy, isn't it?" I asked.

"At this point," she replied, "I think just about anything is possible."

I couldn't have agreed more.

Someone pounded on the cabin door and when I jerked it open Hank stood in the gangway looking like a storm cloud. "Them cops," he fumed, "are messin' with my investigation. They got themselves a damn search warrant and they're all over the *Mirage* like fleas on pelicans."

"Do you want to come in?" I asked, hoping to find out what was going on.

"No," he answered. "I been sent to tell you all to just git. Them weasels want y'all to get out of their way. You're s'posed to go up to the bar and wait for them to be finished."

The expression on his face told me more than words could have how he felt about the interlopers from Key West.

He looked ready to detonate. We grabbed our things and scurried back to the dock with Hank escorting us. Once we were safely off the *Mirage*, Hank turned his back, stomped back aboard the boat and disappeared below.

"Are we going to just go and sit in the bar? Again?" Sandra demanded. "I am getting sick and damn tired of all of this."

"This is our vacation," Ellie cried. "This stinks."

"Yeah, it kinda does." I apologized. "I feel like it's all my fault. I got us on the *Mirage*. We could have just spent our vacation in the Keys or shopping in Miami."

"Don't blame yourself, Katie love," soothed Mel. "I have my computer. Let's see what I can come up with while we wait for Hank and the Key West guys."

We hadn't been at the bar long when Hank blew in sending the bead door flying. He didn't look happy, but he was calmer than he had been. With a huge sigh he sank into a chair and started talking. He was a bit reticent at first, but he became more animated as he got into his story. "Them cops pure and simple trashed the *Mirage*. Turned the place upside down. Even went through your stuff."

At the horrified looks on our faces, he interrupted his story to say, "Now, now. Don't worry. I'll send Flo down there to put things back together."

"Not good enough," I objected. "What the hell were they thinking? Are we suspects? What on earth could be our motive?"

Bad enough that we were involved in this murder mess, but to have cops touching our stuff was the last straw. I may not be a neat freak but I prefer to create my own disarray, not have someone else do it for me.

Sandra was appalled. Shoving one strand of shiny dark hair behind her ear, she stood up and brandishing her cell phone declared hotly, "My husband is an attorney. Maybe I'll just call him and see what he has to say about this. Suspects? The only thing we're guilty of is bad judgment." She glared at us. "I told you we should take a regular cruise. We wouldn't be in this mess if anyone had listened to me."

"Now, Miss Sandra," Hank said, "give me a chance to explain. You aren't suspects. Ain't no one thinks you are. They just dusted the entire boat for prints and they were lookin' for clues as to the whereabouts of Miss Svetlana and that husband of hers."

Slightly mollified, Sandra dropped back into her chair and huffily awaited Hank's next disclosure. If we thought we'd been shocked before, Hank's next words paralyzed us with astonishment. "It seems," he said, "that we have the perp."

"What perp?"

"For Skippy's murder. They got prints from Glenn's cabin and they matched Skippy's."

"So, Glenn is the perp?"

"No, actually not," Hank continued. "Seems that Skippy's prints weren't just in Glenn's cabin. Found them some other places as well. Found them in Martha and Miguel's cabin."

We were dumbstruck. "Miguel and Martha are the perps?" My voice was a squeak.

"Not Martha," Hank said. "They say Miguel done it. Miguel killed Skippy."

"But why on earth . . ." I blurted.

"Let me finish," Hank said. "Turns out they had Miguel's prints in the system. Him being an alien and all. So they compared prints from Glenn's cabin and found not only Skippy's prints but Miguel's. That's not enough to convict him, but when they confronted Miguel, he just plain broke down and confessed."

"But why . . ." we said, confounded by this unexpected turn of events.

"Okay, now this is just gonna blow you away," Hank explained. "Miguel had a thing for Glenn."

Five identical looks of disbelief showed on our faces. "Now, I know you might think this is pretty farfetched," Hank said, "but apparently true. So when Miguel found Skippy and Glenn having a heated argument he just couldn't help but get himself involved. Took matters into his own hands. Says they fought and he hit Skippy and he fell and hit his head."

"Wait," I asked. "Couldn't it have been Svetlana that Miguel was lusting after? Not Glenn?"

"'Peers that it was Glenn. That's what he said anyway. And those Key West fancy pants believe him. Or at least they plan to take him to Key West for questioning."

Sure enough, at that moment, we saw Good Cop and Bad Cop leading Miguel down the dock toward the police boat tied up nearby. He was a pathetic sight. His hands were shackled behind his back and he hung his head. Martha followed behind loudly proclaiming his innocence and demanding his release. As the cops loaded Miguel onto the boat, Martha stood on the dock sobbing while Flo tried to comfort her.

"So, what happened to Skippy after he hit his head?" I asked.

"Well," Hank said, "Miguel says he didn't wake up and didn't have a pulse so they figured he was dead."

"Who figured that?" Sandra asked.

"Glenn and Miguel. So they got that rug from Ned's cabin and rolled him up in it. Dragged him up to the deck. And tossed him over. Then, according to Miguel, they took the rug back to Ned's cabin and went about their business."

I recalled the noises I had heard that night. The strange thud and the shushing noises coming from the hall. It fit, I guessed.

"But doesn't that make Glenn guilty too?" Julie asked.

"Yep," Hank agreed. "Guilty of being an accessory. The charge would have to be manslaughter, but Glenn didn't want to take a chance on that so as we got closer to figuring it all out, he just up and vamoosed."

"Couldn't Miguel have confessed because Glenn did it and he wanted to protect him?" I asked.

Hank scratched his chin. "I s'pose it could have gone down that way. Them Key West guys will have to sort it out."

"But where does that leave your investigation into Captain Fairweather's death or disappearance?" I persisted.

"Doesn't really mean a thing," Hank said. "One crime isn't necessarily connected to another." The look on his face said he was skeptical, but he wasn't about to share confidences at this point.

"So, now what?" Ellie demanded. "When can we go home?"

"Yeah," chorused the others. "We can't hang out here forever."

"We have families. We have husbands," said Ellie.

"Well, some of us do," Julie added darkly.

"Can you ladies give me just another day?" Hank pleaded. "I think I can wrap it up by then."

Given that we had no choice in the matter, we agreed.

Hank's cell phone chirped and he snapped it open and pressed it to his ear. His expression was grim and after he completed the call he said, "I have something in the office that needs to be taken care of. Can you all stay put for a couple of minutes. I'll be right back."

The atmosphere in the bar was melancholy after Hank left. This vacation had definitely not turned out to be the carefree adventure we had anticipated. Grey and depressing Winslow, Ohio, was looking very attractive at the moment. Coconut Key may have been idyllic, but the circumstances were not.

"I have an idea," Ellie said. "Why don't we call home and have everyone come down here?"

"Sure." Julie's voice dripped sarcasm. "Why don't we book airline tickets for everyone? Who was it who won the lottery again? Sure wasn't me."

Suddenly Mary Linda, who had been pecking at her computer, whooped. "You guys! You guys, come here. Look at this."

We crowded around the screen. "Is that who I think it is?" Ellie asked.

"You gotta love Google," Julie said.

Sandra and I exchanged knowing looks. "I knew we'd find a connection," I crowed.

There on the screen was a much younger Svetlana mugging outrageously for the camera. It was a photo of the Tri-Sigma sorority girls from 1987. Svetlana and another girl, arms around each other, were dressed in Gibson girl type costumes and laughed as the other girls looked on.

"Who is that other girl?" Sandra asked.

"That's almost the best part," Mel said. "Let me explain."

"Tell!"

"I Googled Ned's father. Nigel Senior. And there is lots of info on him. Big billionaire and all. And there is a very nice bio. In the bio, of course, is the name of his wife."

Mel paused for effect. "Drum roll please," she said. "And the wife is one Alison Stanford Fairweather. So then I went to the Berkeley site for the years that Ned should have been there and looked for an Alison Stanford. I knew that Kate said they met at school. So I was surfing along and hit on this sorority picture and there is Alison in all her glory with . . ."

"Svetlana," we finished in unison.

"So, this means," Mel concluded, "that Svetlana must have known Ned. She was in the same sorority with his ex. Surely they must have at least met. Even if they were just acquaintances back then, why would they act like total strangers on the *Mirage*?"

"Unless," I said, "they didn't want anyone to know they knew each other. Pretty much what Svetlana said when we told her we'd seen her with Ned in Key West."

"Which brings us right back to the same old question," Sandra said. "What were they all up to?"

"I guess we know they were involved in Skippy's murder and we can presume that Skippy was blackmailing Glenn," Ellie said.

"We know that Glenn would inherit the company if Ned was out of the picture. And that Ned wasn't interested. And that Glenn had to be straight," Julie went on. "What if they knew all this back in the day? And always intended for Glenn to inherit. They'd have to come up with a way for him to look straight even if he wasn't."

"So," I guessed, "maybe Svetlana comes into the picture when Ned and Alison break up. She isn't in love with Glenn and hooks up with his brother, Ned. To help out both of them she marries Glenn, but continues her affair with Ned."

As the entire plan began to come into focus, we all spoke excitedly, interrupting each other.

"And then," I said, "Dad gets sick and it looks like this is it. They have to get rid of Ned so he won't be available to inherit. They come onboard the *Mirage* as the Livingstons and pretend not to know Ned. They know that if they stage Ned's death, Glenn is totally capable of sailing the *Mirage*. They plant Ned where I'm sure to find him."

"And little sleuth that you are, you fall right into the trap. You scream bloody murder and the games begin." Sandra beamed at me.

"Yes," I said, "but even better we have Hank all set to do the big favor for his benefactor, Ned. He agrees to declare that Ned is not just missing, but likely is dead. But he doesn't want to have to arrest Glenn for the crime because that would mess everything up, so he is royally pissed when Glenn gets himself involved with Skippy. He couldn't stay away from the gay bar in Key West and makes himself look all kinds of guilty."

"Which means that Hank has to try to keep the Key West cops out of the picture until he can conclude his own investigation into Ned's disappearance," Mel said. "But, stupidly, Glenn brings the cops down on his head and the whole plan is about to go up in smoke."

"And Glenn and Svetlana flee to avoid being arrested," I said. "Which is majorly stupid since they are sure to be tracked down. I don't think Good Cop and Bad Cop just fell off the lobster boat here. They may not have identified Glenn yet, but it's just a matter of time 'til his prints are traced."

I sucked in a breath and stared blankly at my friends. Where did all of this leave us? And where had Ned gone? And Glenn and Svetlana?

Chapter
Twenty-Seven

As if the day hadn't been astounding enough, Hank had
another surprise in store for us. Tired of cooling our heels
at the bar, we were debating going back to the *Mirage* in
spite of Hank's dictum to "just stay put." A bunch of liberated, not to mention restless, women like us couldn't be
ordered to follow directions. Grumbling among ourselves
we were perched on the edges of our chairs about to split
when Hank stomped into the bar.

Close on his heels were two unexpected visitors. The
first was a tall, dark-haired, dark-eyed man of Hispanic
descent. Clad in a sparkling white golf shirt with a logo
on the breast, he was all smiles as he strode over to us. As
he got closer, I could see that the logo was for Sunshine

Tours, the very company which had arranged our ill-fated cruise. It took a moment for my eyes to adjust as the second man entered the dim bar from the bright sunlight. But when they did, I recognized him immediately. It was Tony! The wild jeep driver from Fort Lauderdale.

"Tony!" we shouted.

He grinned at our shocked faces. "Hola, amigas," he said. "Como estan ustedes?"

Then he introduced his companion. "This is my father, Ricardo Moreno. He is the president and CEO of Sunshine Tours. He came down here to see what he can do to help you out of your predicament."

We were mesmerized by the sudden appearance of these two extraordinarily good-looking men. We did not know what to expect from them. Hank leaned against the bar, the expression on his face reminiscent of a proud father who has produced a pony for his children's birthday gift.

Ricardo began speaking and we hung on his words. "First of all, let me apologize. Profusely. For the circumstances you are in. Obviously, we couldn't have known what was going to happen when you set sail. And, quite frankly, I didn't find out about all of this until yesterday."

He glared at Hank with ill-disguised fury. "The sheriff here didn't even call us until last night. If he had made the call when you first put in . . . well, let's just say that I'd have been here in a flash."

Julie grinned at the irony. "With Tony driving? In a New York minute."

Ricardo Moreno clapped his son on the back, his anger dissipating when it appeared that his customers were not going to tar and feather him.

"Driving with Tony is always an adventure," he said. "Anyway, I have told the sheriff that he cannot hold you prisoner in Coconut Key and he agreed that he sees no real reason for you to stay here any longer."

"The thing is," Hank interjected, "the *Mirage* is still in police custody. I think it might be released by tomorrow."

"Good," Moreno said. "Then we'll wait 'til then and Tony can sail them back to Fort Lauderdale."

"We were supposed to go back days ago," I told Moreno. "What about flights home?"

"Sunshine Tours will arrange everything," he said. "We will get you where you want to go and you won't have to pay anything extra. Furthermore, we at Sunshine Tours regret what has happened and we want to offer you a full refund on your money as well as vouchers for a future sail at the time of your choice."

That seemed more than fair to me. And the others plainly agreed. In fact, the mood in the bar improved dramatically with Ricardo's announcement. Everyone began to speak at once, excitedly making plans for our return to civilization.

"We can finally go home and stop playing detectives," Julie said. "Or not. I still have to find out what Robert's up to."

Hank cornered Tony and his father in the back of the bar to have an animated discussion. Maybe about our status. Maybe about the Captain. I was itching to get within earshot to find out. And I might have if Mary Linda hadn't chosen that moment to drop her own personal bombshell.

Looking embarrassed, she started to speak and then stopped, a variety of emotions crossing her face. Confusion, fear, joy and shock warred with each other and her deep blue eyes were full of tears. She finally took a deep breath and blurted, "I have something to tell you guys." She looked at me and I nodded encouragement.

Mel obviously had second thoughts about making a big announcement, but having begun she was committed to going through with it. She hemmed and hawed and finally confessed. "I'm afraid that. I mean, I think I might be. I don't know if I am but I could be. I'm not really sure."

"What? We don't have all day."

"I think I might be pregnant." Mel scowled at us, daring anyone to say anything.

"I'm late," she announced in a dramatic tone. "And I'm never late."

"Too unscheduled, huh?" Sandra asked.

Mel giggled in spite of herself. "You gotta keep to a schedule. Apparently I didn't though."

Ellie vaulted out of her chair and hugged Mel before Mel even finished her announcement. "A baby. I love babies. And you will be a fantastic mom. Well, you already are but . . ."

"I'm not even sure yet," Mel told her. "I bought the testing kit thing, but I've been too scared to use it."

"Have you told Don?" Sandra asked.

Mel's face fell about a mile. "No. I didn't want to say anything until I was sure."

"He'll be over the moon," Julie said.

"I don't know. We never discussed kids. I mean, we have our own, but together we never talked about. And we're too old. I'll be wearing Depends before the kid is in elementary school."

"How long have you been sitting on this news?" Ellie demanded.

"Since the trip began," Mel admitted. "I did tell Kate before the Captain disappeared and since then it hasn't seemed like a good time for it. But with us going home soon, I just had to tell you."

Mel's news mobilized us. "Get that kit this minute," Ellie said, "and we'll do a group pregnancy test."

We started to go back to Mel's cabin to get the kit when we realized that the *Mirage* was still off limits. Key West investigators swarmed over the boat and we were stranded ashore.

"I bet we can get another kit in Coconut Key," Julie said. "Then we can do it now."

"Wait just a darn second," Mel protested. "Even if we buy a new kit, where are we gonna do the test? I don't think I want to find out I'm having a kid while I'm standing in the stall at the Seven-Eleven."

"It's not like you are giving birth at the Seven-Eleven," I said. "Do you or do you not want to know once and for all?"

Mary Linda rolled her eyes and then smiled. "I do. And I want you all with me for moral support. Let's do it."

At that we trooped out of the bar in search of a pregnancy test kit. We canvassed the few stores on the main street and then hit pay dirt at a tiny grocery on Ocean Avenue. Julie, who had been delegated to search the shelves while the rest of us paced the sidewalk, darted out the door clutching a brown paper bag. She called to us in triumph, "Voilà. I've got it." And she thrust the bag into Mary Linda's reluctant hands.

Mel sneezed as she pulled a dust-covered box from the bag. "You expect me to use this," she objected. "It's all dusty. It's probably a hundred years old. It won't work."

I snatched the moth-eaten box from her. "See, it's still good. Doesn't expire for months yet." I waved the box under Mel's nose and she recoiled as if I had stuck a spider in her face.

"Let's go back to the Coconut Bar and do it," Ellie said.

We surrounded Mary Linda and herded her, protesting every step of the way, toward the bar. It was a bit cramped in the bar's restroom. Four of us crammed ourselves into the meager space while Mary Linda eased into the only stall and closed the door. The only sound was the tick tick of the battery-powered Flamingo wall clock and the rustle from behind the stall door.

Finally, Mary Linda wailed plaintively, "I can't go with you standing there. Can't you go outside or something?"

After a brief consultation, we decided that I would stand watch in the bathroom while the other three would go outside to hover. And it wasn't long before Mary Linda came out of the stall, zipping her capris over her flat stomach and clenching the stick in a death grip. I stuck my head out the door and signaled the others so that the five of us were stuffed into the claustrophobic bathroom when the stick turned blue and Mary Linda's face turned green.

"Oh, my God," she breathed. "I'm gonna be a mommy." And then it struck her. "And Don is gonna be a daddy."

By the time we emerged from the restroom, Hank and the Morenos had retired to Hank's office to iron out the details of our departure from Coconut Key. Giddy with excitement and, in Mel's case, apprehension, we swarmed outside and plunked ourselves down at one of the umbrella tables to figure what to do next. A much subdued Flo approached us and said glumly, "Can I bring you anything?"

One look at her face was all anyone needed to see that usually exuberant Flo was not herself. Ellie asked, "Flo, are you all right? You don't look too good."

"Oh, Miss Ellie, I'm sure not," Flo said. "This thing with Martha is just heartbreaking." And Flo did look as if she might burst into tears.

"Sit down, Flo," I said. "Can we help?"

Flo sank into the remaining chair and put her head in her hands. Her face was tear-stained when she looked up. She scrubbed her face with shaking hands. "I just feel so dang bad for them. Martha and I kind of bonded last night, you know, and she told me stuff about her life that made me feel so ashamed of myself. Here I was all mean and snippy with her because I didn't want her on my turf and you wouldn't believe how amazing she is."

We waited for Flo to continue, and when she didn't I prompted her, "How is she amazing actually?"

"Oh." Flo snapped out of her reverie. "Well, I trust you not to tell a soul what I'm about to tell you. Do you promise?"

"More secrets," Sandra said. "Too many if you ask me."

"We didn't," Julie said. "Tell us about Martha, Flo. We won't tell." She glared at Sandra daring her to say another word.

"Okay," Flo said. "I feel like I'm going to suffocate if I can't tell someone. Martha and I really hit if off. You could have hit me over the head with a lobster trap, I was so surprised. I thought she was all hoity- toity, but she wasn't. Well, yeah, at first she was a bit snotty, but when we started cookin', we had a good old-fashioned gal gabfest. She even shared her recipes with me. The thing is she told me about her and Miguel. When she was head chef at one of them fancy restaurants in New York City, she had a real good friend. This friend, Rosa, come from Mexico and had her visa and all that. She was legal. But Rosa had this brother who couldn't get a visa, cuz he done some crime when he was just a boy in Mexico City. His record was keepin' him from coming to the United States. And he had nothin' in Mexico and Rosa knew he could do better in the States. You can probably guess what came next."

"Maybe," I said, "but tell us."

"Martha has this great big ole heart and she and Rosa talked about it for a real long time before Martha volunteered to go down to Mexico and get him to the States the only way the two of them could figure. She went and married him. Got him a Green Card and got him to New York. Fooled them officials at Immigration. Them with all their questions. And convinced them that Martha and Miguel were in love and the marriage was legit."

"Well, what Martha didn't know when she married him was that Miguel is gay. But she loved her friend Rosa so much that she just played along with the wedding story and so she and Miguel was gonna live 'happily ever after.' Course she wasn't too thrilled when she learned that Miguel didn't like girls, but what the hell, she figured she would stay married for the five years 'til he can get his citizenship and then she'd be able to divorce him. Wasn't like, she said, that she had some hottie hangin' around wanting her."

"So, anyway, they were in New York for a while and Miguel found some jobs. Nothing too great but it kept him off the streets. He even thought about going to school, but he had to learn English first and, before too long, Martha got offered the job on the *Mirage*. They needed a deck hand too, so Miguel and she came on as a pair. She is fond of him, she says, but more like a little brother. Still, she's pretty devastated about this turn of events. She claims that Miguel is too soft-hearted to have killed anyone."

"Martha says she suspected that Miguel had the hots for Glenn, but she told him Glenn was off limits. She was totally shocked to have the cops look at Miguel as a suspect, and then he up and confesses that he killed Skippy."

"I hate for her to be in this mess. And poor Miguel. Y'all shoulda seen him. He looks like he don't even know where he is."

"Wow," I said. "That is quite a story. Does Martha think Miguel really did it?"

"She's pretty sure he didn't do it. Says she thinks he mighta confessed just to take the heat off Glenn. Or he coulda done it cuz Skippy was making trouble and maybe things got out of hand. No way he would have done it on purpose. If he did it, it was an accident, Martha says."

"I do know one thing," Sandra said. "Miguel needs a good lawyer or he'll end up behind bars for sure."

Flo looked discouraged for her new friend. "How's he gonna find a lawyer let alone pay one? They don't have money for that."

Sandra tucked a strand of hair behind her ear. "Let me call Allen. That's my husband," she told Flo. "He's a lawyer and maybe he knows someone who knows someone. We can try to get them some help."

Relief lit Flo's face. "Would you do that for them? Them two are about to be plumb crushed by the system."

Sandra, cell phone in hand, set off to find a spot with good reception to make her call. Leaving the others huddling with Flo, I went after Sandra. She was just closing her cell phone when I found her propped against the side of the office building, legs stretched out in front of her. I sank down beside her and leaned my back against the warm wooden siding. I pulled my sunglasses from my pocket, put them on, and peered absently at the blue cloudless sky and the bright Florida sun. We sat in silence for a moment enjoying the warmth and the solitude. Finally, Sandra said, "I got a couple of names from Allen. I kind of remembered that he had some law school buddies who live in Florida. They aren't in the Keys, but might be persuaded to come down to help out. Allen was going to call both of these guys and see if either one is available. I can give the names to Martha. She'll need to contact them."

"That's really great," I said. "Helps to have friends in high places."

Sandra grinned. "Twarn't nothin'. I don't even know if they can help, but it's a start."

I scratched a peeling spot on my leg and gazed at the ocean. "That was some story Flo told us."

"I imagine it was true. I don't think Flo is capable of making up something like that."

"I believed her, too. Or I believed that she believed Martha anyway. There is a difference."

"Too true. Now what do we do?"

Before I spilled my idea, I wanted to hear what Sandra had in mind. So, I said, "Go home?"

"Possible," she said, "but I hate to leave before we finish what we started."

"Are you saying that you want to continue our investigation into Ned's disappearance and Skippy's untimely demise? I was under the impression that you thought I was a nut case."

"Not so much," she said. "And I don't have anything urgent to make me want to go home. Neither of us has kids at home like Ellie and Julie."

"Or one in the oven," I added in amusement, "like Mary Linda."

"Actually, I was thinking of staying down here for a few more days," she said. "Tony's dad said he'd fly us home, so airfare shouldn't be an issue. And I hate to run off and leave things in limbo. Frankly, this is more interesting than anything in Ohio."

"Except Allen, of course," she added with a wink.

"Yep," I said. "We do need closure. And Scott will be okay with it, too."

"So, we stay?"

"We stay. Let's go tell the others."

Ellie, Julie and Mel were still sitting under the shade of the umbrella with Flo. They were drinking iced tea and didn't appear to have a care in the world. Until you got closer and could see their faces. Mel was an unbecoming shade of green. Her eyes were hidden behind dark glasses, but she perched on the edge of her chair like a bird about to take flight. Hopefully she had a direct shot at the restroom. Ellie scribbled notes in her notebook, while Julie had once again retreated into her own world. Flo dictated recipes to Ellie, but kept glancing around distractedly as if she expected to be interrupted at any moment.

They snapped to attention when they spotted us. "Did you have any luck?" Flo asked. Sandra handed her the slip of paper with the names and phone numbers and explained what she had learned. Flo bounded from her chair and gave Sandra a quick effusive hug. "I'll just take this to Martha," she said as she rushed toward the police boat tied to the dock.

"I'm really sorry I got us into this," I apologized for the zillionth time.

"You didn't know," Ellie assured me.

Mel said, "I pretty much made my own mess." She hesitated and added, "Or my own miracle. Whatever. But I can't wait to tell Don, so I want to get home as soon as I can."

"Don't worry, Kate," Ellie said. "I never would have thought of doing a cookbook if it hadn't been for this adventure." She ran a hand through her spiky hair. "Or gotten this new look. Or a tattoo, either, for that matter. It's all good for me."

That left only Julie and as she was about to speak her cell phone played its distinctive tune. She glanced at the caller ID and a look of pure joy crossed her face. "It's Robert," she exclaimed. "I've got to take this. 'Scuse me, guys."

"Robert," she breathed into the phone, "I've been trying to reach you for ages."

And she hurried to the dock to find some privacy.

Chapter
Twenty-Eight
Julie

Julie snapped her cell phone shut and scowled at it. The call from Robert hadn't gone well from the outset. He was furious with her. What with static and generally poor reception, she wasn't positive whether Robert was more angry because she had spoiled his surprise or because she hadn't trusted him. Undoubtedly the latter. How, she wondered, would any sane woman trust a man who for weeks (weeks!) went out the door every morning and returned every night and let her assume he was going to his job when he'd been laid off? She was well within her rights to be upset and hurt, and yes, dammit, angry.

They'd both let off steam and said some things they regretted, but they were cut off before they could resolve anything. Robert had been trying to explain something complicated about ovens and leases when suddenly he was gone. Julie re-dialed and re-dialed again, but it was no use. Robert was gone and nothing, absolutely nothing, was clear to her.

Still seething, Julie paced from one end of the dock to the other. Okay, she fumed, I guess I can assume he isn't having an affair. Or at least one of the heart. His affair seemed to be more one of the kitchen. But the Robert she knew and loved all these years didn't cook. He had never shown one iota of interest in doing so. Even the traditional guy thing of cooking steaks on the grill held no appeal. I don't get this at all, Julie fretted.

The only way to get to the bottom of this, she concluded, is for me to get home. No more frittering away her time in this Godforsaken tropical hole-in-the-wall. Julie decided she had to be on the next plane heading north.

Julie decided to find out what progress Hank and the Morenos had made in orchestrating their departure. Feeling a bit more in control of her emotions, she let herself into the ramshackle office building. She saw Hank, Tony and Ricardo in Hank's office. She heard them talking, but couldn't make out what they were saying. They hadn't heard her come in, and she leapt at the chance to do a bit of creative eavesdropping. She congratulated herself on having worn her sneakers as she sidled soundlessly to the door and backed out. She scuttled around the side of the building and positioned herself under the window so that she could hear their conversation.

"I guess that's it then," Ricardo Moreno said.

"I just wish things had turned out different," Hank said. "Ned was a good friend to me and Flo."

"Ned was a good man," Tony agreed. "Damn shame about him."

"It wasn't supposed to turn out like this," Hank said.

"What do you mean?" asked Ricardo. "How was it supposed to turn out?"

Hmm, Julie thought. Perhaps Hank hadn't meant to say so much.

"I just never thought old Ned would die on the seas," Hank said. "That's what I meant."

Julie chanced a quick glimpse through the window. Ricardo stared at Hank as if trying to read his mind. "I'm sure that's all you meant."

Julie scrunched lower beneath the window and motionless tried not to make a sound. She held her breath until Ricardo spoke again. "Hank, you can tell Tony and me if you know more. I'm gonna deal with the family and insurance and I need to know everything."

There was a pause and then Hank said, "I don't know nothin' 'bout nothin'."

"Come on, Hank," Tony urged him. "There's something you aren't telling us."

"I'll just say this," Hank said, "you don't need to worry 'bout the family or insurance. Ned took care of his own."

"Meaning?" Ricardo asked.

"Nothing," Hank repeated stubbornly.

Julie peeked through the window and then quickly ducked back down. How was she going to explain herself if they discovered her skulking out here? Oh well, she'd think of something.

"Okay," Ricardo said, "I'm asking you one last time. You're in charge of the investigation into Ned's death or disappearance. What do you think happened to him?"

"My evidence tells me . . . supports the theory . . . that he's dead."

"Very convenient for his brother then isn't it?" Ricardo suggested.

Taken off guard, Hank asked, "What do you know about any brother?"

"I've done my research. You think I wouldn't know that one of my captains was a member of the infamous Fairweather family and that he was in line to inherit a gazillion bucks some day? Or that he had a brother in line to inherit if Ned didn't? Don't you suppose I can put one and one together and come up with at least two billion? Easy to see who's going to gain the most by Ned's death, isn't it? If Ned is dead, I'd bet my ass that his brother is behind it."

"Okay," Hank admitted, "it does look bad for the brother. If the brother had been anywhere around, we'd be looking at him as a suspect. But since that wasn't the case, well, I guess we can just leave it as a mystery. Nothing to prove exactly who might have done it."

Ricardo drummed his fingers on the desk. "Right. I guess you considered that one of those women might have had a fling with Ned. He was a good-looking guy. Maybe one of them killed him."

Julie gasped in outrage. One of them! How dare he! We're from Winslow, Ohio, she thought. We're nice people. The nerve.

"No. No way. Them ladies are a class act. They wouldn't a done it. And no motive. Nothing to make me look at them."

316

Well, Julie thought huffily, at least Hank is a gentleman. She remained paralyzed in her hiding place.

"Well, then, maybe it was Martha or Miguel," Tony said. "The police in Key West think Miguel killed some gay grifter type. What's another killing if you've done one?"

"You two are barking up the wrong damn tree," Hank shouted. "It wasn't like that."

"Then how was it?" Ricardo demanded.

Julie heard the wheel on Hank's chair squeak and she peered over the window sill and saw Hank slumped unhappily in it.

"Dang it," Hank said. "Just what do you want from me, Señor Ricardo?"

"How about the truth?"

Hank heaved a sigh. "You ain't gonna give up are you?"

Ricardo answered, "I'm not going to do anything to jeopardize my company or Ned's family. I just need to know the truth so I can deal with it."

"Oh, all right," Hank said, "I'll tell you everything I know. But keep in mind that I'm the sheriff here and I will close this investigation how and when I decide. Got it?"

"Of course."

"Ned came to me and said he was in a jam. He said he was gonna be forced into the family business if he didn't do something about it. He said his dad had issues with his little brother and would never let his brother take over as long as Ned was alive. I asked him why he couldn't just turn it down, and he said that his dad had fixed it so's Ned's sons would get nothing if Ned walked out. The only way he could protect his sons and make sure his brother got the business was for him to die."

"Naturally, I didn't know what Ned wanted, so I said I'd do whatever I could to help. See, I owed Ned a huge favor. He loaned me and Flo the money to buy the Fresh Ketch and the Coconut Bar, and he never asked for one penny of interest and he gave us all the time in the world to repay the loan. I owed him."

"Go on."

"So Ned said if he vanished off the *Mirage,* would I see to it that he was declared dead? He said he'd arrange it so's the whole thing took place in my jurisdiction. All I had to do was announce that he was dead. He said he'd be able to set himself up somewheres else. He could get papers and all that. All I had to do was say he was dead."

"Now, how," he asked, "was I supposed to turn him down?"

"Did he by any chance mention how he'd disappear or what would happen to the passengers and to the *Mirage?* Trivial details like that?" Ricardo asked.

"No. We agreed that the less I knew, the easier it would be for me to just declare him dead."

"And that's it?" Ricardo wanted to know.

"Not quite," Hank replied. "I figured out one piece of this that Ned didn't tell me. Seems there was a vacant cabin on the *Mirage* before this last trip. And so Ned called his brother, and he and his wife hustled down here from Nebraska and hopped on board. Didn't call himself Fairweather, though. But I recognized him right away. Not going to forget that little twirp."

"I saw him one other time when Ned was down this way. He didn't leave the boat, but I saw him anyway. And I never forget a face."

"Anyway," Hank continued, "when the *Mirage* put in to the Fresh Ketch to get some repairs done, there he was. Ned's brother in the flesh. Name of Glenn. Course he was calling himself by another name and he had that doctor lady with him, but I knew it was Ned's brother."

"Doctor lady?" Ricardo asked.

"Oh, that's another thing," Hank said. "One time Ned came down on the *Mirage*. Just him and this doctor lady. She seemed nice enough and she looked at Ned like she wanted to eat him for dessert. Didn't see her 'cept that once, 'til she turned up on the *Mirage* with that Glenn and said she was his wife. Talked funny, too, but it was the same one. Like I said, I never forget a face."

"Shit," Ricardo muttered, "Shit, shit, shit."

"You got that right, Dad," Tony said.

Julie didn't dare move. She didn't want the men to discover her and maybe they'd reveal something she didn't already know.

"So what you're saying," Ricardo concluded, "is that Ned's brother and his wife, who presumably was also Ned's girlfriend, came down here and got on the *Mirage* pretending to be ordinary passengers."

"Yep."

"And I'm not so stupid as to think they didn't have an ulterior motive for being here. I imagine that you think this brother, what's his name, was here to help stage Ned's death."

"Yeah," Hank admitted. "His name's Glenn. But it got a bit sticky when Glenn did some real dumb stuff. Really pissed me off him being so stupid. Dated this Skippy. The one who turned up dead in his gold skivvies. Then this here Miguel, the deck hand, confesses to killing Skippy.

But no one with half a brain really thinks Miguel did it. I personally think Glenn did it and Miguel is covering for him. Skippy, according to them Key West types, was a bad dude. Possibly blackmailing Glenn. The cops don't know . . . yet . . . that Glenn is Ned's brother. Won't take them long to figure it out, though. So, the quicker I act the better."

"Oh, my God," Ricardo moaned. "This just gets better and better. It can't play out any way but that the authorities will bring the brother, Glenn is it, into custody and he'll end up in prison and this whole thing will be for nothing. And my company gets all this bad publicity. Gay dead guys. Missing captains. No one will ever want to take a Sunshine Tour again."

Julie wriggled to a more comfortable position crouched beneath the window. Her back ached and her quads burned. Definitely need to do more Jazzercise when I get home, she decided. She wasn't sure how much longer she could stay there before her muscles collapsed. She was formulating an escape plan when Hank's phone rang. She froze. This spying business was sure tough on the body.

Julie pressed her ear against the wall hoping to hear more clearly. Hank's voice was low and troubled. From Hank's end of the conversation, Julie could tell only that someone on the other end of the line was offering him information. "No," she heard him say. Then, "No, I didn't. I haven't heard that. Send me the manifest. Yeah, I will. Thanks a lot. Sure thing. Bye."

There was silence in the office, the only sound the thunk of a beer bottle as it smacked a surface. Finally, she heard Tony say, "Hank, what is it? You're white as a sheet."

Hanks's reply made Julie bolt upright in astonishment. She cracked her head on the window sill and toppled over in a heap. Struggling to get to her feet, she held her aching head with one hand and pulled herself up by holding the window ledge. Unfortunately, her right foot had fallen asleep and collapsed when she put her weight on it, throwing her forward into the hibiscus. The noise drew Hank and the Morenos to the window and they spotted Julie sprawled in the hibiscus bushes.

"So, little lady," Hank said, gazing down at her, "did you hear everything you wanted to hear?"

Julie pushed a twig out of her face and tried to regain some semblance of dignity. Rubbing her head, she disentangled herself and stumbled to her feet. "I don't know what you are talking about," she said haughtily. "I was just taking a stroll and thought I'd pick a few of these flowers."

"Sure you were," Hank said. "Why don't you run along and tell the other ladies what you heard. It's gonna be big news real soon anyway."

Julie looked him in the eye. "I have no idea what you think I heard."

She started toward the bar and then turned and called back to the three dumbfounded men still staring out the window. "And I certainly hope that you have made all the arrangements to get us out of this place." Then she limped off with as much poise as she could manage with twigs in her hair and dirt stains on her shorts.

"What was that?" Ricardo said.

Chapter
Twenty-Nine

Good Cop and Bad Cop finally finished their CSI work on the *Mirage* and cleared us to go onboard. We retreated, flip flops dragging with dread, to our cabins to pack. We felt violated by the ordeal. After all, we weren't the criminals. We just felt as if we were treated that way.

Mel and I had our cabin to ourselves and she immediately vanished into the head. I heard water running and splashing. I was re-folding a stack of tank tops that had been tossed aside by the overzealous cops, when Sandra materialized in the doorway.

Holding a hair pick in one hand and a tube of gel in the other, she looked strangely perplexed. Evidently she had been halted in the middle of doing her hair. Since there is almost nothing that would prevent Sandra from being seen in her usual put-together state, I knew something was definitely amiss.

"Nice 'do," I told her. "You trying a new look?"

She glanced at herself in the mirror. "Oh, this. I got distracted." She looked bemused. "Kate, I just heard something on the radio."

"Yes," I said. "A Jazzercise song?"

"Be serious. A news bulletin."

Now she had my attention. "They just said that a small commuter plane had crashed into the ocean and all aboard were missing and presumed dead. Took off from Key West last night," she said.

"Well, that's too bad. I hate it when that happens, but why do you look like your mother was onboard?"

"Not my mother. Ned!"

"What? You must be kidding. They said that? How do you know that?"

"It was on the news. The news guy said that one of the passengers was one Nigel Edward Fairweather."

"But that's not possible. Or is it?"

Mary Linda came out of the bathroom in time to hear Sandra's pronouncement. She leaned against the bunk and looked at us oddly. "Um," she began, "you guys I have kind of a confession to make."

"You're having twins?" Sandra guessed.

Mary Linda gazed at the stick in her hand as if she had forgotten she was clutching it. "No, not that. Although I did just do the pregnancy test again. The one I had. And . . ." She waved the blue stick in the air. "I'm still pregnant."

Our attention diverted from the news bulletin, Sandra and I pounced on Mel and twirled her around the room in celebration. "No," she protested. "Wait. Stop. I have to tell you something."

We stopped spinning and regained our composure. "Sorry," I said, "we do tend to get carried away."

"You think?" Sandra said. "What big confession do you have to make, Mel?"

Mel looked at me. "Remember the number you found scribbled on that bank envelope? From Ned's cabin?"

"Definitely. I thought maybe it was some kind of confirmation number. For a flight or something. I wanted you to check it out on your computer."

"Here's the thing," Mel said. "Yesterday I was going to check it out, but the battery went dead on my laptop. And I figured I could borrow Hank's computer. In his office?"

"Hank caught me and I told him about the number and he said he'd check it out and for me not to worry and I just wanted to get out of his office and I just said he could do it and I figured nothing would come of it anyway so I. . . ." She ran out of breath and trailed off.

"So what you're saying is that Hank could have found out the flight or whatever that matched the number?" I asked. "He probably didn't bother, but how would that change anything if he had?"

Before Mary Linda could answer, Julie rushed in looking like she had done battle with an irate shrub. Hair full of twigs, one knee scraped and bleeding.

"What happened to you?"

"Long story. But not important at the moment. I've got other news that will rock your world."

More news? Things were happening way too fast. "What news?" I asked. "What could have happened more earth-shattering than the news bulletin Sandra heard that Ned died in a plane crash?"

Julie looked deflated. She sank onto the floor in exhaustion. "Damn. That was my news."

"Where did *you* hear it?"

"I was kind of listening . . . snooping . . . outside the window of Hank's office. And Hank got a call. After he hung up he was talking to Tony and his father." She paused. "He said, 'well now they won't never find him. Ned's dead. He died in a plane that went down.'"

"Did he seem surprised?"

"More like devastated. They must have been real good friends."

We stared at each other. Ned was dead? But not murdered on the *Mirage*? Killed in a plane crash? How?

The four of us found Ellie in the galley humming to herself and rummaging in the well-stocked cupboards and refrigerator. She had the place to herself since Martha was accompanying Miguel on the police boat transporting him to Key West. She stopped paging through Martha's recipe file and looked up as we entered. Her face fell at our expressions.

"Oh, no," she said. "You look like you just lost your last friend."

We settled ourselves around the galley table and I broke the latest news. I had just finished when Hank stomped in. He took in the scene before he said a word. His face was pale, his hands trembled and his eyes were glassy with despair. Wow, I thought, he really must have been a lot closer to Ned that we realized. Hank sure did look like he had lost more than a business associate.

Finally he said in a gravelly voice, "I 'spose Miss Julie told you 'bout the plane crash."

We nodded. Five bobble-head dolls. "Not much left for me to say," he went on. "Captain's dead for sure. I can close this investigation and you all can get back to your lives. Should be wrapped up soon."

He turned to leave, but I stopped him. "Wait a second. If you are saying that Ned died in that plane crash, then what was he doing lying on the floor all bloody? Where did he go between then and last night when he went down with that plane? Aren't you going to find the answers to those questions?"

"Nope," he said. "Ain't none of my business. He's gone. Case closed." He hitched up his baggy shorts, turned his back and retreated, leaving us staring at empty space.

"He's sure upset," Ellie said.

"Seems more upset than I would have figured him to be. When he hung up the phone after he learned about the crash, he was crushed. Was Ned that good a friend?" Julie observed.

"Must have been," I said.

Fifteen minutes after Hank's abrupt departure, we regrouped on deck in our bathing suits. With our days in the Florida sun numbered (perhaps to only one or two) and the prospect of the cold, grey Ohio winter looming ahead, we voted unanimously to take advantage of the sun while we still could. We felt guilty soaking up rays while death and despair lingered in the air, but we weren't going to let that stop us. Not after the last few days that we spent being grilled by Hank and the Key (Stone) West cops.

The sun worked its magic and soon we were in better spirits than we had been for days. The end of our "vacation" was drawing near and there was a general sense of relief. Julie, Ellie and Mel were anxious to leave Florida behind. Sandra and I disclosed our plan to stay behind for a few days to "wrap up our investigation." I believe we used the word "closure."

The others hesitated to abandon us (their words), but didn't take a lot of convincing to agree that we needed to finish what we had started. We pointed out that the three of them had pressing concerns at home, while Sandra and I had no immediate need to return.

The welcome aroma of suntan lotion wafted in the air while we sprawled in deck chairs and paged through the fashion magazines that had gone untouched while we played detective. We avoided any discussion of Ned or Skippy. No one, it seemed, wanted to disturb the tranquility of the afternoon.

Before long Tony and Ricardo Moreno came by to explain our options. They felt that it was best to sail the *Mirage* to Key West rather all the way back to Fort Lauderdale. Something about weather and the length of the trip. We could catch a flight from Key West to Miami and from there to Ohio. It could all be arranged quickly if we agreed. When Sandra and I advised Ricardo that we wanted to stay a bit longer, he was eager to accommodate us. He offered to book rooms in a small hotel that would put us up for as long as we wished. It was settled that Tony would pilot the *Mirage* and we would leave for Key West the first thing the following morning.

We spent the rest of the afternoon doing nothing more taxing than pouring a drink or reapplying sunblock. As the sun began to sink and the temperature dipped, we stirred ourselves and apathetically considered going below. It was at this moment that Flo bustled down to the *Mirage* and broke into our self-imposed stupor by flinging the day's edition of *The Coconut Keynote* (the local newspaper) at us.

"HEIR TO FAIRWEATHER ELECTRONICS PERISHES IN PLANE CRASH," screamed the headlines.

"Thought y'all would want to see this," Flo said as she came aboard. She was puffed up by her role as bearer of bad tidings.

I snatched the paper and began to read it aloud while the others crowded around and tried to read over my shoulder.

A small commuter plane carrying six passengers in addition to the pilot and co-pilot crashed into the ocean last night approximately 30 miles south of Key West, near Coconut Key. The Key West Charter plane, a Beechcraft King Air, disappeared about ten minutes after take-off. Flight controllers state that the pilot had declared an emergency and asked for clearance to return to Key West. The plane went down in the ocean before it could land at Key West Airport. The Coast Guard and Key West police boats have been on the scene and have found no survivors.

Among the passengers aboard the ill-fated plane was Nigel Edward Fairweather, 41, Lincoln, Nebraska. Fairweather was the son of Nigel Edward Fairweather, Senior, President and CEO of Fairweather Electronics, a multi-billion dollar electronics empire. Fairweather Senior, is reportedly critically ill at his home in Lincoln and expectations had been that the younger Fairweather would take over upon his death.

Nigel Fairweather Junior, had been the subject of a police investigation in Coconut Key. The captain of a chartered sailboat, the Mirage, *owned by Sunshine Tours, Fairweather had been reported missing and presumed dead. Sheriff Hank Dayton, of Coconut Key, stated that he believed Fairweather was the victim of a criminal attack onboard the* Mirage. *Dayton told the* Keynote *that he considered the case to be closed and that he did not expect any survivors of the crash.*

"All we have found is an oil slick and some personal items floating on the water. The National Transportation Safety Board (NTSB) is on its way down to investigate, but we are certain this accident was caused by engine failure and that all aboard, unfortunately, died," Dayton told the Keynote.

The article went on to list the names of the other passengers and the pilots of the plane. There wasn't any mention of Glenn or his role or of the future of Fairweather Electronics, but we knew it couldn't be long before his name popped up and questions about his whereabouts were asked. I finished reading the article and looked up into the stunned faces of my four friends.

"There it is in black and white," I said.

"Hank's holed up in his office with Ben Gullion of the *Keynote*. Been there all afternoon. The press is on this story like racoons in a garbage pail." Flo was eager to tell us everything she knew.

"This is some story," I said. "I think the national media will pick it up in no time and then there will be all kinds of reporters asking us what we know. Better for us not to be here when that circus begins."

"Good thing we're leaving tomorrow morning," Julie said. "I really don't want to talk about this."

No one disagreed.

That evening we hosted an impromptu farewell party aboard the *Mirage* with Hank and Flo as our invited guests. Ellie chose recipes from Martha's extensive file and raided the freezer and cabinets for supplies. We wanted Flo to be our honored guest to repay her for her kindness over the last few days, but she refused to be waited on. She preferred to pitch in to help Ellie in the galley.

Ellie read and rejected several selections and called to us, "Salmon? What about salmon with an apricot glaze?" or "How about some grouper in a macadamia nut crust?" or "Can I bring you some crab puffs?"

We cracked open several bottles of good wine we found stashed in the larder. And since Ellie locked us out of the galley, we lounged on the deck sipping wine and enjoying the sunset. Even Mel looked perkier as she drank water adorned with a lemon slice. Thoughts of going home buoyed us.

Hank, though, was not his former outspoken self. He was dressed in neat khakis and a conservative golf shirt and was somber and subdued. Even sad. He tolerated each of us hugging him and thanking him for his efforts, but he gruffly shoved us away in turn. He seemed embarrassed by our gratitude. "I ain't done nothin'," he protested time and again.

He accepted a beer and then, lost in thought, sank into a deck chair. Occasionally his cell phone rang and he answered questions and issued orders in a crisp authoritative voice. "The news is out," he told us in a melancholy tone. "Everyone and his Great Aunt Sally is heading to Coconut Key. That plane crash and Ned bein' on the plane is major news."

We cringed at the thought of hordes of newspaper and television reporters and photographers and film crews descending on the little town of Coconut Key. It didn't take a rocket scientist to figure out that we would be the target very soon. It wasn't a heartening notion.

In spite of everything, we managed to enjoy a peaceful and pleasant dinner. Flo and Ellie emptied the pantry in honor of our last night in Coconut Key. One platter followed another and wine flowed freely. Shrimp dusted with Florida spices, grouper stuffed with crab, fresh wahoo sauteed in garlic butter, fresh baby asparagus in a light lemon sauce. Enough food for the navy. Tony and Ricardo stopped to offer us their assistance and stayed to savor the repast.

We had an unspoken agreement not to speak of depressing things, but as we finished the meal and settled back with glasses of wine or cups of coffee, the talk drifted to the strange vacation cruise we had nearly completed. Five inquisitive women couldn't possibly avoid the topic forever.

"Where on earth do you suppose Glenn and Svetlana are?" Julie asked. We knew they hadn't shown up yet in Key West. The *Honor* docked there without them aboard. The captain, according to Hank, told the Key West authorities that he put them ashore some twenty miles from Key West.

Julie giggled. "Can you guys imagine Svetlana hacking her way through the mangroves?"

"In four-inch heels," said Mel.

"And a sarong," said Sandra.

"And poor Glenn," I said. "He'll get scratches all over those scrawny legs of his. I can see him fighting off snakes with his bare hands."

"No," Sandra said, "that would be Svetlana. I can see her as Jane of the Jungle."

"Truthfully, I wouldn't want to mess with her," Julie said. "She is the tough cookie."

We grinned, remembering Svetlana's phony accent. I figured that it would take more than a mere mangrove and some snakes to stop her.

Picturing the two of them in some godforsaken swamp might have been funny in a demented way, but we knew that wherever they were they weren't laughing. They were on the lam.

Hank told us an all-points bulletin had been put out for them and they were wanted for questioning in the death of one Reginald Anderson MacComber III (known to us as Skippy). He was certain that it wouldn't be long before the Key West cops captured them. They didn't have the outdoor skills necessary to hide out in the mangroves for long.

It was late before we called it a night. We assured Flo that we would check on Miguel and Martha and call her with a report. Hank scurried off to deal with the incoming press corps and to schedule a press conference to discuss Ned's mysterious disappearance. Thankfully, it wouldn't take place until after the *Mirage* departed. Not that we believed we would totally escape the clutches of the eager press, but we might delay the confrontation until we reached Key West. We still harbored the blind hope that something else might divert the press from our trail.

Tony said goodnight and promised to be ready to set sail at first light. The final leg of our journey was about to begin.

Chapter Thirty

The next morning we were all up before daylight. I jumped out of my bunk and dressed hastily. I grabbed a cup of coffee from the galley and made my way to the deck in order to be there before Tony arrived. I wasn't alone. Sandra and Ellie were there already. We had barely said hello when Mel and Julie joined us. We were eager to set sail.

It was only a few minutes before Tony sauntered down the dock, accompanied by his father and a boy of about sixteen. The teenager wore baggy surfer shorts and a spotless white Sunshine Tours t-shirt. His dark hair was tied back in a ponytail and he sported an assemblage of earrings and silver chains, but he was showered and shaved and cheerful. Tony introduced him as his brother, Tommy, and told us he would act as crew on the *Mirage*.

Tony hopped on board and, with Tommy's assistance, was ready to set sail in record time. The sails were rigged, the gear stowed and Tony was about to fire up the outboard motor when Flo came running down the dock. Red-faced and puffing, she halted by the boat slip. "I just wanted to say goodbye again," she said, "and to tell you I hope you will come back to Coconut Key under happier circumstances. The bar is always open to you and your families."

Once again, we hugged Flo goodbye. We jumped back onboard and Tommy untied the lines and prepared to leap onboard himself as Hank dashed up. "Thought you'd want to see this morning's paper," he said. "And I wanted to wish you well." He tossed the paper onto the deck of the *Mirage*, and put his arm around Flo's shoulders.

"Good luck and God bless," they called as the engine sputtered to life, and Tony steered us away from the Fresh Ketch Marina and toward the ocean and Key West.

I picked up the newspaper and unrolled it. The story of Ned and his fatal final plane trip was still the front-page story. Today's headline just added a few more gory details. Next to a picture of Ned was one of an older man who bore a striking resemblance to our former Captain. The older man, though, wore a look of impatience and scowled fiercely into the camera. One could imagine that his was not a warm and winning personality. Under the two photographs the headline declared, "HEAD OF FAIRWEATHER ELECTRONICS CRITICALLY ILL. HEIR PRESUMED DROWNED IN FATAL CRASH." In a tiny font much farther down the page, the headline announced, "YOUNGER FAIRWEATHER SOUGHT IN UNRELATED CRIME BY KEY WEST POLICE."

"Damn," I said. "They've made the connection. It didn't take long, did it?"

"They've got some of the facts, " Sandra said. "I guess the Livingstons' cover is blown."

"Right," I said. "How is Glenn going to show his face to stake his claim to the company? If he does, he'll be arrested as an accomplice in Skippy's murder."

"And if he doesn't," Mel said, "there goes fame, fortune, and the whole plan is up in smoke."

No one had anything further to add. As we sailed into the sunrise each of us was preoccupied with her own thoughts.

A nice breeze caught the big white sails and they billowed and filled as Tommy hoisted them. We skimmed across the ocean as the day grew warmer and the sun rose higher. It was a Chamber of Commerce day in South Florida, perfect for our final sail on the *Mirage*. We made good time and soon recognized Key West on the horizon. It seemed like a lifetime ago that we had last been there. It was hard to believe that only a few days ago Ned was alive and Glenn and Svetlana masqueraded as a happily married couple. Martha indulged us with an unending array of goodies while Miguel silently kept the *Mirage* in tip-top condition. Things had changed so much, but Key West hadn't changed at all.

Tony dropped the sails and motored the *Mirage* into the mooring, and we spotted Wil waiting on the marina dock waving frantically. He was wearing an electric blue shirt of some silky material and skintight white jeans, his pedicured feet shod in kino sandals.

We agreed to accept Ricardo Moreno's offer to put us up in a hotel for our last night together in Florida. Our time on the *Mirage* had been interesting, and even fun, (when we weren't either frightened to death or seasick) but it was time . . . past time . . . to abandon ship and seek refuge on dry land.

We'd packed our bags and Tony planned to deliver them to the hotel, so there was nothing left for us to do onboard the *Mirage*. Tony directed Tommy to ferry us into the marina in the No See 'Em.

"Tony," Ellie said, "we're going to have dinner tonight at a place called Boys Will Be Boys. (This was news to the rest of us, but it did seem appropriate to have one final meal there.) Would you like to join us?"

Tony grinned gallantly and shook his head. "Thanks, but that isn't really my scene. I have some final arrangements to make for your return trip anyway. But thanks, Ellie, I appreciate the invitation."

Tommy maneuvered the dinghy close and we clambered aboard, giving the *Mirage* one final look before turning our attention to the dock and Wil who hopped up and down in anticipation. Ellie was the first to leap onto the dock and directly into Wil's arms. The two of them hugged and danced in a circle as the rest of us looked on in amusement.

We made a beeline for the Schooner Wharf Bar, sagged into chairs around a round wooden table and ordered drinks. We compared notes with Wil, bringing him up to date on our adventures, and he sat spellbound until Ellie turned to him and said, "Okay. Now I need to ask you something. Your e-mail said the police suspected you in Skippy's death. Why on earth would anyone think you killed him?"

"They just don't know me like you do," Wil said.

It occurred to me that we really didn't know Wil all that well. What had we done but share a few meals and a few minutes of conversation? Sure, he'd been Ellie's staunch-est ally when she traumatized herself with her haircut and tattoo, but did that constitute actually knowing him? I didn't think so and said as much. "How well do we really know you?" I asked him.

"Kate!" Ellie was shocked by my temerity. "Wil would not kill a fly, let alone a man."

"Excuse me," I said. "And you would know this exactly how?"

"I cannot believe you would suggest . . ." Ellie began in a huff.

"No, wait," Wil said. "Kate's right. You don't know me that well. And there might have been a teeny little reason why the police thought I could have been involved."

The waitress brought our drinks and we waited for her to leave so Wil could continue his story. It was deathly silent at our table as we sipped our drinks. Wil played with his glass and gave us a shamefaced look. "I think they might have suspected me because I was kind of dating Gino for a little while. Before he met that slime, Skippy."

"You did what?" Julie exclaimed. "Gino?"

"Yeah," Wil admitted. "Gino was a sweet boy before Skippy got his claws into him. I met him at Boys Will Be Boys and we were an item briefly. He really was a dear."

"And then what happened?" Ellie asked.

"Well, Skippy blew into town. Literally. On that sail-boat of his. He went around flashing cash. Probably stole it. Dressed fit to kill. He was good-looking in a sleezy way. Gino and I met him one night and Skippy made a play for Gino. Gino was an innocent and fell hook, line and sinker for Skippy. The rest is history. Gino and I broke up, and Skippy and Gino became an item."

Julie said, "Break-ups happen. Why would they think you murdered Skippy?"

Wil looked embarrassed. "I didn't take it all that well. I had been very fond of Gino. So, one night when they had the nerve, the unmitigated gall, to come into the bar while I was working, I kind of lost it. I mean I had a real hissy fit. If I recall correctly, I told Skippy he was a worthless slug and he had better watch himself, because I was going to beat him over the head with his own mast and stuff his undies in his mouth and toss him overboard."

"Uh, oh," Mel said.

"I was pretty unhinged," Wil said. "I wasn't going to hurt him, but there were lots of boys there that night who heard me. One of them might have mentioned it to the police and so . . ."

"But you aren't a suspect now are you?" Ellie asked, ready to do battle for her friend if necessary.

"No." Wil hung his head. "I had an alibi for the night Skippy vanished. I was with another boy." He paused, trying to gauge our reaction. "And he just happens to be the mayor's son. That was the end of the investigation."

"I guess it would be," Julie said.

When we finished our drinks we headed for the Key Rest Inn on Duval Street where Señor Moreno had arranged for us to stay. We found it easily and crowded through the door into a tiny lobby furnished with whitewashed bamboo chairs with floral print cushions. Matching curtains shaded the lobby from the sun and fresh flowers filled the air with their scent. Behind the counter a woman who could have been Flo's older sister, sat with her feet propped on the counter, a pencil stuck in her frowsy hair and a romance novel balanced in her lap. When we entered she leapt to her feet, simultaneously tugging her skirt down and running her hands through her hair. "I'm sorry," she said. "We don't get much activity around here this time of the week. I was expecting you, though." She pointed at the stack of luggage that took up most of the minuscule lobby. "Your stuff arrived an hour ago. Your rooms are ready."

"By the way," she added, "my name is Inez and I'll be here to help you any way I can. I've given you adjoining rooms on the third floor. I understand two of you will be staying a few days longer, so I gave you one of our best rooms. It overlooks the courtyard, so it's much quieter than the front-facing rooms."

Our rooms were sunny and cheerful with brightly colored bedspreads and more of the whitewashed furniture. Framed prints of the Keys decorated the walls. Sandra and I each sank gratefully onto one of the twin beds. "It's not moving," Sandra sighed.

I stretched out on my bed. "I hadn't realized how good it would feel to have solid ground under my feet."

Before we could relax too much, we were interrupted by banging on the door that connected our room with the one shared by the others. "Open up," Julie demanded.

I unlocked the door and let them in. Julie waved a piece of paper in my face, bursting with excitement.

"Tell them, Jules," Mary Linda prompted her. "Tell them what you found."

"What's the big deal?" Sandra asked. "Give it up."

Smugly, Julie produced the piece of paper. "I found this tucked into the outside pocket of my bag."

"Read it," Ellie said.

Julie cleared her throat, smoothed the paper, and began reading.

"Dear Julie, We didn't get the chance to say goodbye. Glenn and I had to leave in a hurry, but I wanted you and your friends to know that we're okay. Don't worry about us. It was great meeting you. I hope we can meet again some day. Lana."

I was stunned. "Where did that come from?"

"I told you. It was in my bag. And I know it wasn't there this morning. Someone put it there since our bags left the ship."

"Let's assume it was slipped into your bag before we got here," Ellie said. "Our bags sat around for at least an hour or two before we arrived."

"If that's true," I said, "maybe Svetlana or Glenn was here and left it. Maybe Inez noticed someone hanging around. Come on, Julie, let's go down and ask her."

Inez was engrossed in her novel when we approached the desk. She jumped when Julie cleared her throat. "Caught again." She grinned. "I'm just at the good part." She winked. "Can I get something for you?"

"We have a question," I said. "Before we got here did you notice a woman hanging around the lobby?"

Inez shook her head. "Nope. And I couldn't miss seeing anyone. This place isn't that big."

We gazed at the lobby. No one could hang out unobserved in the tiny space.

Inez looked thoughtful. "But now that you mention it, there was a rather odd gentleman who stopped by."

"What did this gentleman look like?" Julie asked. "Did he stay long?"

"Well," Inez said, "what I noticed was that the guy was tall and wearing the usual . . . you know, baggy cargo pants and a tropical shirt, baseball cap and sunglasses. I couldn't describe him any better than that."

"Did you speak to him?" I asked. "Did he say anything at all?"

"No," Inez said. "That's odd. I don't think he said a single word. In fact, he came in and sat on the loveseat and I thought he was waiting for one of the guests. I had to take some towels up to one-oh-three and when I came back he was gone. I never gave him another thought."

We thanked Inez and stepped into the elevator. As the door closed we looked at each other triumphantly. "Svetlana!"

"Must have been," I said.

Julie agreed. "She's tall enough to look like a man and in those clothes her . . . um . . . assets wouldn't be obvious."

"But why on earth would she take such a big chance? Why show up anywhere in Key West when she has to know that the cops are hunting for her and Glenn?"

Julie shook her head and shrugged. As the elevator reached the third floor, she said, "Friends don't let friends worry if they can help it. And we were friends. Sort of."

Chapter
Thirty-One

That evening at the farewell dinner at Boys Will Be Boys, we reminisced about the cruise and our former shipmates. "Where do you think Glenn and Svetlana have gone?" Ellie wondered aloud.

"And how will Glenn be able to take over Fairweather Electronics?" Julie asked. "They'll have to come out of hiding sooner or later, and then they better have alibis for the time of Skippy's murder."

"And the Captain's so-called disappearance," said Mary Linda. "Since he's gonna inherit a billion dollar enterprise, you'd think the authorities would be a bit suspicious. He might have killed Ned to get the company. People have committed murder for less."

"But," I said, "if Ned didn't actually die until that plane crashed, then Glenn couldn't have done it. Could he?"

"What about this?" I went on. "What if he helped Ned plan his disappearance, but then somehow sabotaged the plane he knew Ned would be on?"

"Yes," Sandra said. "Glenn is an engineer and he knows boats. I suppose he could have done that. But somehow I doubt it."

"Why?" I was determined to be devil's advocate. "That would account for what happened. Not to mention that Ned was involved with Glenn's wife."

Julie ran a hand through her dark curls. "So, what you're suggesting is that Glenn plotted with his brother to help him fake his death and then disappear. Then Glenn really killed Ned by causing a plane crash in a fit of jealous rage."

Wil picked up his half-empty wine glass and drained it. "That doesn't make sense. Glenn is gay. He didn't give a rat's ass who Svetlana slept with. And what about all the other people on that plane? Do you really think Glenn would have killed them too?"

Mary Linda toyed with the silver bracelet on her wrist. "But with Ned conveniently out of the way, he still is in line to inherit a billion dollars."

We all considered for a few minutes, an island of silence in the noisy restaurant. Finally, I said, "I seriously doubt that Ned cared about the money. I'd be willing to bet he would have gladly turned it over to Glenn. But if dear old Dad wouldn't do that if Ned was alive, well, then he'd just have to play dead. So, Ned disappears and 'dies' in a plane crash. Glenn inherits the fortune. What happens to Svetlana?"

"And, furthermore," Julie said, "who killed Skippy? Was it really Miguel or did Glenn do it?"

Wil looked over his shoulder at the crowded dining room and said quietly, "My money is on Miguel. He had a crush on Glenn and wanted to help. Things got ugly. I don't believe he meant to do it. I'd say it was accidental. But Glenn couldn't take the chance of having the spotlight turned on them before Ned could make his escape. One thing led to another and then things got out of his control."

Sandra shoved her dinner plate away and pushed back her chair. "That is one of the stupidest plots I've ever heard. Do they not watch television? Three college graduates who devise a plan as idiotic as that deserve to get caught. Personally, I'm going to the restroom." She marched away, her heels clattering on the tile floor.

"She does have a point," Ellie said.

I tossed around the various theories. "But they never expected anyone to actually investigate their so-called crime. Hank was onboard with the cover-up. He was ready to declare Ned dead, and then Glenn could go home and inherit. Glenn messed up big time when he got involved with Skippy."

Wil interrupted. "He wasn't exactly involved with Skippy, was he? I mean, Skippy was blackmailing him. I think Glenn just got caught in a bad situation. Wrong place. Wrong time."

Mary Linda scratched a peeling spot on her nose. "Glenn knew that dear old Dad wasn't going to be one bit happy about that old scandal resurfacing after he thought he'd buried it. And Glenn must have felt he deserved to be CEO of the company. After all, he worked there for years while Ned was sailing on the high seas."

"And sleeping with Svetlana," Julie said.

"What about Svetlana?" Ellie asked. "What happens to her now?"

I recalled the scene on the beach and the vision of Ned and Svetlana on the porch of the house in Key West. "My guess," I said, "is that she volunteered for all this to help Ned. And Glenn. We know they were all in college together. Svetlana and Ned were an item, but when they concocted this stupid plan, she married Glenn so he'd appear straight. Then Ned dies, Glenn inherits and, after a suitable amount of time, Svetlana divorces Glenn and vanishes. No one cares by that time and she can meet Ned wherever he is. They have new names, new identities, a new life."

Julie shook her head. "Katie, my love, you need to get a life. You have quite the imagination."

"But, couldn't that be the whole idea? Everyone wins. Except it appears, and I stress appears, that Ned died in a plane crash. Glenn and Svetlana are on the run, and when they get caught Glenn will be charged with murder or as an accessory. Dad will never relinquish the company to him then. The perfect plan has gone up in smoke."

"Hank sure looked devastated when he heard about the plane crash," Julie said. "Maybe he knows more than he's saying. Someone needs to talk to him. And to Flo. I have a feeling they are hiding something."

Sandra slid back into her chair and sighed. "Same topic, huh? Well, Kate and I will stick around and see what we can figure out. You three need to go home to your husbands and kids."

Later that night, Sandra and I sprawled on our beds in our pajamas and brainstormed. We had just formulated our plan of action for the next day's sleuthing when there was a knock on our door. We opened it to find Julie, Mel and Ellie standing there bearing a tray on which there was a bottle of wine, a bottle of sparkling grape juice, an array of fruits, cheese and crackers and five wineglasses bearing the logo of Sunshine Tours.

"The card says, 'Please accept our apologies. Come back anytime and enjoy a complimentary cruise.' And it's signed Tony, Ricardo and Tommy Moreno. Sunshine Tours," Mel told us.

"You can't beat that offer," Sandra said. "But do we want to take them up on it?"

"Maybe not right away," Ellie said. "But later . . . who knows?"

"I think I might have to find a more family-oriented cruise," Mel said.

"With babysitting services," I said. "Can you picture Martha babysitting?"

"I can," Julie said. "Probably makes homemade baby food."

"With recipe cards," Ellie added.

Laughing, we jammed into our tiny room and polished off the tray of goodies.

Chapter Thirty-Two

Early the next morning, the five of us congregated on the sidewalk in front of the Key Rest Inn surrounded by an odd assortment of suitcases and shopping bags. Ellie, Mary Linda and Julie wore traveling clothes, but Sandra and I dressed more flamboyantly. Sandra's skintight strapless, red dress and matching stilettos were on loan from Ellie. And I paired an orange, fuchsia, and lime green floral print sundress with towering three-inch platform sandals and huge sunglasses. The night before, fueled by wine and influenced by all those detective novels I like to read, Sandra and I devised a brilliant plan. We decided that as part of our covert operations we would pretend to accompany the others to the airport. Our outfits were designed to be so outrageous that anyone seeing us would be sure to remember us getting into the limo with the others. It seemed like an inspired idea at the time.

The Sunshine Tours limo pulled up to the curb, and Tony hopped out of the front seat. He grinned appreciatively at the two of us. "Just getting home from a night out?"

As the driver loaded the luggage into the trunk, Tony opened the rear door and ushered us into the plush interior. We sank into the buttery soft leather seats and Tony popped the cork on a bottle of champagne. As the others toasted and the limo pulled away, Sandra and I grabbed the duffle bag Mel handed us and climbed into the back seat. We closed the partition and slithered out of our gaudy dresses and high heels and changed into the baggy cut-offs and the Margaritaville t-shirts we had stowed in the bag. Within a few minutes we metamorphosed into typical, and we hoped unremarkable, Key West tourists. Stuffing our dresses into the duffle bag, we pulled on tennis shoes. I handed the bag to Mel and asked, "Do we pass?"

Tony's mouth dropped open and he started to laugh. "I never know what to expect from you guys. What are you doing? Going fishing?"

"In a manner of speaking, that's exactly what we're going to do," I told him. And to the others, I said, "Wish us luck!"

"I hope this works," Ellie said. "Good luck."

"Let us know what happens," Mel said. "We want to know everything."

We hugged and then I called to the driver, "Could you pull over here? We won't need to go all the way to the airport."

Tony conferred with the driver in rapid Spanish. "I hope you aren't going to get yourselves into more trouble. I'm going back to Fort Lauderdale and Dad's already gone. There isn't anyone to bail you out of jail."

The driver pulled over and Sandra and I slipped out of the limo onto the sidewalk. As the limo pulled away we heard a trio of tearful goodbyes and then silence.

"You gotta love it when a plan comes together," Sandra whispered.

We surveyed the unfamiliar neighborhood curiously, taking in the typical Key West bungalows and tropical vegetation which lined the quiet side street. I dug into my backpack and produced a map of Key West and handed it to Sandra. I tend to be geographically challenged and appointing me as navigator is the equivalent of selecting a blind man to lead a trip through the New York subway system. Sandra studied the map for few minutes and said, "Okay. I think I can find that house again."

It was still early and we saw few people as we hurried along. With the others gone and only Sandra as my companion, I felt isolated and my stomach knotted nervously as I reconsidered our (undoubtedly insane) plan. Neither of us spoke for some time. We planned to show up at the house before anyone left for the day. We hoped the element of surprise would work to our advantage. To this day I am not certain what we expected to find. Maybe Svetlana and Glenn. Or perhaps Ned. At the very least, we thought we would get some answers. All we could say for sure was that we had seen Svetlana and Ned bidding goodbye to someone inside the house on Bougainvillea Lane, and we wanted to talk to that mysterious someone.

As we got nearer to the street, we quickened our pace and watched over our shoulders for anyone following us. Cleverly disguised as typical tourists, we hoped that we wouldn't attract any attention. As we turned the corner onto Bougainvillea Lane, two things happened simultaneously. Peering into the early morning sun, I squinted and then gasped. "Do you see what I see?"

Sandra grabbed my arm and began to trot toward the house. "Glenn and Svetlana," she said, breathing heavily as we ran toward them. We might have been able to catch them if, at that exact moment, Good Cop and Bad Cop hadn't suddenly appeared at our side.

"Going somewhere, ladies," Good Cop began when he, too, saw the pair standing on the porch. It took him only a moment to react, but it was just enough for Glenn. Glenn had turned to leave when he spied our unlikely foursome half a block away. He seized Svetlana's arm and sprinted down the steps and raced down the street with Svetlana clinging to him. This morning Svetlana wore a pastel sundress with her customary three-inch platform sandals. Not exactly running attire. As Glenn dragged her along, she kicked off her heels and, barefoot, ran like the college track star she had been.

Good Cop hightailed it after them with Sandra and me hot on his heels. He was a decent runner but Glenn and Svetlana had a head start and managed to disappear around the corner before we reached them. Bad Cop huffed and puffed as he brought up the rear. I was glad we had worn tennis shoes and grateful for our Jazzercise training. Good Cop had only a slight lead on me as we tore down the street after the pair.

I would never have imagined that Glenn could run so fast, but perhaps fear was a good motivator. He rounded the next corner and vanished into thin air. Gasping for breath and sweat dripping from every pore, I bent over and tried to suck in enough air to keep from passing out. Good Cop halted, too, and scanned the street anxiously trying to guess which direction our prey had taken. Panting, we looked at each other. Sandra jogged up and joined us while Bad Cop straggled behind.

Good Cop loosened his tie and wiped his forehead with his sleeve. I really thought Glenn and Svetlana had made a getaway when Good Cop bolted. A flash of sunlight caught the swirl of Svetlana's dress and I realized they were heading for the marina. I raced after Good Cop, followed closely by Sandra and, still further back, Bad Cop.

I was at Good Cop's heels as he sprinted down Duval; passers-by scrambled to get out of his way. "Stop," he yelled. "Police. Stop." He might have caught them, but the excitement drew the few pedestrians into the street and our path. We were slowed just enough that Glenn reached the dock and the Just Jet Ski rental office before us. A teenager was putting out the jet skis and stepped off a bright red jet ski as Glenn approached. The key was still in the ignition and Glenn leapt onto the watercraft and Svetlana flung herself onto it behind him. Glenn turned the key, the craft sprang to life and they raced away from the dock into the harbor.

Good Cop reached the startled kid, shoved his badge in his face and demanded, "Police, I need a jet ski." Tongue-tied, the kid pointed at a blue watercraft. Kevin . . . I decided on the spur of the moment to think of him as Kevin not Good Cop, since I was putting my life in his hands . . . jumped aboard and I vaulted onto the jet ski behind him, fortunate not to have either missed completely or broken every bone in my body. Gasping from terror and exertion, I clung to Kevin as we sped across the water in pursuit. The wind whipped my hat from my head, and as we bounced over the waves, I was drenched by cold sea water. I chanced a look back at the marina and saw Bad Cop . . . guess he'd better be Steve . . . and Sandra board another jet ski and follow us.

Up ahead the red jet ski headed pell mell for a cruise ship at the dock. We lost sight of it as it skimmed around the bow of the ship to the other side. Trapped, I thought. There's nowhere for them to go. I had mixed emotions about the whole chase thing. Most of me cheered for Glenn and Svetlana to escape, while a tiny part wanted answers only they could give.

Undaunted, Kevin flew around the cruise ship and we saw only empty docks. No red jet ski. The water in this protected area was undisturbed. It was as if Glenn and Svetlana had never existed. I heard only the slap slap of water against the hull of the cruise ship. Kevin cut the engine and we drifted into the dock area and cautiously peered from side to side. I swiped my wet hair out of my eyes and loosened my death grip on Kevin. "Where the hell . . ." he muttered.

For a few minutes, which felt like hours, we searched methodically for the red jet ski and then Kevin steered our ski back the way we had come. "Now, where in the . . ." he began when we both spied the red jet ski. It emerged at the stern of the cruise ship and drifted toward a secluded beach area marked with orange construction buoys. We might have missed it if the sun glare hadn't reflected off it.

Kevin kicked our ski into high gear and tore through the water toward the slow-moving red ski. Glenn had nowhere to go. The jig, as they say, was up. We pulled up beside the red ski. Glenn was soaking wet and defeated. But Svetlana, behind him, sat ramrod straight and glared at us, sea water glistening on her bare shoulders. Kevin glanced at her with awe and then transformed back into Good Cop and read Glenn his rights, "Glenn Fairweather, you are under arrest. And you, Svetlana Fairweather, are under arrest as an accomplice. You have the right . . ."

Glenn refused to speak or look at us and Svetlana simply stared into space. Steve, with Sandra's arms wrapped around his ample waist, roared up and the wake rocked our little crafts. He had his cell phone in his hand, calling for reinforcements, I supposed. Sandra looked like a drowned rat, but her brown eyes sparkled.

"That was a hell of a Plan B," she whooped.

"Totally," I said.

Within moments a police boat thundered up and cut the engine and the wake threatened to swamp us. The officers dragged Glenn and Svetlana aboard. Neither spoke as the transfer was made. Once they were safely onboard, a policeman handcuffed Glenn's hands behind his back. Silently, he sank onto the bench that ran along the side of the boat and contemplated the deck. Svetlana glowered at the policemen, daring them to touch her. Wisely they stayed clear and didn't attempt to cuff her. Mutely, I watched the proceedings. As the police boat started toward shore, Svetlana caught my eye and smiled the tiniest of smiles and nodded slightly. I wasn't sure what she was trying to tell me, but I was oddly reassured.

Kevin settled himself on the seat of the jet ski and turned the ignition key. "I'll just run you back to the dock. Not enough room on the cruiser."

He powered the jet ski back to life and raced full-speed back to the Just Jet Ski dock with Steve and Sandra bouncing along in our wake. The teenaged attendant at the ski dock paced anxiously. When he saw us returning, his relief was obvious.

Kevin steered our jet ski into its space at the dock and climbed off, offering me a hand up. We waited for Steve and Sandra and when they were safely ashore, Kevin glowered. "We need to talk with the two of you. Do not leave town. I'm not kidding. We would just as soon arrest you. You can go back to your hotel and change, but I expect to see you at the police department in an hour."

We nodded meekly and squished toward the Key Rest Inn leaving wet footprints on the sidewalk. Neither of us spoke as we clomped down Duval Street, trying to ignore the curious glances directed our way. When we glimpsed our reflections in a store window, we realized what a picture we made. Suddenly the whole episode seemed terribly funny, and we collapsed in helpless laughter on a sidewalk bench. Sandra wrung sea water from her t-shirt and grinned. "What were we thinking?"

There's nothing like a hot shower and dry clothes to improve one's outlook, so Sandra and I were in a better mood when we reported, as ordered, to the Key West Police Station. The officer on duty ushered us into a small, sparsely furnished office and admonished us to wait for Sergeant Goodman (Good Cop/Kevin did have a last name) and Officer Polarski (obviously Steve/Bad Cop).

We didn't wait long for the two cops who fixed us with no-nonsense looks. Uh, oh, I thought. I gulped and Sandra's expression was apprehensive. Kevin had forsaken his role as the good cop and obviously was in no mood to tolerate our interference in his case. "So, ladies, are you ready to talk now?"

I bobbed my head at him, afraid to speak in case my voice came out as nothing more than a pitiful squeak. I doubted that Stephanie Plum or Nancy Drew would be unnerved in this situation, but I sure was. Face it, Kate, I thought, you are just a tennis-playing, Jazzercise addict from Winslow, Ohio. What made you think you could catch a murderer?

Kevin riffled through a stack of papers on the desk and then stacked them neatly. Even if it was a performance, this silent treatment was beginning to freak me out. Finally, when I thought I couldn't stand it any longer, he exploded. "What in the name of all that's holy were the two of you doing this morning? Beside interfering in the investigation of a criminal case and putting yourselves at risk?"

"Going for an early morning walk?" I ventured. Steve glared.

"Come on, Kate," Sandra said. "Let's tell them what we know and get out of Dodge. I, for one, am more than ready to retire from the girl detective business."

I was aware that Sandra would no more quit our quest than she would wear sandals without a pedicure, so I decided to play along. "I agree. Let's fill them in on our investigation. It isn't going all that well anyway."

An hour later Kevin's good humor was restored because we had told him everything (well, almost everything) we knew about Glenn and his relationships with Skippy,

Svetlana and Ned. Even Steve seemed less Bad Cop than weary and overworked. He sighed. "Just like my wife. Can never leave things alone. Always needs answers."

I wasn't sure if he was referring to us or to his wife. I pictured a tired, slightly overweight woman with no sense of style. Kevin gestured at a framed photo of a slim, smiling blonde in tennis clothes on the credenza behind the desk. "That's Gloria. His wife."

My face must have registered surprise, because Steve said, "Yeah, I know. Everyone has the same reaction. No one can imagine someone like me with someone like her."

"Stranger couples have happened," I said.

"Not to interrupt your little chat or anything," Kevin interjected, "but we need to finish up here. I'm sure you have better things to do than sit around our humble police station."

He scratched his head and thought for a moment. "So, let me review. You're saying that you think Glenn Fairweather had a prior relationship with the deceased. In college. And that they renewed their acquaintance during that beach party. You're guessing that the deceased was blackmailing Glenn over some youthful indiscretions in college. You say you saw the two of them together at Boys Will Be Boys. Am I right so far?"

We nodded and he continued. "But Glenn Fairweather and his wife, Svetlana, came onboard the *Mirage*, apparently a happily married couple using the name Livingston. Never mentioned he was the Captain's brother. What made you suspect them?"

"We didn't," I said. "That's the thing. If we had never seen Glenn and Skippy together, I doubt if we would have thought anything was at all funny." I conveniently failed to mention that I had overheard Ned and Svetlana's mysterious conversation on the beach. Or that we had seen Ned and Svetlana together at the house on Bougainvillea Lane shortly before the *Mirage*'s final sail. I didn't intend to cast any light on Ned's death or disappearance. That was none of their business.

Almost as if he could read my mind, Kevin asked, "Then why were you heading for Bougainvillea Lane this morning? How did you know the Fairweathers would be there?"

"We didn't. We already told you about seeing Svetlana." I hesitated for a heartbeat and then continued. "We told you we saw Svetlana there and we figured we might find out something from whomever lives there."

Steve picked up his coffee mug and deliberately took a sip. "That is what you said. But is that the whole truth and nothing but? Didn't you maybe have some other reason for going there?"

Kevin added, "And why the subterfuge? Not that we don't appreciate a good show, but why the change in clothes before you headed for the house?"

Sandra and I exchanged looks. "Too many detective novels, I guess," I said. "It seemed like a good idea at the time."

The two cops sat back in their chairs and considered all we had told them. Then Kevin leaned forward. "Is that all you want to tell us?"

"There isn't anything else," I said. "We've told you everything."

Steve eyed us with suspicion. "Are you absolutely certain?"

We nodded at him like a pair of bobble-head dolls.

Kevin pushed his chair back. "Okay, you can go. Just stay out of trouble."

"Wait a second," I said. "We've told you what we know. Now can I ask you a question and a favor?"

"Shoot."

"Well, who exactly lives in the house on Bougainvillea Lane? Just wondering since Svetlana made two visits there?"

Kevin took a moment to decide, but then said, "I can't see any harm in telling you. We have the Fairweathers in custody after all. The house belongs to one Mabel Lentz. Age eighty-two. She's known in these parts for her skill in sewing and needlepoint. Things like that. But she's better known to us cops for her cottage industry. In her spare time she designs new identities for her customers. The old gal is real skilled at that."

It didn't take a mastermind to figure out, then, what business Ned and Svetlana had with Mabel Lentz. New identities, huh? That made sense. Ned Fairweather is declared dead by his good buddy Hank and he turns up God knows where as someone else. Perhaps with a gorgeous six-foot Slavic wife? I didn't dare meet Sandra's eye for fear of giving something away, so I just gazed innocently at Kevin.

"And what is the favor?" he asked.

"Oh, I almost forgot. Would it be possible for us to talk to the prisoners?"

Sandra added, "We wouldn't take long, but we promised Hank's wife, Flo, that we'd check on Martha and Miguel. And while we're at it we'd like to say goodbye to Glenn and Svetlana."

Kevin examined us skeptically before he said, "Okay, don't see what it could hurt. I can let you see the women, but the men aren't available for conversation. I assume you aren't hiding any weapons under those t-shirts." Was that a leer I detected on the face of well-mannered Good Cop? Nah, couldn't be. "Okay. I think Officer Polarski and I are finished here. Must say its been interesting spending time with you."

Steve escorted us down some stairs and through a series of locked doors to the holding cells. He gestured to the left with one hand. "The women are in this area." He pointed to the right. "The men over here."

He scooped up a set of keys from a desk and unlocked the last door, standing back to let us precede him into the cell area. There were four cells . . . two on either side of a narrow walkway. Three were unoccupied, but Martha and Svetlana shared the fourth. I was certain that when they met and became friends on the *Mirage*, they never would have imagined they would end up roommates in a jail cell. They looked up inquiringly as we entered, but neither showed much emotion. It was almost as if they were expecting us. If Martha had whipped out a platter of hors d'oeuvres and a recipe card, I wouldn't have been shocked.

"Ladies, you've got visitors."

"Wait," I whispered urgently, my hand on Steve's coat sleeve, "is Martha under arrest? Why is she in a jail cell?"

"She's not under arrest, but she refuses to leave as long as Miguel is here. We figured it was better to give her a place to sleep and eat than to trip over her sacked out on the floor upstairs."

I doubted that most police departments would run a halfway house for wives of their inmates, but Steve didn't seem to think this was any big deal. And what did I know?

"You've got fifteen minutes," he told us and withdrew, locking the cell door behind him.

The four of us stared mutely at each other. In a strange way it didn't feel all that different from a coffee klatch in the *Mirage*'s salon. "We've got to quit meeting like this," Sandra said. Martha smiled wanly and Svetlana drew a worn blanket more snugly around her shoulders.

"Flo wanted us to check on you, Martha," I said. "She's pretty worried about how you're being treated."

"Well," Martha said, "the food isn't too bad." With Martha, I guess, everything boiled down to food.

"No," Svetlana agreed. "Not bad if you like rubber chicken and cold gravy and undercooked vegetables."

"Now, now," Martha chided her, "that Eggs a la Goldenrod I had this morning before you got here was really quite tasty. I asked the officer who brought breakfast for the recipe. It would be great . . ."

"I don't believe it," Sandra interrupted, laughing. "You'll never change."

"What you're saying, then," I said, "is that the food here won't give you the fat butt?"

We all laughed briefly and then I asked, "Why are you locked up in here anyway, Martha? I didn't think you were under arrest."

"I'm not, but Svetlana is. And when they brought her in I asked to keep her company until they figure out what to do with her."

"Is there anything we can do for you? Either of you?" Sandra asked. "I called my husband and he asked a couple of his law school buddies who practice down here to come by to see you. Have they been here yet?"

Martha nodded. "A lawyer was here yesterday and talked to Miguel and me. He told us he'd do some investigating and get back to us. He didn't think there was enough evidence to hold Miguel. But I'm really worried about the whole immigration thing. He could be deported."

Tears rolled silently down her plump cheeks and her hand shook as she brushed them away. Svetlana dropped her blanket and squeezed Martha consolingly. She looked over Martha's head and said, "I don't think they have anything on him. There weren't any witnesses."

"If you don't mind our asking," I said, "what did happen on the deck that night? Who killed Skippy?"

Martha and Svetlana exchanged enigmatic looks, apparently reaching an unspoken agreement not to reveal anything to us. "I haven't any idea," Martha said. "I wasn't there."

"Yes, but you've talked to Miguel." I looked at Svetlana. "Surely you have some idea."

"That lawyer friend of your husband's," Martha told Sandra, "advised us not to say anything about it to anyone. But I will say this . . . Miguel didn't commit any murder. Skippy fell and hit his head and fell off the deck."

"What part did you and Glenn play?" I asked Svetlana.

Cool green eyes met mine. "Skippy fell and hit his head and fell off the deck. That's all you will ever hear from me."

"Have you hired an attorney yet?" Sandra asked.

Svetlana gave a disgusted snort. "You *know* who my husband's father is? Even from his deathbed he is orchestrating things. The Fairweather attorney is at this very moment on the company jet winging his way to our rescue. Or, more likely, to the rescue of the company's good name.

It wouldn't do to have Glenn be an embarrassment again. I wouldn't mind some dry clothes though. I doubt if the company attorney will be willing to shop for me."

"And," she added with her familiar heavy accent, "I'm so not liking this wet dress."

"Those were the days, huh?" I said.

Svetlana sank down on the barren cot and put her head in her hands. "God, we sure made a mess of things, didn't we? If I could just go back . . ."

It was Martha's turn to comfort Svetlana and she patted her back sympathetically. Just then Steve returned, "Time's up, ladies."

Sandra and I turned to leave. "We'll get some clothes to you. What size are you? A two?"

Svetlana smiled her old beguiling smile. "Anything will do. I am so not the fashion plate in here."

The last thing we saw as we left the cell was Martha with her arms around Svetlana, who was shaking, whether from the cold or from fear we never would know.

A few minutes later we bid Steve goodbye and emerged from the shadows of the police station onto the sunny sidewalk. It was surprisingly warm under a cloudless sky. But I shivered. "Now that was depressing."

We wandered down the street dodging pedestrians and peering aimlessly into shop windows. We came to a standstill in front of a display of Key West t-shirts and souvenir paraphernalia. "Now what?" Sandra asked, her eyes glued to a gaudy orange t-shirt.

I settled my sunglasses firmly on my nose. "I have an idea. I think we should go back to Bougainvillea Lane and try to catch . . ." I fumbled for my notebook. ". . . a Mrs. Mabel Lentz and have a chat with her."

"The forger?"

"No, the identity designer."

Sandra faced me and hitched her purse up on her shoulder. "Let's go." She strode off, a woman on a mission.

I hustled after her and caught up a few stores down the street. "Hey, slow down. Are we in a hurry? You don't move this fast unless you're running for the big shoe sale at Nordstrom."

"Gotta make time. Shoes and Mabel wait for no woman."

Chuckling, I hurried after her. We made it back to Bougainvillea Lane in record time, and then halted on the sidewalk in front of the bungalow that was Mabel Lentz's home . . . and office. "Do we need a plan?" Sandra asked. "Or do we just fly by the seat of our pants?"

"I'm thinking of taking the whatever happens route," I replied.

"Let's do it," Sandra said and started up the steps.

I had my hand on the ornate brass door-knocker, when the door opened and we came face to face with a petite, white-haired woman with brilliant blue eyes and a startled look, who could be none other than the infamous Mabel Lentz. "Oh, my," she gasped, a hand to her chest. "You scared the life out of me. I nearly wet my pants."

"I'm so sorry, Mrs. Lentz," I said. "We didn't mean to startle you. We just wanted a few minutes of your time."

The diminutive woman dressed in a pink polo shirt and a pair of bright floral capris with matching pink Keds on her small feet, studied us with a piercing gaze. "You seem to know who I am," she said finally, "but I have no idea who you might be."

"I'm Kate Kelly. And this is my friend, Sandra Klein. We're from Winslow, Ohio. (I confess I don't know what our hometown had to do with it. Perhaps I assumed it made us look respectable. Or maybe I was just nervous.) We are friends of Glenn and Svetlana Livingston (a slight exaggeration). Maybe you know them as the Fairweathers, though."

As Mrs. Lentz continued to examine us, I babbled on, "We also knew Ned Fairweather before he died. And we heard you might have known him and . . ." I ran out of breath and stopped. Thank goodness.

Finally she made a decision. "I was on my way out to a lunch date, but come on inside and get out of the heat and we can talk."

She backed into her house and beckoned for us to follow her. Mrs. Lentz's home was cool and immaculate, nothing out of place. She led us through the living room and into the kitchen that extended across the entire back of the house. Sunlight poured into the room from a skylight and from glass sliding doors that covered the width of the room. Tiny pink and yellow flowers danced across the wallpapered walls and a round glass table surrounded by comfortable-looking chairs dominated the space. She gestured at the table. "Sit down, sit down. Would you care for some iced tea? I get my tea special ordered and with my homegrown lemons . . . Hmm. It's sure good."

"That sounds great," we said.

Mrs. Lentz busied herself getting out glasses and ice and poured tea, adding a sprig of fresh mint to each glass. "Now then . . ." she said as she settled herself in a chair and looked quizzically at us.

I took a sip of tea. "This is good, Mrs. Lentz. Thanks a lot. It is hot out there."

"You're quite welcome and please don't call me Mrs. Lentz. My name is Mabel, but my friends call me Belle. How can I help you young ladies today?"

In spite of the fact that she claimed she was on her way to a luncheon date, Belle seemed ready to spend the afternoon chatting. Taking a deep breath, I launched into the tale of our cruise and how I found the Captain dead on the floor of his cabin. About how the body vanished. And all about the storm. And Glenn and Svetlana and how they pretended not to even know the Captain when really he was Glenn's brother. And about Skippy and the beach party and Key West and then how Skippy had been murdered. I went on and on, barely pausing for breath. All the while, Belle's intelligent blue eyes remained focused on my face. I told her about Hank and Flo and the investigation of Ned's disappearance and how we decided to stage our own investigation. I told her everything I could remember and maybe it was a bad idea. But when I finally finished, she nodded and said, "That is quite a tale, young lady. I don't think you could possibly have made all that up."

Sandra assured her that it was the whole truth and nothing but the truth. In fact, it was a more complete accounting of the story than we had given to anyone. Including Hank or the Key West cops.

Belle fixed us with her steady gaze and said, "I do believe you. But I ask you again, what can an old woman like me do to help you?"

I explained that the police confided in us that she was quite talented at creating new identities for people. Since we had seen Ned and Svetlana, and later Glenn and Svetlana, on her doorstep, we put two and two together and concluded that she had created new identities for them.

"My, my, my," she said with a twinkle in her eye. "You do have quite the imagination. I'm just a helpless little old woman. Why, I'm nigh onto eighty-three years old. Me, an identity, what did you call it? Designer? Only thing I design is patterns for my needlepoint."

We waited. It was quiet in the sunny kitchen . . . the only sound the ticking of her clock and the chirping of birds gathered on the feeder hanging outside the window. I took a sip of tea and rubbed the condensation from the glass.

"Let's just say that someone. And I'm not saying it's me. Did do what you claim. How could that person do anything for you all?"

"Mrs. Lentz. Belle. We aren't looking to get anyone in trouble. We just want to know what happened. Is Ned, the Captain, dead? Or is it possible he simply staged his own death and subsequently his disappearance? I guess we'd feel better knowing he was okay."

Belle contemplated, stalling for time by hopping up to refill our glasses and to arrange a plate of cookies and place it on the table. "Honestly, " she said, "and this is God's own truth, I can't tell you if he's dead or alive. I saw on the television that he died in that plane crash the other night. Terrible tragedy. If I had given him a new identity, and I'm not saying I did, then he obviously didn't use it, now did he?"

"I guess that's where we get lost too." I put my elbows on the table and leaned toward her. "The thing is, we think he and Svetlana are lovers. She may be married to Glenn, but she doesn't love him. Not like that anyway. We think this whole thing was part of a plan to win Glenn control of Fairweather Electronics. Glenn's gay you know."

Belle didn't seem surprised by any of this.

I pressed on. "Can you at least tell us if Glenn and Svetlana stayed here last night? We saw them coming out of your house earlier this morning. Did you know they are both in custody at the Key West jail?"

This obviously was new information for her. The shocked look on her face certainly seemed genuine. "Oh, my stars," she exclaimed. "In jail? Those two children? Oh, my."

"Yes," Sandra said. "In jail. Under arrest for murdering Skippy."

"Oh, dear. Yes, I did put them up last night and the night before that. I have plenty of room now that Harold is gone. They turned up on my doorstep and looked so pathetic I couldn't turn them away."

"Is Harold your late husband?" I asked.

"Oh, my no. He was my cat. Died a bit ago of pure old age and meanness. That was one bad cat, I tell you. With him in the house, I could never have guests." She chuckled. "He would have scratched their eyes out."

"Look," she went on, "you seem like nice girls. Let's just say that I like to make people happy. And if they aren't happy with who they are, well, I try to fix that. Make them someone they can love being. It's a blessing and a service."

"You do that here?" I asked.

"I can't tell you more. I have my ways and I have my helpers. And I do a job that helps lots of people. My Ralph would have been proud."

"Another cat?"

"No, Ralph was my husband. He was a Professor of Criminal Justice and when he retired from the New York City Police Department as a consultant, we moved down here. When he died, I needed to do something to contribute. My kids are grown and live up north and I wanted to do my share. And I believe I have."

"Creating new identities for people?"

"I have used my God-given talents for the greater good. I'll admit to that much." Belle reclined in her chair and folded her arms across her chest.

"I guess you wouldn't tell us where Ned might have gone or what name he might be using if he is still alive," I ventured.

"That would be under the heading of privileged information," she scolded me. "And I certainly never am privy to private destinations of my clients. That would be a really dangerous situation for me. I need to protect myself now that Harold and Ralph are gone."

I doubted that Belle had ever needed the protection of either cat or husband. She certainly appeared quite capable of taking care of herself.

"Could I ask you one more question before we go?" I asked.

"What did you want to know, sweetheart?" Belle said.

"Just how did you come to know Ned and Glenn and Svetlana. They wouldn't have exactly looked you up in the phone book."

Belle chuckled. "Not in any regular phone book. I work by recommendation only. If one of my . . . um . . . sources refers a client to me, then I'll help out any way I can."

"Do you remember who referred the Fairweathers to you?"

Belle pondered for a moment. "Well, you know I'm not as young as I once was. Sometimes names just plain slip my mind." She hesitated, apparently lost in thought, and I believed for a second that she had nodded off. Then she blinked and said, "Must have been Hank Dayton, Ned's brother, that is, who sent them on over."

"But Ned's not Hank's brother . . ." I began, and then concluded it didn't really matter. Hank had undoubtedly come across Mrs. Lentz during some criminal investigation and used the information to help his friend Ned. Hank was definitely in this thing up to his eyeballs.

"Well, we have taken up a lot of your time," I said. "Thanks for talking with us. And for the tea and the cookies. I can't tell you how much we appreciate it."

Belle gathered the glasses and cookie plate from the table and began to wipe it with a sponge and lemon spray. "No problem. You two do seem to have had a time of it. If you ever need to get away, just let me know. I can fix you up in a jiffy." And she winked.

We thanked her, but assured her that we were quite happy and wouldn't be needing her services. We gathered our things, said goodbye and stepped outside. As we walked away, Belle stood on her step watching us. "Toodle ooo," she called. "Have a nice trip back to Ohio."

"Wow," Sandra whispered, "criminals sure come in all shapes and sizes."

"She is *not* a criminal. Just ask her. What she does, she does for the greater good. She just fills a need."

We began to giggle as we hurried down Bougainvillea Lane away from the charming house of Mrs. Mabel Lentz. We sped down the street as if we were on our way to a half-price sale at a local jewelry store, rounded the corner and came to a halt, breathing heavily. "Rum Runner?" Sandra asked.

"Margarita," I answered. And we dashed toward the Schooner Wharf Bar and the promise of liquid refreshment.

Chapter
Thirty-Three

We found a table at the Schooner Wharf and sank into the rattan chairs in relief. The bar was busy and a local musician was entertaining the lunch crowd. The decibel level was high enough that no one could overhear our conversation. The blonde, pony-tailed waitress who bustled over to our table was a familiar face. I didn't need to read her name tag to know her name was Stacey. "Margarita?" she asked me. I nodded. Stacey turned to Sandra. "You'd be a Rum Runner?" Sandra nodded.

"You know you've got a problem," Sandra said as Stacey hurried away, "when the waitress in a bar knows your drink choice."

I glanced around but no one seemed to be paying any attention to us. Stacey brought our drinks and I took a big gulp of my margarita and then licked the salt from the rim. "Um." I sighed. "Now that's good."

"What did you think of Belle?" Sandra asked.

"I liked her. And I think now we know what happened."

"Review it for me."

"The three of them, Ned, Glenn and Svetlana, cooked up this scheme where Ned stages his own death so that Glenn inherits the company. Hank gets involved because he owes Ned money. Hank is a law enforcement guy and he knows Belle and her business, so he sends Ned to see her. Ned gets all fixed up with a new identity and plans to disappear after he 'dies'. All Hank has to do is declare Ned dead. But before the plan can actually be carried out, Glenn blows it by being recognized by Skippy who decides to blackmail him and then somehow gets killed and gets the cops chasing them. I'm not sure if Glenn killed him or Svetlana or Miguel. We might never know. We saw Ned and Svetlana at Belle's the other day, probably collecting his new identity. And yesterday Glenn and Svetlana had the bad luck to be caught leaving. I'd guess that with the cops after them they called on Belle to hide them. Only because she was the only person they knew in Key West. Wrong place, wrong time, and we led the cops right to them. That's it in a nutshell. End of story."

Sandra sipped her Rum Runner thoughtfully. "I just have a feeling we're missing something. For instance, Ned dies in a plane crash. But it's days after you found him lying on the floor of his cabin, supposedly dead as a doornail.

Why? If he's already staged his death, why is he getting on a plane using his own name and not his new one?"

"I know," I said. "I'm confused too. Unless maybe he figured he could use his credit cards and stuff one last time before he vanished. Doesn't make sense, though, does it?"

"What if," Sandra suggested, "someone else was using his identity?"

I nodded. "Pity the poor identity thief. He steals Ned's credit cards, books a flight out of Key West, expecting to create a new life for himself using Ned's name and credit. Alas, he picks the wrong plane and it goes down. End of him. End of story."

"Say that Belle creates new identities for her clients, but doesn't want the old ones to go to waste, so she sells them to other clients. Kind of a clever scam." Sandra looked proud of herself.

"I never would have thought of that," I said. "That would solve the mystery of why Ned was on the plane. It wasn't Ned, after all."

"Hank was pretty upset, though," Sandra said. "Maybe even he didn't know."

"Yeah," I said and then stopped. "Look. Would you mind if we went back to Coconut Key and the Fresh Ketch one more time? We could ask Hank a few more questions and see if we can get some final answers. We could rent a car and drive. I'm not about to get back on a boat right now."

Sandra played with the clasp on her gold bracelet. "Why not? Let's go tomorrow and see what we can find out from Hank." She paused. "And Flo."

We grinned at each other conspiratorially.

After lunch we dawdled along Duval Street. As we drew near the Key Rest Inn, I spotted a reporter and a photographer lurking in the shade of a palm tree in front. I stopped and grasped Sandra's arm. I pointed. "Looks like the press hasn't totally given up on us. Do you want to cut and run?"

"Nah," she said. "Let's not hide. We can get our fifteen minutes of fame."

"More like five," I said, and we marched, kino sandals slapping the hot sidewalk, toward our appointment with posterity.

Since our arrival we had dodged the press corps camped in front of the Key Rest. When the son of a billionaire tycoon disappears, it is big news. Since we had been involved, in whatever small way, we were big news too. I had always hoped that if and when I became famous, it would be because of some noteworthy book I had written or because of my great humanitarian efforts. I never thought my opinions would be sought because I knew something about an alleged crime. Go figure.

Abruptly Sandra pulled me into a doorway. "Oh, God," she exclaimed in panic. "How do I look? I see a photographer. That means pictures. I'm not doing this unless I look good."

I looked her over. "Sandra, I have never seen you look less than perfect. Well, almost never. You look fine."

She rummaged frantically in her purse. "I need lipstick. I need to fix my hair. Do I have time for a face lift? A tummy tuck? A diet?"

I handed her the mirror I always carry in my bag. "Really, you look fantastic. Me, on the other hand . . ."

And I realized that I was a disaster. Hair in disarray. Make-up non-existent. In an agitated state, we stepped into the Oodle Too Toy Shoppe and, much to the amazement of the proprietor, proceeded to do a quick make-up and hair repair. As he looked on, first with concern and then amusement, we readied ourselves for our confrontation with the media. Finally, we pronounced ourselves camera ready, and strolled casually (calm, cool, collected, the image we hoped to portray) toward the gathered press. We discovered quite a congregation waiting. Not only that, but one of them was wielding a television camera.

"Television crew," Sandra cried. "Oh, God. I am so not ready for prime time. The camera adds ten pounds, you know."

I had to laugh. Either that or cry. "Come on. Let's just get it over with."

Resurrecting the talents she had used first as a congressional assistant and then as an attorney's wife, Sandra boldly marched up to the first reporter she saw. "I'm Sandra Klein. This is Kate Kelly. I understand you have some questions for us."

Sandra drew herself up to her full five feet four inches. I made a feeble attempt to hide behind her, but since I am a good five inches taller it wasn't possible. So I took a deep breath and turned to face the assembled press with as much aplomb as I could summon.

For the next fifteen minutes we fielded questions. As word got out that we were holding an impromptu press conference, more reporters and photographers showed up. Before long we had attracted a mob. We created quite a commotion and passers-by stopped to see what was going on. It was a brief introduction to what it must be like to be a celebrity, and I confess I found it overwhelming. Our refusal to divulge anything new about what they called The Case of the Missing Heir frustrated them and the media frenzy increased.

Fortunately, our cop friends materialized out of thin air, and elbowing their way to the front of the crowd, corralled us and pushed us into the lobby of the Inn. The tiny lobby was a peaceful oasis after the din outside.

"Whew," I exhaled. "That was getting scary."

Sandra straightened her skirt that had been pulled askew during our escape. "Vultures," she spat.

"Are you two okay?" Kevin asked with concern.

"We are," I said. "But we wouldn't have been if you hadn't come along. They never would have let us go. Thanks very much for the rescue."

Safely back in our room, I propped myself up on the bed with the fluffy pillows and turned on the TV. "Want to see if we can get *All My Children*?"

Sandra checked her watch. "Too late for that, but maybe we can catch some news. I hate to admit it, but I want to see our little press conference."

It wasn't too long before the local channel aired a news bulletin, and, sure enough, there we were in all our glory. We watched for a few minutes before Sandra moaned. "Oh, God, I look awful. My hair is a disaster and those shorts make me look fat."

I wailed. "I look like an Amazon next to you. And my hair? What was I thinking when I cut it?"

As absorbed as we were in our fashion and hairstyle faux pas, we almost missed the fact that we had handled ourselves remarkably well. Our answers were coherent (mostly) and once we got over how awful we looked, we congratulated ourselves on having survived the ordeal with our dignity, if not our clothing, in tact.

"I'm going to call Scott," I said. "I bet this will make the national news. I can't have him miss my five minutes of fame."

"Good plan," Sandra agreed. "I'll call Allen and get him to record it for us."

"Hey," I said to Scott when I reached him. "You'll never guess what we did today." (Beside taking part in a chase that ended with the apprehension of two fugitives, a visit to the jail to talk to the inmates, a social call on an "identity designer" and holding a press conference, it had been a fairly average day.)

It took a lot of cell minutes to bring Scott up to date on the adventures and misadventures of his Girl Detective wife. As I have mentioned before, Scott doesn't get upset easily, remaining unperturbed at most of my shenanigans. This, though, was more than even he could tolerate. He remained unusually quiet through my tale, but when I stopped, he began to yell. "Kate Kelly, what on earth are you thinking? You shouldn't be getting involved in stuff like that. Police chases? Tracking down murderers? You could get hurt."

I tried to reassure him, but he wasn't listening. "I'm getting on the next flight down there and I'm bringing you home. I can't believe that Allen is allowing Sandra to stay."

Now he had flipped my trigger. "Allow," I screeched. "Allow? No one needs to allow us to do anything. In case you aren't aware of it, we are grown women. We can handle ourselves."

"Grown women, are you? Then act like it."

Oops. Wrong thing to say. Our conversation took a not so pleasant turn and we said unkind things to each other until, out of insults, I called my beloved husband a rotten chauvinist poop, and we both began to laugh. The tension eased and we managed to end the call on fairly amicable terms. I promised him I wouldn't "do anything stupid" (other than driving to Coconut Key to grill a police chief, but I wasn't sharing that information) and that I would call the next day to report.

We said goodbye the way we usually do. Scott suggested, "Come home, woman, and you can have your way with me."

And I answered, as always, "What way is that?"

"Any way you want," he finished. "Love you, bye."

I snapped the phone shut, annoyed with both Scott and myself. Him for being such a jerk and with me for confessing so much. What he didn't know would not hurt me.

Sandra had much the same reaction to her phone call. "Men," she groaned. "Can't live with them, can't live with them."

"I take it Allen's not any happier about us being here than Scott is."

"Not one iota. He says either I come home or he's coming here."

"Yeah, I basically had the same conversation. But it backfired. Now I am more determined than ever not to go home until we figure this whole thing out. Or at least until we figure out what happened to Ned."

Sandra poured two glasses of wine from the bottle on the dresser and handed one to me. "Here's to a successful investigation by the Jazzer-detectives." And we clinked our glasses in a toast to triumph over adversity in whatever form . . . overprotective husbands, overbearing policemen or calculating criminals.

Chapter Thirty-Four

After breakfast at Two Friends the next morning, we picked up our rental car, a cherry red Chrysler Le Baron convertible . . . the quintessential Florida tourist car. We had a brief scuffle over the keys before I won the driving rights and Sandra was relegated to riding shotgun. In spite of the fact that it was a cool, grey day with the promise of rain hovering in the air, I put down the top and fired up the engine. We had barely slept the night before, anticipating the trip to Coconut Key and perhaps the end (finally) to our Florida adventure, and we were exhilarated as we set out.

Sandra navigated as I drove through the still-sleepy streets of Key West to Highway One, which would take us to Coconut Key and the Fresh Ketch. We hadn't called Hank or Flo to forewarn them that we were coming, figuring we might catch them off guard. Who knew if we might surprise them into revealing some new information? As we left Key West and headed up Highway One, I reveled in being behind the wheel of the snappy little car. Driving along with the humid air whipping our hair into tangles, I enjoyed a sense of freedom I hadn't experienced since we left Winslow. I tend to drive fast . . . waiting for that blue flashing light to appear in the rear view mirror . . . on an ordinary day, but today I sped along happily ignoring the speed limits out of sheer exuberance.

The scenery beside Highway One was pure Keys wilderness, wild and tropically beautiful. Tall, brownish gumbo limbo trees with tangled and twisted limbs sprouted out of the mangroves that flanked the highway and bougainvillea blooms added bright spots of color. The ocean beyond lay grey and strangely calm. We spotted an occasional egret or other bird and half-anticipated coming upon a lazy alligator straddling our path. The alligator never showed up, which was undoubtedly a good thing, and we covered the thirty-five miles of highway in no time.

"We're here," Sandra said, and pointed at a tiny weatherbeaten sign nearly hidden in an overgrown mangrove swamp. "Coconut Key. Population 431."

I cruised down the almost deserted strip of asphalt that was Coconut Key's main drag. It was eerily familiar. I shivered. It was weird being back in this rundown little town.

"There." Sandra pointed and I saw the Fresh Ketch Marina sign to my right. I found a place to park in the dirt parking lot next to the dock and turned off the engine. Reluctantly, we climbed from the car, not really wanting to disturb the peace. I dug into my bag and retrieved my brush and tried my best to repair the damage the wind had done to my hair while Sandra yanked a comb through her wind-tossed 'do. We weren't in any hurry. Finally we hoisted our bags onto our shoulders and headed for the Coconut Bar.

Nothing had changed. That shouldn't have surprised me; we had only been gone a couple of days. But it felt like years. We found the entrance to the bar blocked by a tangle of hoses and equipment. A strange whoofing noise came from the bar and we stood on the deck debating. We were about to head for the office when a man wearing a strange contraption on his back came out of the bar and saw us. "Can I help?" he shouted in a distinctly Spanish accent. "You need Señora Flo?" We nodded, unable to make ourselves heard over the noise his backpack was making. He disappeared inside and moments later Flo bustled out, a huge smile on her face.

"Carlos," she yelled. "Callete!" And the noise ceased.

In the sudden silence, I could hear only the ringing in my ears. Had I gone deaf? I shook my head to clear it and realized that Flo was speaking. "Bugs. Pest control."

"We have red ants in the kitchen," she continued. "And roaches in the bathroom."

I shivered again. This time from revulsion. "Ick," I said.

Flo was delighted to see us. "I'd ask you into the bar, but Carlos and his helper are spraying and doing some serious bug exterminating. The fumes would kill you." Her face fell. "I would have loved to make you breakfast. Home fries, sausage, eggs, toast. But it's out of the question."

"That's okay," we said, remembering the calorie count of her cooking. "We've had breakfast."

"Oh," she said, disappointed. "I didn't think I'd see you girls again so soon. What brings you to Coconut Key? Do you have news about Martha and Miguel? Have you seen them? Are they okay? Are they eating? Is Miguel in jail?"

"Whoa," I said. "One thing at a time." And I told her about our visit to the jail. I reassured her that Martha was doing as well as could be expected and that the attorney Allen had called was doing his best to get Miguel released.

"But," I continued, "we also wanted to talk to you and Hank. We have a few more questions to ask before we go back home to Ohio."

"Hank's working on a boat this morning." Flo pointed to a slick powerboat tied in one of the slips. "It might take him awhile to finish up."

"We can wait," Sandra said.

"I'd love for you to wait in the bar, but . . ." Flo said. "Why don't you go up to Hank's office and wait for him there? I'll talk to the Pest Control guys and bring you some coffee."

The door to the ramshackle building creaked as we opened it, and we hesitated in the doorway as we surveyed the interior. With no lights, it was dim and gloomy. I started for Hank's private office. What happened next can only be chalked up to cosmic interference. Had I not been wearing my new three-inch platform sandals, we might never have learned what we did.

I put on those trendy sandals because I knew I wouldn't be on my feet much. All I can say, hindsight being 20/20, is that it was serendipitous that I did, because as I stepped into the office, I tottered on the high heels, clumsily caught my toe on an uneven tile and launched myself into the air.

Frantically I scrabbled for something to break my fall, and landed half on Hank's desk and half off. The desk skidded a short distance and slammed into the shelf behind it and everything on it came crashing to the floor. I ricocheted from the desk and toppled in a heap onto the hard tile floor.

"Ouch," I moaned feebly.

Sandra knelt beside me. "Kate. Oh, my God. Are you okay? Did you break anything? Do I need to call 911?"

"Wait a minute," I said. "I don't know yet." I sat up cautiously and tested my arms and legs and other body parts. "I think everything works."

It was my lucky day because, other than a few bumps and what would be some awesome bruises and my pride, I was uninjured. "Turn on the lights," I said. "I can't see a thing."

Sandra flicked the switch and illuminated the office. I picked myself up and gingerly moved around expecting to find at least one broken bone. When I concluded I had escaped serious injury, I turned to inspect the mess I had made. Everything from the shelf was scattered across the floor. Carefully I began putting things back in place. I scooped up some odd-shaped shells and a file box and replaced them on the shelf. It appeared that nothing was damaged until I noticed the broken picture frame lying upside down.

"Oh, no," I exclaimed. "That was Flo and Hank's wedding photo." I had admired it every time I had been in Hank's office. A much younger and thinner Hank and Flo beamed out at us; Flo in a fancy wedding gown and Hank in a matching white tuxedo. I always felt good when I saw that photo. Just a sucker for the warm and fuzzy, I guess.

I bent to retrieve the frame and broken glass shattered on the floor. Painstakingly, I pried the photo loose from the shards of glass and placed it on the desk. Then I examined the rest of the ruined frame. The backing for the photo was upside down and when I grasped it I saw another photo hidden behind the wedding photo and stuck to the cardboard backing. Careful not to tear it, I pulled it loose and held it up to get a better look. And my heart stopped.

"Sandra, come look at this." We peered at an old photo of Hank and Ned. They were merely boys and squinted into the sun, arms around each other, holding up a huge trophy.

"I guess that proves they knew each other a long time ago," Sandra said. "How old do you think they are?"

I flipped the photo over to see if there was a date written on the other side. Sure enough, there was a date, but the inscription said, "Hank and Alec, 1977."

I showed it to Sandra. "Alec?" she asked. "Was Ned called Alec when he was a boy?"

"Must have been," I said. "No doubt this is Ned."

We were still studying the photo when Flo darted through the door bearing a carafe of steaming coffee and two mugs. She took in the disarray in the office and the looks on our faces. "What happened? Are you hurt?"

"No," I said. "I tripped and fell. I'm so sorry about the mess, but . . ." I held the photo of Hank and Alec/Ned out to her. "Who is that?"

"Why, that's Hank and his brother, Alec. But I've never seen that picture before."

"Hank's brother?" I asked. "That can't be his brother. That's Captain Ned."

"No," Flo said, "Alec is Hank's brother."

"But he looks just like Ned's . . ." I began, and Sandra and I finished together. "Twin!"

We stared at each other in open-mouthed disbelief. His twin brother? Did Ned have a twin brother? What on earth had we stumbled upon?

"Flo," I said, "tell us everything you know about Hank's brother. Alec, is it? Don't leave anything out. We want to hear it all."

"Stop." Hank's voice came from behind us. "Don't badger her." Hank, grimy and wiping grease from his hands with a dirty rag, loomed in the doorway. "It's okay, honey. I'll talk to these young ladies. You go see to the pest guys."

Flo, undecided, hovered for a moment, looking up at Hank in silent appeal. "It's really okay," Hank told her. "It's probably time to get this out in the open. Go on." And Flo slipped quietly from the office, leaving the three of us staring at each other.

Hank slumped into the chair behind his desk and poured himself a cup of coffee from the carafe Flo left behind. He took a couple of sugar packets from his desk drawer, stirred them into the mug and then added creamer, making a big production out of it. He smiled a small, humorless smile and said, "I guess it's way past time I told someone this story and you girls deserve to know. I can't keep covering for him forever. After I tell you everything, you can decide for yourselves if you need to tell anyone else. I'm tired of the lies and the pretending."

Hank held his head in his hands and said nothing for a few more moments. When he did raise his head, his face reflected despair. "I'm not sure where to begin, but I guess I'll just start and see where I end up."

We were spellbound, our eyes glued to his face.

"I guess the beginning would be way back when old man Fairweather, Nigel Senior, married little Charlotte Ann Kilgore. Even then, Fairweather had big plans and big ambitions, and little Charlotte Ann from Nowhere, Nebraska, fell head over heels for him. She saw him as her knight in shining armor. The way out of Nowhere to bright lights and fortune. Charlotte Ann was beautiful and innocent and Fairweather believed she would look real pretty on his arm. So they got married and started to live happily ever after. Except that Charlotte Ann discovered her knight wasn't such a hero after all. Sure, he founded his company, Fairweather Electronics, and began to make money. Pots of money. And he started to live in the fast lane. Parties and late nights and other women. Charlotte Ann still loved him, but hated the life he was leading. Without her. One night when she came home from visiting her mother and found him dead drunk with another woman, in her bed, she ran away.

Hank sipped coffee. "Well, anyhow, Charlotte Ann packed her bags and got herself to the bus station and headed out of town. She hid her tracks pretty well and escaped before Fairweather was any wiser. Ended up in a small town in Kansas. She was running pretty low on funds when she walked into Sam's Diner and asked if Sam needed a waitress. Sam took pity on the girl and hired her on the spot. Not only that but he offered to let her stay in the room above the diner for as long as she wanted. Charlotte Ann took him up on that offer right quickly."

Hank looked us in the eye. "What do you suppose Sam's last name was?" When we shook our heads, he said, "Sam Dayton. My dad. Good, old Dad always had an eye for a pretty girl and a soft heart to boot. So, Charlotte Ann moves in and starts workin' for him. One thing leads to another. See, Dad was in kind of a bad patch with my mom. She was so busy with her sewing business and raising kids and all she didn't have time for him. And, as I said, Dad did love a pretty girl. Wasn't long before him and Charlotte Ann were spending a lot of time together. Some of it in the bedroom."

"When no one came looking for Charlotte Ann, she figured she was in the clear and she fell in love with Dad. Thought the world of him, to hear him tell it. I was just a young 'un, but I remember the two of them together. Well, Charlotte Ann got herself pregnant and she was real happy. But Mom blew a gasket when she found out. Left Dad and took us kids . . . there were three of us. I'm the youngest. Still, Dad and Charlotte Ann was happy as two clams. But Charlotte Ann's pregnancy didn't go smooth. She was in trouble from the beginning and then they found out it was twins."

Sandra and I exchanged looks.

"She was in the hospital waiting for those twins to be born when Charlotte Ann's husband decided it didn't look good for her to have run out on him and he hired some private eye. Didn't take long for him to find her either. Charlotte Ann had the twins, boys, and was ecstatic. That is, 'til she learned that one of them boys was sickly and needed one of them incubators. The other was a big healthy boy."

"And then it all came apart. The detective tracked her down and Fairweather came to town to drag her back home. My mom was on the warpath and Charlotte figured it was best for everyone if she left with old man Fairweather. Dad begged her to say, but she said she couldn't do that to Mom and us kids."

"Remember I was just a little kid myself, so I can't say how the rest of it happened exactly. But one of those twins, Ned, was healthy and the other, Alec, was ailing and needed to be in the hospital. So, Charlotte Ann up and took the healthy boy and went back with Fairweather. She left the sickly twin with my dad. I think she maybe intended to come back for him, but time went on and it never happened. Fairweather, I think, wanted an heir and he and Charlotte Ann couldn't have kids. Leastwise, that's what they thought at the time. So, he let her bring her bastard twin home and he pretended he was the dad. Even adopted him. Alec stayed here and Mom and Dad raised him like one of their own. My mom forgave my dad and life went on like always. 'Cept we had a new baby brother."

"Alec got over being puny and grew up to be a big pain in the ass. No one ever told him he wasn't pure Dayton, but somehow he figured it out. We called him Smart Alec. He always thought he was better than us. Smarter. He was always looking for a way to get out and make big money. His idea of success. Maybe none of the rest of this would have happened if Ned's mom, Charlotte Ann, hadn't taken ill and died."

"The twins must have been about twenty-one when she got the cancer. She got sicker and sicker and, finally, she called Ned to her deathbed and confessed everything. She told him Nigel Senior wasn't his real dad and that he had a twin and where the twin was. After she died, Ned decided to find his twin and his biological father. He'd never been real tight with Old Man Fairweather, so he figured he'd latch onto a new family. By that time Dad had passed, too. But Alec was here and when Ned come lookin', Alec was more than happy to be brothers. New best friends and all."

"That's how I come to know Ned. Even though Alec was his twin, Ned and I was brothers too. We hit it off right away. I can't say when Alec came up with his big plan, but he reckoned maybe he could find a way to use his being a twin to get hisself some big bucks. He learned everything he could about Ned's life. He asked more questions than you could shake a stick at and memorized every tiny detail. Ned never suspected a thing. I'm not sure why Ned never came out in the open about his twin. For his part, I think he wanted something private that was all his. He didn't want any part of the Fairweather billions. Give him a sailboat and a beer and he was happy."

"As for Alec, I guess he was just biding his time. Waiting for the perfect moment to step into Ned's life and take over. I can't say he planned to murder Ned. He never talked to me about none of this. All I know for sure is whenever Ned showed up, Alec spent hours with him. Always asking questions."

"Maybe none of the rest of it would have happened if Glenn hadn't been gay. I mean, he is Fairweather Senior's biological son. Not adopted like Ned. Glenn come along unexpected after Charlotte Ann went back. And he probably would have been the logical heir but for the gay thing. When Glenn messed up in college and got involved in this big scandal, he pissed off the old man. Ned told me all about it when he hatched the plan. You know about that plan, don't you?"

I asked Hank to explain it to us. "Miss Kate, Miss Sandra," Hank said, "I think you have probably made some pretty good guesses about the Big Plan. One day about six months ago Ned showed up at the Fresh Ketch. He helped me buy it a few years back, and he used to show up here from time to time. Usually he was alone. But this time he had Miss Svetlana with him. It didn't take a genius to see how they were with each other. Couldn't keep their hands to theirselves. I could see they had something special. So, one night while Svetlana was helping Flo in the kitchen, Ned started talking. He said that his father, I mean old man Fairweather, was real sick. He'd been to a whole slew of doctors and he wasn't gonna get better. Ned might have told me what the sickness was, but I didn't quite catch it. All's I know is it was serious. Ned told me when the old man died he, Ned, would inherit Fairweather Electronics and all the billions of dollars. I asked him about Glenn. After all, he was the real son. But Ned said his dad would have none of that. His being gay was the problem. Dad would never forgive him for the way he embarrassed him with that college scandal. Ned claimed there was no way Glenn could ever get his hands on the company if he, Ned, was still alive. I guess there was more to it than that. I think maybe Glenn had to be straight and not cause any more embarrassment. Here's where I'm a little fuzzy. Ned told me how Glenn is married to Svetlana. What? I said. You and her are obviously crazy about each other. All part of the plan, he said. Glenn has a marriage in name only that solves one of the problems. Ned's being alive was the only problem left to solve."

"So he tells me that he and Glenn and Svetlana are gonna make it look like Ned is dead. He didn't give me specifics at that point. What he wants from me is to have me declare that he's dead when the time comes. He says

I'll know when it happens, and I just need to act like the sheriff and issue the death certificate. Well, I owe Ned big time for the place here, and he's my brother, so I said sure I'd do it. I admit I thought it was a stupid plan, but Ned is smarter than me and I figured he would pull it off."

Hank stopped and went over to the water cooler for a glass of water. I noticed that Flo had stolen back into the office and perched on a chair, listening intently. She clutched a tissue in one hand and occasionally dabbed at her eyes.

Hank dropped into his chair and continued. "Some of the rest of this I am kind of guessing. Ned didn't want me to know everything. He was protecting me, I think. So I don't know exactly how Alec found out about the big plan. Maybe he overheard us talking. Or maybe Ned confided in him. Ned always was too trusting for his own good. I just know that not too long before Ned had his accident, Alec let it slip that he knew what was going on. I swore him to secrecy, but that wasn't necessary. Alec never would have told anyone that Ned was staging his own death. No way. Alec was too clever for that. I think he figured his time had come. All he needed to do was make sure Ned was *really* dead, but make it look like Ned staged his own death. Then Alec, calling hisself Ned, could magically reappear. Say, I reconsidered and here I am alive and bingo . . . he's Ned. No one to argue. Well, except me and Glenn and Svetlana, but I guess he was hoping no one would believe us. Glenn would have a real motive for lying, wouldn't he? Since if Ned is dead, Glenn gets Fairweather Electronics."

Hank shook his head. "Crazy. The whole thing. And I don't have any proof of any of it. Now Ned is God knows where. And Alec vanished too. Glenn and Svetlana are under arrest for murder. When Glenn messes up, he messes up big. This whole Skippy thing. Nuts. Just plain nuts."

He spread his hands helplessly. "That's about it. I don't know any more than that. I did my part. I investigated Ned's so-called death and interrogated you all and then made the call. I declared him dead. Supposed to be the end of the story. What to do now is way beyond me."

There was dead silence in the office after Hank concluded his story. My mind raced as I tried to fit it all together, but I still had questions. "But Hank," I said, channeling Stephanie Plum, "what about the plane crash? Someone used Ned's credentials. The authorities believe that he perished in that crash. How does that fit?"

"Not sure of that myself," he answered. "One possibility is that Ned himself found out what Alec was up to and so he 'killed' himself all over again. Or maybe Alec really killed Ned and was skipping town using Ned's identity, hoping he'd be discovered and brought back. Then he'd just say, sorry, and go back to Nebraska and take over the reins of the company when the old man kicks. If the first scenario is correct, then it's possible Ned arranged for the plane crash. He had the means and the opportunity, but I can't see him killing all those people just to stage his own death. If it was Alec, then he got caught in the wrong place, at the wrong time. Died on that plane. Either way, both my brothers are gone."

Flo hurried to Hank and wrapped her arms around him. "Hank's told you everything. Now you decide what you have to do."

We didn't really need to *do* anything. We'd been merely playing at being private investigators and we might have found all the answers we ever were going to have. I couldn't see any purpose in exposing the whole plot to the authorities. Glenn was in enough trouble already. Adding fuel to that fire wasn't going to bring us any satisfaction. And if you asked me, Skippy probably deserved whatever he got.

"Thanks for telling us, Hank. I know it wasn't easy," I said.

Flo pulled Hank aside and whispered in his ear, showing him a piece of paper in hand. Hank glanced at it and said, "I need to make a call. Can you wait while I do?"

"Not a problem."

Curiously, I watched him punch in a number on his phone. "Hank Dayton here." He listened to whatever message was being relayed. The look on his face said it was not good news. "Okay. All right. I will. Soon as I can. Thanks. Bye."

Hank swiveled his desk chair away from us and took a few moments to compose himself. When he turned back, grief was written all over him. "That was the NTSB. Seems they got one bit of evidence from the plane crash site this morning. Some DNA. The lab did a rush job and identified it as Nigel Fairweather. Ned."

"You do know," Sandra pointed out, "that twins have the same DNA. So, it could be either of them."

"I know." Hank's voice was weary. "But I'd kind of been hoping it was a mistake and neither of them was on that plane. Damn. Damn. Son of a bitch."

I wasn't about to ask about the DNA evidence. Visions of wreckage and bodies came to mind and it was too gruesome to consider. I shuddered at the thought.

That was the end of any meaningful conversation with either Hank or Flo. Both wore a shell-shocked look and neither was in the mood for further discussion. As quickly as we could Sandra and I offered our condolences, both of us secretly hoping that Ned hadn't been on that plane. We promised to stay in touch and left them in each other's arms.

A light mist was falling when we emerged from Hank's office, so we didn't waste any time getting back to the rental car whose top we had left down. We had reached the car and mopped the damp seats with paper napkins we found in the glove compartment when the memory that had been floating at the edge of my mind came into focus like a bolt of lightning. I stood up, nearly decapitating myself on the car door. "I just remembered something. I have to talk to Hank." And I lurched down the dock with Sandra hot on my three-inch heels. I rounded the corner and burst into the office building with Sandra close behind. Hank was slumped in his chair, his head buried in his arms. Flo stood behind him rubbing his back. When Hank looked up his face was bleak and his eyes red.

"Hank," I gasped. "I'm sorry to interrupt, but I just remembered something I have to tell you. First, I need to ask you a question."

"Shoot."

"Well, you knew the twins better than anyone else. Could you tell them apart?"

Hank nodded. "Sure. Not from a distance, maybe, but up close, I could tell who was who. Why?"

I persisted. "How could you tell them apart? What made them look different to you?"

"Easy. Alec is the cynical one. He thinks he was cheated out of the life he deserved. I've heard him say it a million times. Why was Ned the twin that got to be a Fairweather?

Why wasn't it him? How come Alec ended up in a family that had to struggle to put potatoes on the table when Ned got caviar and champagne? Alec was bitter and that made him mean."

"Go on. What else?"

"Ned, on the other hand, was more easy going. Maybe because he never had to worry about money or any of that. I don't know. But he was a much easier person to be around. I could tell the twins apart by their eyes most of all, I guess. Alec's eyes were cold and calculating. Almost . . ."

"Evil?" I finished.

"Exactly. Evil. That would be Alec. Now tell me why you're asking."

"Okay," I said. "The very first day on the *Mirage* when we all met the Captain, my friends were all gushing over him . . ."

"I did *not* gush," Sandra interrupted. "I *never* gush."

"Shush," I said. "We can debate the gushing later. While they were, um, falling for his good looks and smooth line, he gave me the chills. It just came back to me. I remember thinking he had the coldest, most evil eyes I had ever seen."

"So?" Hank said.

"That was the first day. But later I would be talking to him and I'd think I had misjudged him. He wasn't such a bad guy after all. I'd no more than decide that I sort of liked him, then he'd be all creepy and obnoxious again. First one and then the other. I had him pegged as being a sort of a double personality. But what if it wasn't a double personality? What if it was two people? Maybe Ned and Alec were doing the twin thing and Alec was substituting for Ned?"

Hank rubbed his bearded chin thoughtfully. "I think you might have something there. Ned wouldn't have hesitated to confide in Alec. Ned would never have believed that his brother was planning to kill him. And having Alec around to take his place might have been real handy. That way Ned can set up his whole plan behind the scenes while Alec plays Captain. Works for me."

"And," he continued, "Alec would have jumped at the chance. Since that's what he wanted to do for real. Ned offers him the perfect opportunity and Alec doesn't have to do anything except pretend to be Ned until he can take over Ned's life for good. All he has to do is wait and everything Ned has will be his. That's exactly what Alec had been hoping for all along and Ned handed it to him on a silver platter. That little shit, Alec."

We debated the possibilities, but with nothing more than my woman's intuition to go on we couldn't come to any definite conclusions. "Too bad," Flo said, "that one of them twins didn't have some birthmark or scar or something."

"But one of them did," Hank said. "Alec did. He fell out of a tree when he was a little kid and landed flat on his back on a shovel. Made a great big scar on his back. I plumb forgot that."

"I saw that scar," Sandra said. "The Captain . . . or I guess it must have been Alec . . . was working on deck the day before we sailed. I came up and saw him and I was . . . okay, okay, I'll admit it, I was admiring his studly body and I noticed the scar on his back. I remember thinking it looked like he'd been in a sword fight and lost. Kind of sexy, though."

"Ned didn't have a scar on his back," Hank added. "It had to be Alec. Them two playing tricks. Only it wasn't just a trick for Alec. He had bigger things in mind."

"I guess that means Ned told Alec his and Glenn's plans then. Why else would he need a stand-in?" I said.

"'Fraid we're never gonna know for sure," Hank concluded. "Less one a them shows up again. And I don't see that happening. My brothers are gone."

"I know," he went on, "if Ned's alive, he'll find some way to let me know. He wouldn't let me just wonder. So if I don't hear anything, I'll know they are both dead. Until then I am going to assume that both twins are gone. One lost at sea, maybe murdered by the other one. And one lost in that plane crash. I can't go on hoping and hoping."

Flo patted his shoulder. "You never give up hope, honey. But we gotta get on with our lives."

Sandra and I bid them goodbye again, and in somber moods made the drive back to Key West. The leaden skies did nothing to lighten our spirits and I wasn't surprised when Sandra announced, "I've had it here. I just want to go home. It's just too depressing." I couldn't argue that point and as we drove, the rain fell more heavily, obscuring our view and turning the world a sodden grey. "I do, too," I agreed. "Let's get the hell out of Key West."

We dropped the rental car off and walked back to the Key Rest Inn in the rain. Soaked and dripping, we entered the lobby, wanting only to change into warm, dry clothes. Inez, at the desk, greeted us. "Got a message for you two. And you have a guest." She gestured toward the loveseat in the corner. There, scrunched into one corner, sat Martha.

"If she offers you a recipe card or a snack, run," Sandra whispered.

Martha stood when she spotted us. "I hope I'm not interfering." She reached into the large bag she was carrying.

"I told you," Sandra said under her breath. "Recipe cards!"

Sure enough, Martha was pulling out something which looked very much like one of her recipe cards. She handed it to me, and I looked at it, trying to figure out what she was giving me. Not a recipe card, that's for sure. "What's this?"

"Just my way of saying thank you," she said. "Mr. Stone, the attorney, is having Miguel released tomorrow morning. He convinced the police there is no reason to hold him. And since there are no witnesses to the crime, he is pretty sure the charges will be dropped."

I turned the card over. Not a recipe, but close. It was a gift certificate to a New York restaurant . . . the one where she had previously been employed, I assumed.

"I don't have any money to give you. I gave everything I had to Mr. Stone. But I wanted to show our appreciation."

"What about Glenn? Is he being charged with Skippy's murder?"

Martha shook her head. "A whole team of lawyers showed up on the Fairweather jet. In no time at all they had Glenn and Svetlana out of jail and on the jet back to Nebraska. I guess no one is going to do time for Skippy."

"But someone killed him," I protested.

Martha narrowed her eyes. "Maybe it was just an accident. I don't know. All I care about is Miguel. He's pretty upset. Do him good to go back to New York and forget this nonsense."

She scooped up her large bag, hugged us and evaporated into the rain, leaving behind the faint aroma of vanilla. After Martha took off, I remembered the message

I clutched in my hand. "Good Cop wants us to call him," I told Sandra. "Now what do they want?"

We went up to our room and while Sandra showered I called the police station and asked for Sergeant Goodman. When he came on the line, he confirmed what Martha had told us. "Just wanted to let you two Nancy Drew wannabes know we are dropping all charges against Glenn Fairweather and Miguel Santos in the murder of Reginald MacComber, aka Skippy."

"But why?"

"Let's just say that with no witnesses to the alleged crime . . . at least none that were willing to talk . . . we don't have enough evidence to convict. We have no murder weapon, nothing but MacComber's blood on a piece of carpet. I have my suspicions, but I'd have a hard time proving it in a court of law."

"So, Glenn and Svetlana were released?"

"Money talks," Kevin said shortly.

I hung up and sighed. If the police were choosing to let it go, who was I to disagree? Although I couldn't prove it, I would have bet my life savings there was an altercation over Skippy's blackmail, and someone (my guess, Svetlana) bopped him over the head and then the three of them (Glenn, Svetlana and Miguel) pitched him overboard. This crime solving stuff is really tough. In books it always seemed so much easier. Cut and dried. Here's the crime. Here's the perp. Here's the evidence to prove he did it. One, two, three. Stephanie Plum never had to guess who done it.

I repeated Kevin's message to Sandra and then stepped into the shower. I was drying my hair when Sandra shouted at me over the noise of the hairdryer. "Kate. You'll want to see this. Come in here."

Sandra had been watching a rerun of Law and Order on TV (is that appropriate or what?) when the program was interrupted by a news bulletin. Positive proof of Nigel Fairweather Junior's death had been found. DNA evidence recovered just this morning. Blah, blah, blah.

"That was quick," Sandra said.

"I keep thinking about the evidence. What exactly was it? Something gruesome, no doubt."

"Don't even go there," Sandra cautioned. "Let's just accept the fact that one of the twins, Ned or Alec, was on that plane when it went down."

Home was sounding better by the minute. My own bed. My own bathroom. My own closet full of clothes that I hadn't worn over and over again. I wanted to eat in my own kitchen. Drive my own car. Go to Jazzercise. Play tennis. I'd had enough of this adventure. It was time to move on.

We called Sunshine Tours to ask them to arrange for a flight to cold, grey, boring, but oh so nice, Winslow, Ohio. It wasn't long before the tour office called us back to report that our flight to Miami and then home would leave at three the next afternoon.

We spent the rest of the afternoon watching daytime television (nothing more soothing than a good dose of Oprah) and packing. Since we'd skipped lunch, we decided on an early dinner at Sloppy Joe's. One last trip down memory lane. As we sipped margaritas and watched the few pedestrians hastening down the street, we were both strangely sad, and yet very happy, that we were leaving the next day.

One margarita led to two as we lounged at our table absentmindedly staring at the rain pelting the front window. For the umpteenth time we speculated about Skippy and Ned and Glenn and Svetlana and the entire cast of characters we had been teamed with and against during our stay in the Keys. "What I just don't get," Sandra said as we consumed the last of our veggie burgers and sucked down the last drop of margarita, "is how someone like Stephanie Plum always gets her man. Or woman as the case may be."

"My sentiments exactly," I replied. "Be careful what you wish for, I suppose. I am forced to admit that I am not Stephanie or Nancy or any of those purely fictional super-chicks. I am plain old Kate Kelly from boring old Winslow, Ohio, and I am totally over the whole private eye thing."

"Right on, Kate Kelly," Sandra said. And we clinked our empty margarita glasses together.

"Next time I come to Key West," I concluded, as we headed into the rainy night, "it's going to be with Scott and it will be all about shopping, sand and sex. In that order!"

Chapter
Thirty-Five

I woke early the next morning after a restless night. I hopped out of bed and padded to the window to find that the rain had stopped and the sun was shining brightly. A good omen.

Sleepily, I wandered into the bathroom and took a long, hot shower, lathering my hair twice and taking the time to leisurely shave my legs. I sighed at the pallor of my skin, but rationalized that at least I had avoided potential sun damage. All in all, I felt pretty good. When I returned to the bedroom, Sandra was sitting up in bed with a mug of coffee watching the *Today Show*.

I poured myself a mug and plopped down next to her to see the morning's news. I wasn't paying much attention to Ann Curry as she read the day's headlines. I was daydreaming, lost in my own world, when Sandra nudged me with enough force to cause me to slop hot coffee on my hand. "Ouch," I protested. "What on earth?"

Mutely, she pointed at the screen and grabbed the remote to punch up the volume. "Died last night," Ann was saying. "Nigel Fairweather Senior, was seventy-five years old, the founder and CEO of Fairweather Electronics, the billion dollar Nebraska corporation. Fairweather was preceded in death just a few days ago by his son Nigel Junior. The younger Fairweather, the captain of the sailboat, *Mirage*, died in a plane crash near Key West. It had been assumed that Nigel Junior would take over the reins at Fairweather Electronics. Now sources say the role will be filled by Fairweather's younger son, Glenn. Glenn Fairweather has just returned to Nebraska after being held as a suspect in the death of a former classmate, one Reginald MacComber. No charges have been brought against the younger Fairweather at this time. Now, let's go to Al and the weather."

Sandra punched the mute button. "Oh, my God! They actually pulled it off!"

"So far, so good, I guess," I said. "Unless they charge him, but Kevin said they wouldn't. Case closed, he said. Money talks, he said." I knew I was babbling, but it was all I could manage. Coherent speech, let alone thought, was beyond me.

"I believe I've said this before," Sandra pointed out. "But you have to love it when a plan comes together."

There didn't seem to be much to add. Sandra showered and dressed, while I monitored the television for further developments. I channel hopped, but none of the other early shows had more details. Bottom line . . . Dad was dead and Glenn inherited the company. But was Ned really dead? I hoped not, but who knew for sure? I wondered what would happen to Ned's ex and his twin sons. And Svetlana? Was she destined to be Glenn's trophy wife until death they did part? All questions that had no answers.

"Hey, Kate. I have a great idea." Sandra was dressed in a sleeveless navy top and spotless cream linen capris. Her hair and make-up were perfection. She had the impeccably elegant look of, dare I even think it, a political candidate.

"You look fantastic." I complimented her. "How do you pull that off? I look like an unmade bed, a king-sized unmade bed."

She accepted my flattery with a modest smile. "I have one final thing I'd like to do before we catch our flight. Are you game for something out of the ordinary?"

"Sure. I'm game for anything."

"Okay, then, come on." Sandra grabbed her purse and opened the door. "Let's take Key West by storm one last time." I followed her to the lobby and out the door. On the street she looked first one way and then the other, searching for something. Then she spied what she wanted and set off at a trot. I jogged after her until she halted on the corner.

"Here."

"What are we doing here?" I asked, seeing nothing remarkable.

"Him." She pointed. And then I figured it out. We were loitering in front of one of the many tattoo artists who have set up shop along the streets of Key West. These artists (and many are true artists) make a living by luring tourists into getting a tattoo. The difference between these sidewalk establishments and Tattoo You where Ellie got her ill-fated rose is that these tattoos are not permanent. Done with henna and a transfer, they will last for perhaps six weeks. But they are cheap and fun and tourists flock to the tattoo spots. Sandra grinned at me. "I dare you."

I grinned back. "You're on."

The tattoo artist introduced himself as "The Pirate", a dark-skinned, dark-eyed man who proclaimed he was of Turkish descent. Perfect, I thought. How exotic. We pored over books of tattoos the Pirate displayed. There were tattoos of every shape and size, from tiny to ones large enough to cover your entire arm. Nothing seemed exactly right until we turned the page and simultaneously pointed. "That one!"

The Pirate removed two of the tattoos from the book and asked, "Who goes first?"

I pushed Sandra forward. "Your idea. You go first."

"Okay," she said and casually took a seat.

I watched closely as the Pirate did his thing. He gently placed the transfer on her shoulder and then carefully traced it with a henna pen. He wasn't in a rush; there were no other customers. And he chatted while he drew. I learned a lot that morning, not just about tattoos, but also about Turkish bazaars and the Pirate's family. When anyone asks, I tell them it was a very educational experience.

Finally we both were tattooed and we paid the Pirate. As pedestrians eddied around us, we admired the twin sailboat tattoos, bearing an uncanny resemblance to the *Mirage*, sailing tranquilly across our left shoulders.

"Wow," Sandra said as she scrutinized my arm. "That's perfect. I could never tell it's not real."

"But our tattoos *are* real," I argued. "Real fakes."

Sandra made a face. "This trip has seriously affected your brain."

"No," I insisted, "think about it. There's real real. There's real fake. And then there's fake real."

"Too much time in the sun," Sandra said.

"A mirage is an illusion, right?"

Sandra nodded.

"And our *Mirage* was real. Or was it merely an illusion?"

Sandra touched my tattoo. "Kate, you are so deep."

With that we hurried back to the inn to get ready for our trip back to the "real" world. Or was it? Who was to say what was real, after all.

Epilogue

Scott and I were the first to get to the dock where Tony and Ricardo Moreno greeted us as if we were long lost friends. In a way, we were. "Kate, you look fabulous," Tony said, hugging me.

Ricardo stuck out his hand and grasped Scott's in a firm handshake. "I'm Ricardo Moreno and this is my son, Tony. You must be Kate's husband. Delighted to meet you. Siempre es un placer."

Laughing, I pulled away and asked, "Are any of the others here yet? Or are we the first?"

"You two are the first of your gang," Ricardo told us. "I got a call from Julie earlier, and she and Robert missed their flight this morning. Some problem at the restaurant, she said. But they'll be here in time for departure."

I shaded my eyes with my hand and inspected the 330-foot cruise ship floating regally at her mooring. "The ship is beautiful."

"Elegant," Scott echoed. "Really magnificent."

"Only the finest for Sunshine Tours," Ricardo boasted. "The *Reunion* is our newest, biggest and best cruise ship."

"She sleeps one hundred and twenty-five, has two restaurants, a pool, shops and a workout room. All the amenities of a fine resort," Tony added. "A far cry from the *Mirage*."

"Yoo hoo! Kate! Scott!"

I wheeled and saw Mary Linda and Don hurrying toward us. Each balanced a squirming baby and an unwieldy collection of baby paraphernalia. Red-faced and perspiring, Mary Linda joined our little group. The diaper bag she was carrying slipped out of her grasp and landed on the dock with a thud. She let out her breath with a whoosh and handed the chubby, little girl with blonde curls and blue eyes to me. "Take your namesake, will you? She weighs a ton."

I hugged the baby to me and gave her a kiss on her smooth cheek. "Do you remember me, Mary Kate? I'm your godmother."

Mary Kate gurgled in delight and blew spit bubbles. Putting her pudgy hands on my cheeks she said proudly, "Kiss." And planted a wet baby kiss on my cheek.

Mel grinned at me. "Her latest trick. Be prepared."

The baby on Don's hip began to cry, trying to steal attention from her sister. Mel fumbled in her bag, tossing its contents on the dock as she searched. "Where on earth is her binkie?" she demanded of Don. "Do you have it?"

Trying to console his screaming cargo, Don said, "It's in the bag somewhere."

I watched Mel scrabbling desperately through her bag while the baby continued to yell. "I remember the days when you had everything in your purse organized by size, shape and color," I commented.

Brushing damp hair out of her eyes, Mel said, "Those were the days, huh?" But the look on her face said otherwise. She found the binkie and handed it to Don who in turn stuck it in the baby's mouth. Suddenly it was quiet. Don patted the baby's back while she slurped on her binkie. "There, there Jelly," he crooned. Dark-haired and green-eyed, little Julia Elinor (named, of course, for Julie and Ellie, but nicknamed, perhaps unfortunately, Jelly) and her blonde twin (my namesake) Mary Kathleen had turned life at the St. Clair house inside out and upside down. But neither parent had any complaints. I'd never seen either of them happier than they were with their bonus twin girls.

Mary Kate tugged happily on one of my hoop earrings and burbled at me. "She's missed you while you've been away," Mel said. "A month is a long time."

"Where are Ellie and Ted anyway?" Don asked. "Aren't they with you?"

Ellie and I had just completed a book tour to promote the book we had collaborated on, *The Captain and the Meal, A Novel of Crime and Cuisine on the High Seas*. Based loosely (very loosely, I must say) on our adventures aboard the *Mirage* and incorporating as many recipes as Ellie could badger me to squeeze in, we had created a novel that was attracting a modest following. I didn't think we would ever make the *New York Times* bestseller list, but soccer moms and crime buffs who like to cook were buying the book, and we had some not-terrible reviews.

We approached a publisher with our idea right after we got home from our harrowing cruise on the *Mirage* and found ourselves being rushed into print to cash in on our brief fling with notoriety. The only condition was that we had to travel throughout the United States for book signings and the occasional appearance on a local television show.

Now I explained to Don and the Moreno men, "Ellie and Ted are enjoying a little couple time. The boys are coming down for the cruise with Julie and Robert and the girls."

The Moreno men excused themselves, and we began to gather up babies, bags and ourselves to board the spanking new cruise liner and find our staterooms. After nearly two years, we were finally taking the offer of a free cruise on Sunshine Tours. Since we wanted to include everyone, and Mel and Don wouldn't leave the twins behind, we opted this time for a larger, more baby friendly ship. With daycare.

We had no more than made our way up the gangway and been ushered aboard by white-coated crew members than we saw Ellie and Ted on the dock below. They looked up and saw us at the rail and waved. Ellie called to us, but just then the ship's horn sounded and her words were drowned out. We had to wait for the pair to board the ship before we could hear her. "Where are the boys? I haven't seen them in ages. Did they make it?" She scanned the milling passengers, anxiously searching for a glimpse of the three sons she had been forced to "abandon" while we did the book tour.

We assured her that Julie and Robert and the kids would arrive soon and Ellie relaxed a little. The tour had been good for the Francis family, and for Ellie especially. After a lifetime of being the good girl, the good wife and mother, and burying herself in the lives of her family, she had found an identity of her own. And when she could get over the guilt, was reveling in it. It was a work in progress, but she was gaining on it. Her red hair and the rose tattoo on her shoulder had been her first declaration of independence and tangible proof (to her) that she could make decisions on her own.

Mel and Don, struggling with the squirming babies, decided to find their cabin and get settled. Ellie and Ted followed, hand in hand. So Scott and I were alone on the rail when we spotted a black airport limo parked in front of the gangway. The driver hurried around the vehicle to open the door and a glamourous couple stepped out. I was admiring her fashionable white silk suit and turquoise camisole and wondering how much it might have cost, when I was shocked to recognize my good friend Sandra. As she smoothed her skirt and slipped on large dark sunglasses, Allen emerged from the limo. He could have stepped straight from the pages of *GQ*. I punched Scott's arm to get his attention and realized that he, too, was mesmerized by our friends. "Is that who I think it is?" he asked. "I don't believe it."

"It is, indeed," I said. "Ohio State House of Representative Sandra Klein and her brilliant campaign manager, Allen Klein. In the flesh."

I hadn't seen Sandra since the election. I'd been on the book tour and she had been in Columbus checking out her new office space and organizing her staff. "She looks amazing, doesn't she?"

No doubt the political life agreed with Sandra. When they came on board and we exchanged hugs, it took only one look to see that Sandra was in her element. She was beaming. "Kate, I can't believe we're really here. It seems like a century ago that we were on the *Mirage*, doesn't it?"

"How is Columbus?"

"How was the tour?"

"You go first."

"No, you go."

Scott and Allen squeezed between us. "Let's go find our cabins before we weigh anchor," Scott suggested.

"We can come back up here to watch when we do leave port," Allen added. So, frenetically trying to catch up on the gossip and news, we went seeking our cabins.

The Morenos had secured a block of six cabins for us (Ellie's boys had one of their own and were in seventh heaven). Each cabin was beautiful. Done in polished teak and the calm colors of the sea, our cabin was indeed elegant. The *Reunion* was a smallish cruise ship, sleeping only 125, but it was as luxurious as a much larger ship might be. No detail was ignored. The Morenos had done themselves proud with the latest addition to the fleet.

"I guess this is a little different than the *Mirage*," Scott said as he unlocked the door and stepped inside.

I vividly recalled our cozy, some might say cramped, cabin on the *Mirage*. "No comparison," I told him.

From across the hall, Sandra called, "Whoo-eee, Katie. This is my kind of a cruise. If you all had just listened to me in the first place."

"I know," I said. "But would you be where you are now if we hadn't taken that cruise?" The Congressmen she met in Key West had been a huge influence on Sandra, and through them and the doors they opened for her, she ended up in the Ohio House of Representatives."

"Point taken," she said. "But you gotta love this."

I couldn't argue. I closed the door to our cabin and with my back against it crooked my fingers at Scott. "Come over here, you," I said, and snuggled against him when he did as I asked. "This is the life."

414

He kissed me. "Do you want to test the bunks?"

"Mmm," I whispered, but the mood was shattered by noises coming from outside our door. A series of bumps, thuds and giggles erupted and then I heard Julie's boisterous laugh. "Robbie, Kevin, Michael, watch it. Stop banging on those doors. Your cabin is right here." More thuds and then more giggles. "Alexa, help your sister," Julie exclaimed.

I threw open the door and toppled into the hallway. "Julie," I shouted, "you're here at last."

Ellie, Sandra and Mel heard the commotion and burst into the hall for an exuberant reunion. We created quite a racket . . . hugging and kissing each other. A crew member started our way, but taking in the raucous scene reversed direction and retreated. We all started laughing again. Finally, Sandra took charge. "Let's get settled and then go up to the deck for the launch." She glanced at the obviously new and expensive watch on her wrist. "We're leaving in thirty minutes."

Half an hour later, the five of us, with our husbands and assorted children, lined up along the rail to watch Fort Lauderdale grow smaller and smaller as the *Reunion* steamed out into the Atlantic. On shore I admired tall hotel buildings and palm trees lining white sand beaches. It was impossible not to think of the other cruise on the *Mirage*. From their expressions, I knew the others were doing the same thing.

"Strange, huh," Sandra said to me. "I can't believe we're back here."

The twins began to fuss and Mary Linda and Don went to their cabin to feed them. Ellie's sons set out to explore the ship. Ellie and Ted, arm in arm, still basking in a honeymoon glow, followed them. Robert and the girls found the pool and the girls splashed and screamed in delight. Scott and Allen sprawled in deck chairs and were deep in discussion about, presumably, "guy things." This left Sandra, Julie and me leaning against the rail, the tropical breeze ruffling our hair and the sun warm on our shoulders.

"I'm so glad you guys made it," I said to Julie. "What happened that you missed the flight?"

"Something always happens at the restaurant," she replied. "This time it was a major plumbing leak. We had to wait for the plumber to get there and fix it. Thank heavens for Martha and Miguel. We never would have been able to leave if they weren't in charge. Miguel was manning the mop and Martha was cooking up a storm when we finally managed to sneak out."

"So they're working out then?"

"Oh, my God," Julie exclaimed. "I don't know how we could have done it without them. The phone call I made to ask Martha to come cook for us was inspired, if I do say so myself. When Lana wrote to say that things weren't going well for them in New York, it hit me like lightning. Martha's cooking and Miguel's handyman skills are keeping us afloat."

"It's going well?" Sandra asked Julie. "Last time I was there it was jammed."

"Business is unbelievable," Julie said. "Robert is awesome. Three years ago he couldn't make toast and now . . ." She spread her hands. "A gourmet chef. As he explains it, it's all just chemistry to him. And Martha . . . well, you know her cooking. She still has the recipe cards, but they're a big hit too. Maybe that's Ellie's next book."

"I think you've done wonders with the place," I told her. "I love all the stained glass and the Tiffany lamps and the decor is amazing. Who'd believe that it was once a gas station?"

"We couldn't afford to put gas in the car so we bought the station," Julie joked.

"No, really," Sandra said. "It's an incredible place."

"It really helped, you know," Julie said, "that you guys have all had events there. The election night party, the book signings, and the twins' christening. It gets people talking. And people talking to other people is how restaurants make it."

"And to think," I said, "that you thought Robert was having an affair."

Julie laughed ruefully. "I was an idiot. What can I say?"

"Who would have thought we'd be where we are today," Sandra said.

Later that evening, after a rowdy dinner at the Captain's Table (the Morenos were giving the survivors of the *Mirage* debacle the royal treatment) complete with babies smearing food in their hair and the little girls giggling at the older boys, the five of us declared we needed some serious girls-only bonding. The rest of the gang would have to fend for themselves. Mel left Don in charge of the freshly bathed and diapered twins, while Julie sent Robert and the girls off to the movies. Ted and the boys discovered the game room and were happily engaged in computer warfare. I shooed Scott out of our cabin and he and Allen sought entertainment, if not exactly peace and quiet, in the lounge where some cheesy Britney Spears wannabe belted out songs.

The five of us changed into scuzzies and then crowded into my cabin. I opened a bottle of Merlot and poured.

Glasses in hand, we toasted. "To the Jazzer-detectives, together again." (That was my toast) "To the five of us." (Ellie, the sentimental one) "To prosperity." (Julie, worried about the bottom line) "To world peace and cheap gas." (Sandra, the politician) "To long naps and sleeping at night." (Mel, the new mommy)

Several months had passed since the five of us had been together. One of us was always too busy with our new lives. So we were anxious to get caught up. I opened a second bottle of wine and we lazily sipped and drifted from one topic to another. Finally, someone asked, "So, Ellie, what do you hear from Wil?"

"Kate and I saw him when we did the book signing in Lincoln," Ellie said. "You know Lincoln is where Fairweather Electronics is headquartered?" Three heads nodded. "So, when I knew we'd be there, I called him. He came to the signing. He said he loved his new job."

"What new job?" Julie demanded. "What did I miss?"

"Didn't I tell you?" Ellie said innocently. "He works at Fairweather. He's Glenn's assistant. I gather he likes his job almost as much as he likes Glenn."

"Good Lord," Julie exclaimed. "I did miss something. How did that happen?"

"I guess Glenn called him. Right after the divorce and wanted to know if he'd be . . ."

"Divorce," Mel shouted. "Do you mean to tell me that he and Svetlana . . ." Her voice trailed off.

"Well that much I knew," Julie said. "I got a note from Lana and she told me she was leaving him."

Mel glared at Ellie. "So what's the deal with Wil and Glenn?"

"I'm not sure myself how it all came about, but Wil says that he and Glenn made a connection in Key West and Glenn remembered him."

"But a job?" Mel said. "Is Wil even qualified to be an executive assistant at a high-powered company like Fairweather?"

"It appears that way," Ellie said. "Wil did go to college, you know."

"Well, what is Svetlana up to then?" Mel asked. "What did she tell you in her note?"

"She said she was going to Darfur to help there. That's in Africa, you know. Lots of doctors are volunteering. So much poverty and illness." Julie went on to explain what she knew about the situation in Darfur and Svetlana's involvement.

"I wonder if anyone has heard from her since she left?" Sandra asked, and the discussion continued.

While they talked I wandered around the cabin aimlessly. Scott had brought with him from Ohio a stack of "fan" mail which had accumulated during my absence. Our publisher arranged to have all mail addressed to Ellie and me sent to a PO box in Winslow. Our fans tended to be old high school or college friends who wanted to either compliment us or complain. (I tried that recipe, one said, and you deliberately left something out.) Most were amusing and a few annoying. Scott had been in a hurry to leave and hadn't sorted through the stack, so I began to riffle through the letters arranging them in categories: mine, Ellie's, ours. At the bottom of the pile I came upon a weathered postcard. It looked like it had literally been around the world, the edges bent and torn. The scene on the front was of sand, palm trees and a vast expanse of green ocean with a couple under an umbrella. Curious, I examined it more closely. It was a scene of the Seychelles Islands. Odd, I thought, I don't know anyone vacationing in the Seychelles. Absently, I flipped it over to read the message. Stunned, I read it again. And then again. Suddenly the cabin felt hot and claustrophobic. My cheeks burned and there was a strange buzzing in my ears. Heart pounding, I started to speak and could hardly get the words out around the lump in my throat. "Guys," I began. And then more loudly. "Guys!"

Four inquisitive faces turned toward me. The dazed look on my face shut them up quickly. "What . . ." Ellie said, and then stopped.

"Read this," I croaked. And they crowded behind me and read over my shoulder. Hushed, we passed the post-card around, each trying to absorb the message in turn. On the back of the card in concise masculine writing . . ." "*Tell everyone I'm well. N.*" Beneath it in flowing feminine script, "*Me, too. S.*"

No one made a sound. When it seemed as if the silence would stretch forever, Sandra said softly, her tone awed, "I've said it before and I'll say it again. I love it when a plan comes together."

"Here, here," the five of us whispered in unison. And we raised our wine glasses in a final toast to the *Mirage*, the illusion and the reality.

The next morning the five of us and our entourage con-gregated on deck for the ceremony we had devised (aided by more wine than I cared to think about) the night before. "Do you have it?" I called to Mel as she rushed up toting one life jacket clad twin.

Breathless, she passed the wiggling baby to me and dug into her diaper bag. She pulled out two diapers, a bottle of juice, a bag of goldfish and a tube of baby sun block before she found what she was looking for. "Ah, hah," she said triumphantly. "This is the best one I could find." And she waved a photo, with a few cookie crumbs clinging to it, in the air.

Each of us took a turn gazing at the group photo taken (probably by Martha or Miguel) early in the cruise on the *Mirage*. The five of us and Glenn and Svetlana clustered around the Captain and we all were laughing and squinting in the bright sunlight. We wore bathing suits and t-shirts and looked happy and excited. I fingered the photo and noticed something I had never seen before. Ned stood directly behind Svetlana and, partially obscured by her ever-present sarong, I could see their hands entwined. Probably only a momentary touch, but caught by the camera forever.

Julie produced an empty wine bottle, a remnant of last night's reunion. A special Sunshine Tours vintage, it proclaimed, quite appropriately, that it was a product of the Mirage Winery. I handed Julie the photo and she rolled it up, stuffed it into the bottle and pushed in the cork. Solemnly, the five of us made a circle and passed the bottle around. Each of us clutched the bottle in turn and proposed a toast.

Ellie said, "To a happy life."

Mel echoed, "Sunny skies."

"A safe harbor," Sandra added.

Julie grinned. "Lots of little umbrella drinks."

Then I took the bottle and held it up in the sunlight and with all my strength I flung it over the rail and into the sparkling ocean waves. "Bon Voyage," I said.

We watched as the bottle bobbed on the waves slowly washing farther and farther away from the *Reunion*. Long after the others had tired of the vigil, I remained at the rail with Scott's very firm and very real arm holding me close. I blinked as the sun's reflection danced off the water and the bottle drifted toward the horizon. I imagined a distant beach with white sand and swaying palm trees. And on that beach I saw Ned and Svetlana, hands entwined still, waving at me joyfully.